Four Roses for Sarah

By
Gerry Edwards

PublishAmerica
Baltimore

ISBN: 1-4137-3398-0
PUBLISHED BY PUBLISHAMERICA, LLLP
www.publishamerica.com
Baltimore

Printed in the United States of America

Dedication

This book is based on the Greencastle area in which I live, and many of the people in the book are composites of family and friends. The main character Bill is based on my son, Bill Harne, to whom I wish to dedicate this book. I could not have written it without the inspiration he gave me. Bill was a loving, caring, sharing individual with strong ties to his family. Indeed, the special bond he had with his mother almost made them inseparable.

Bill had a deep respect for the area he lived in and the community around him. All those whose lives he touched agree that knowing him greatly enriched their lives. He was a deeply religious man who read his Bible regularly and took the words to heart. He gave generously to the church and those less fortunate.

Like Bill in the book, our Bill had recently felt a strong need to find that special someone with whom to share his life. Unfortunately, our Bill will never experience the joy of finding his Gail. Bill Harne, a real-life hero in my book, died in a tragic motorcycle accident on December 28, 2003, shortly after I completed writing my story.

Bill, I love you and dedicate this book to your memory.

Four Roses
for Sarah

Especially for Sharon,

Gerry Edwards

CHAPTER 1
Return of the Roses

"Those damned roses are back!"

Dottie was jolted awake from a short nap by her sister Kate yelling. Now, Dottie knew her sister and how unpredictable she was, and she knew things would get worse from here. As she opened her mouth to utter calming words to Kate, she was thrown forward in her seat as Kate jammed on the brakes. The wheels locked up and the car slid sideways to a stop in the middle of the road. Behind them Dottie heard a horn blare and the screeching of tires as a car came sliding toward their vehicle. Dottie just knew this was her last day on earth. Not even Kate could get them out of this jam. In an instant the car behind them would crash into the rear of their little Mustang. The car approaching in the other lane had not seen them yet and would never be able to stop in time to avoid hitting the front of their car which projected into its lane.

Even though Kate was 57 years old, her reflexes were top notch and a quick glance over her shoulder told her she had put herself and her sister in a nasty situation. *I need to get us out of this mess real quick*, she thought to herself. She instinctively pushed in the clutch and grabbed the gear shift lever on the floor. As she pulled the lever into first gear her other foot punched the gas pedal to the floor. The V-8 engine under the hood roared to life as Kate popped the clutch. Instantly the Mustang lurched forward and the car behind them slid past. However, the car was still sideways in the road and totally in the lane of the oncoming car which had finally seen them. With no time to turn the car Kate aimed it straight for the two-foot-deep ditch at the edge of the road.

Dottie waited for the crash with the oncoming car and suddenly heard a rush of air as the two cars cleared each other by inches. *It only gets worse*, Dottie said to herself as she realized that they were about to go into the ditch and probably flip the car. The momentum carried the front wheels across the ditch, but then the rear end of the car settled in with a sickening thud.

Suddenly the wheels grabbed and the car careened toward a large tombstone in the cemetery beyond the ditch. Dottie swore the tombstone scraped the dirt off the paint on her side of the car as Kate swerved to the left to miss it. Another even bigger tombstone, impossible to miss, loomed ahead, but by now Kate was pushing the brake pedal with all her might and the front bumper only tapped the base of the tombstone as the car rolled to a stop.

Dottie was shaking and trying to catch her breath as she heard her sister open her door, step out and start cursing again about the roses. Rage erupted in Dottie and she flung open her door. "Kate, you just about got us mutilated and killed—not to mention the scare you put in the other drivers and it hasn't even affected you. What kind of person are you? All you can think of is roses on mother's grave! This is the last time I'll ride with you. I don't know why I agreed to ride out to Lou's with you. What possessed you to pull a foolish stunt like that?"

"I'm sorry, I guess I just flipped. Come and see, Dottie, it's the most beautiful one yet."

Dottie walked around the large monument which blocked any view of her mother's grave site. She had to agree with Kate. This was the most beautiful bouquet left on the grave. As with the others there were four red roses delicately tied with a white ribbon and propped on a ledge underneath the name etched in the stone. This time there were several sprigs of white baby's breath tucked in around the red roses. "Oh, you are right, Kate. It is so beautiful! Can we take it with us to show Lou?"

"No, we cannot do that. Whoever put it here wanted Mom to enjoy it. Come on, we must go tell her that it has happened again."

"What, you think I am riding with you again? You're crazy. I'll walk to Lou's house."

"Don't be a fool, Dottie. Something inside of me just clicked when I saw those flowers. This whole thing has been driving me crazy. Mom never kept any secrets from me. Who is this mystery person that sneaks into our cemetery every year to drop off a bouquet of four roses? I still think it's a case of mistaken identity. This person has Mom confused with someone else."

"And what does 'Mom never kept any secrets from me,' mean? I was just as close to Mom as you were and she always told me everything."

"Yes, well she never prepared us for this. Let's go. I could use one of Lou's whiskey sours right now. Maybe the three of us can figure a way to get to the bottom of this. I know it's driving me crazy."

The rest of the drive was uneventful. Lou, Dottie and Kate's sister, met them at the front door. The house was bright with the summer sun flowing through a large bow window in the front wall of the living room and another in the breakfast nook on the opposite wall. The three women moved through the house to the spacious sun porch behind the dining room.

"Dottie, you are looking a little pale today. Are you feeling alright?" Lou asked as they entered the porch.

"Our crazy sister almost got us both killed out by the cemetery a little while ago, and all over mystery roses at Mom's grave."

Bill, Lou's son, had been dozing on the porch floor. At this point he opened his eyes, sat up and inquired, "What are you talking about, Aunt Dottie? There were no flowers this year."

"Well, sonny, you better get your ass off that floor and drop by the cemetery, because they are there this morning," Kate barked as she slid into the sofa on the porch.

"Kate, that's no way to talk to Bill. He's a nice young gentleman, and he's always tried to help us resolve this mystery. Lou, can you please make our sister a whiskey sour? You know she always needs a couple drinks to mellow out."

Lou went off to the kitchen to prepare drinks. When she returned,

Dottie filled everyone in on the morning's harrowing adventure near the cemetery.

"But it's June third and the flowers never appeared in June before. It's always been April or May," Kate interjected. "This doesn't make any sense. Sarah died five years ago in September and we buried her in the family plot there in the cemetery. The first mystery roses appeared in 1974. Lou noticed them. Lou, what was the date when you saw those first roses?"

"May fifteenth, Kate, I was rushing home from the grocery store to bake Bill's birthday cake. Remember his birthday's on the sixteenth. Anyway, I was thinking about how Mom never forgot his birthday and always sent him a card even as he got older. I looked over at the grave site and noticed the flowers. My curiosity aroused, I turned the car around and parked in the cemetery. There they were—four beautiful red roses. Since there was no card identifying where they came from and everyone in the family said they didn't know how they got there, we thought it was a mistake."

"But it wasn't, as I found out the next year," Kate jumped in. "It was a cold and windy May eleventh, and just like today I was on my way here to Lou's house to get my hair done. I was running late and I cursed the traffic as I left town. It had been a hectic morning and I needed my afternoon drink. That made me think of how Mom always got upset when I drank. That's when I noticed the second bouquet of roses. As with the first time, nobody in the family could shed any light on how they got there and we also checked all the local florists and none delivered them. As always there was no card or clue as to where they came from."

"Well, by the third year we were watchful and every day in May we expected the flowers to appear. As the fifteenth came and went and the days continued it appeared the first two years were a fluke. Then Bill saw the third bunch on the twenty-eighth as he drove to work," Dottie continued. "Last year we didn't even get into May. Eddy and I were coming back on the thirtieth of April from vacation and I glanced at the grave and noticed the roses. Let's see what we know. The dates are random in April, May and June. There are always four roses with a white ribbon. They've appeared five years in a row now and there is no way to predict when they will be put on the grave. To me it gets more confusing each year. Does anyone have any ideas?"

"Mom had a boyfriend who was sweet on her," Lou quipped as she brought a tray of refreshments onto the porch. "Who else would go to all this trouble? Dad died over twenty-two years ago. She just kept her new relationship a secret. Maybe he was a younger man and she was afraid one of us would steal him away."

"Oh, Lou, get serious. We all know our mother and father did not have a great relationship and there was no romance between them. After Dad died, Mom never dated and she told us she was very happy without a man in her life. She was glad to be single and able to devote her time to things she liked to do."

"Dottie's right," Kate jumped into the conversation. "Just look at all the church activities she got involved in. The programs for the elderly and the shut-ins and then there was her work with the handicapped children at the home in York. You all know how she devoted her time to helping others and the smile that came across her face when she talked about her visits to those less fortunate. Mom was never happier than those last ten years of her life. It's a lesson we all could learn from. We crowd our lives with worries and problems and don't really appreciate the blessings we have. By working with the less fortunate, Mom knew her blessing."

"Good drink, Lou, can I get a refill?" Kate continued. "Now the way I see it, there aren't a lot of options here. Mom either had an admirer that she may or may not have known about, or we have a case of mistaken identity where someone is putting the roses on the wrong grave. In any case, this person appears to want to remain anonymous and we will have to respect his wishes and hope he decides at some point to come clean and tell us his story."

"Well I think everyone is missing an obvious explanation," Bill finally spoke up. "Aunt Kate pointed out that Grandma Sarah worked with the sick and shut-ins. Perhaps one of the families she helped is showing their appreciation and remembrance of her work. Maybe we should contact the local paper and see if they would run a story requesting information on our yearly visitor. Someone may come forward at that point and admit he or she is the culprit."

"Say, that might not be a bad idea, Bill," Kate chimed in. "That son of yours is a smart cookie, Lou."

"Of course he's smart, Kate. He's my offspring," Lou joked. "They usually have a hometown news section in the paper. Let me go get last week's paper and see if a telephone number is listed."

"Relax, Mother, I've got it covered," Bill told her. "My friend, Mike Barnes, knows the writer for many of the articles on the local page. I'll go talk to him and get the reporter's phone number."

"I'm not sure we should do this," Dottie broke in. "Maybe there's something in this story that we don't want people to know about. We could wind up opening a can of worms that is best left hidden away on the shelf."

"Oh, Dottie, now you are beginning to sound like Jane, our doom and gloom sister. She wants our whole family history locked away in a safe with the lone key in her pocket. The only way she'd ever let anything out is if she could make a buck on it. She hasn't said a word about this whole situation. Remember how she snuck into Mom's house the day after she died to collect all the valuables before we got there? We need to confront her and find out what she took. Maybe there would be a clue there. Oh look, my glass is empty again. Can you fill it for me, dear?"

"You've had enough, sister," Dottie commented. "You almost killed me earlier today and you were completely sober. I will not ride home with you if you continue to drink. My favorite nephew will take me home."

At this point, Lou led the women into the kitchen to style their hair. Bill lay back on the floor and thought about the conversation that had just transpired. *What did I just get myself into*, he thought. *My big mouth always gets me in trouble.* Yes, his friend Mike knew that girl, Gail, from the local paper, the *Daily Post*, and he was fairly sure that she wrote articles on local news. Mike had dated her for several months. When they broke up a couple of months ago, Mike told him she was too wrapped up in her work and career. Bill had met her one time at Mike's apartment right before they broke up and he didn't like her at all. He recalled that she wasn't much to look at and was very rude to him and Mike that day. *Great, I never wanted to see that woman again and now I have to ask her for a favor. Boy, did I screw up. Well, I might as well ride over to Mike's. If he's home, I'll get her phone number and give her a call, then Mike and I can down a few beers.*

Bill slowly got up and headed toward his room to change his clothes. As he passed the women he overheard their conversation which was now focused on local gossip and beauty secrets. He never could understand how their conversation could swing so fast from one topic to another and never seemed to go anywhere. His mind was analytical, and once into a subject, he liked to take time to dissect it and evaluate the parts to see how they worked before he put things back together and moved on. *Take this rose thing for example*, he said to himself, *there are probably a dozen logical explanations which we haven't even looked at yet. No, wait, that's too much work for a Saturday—let's go back to the original plan, go to Mike's and get drunk.*

CHAPTER 2
The Paper Covers the Story

Bill had worked since graduation in a local manufacturing plant and lived at home with his mother. He was handsome and muscular, 6'-4" tall, with dark brown hair that he usually kept trimmed short. A quiet, somewhat shy man more comfortable in the forest or mountain than in a crowd of people, he usually spent most of his time with his family and close friends.

He walked out the front door of the house and slid into his dark brown Chevy pickup. Since high school his first love had always been his truck. Starting with a beat-up old red Ford, he had progressed from mini to full size and only last week had picked up this top-of-the-line model with all the powered options. He was a man who knew what he wanted and did not waiver until he got it. At 29 years old, Bill was content with his success in life, having worked his way up to a supervisor position in the plant and owning the vehicle of his dreams. Still, recently he realized that he was missing something in life and he felt a lonely emptiness inside.

Bill usually enjoyed the five-mile ride through the country to his little hometown of Greencastle. Along the north and west horizons were the beautiful, lush, wooded Appalachian Mountains. To the east and south spread a fertile farming valley that ran down to the Baltimore and Washington beltways. Greencastle, like many of the small towns that had grown up in this area in colonial times, was originally a manufacturing town with many small industries that supplied the needs of the local area. Indeed, Bill's family had come to this valley in the late 1700s to establish a shop making and selling hats. Succeeding generations of the family had gone on to run the local newspaper, establish a bank, and represent the area in the state government.

Sarah, Bill's grandmother, had always been very proud of the family's history and related the stories to Bill many times as he grew up. At times as Bill walked through town, he could almost feel the tug of history pulling him back in time. On quiet evenings as he walked past the old bank on the square with the brightly lit clock tower, he could almost see his ancestors moving through the old house behind the bank that used to be their home. Sometimes in the winter, when the wind whistled through the alleys and back streets, it almost sounded like they were calling his name—calling to him down through the ages. Bill shuddered as he thought this whole rose mystery may be them calling in a more tangible way. Maybe Dottie was right; things from the past should be left in the past.

Bill's thoughts totally engrossed him today and he was in town before he knew it. In the heart of town was the square, a large open area where the main roads to town met in bygone days. Surrounding this square was the main shopping area of the town. The red brick First National Bank with its old clock tower anchored the one corner. Other imposing old buildings crowded in on the other three corners.

Bill turned left in the square and parked in a lot across from the bank next to a large old building that was one of the hotels in previous times, but recently had been converted to apartments. His friend, Mike, lived on the second floor of the building. Mike usually partied Friday nights and slept in on Saturday. Bill was sure his friend would still be sleeping or recovering from the night before. Bill bounded up the steps to the apartment and rang the bell. He heard a shuffling inside and the door slowly opened to reveal a sleepy-eyed Mike in his underwear and a rumpled tee shirt.

"Hi, man. What brings you here so early in the morning?"

"Mike, buddy, check your clock," Bill informed him. "It's after twelve o'clock. You had another wild night last night, didn't you?"

"Things started out slow, but picked up as the night progressed. I was with that crowd from work. We almost drank three bars dry, and the chicks couldn't keep their hands off me. I think it's that new aftershave."

"Well, it must have failed you at the crucial moment; because I see you are alone this morning."

"Hey, man, I was in no condition to bring a babe home last night. I did get a couple phone numbers though. How about I give you one and I take the other and we see what action we can stir up tonight? Old Mikey is ready to howl."

"To be honest with you, I did come here for a girl's phone number. I need the phone number of the girl from the *Daily Post*. I think her name was Gail."

"That bitch, you don't want her, man. She's trouble, always talking about her work and messing with your mind. Stay away from her. Besides, she's a little chunky and her breasts are too small. Now Vanessa, who I met last night, is just right for you. She's an Amazon in a mini-skirt—at least 6'-3" tall with long, thin legs, a huge pair, and a smile that lights up the room. Here, let me get you her number." Mike went to the refrigerator, grabbed two beers and tossed one to Bill.

As he headed toward the bedroom, Bill yelled after him, "I know what you're saying. I was turned off by the girl from the *Post* also, but my mother and her sisters want the paper to print a story. Someone is mysteriously leaving flowers on my grandmother's grave. A bouquet of four roses are left every year, never on the same date. They think a story might flush out the person or at least get some clues as to who is doing the deed. Doesn't Gail write those types of stories? I was hoping you'd still have her number and I could give her a call. Believe me, it would be business only."

As Mike left the room, Bill opened his beer and poured a big slug into his mouth. Mike returned in a few minutes with a slip of paper in both hands. "This is your decision, Billie boy," he started. "In my right hand I hold Vanessa's phone number. This number will lead you to a night of unending pleasure, the details of which I am sure you understand. In my left hand I hold the phone number of Attila the

Hun, alias Gail Mason, feared by man and beast alike. Now, my friend, which hand will you pick? Will this evening bring business or pleasure?"

Before Mike knew what happened, Bill sprang at him and grabbed both slips of paper. "Now," he said triumphantly, "I can sample both worlds. I can do battle with the evil Gail and then spend a passionate evening with the fair lady Vanessa. Can it get any better than this?"

"Yes, Sir Bill, it can," Mike said as he reached into the refrigerator and threw a second beer to Bill. "Here, drink this can of magic elixir from the gods. It's guaranteed to give you strength to slay dragons and you will need every drop if you are calling Mistress Gail."

After opening his beer and taking a long swig to steel his determination, Bill dialed Gail's number and felt his determination slipping as Gail said, "Hello," on the other end of the line.

"Good afternoon, Gail," he started, trying to begin on the right foot with a cheerful greeting. "This is Bill Henderson. We met at Mike Barnes' apartment a while back." Bill paused and the total silence on the other end of the line made Bill wonder if he should just give up at that point. Taking a deep breath, he plunged ahead, "I have a human interest/mystery story for the paper I want to talk to you about. Can we get together and I'll give you the details?"

"Look, buster, I'm on to your game. This is another one of Mike's schemes and I'm not falling for it. What am I supposed to do—rush to his apartment to hear your story and when I get there you're gone and he meets me at the door naked as a jay bird? You and Mike can take your little games and stick them up—"

"No, wait," Bill broke in, "I do have a story. Meet me at Rosie's in half an hour. It's a quiet place for us to talk, and I'll buy you an ice cream. I know you will want to print this story."

"OK, I have some free time, so I'll play your game, but you better be alone or I'm out of there."

Bill hung up the phone, turned to Mike and said, "Man, that is one nasty chick. What did you do to ruffle her feathers? She wants to tear you to pieces and she has no problem including me for good measure."

Mike sat down, ran his hands through his hair, and stared at the wall a few seconds. "Truth is, Gail and I had a go at a relationship awhile back. For a while she went with me to all the parties and then we started to grow apart as I continued without her. She was never into the party circuit. When she finally broke up with me my ego was bruised. I tried to win her back, and in the process I did some silly, stupid things. Anyhow, I'm over that loser now and ready to rock. Let's have another beer."

Mike jumped up and headed for the refrigerator. Bill also got up and headed toward the door. "Later, man," he yelled after Mike. "Remember, I have an appointment with Attila in a half hour and I need my reflexes at peak performance."

It was a short ride to Rosie's ice cream and fast food restaurant. Bill pulled into the almost empty parking lot at this hour and looked around for Gail. He did not see her waiting for him anywhere. He parked at the back of the lot and slowly walked to the restaurant entrance. As soon as he walked through the door he spied her sitting in the far corner.

As he turned and approached the table, he noted that she was wearing a denim skirt and a white short-sleeve blouse with lacy sleeves. Her dark summer tan complimented her blue eyes and auburn hair and Bill realized that she was a very attractive girl, but as she turned her head and recognized him she did not smile. Instead she seemed to scowl and tense up. Her cold reception made Bill regret insisting they get together to talk.

"Thanks for coming," Bill started as he slid into the seat across from her. "I'm sorry if I gave you some wrong impressions this morning. Mike never told me about his relationship with you. I guess I woke up some painful memories. I didn't intend to do that. I only wanted to talk to you about running a story on a mystery in my family."

"I'm sorry too, Bill, for wrongly accusing you and being short on the phone. Things moved real rapid for Mike and me at first and I fell for him in a big way. It all happened too fast, before we really got to know each other. Then, reality set in and I spent a lot of lonely nights crying my heart out while he would go out and get so drunk he couldn't find his way home. He wasn't going to change his lifestyle and I couldn't live like that, so one day I got up my nerve and told him it was over. He agreed with me and then changed his mind. For weeks I lived in fear day and night not knowing when, where and how he would pop up and try to persuade me to come back. Many times he had been drinking and that convinced me to stick to my decision. I hadn't heard from him in quite awhile. When you called and reminded me that we met at his apartment, I figured he was just trying a new approach. With Mike I have to keep my defenses up and I suspected a trick right away. You need to tell Mike that it's over between us."

"I didn't come here to trick you. Mike told me today that he has no intention of bothering you anymore. Let's start over and pretend this is the first time we ever met. Come with me and I'll buy you that cone I promised and then we'll talk about the story."

For the first time, Gail smiled at him as she slid out of the booth and stood up. Bill was also in the process of sliding out of the booth when Gail stood up. At Mike's apartment he had seen her in an oversized dark blue warm-up suit. Her hair had been tied up in a bun on the top of her head and her eyes were red and puffy, probably from crying he realized now. Surely this tall, thin, well-proportioned girl standing before him was not the chunky bitch Mike talked about this morning. This thought stopped Bill in his tracks.

Gail turned around and saw him staring at her and questioned, "Is something wrong?"

Bill stumbled for words and blurted out, "Err, I didn't realize you were so tall."

"Five foot eleven and finally done growing," she laughed. "My mother always said I inherited my looks and my height from my grandfather. He's over six feet tall and has blue eyes just like me. Sometimes this height can be a real curse. Try going to your prom and looking down at almost everyone in the room. But you probably know what I'm talking about. You're taller than me. How tall are you?"

"I'm six foot four. For a guy being tall is not a problem. Let's go get that ice cream," Bill stammered as he tried to regain his composure. This was not the girl he had come to do battle with in order to get his article published. He had expected a nasty, grumpy, poorly dressed, overweight newspaper reporter who had no interest but the story. Instead there was this tall, gorgeous, blue-eyed woman who had just flashed him a warm smile.

Bill had not been very active on the dating circuit and his shyness usually prevented him from meeting new girls. These thoughts came flooding into his mind and he lost his resolve for a moment. Then he reminded himself that they were here this afternoon to discuss a newspaper article—nothing more. *Stick to the plan and get the article published,* he told himself. With new resolve, Bill slid out of the booth and walked with Gail to the counter.

After ordering the ice cream and returning to the booth, Bill filled Gail in on his grandmother Sarah's death and the yearly appearance of the mystery flowers since 1974, including the bouquet of four red roses this morning. Gail's excitement grew as Bill filled in the details. She assured him that the paper would be willing to run a small article on the mystery, requesting any information from readers in the local area. She needed a picture of the latest flowers, so Bill drove to her apartment to pick up a camera and then they drove to the cemetery. Later they drove back to Rosie's for Gail to pick up her car.

Bill parked his truck and said, "Thanks, Gail, for getting the article in the paper. I hope someone in the area can clear up this mystery for my mother and aunts. Hey, look at the time. It's past six o'clock. We've spent the whole afternoon together and I enjoyed it. Talking to you just seems so easy. I'm usually not very good at striking up a conversation with someone I never met before." He was enjoying the afternoon so much he really didn't want it to end, but he couldn't figure out how to prolong it. Perhaps he would call her sometime and see if they could get together again, if he got his courage up.

"Again, Bill, I need to apologize for how I acted this morning. I shouldn't have pre-judged your conversation. I too enjoyed this afternoon. In fact, I can't remember ever working on an article for the paper and enjoying it so much. Now I really must go." Gail slid out of the truck and yelled back, "Bye, Bill. Look for the article in next week's paper. I'll call and let you know if we get any responses."

Bill pulled out of the lot and thought to himself, *Damn, Bill, why can't you be more aggressive? You didn't even find out if she was dating someone. She sure is sweet and you need a girlfriend, old buddy. Getting drunk with*

Mike every now and then eases the pain, but that lonely spot inside just keeps growing.

Again, Bill had been so deep in thought that he was pulling into the driveway at his home before he realized that he had driven all the way from town. As he walked up the driveway and put his keys in his pocket, he felt the slips of paper from Mike. He pulled the first one out and saw that Gail's name and phone number was written on it. He carefully refolded it and placed it in his wallet. Then he pulled out the second slip of paper and without even looking at it he tossed it in the garbage can as he passed. *Sorry, Vanessa,* he mused, *I'm looking for something more than a one-night stand.*

The following Saturday, as Bill crawled out of the shower and was reaching for his towel, he heard the phone ring. *Oh no. Here we go again and it's Saturday morning,* he thought as he rubbed the towel over his body. *That phone hasn't stopped ringing since the article came out in the paper. It seems everybody in town suddenly knows us and wants to talk about the flowers. Who are all these people that call? I think Mom enjoys the notoriety, but I'm getting a little annoyed.* Bill slipped on his underwear and shorts and was brushing his teeth when his mother knocked on the door.

"Bill, a Miss Mason from the *Daily Post* is on the line and wants to talk to you. Isn't she the girl that wrote the article in the paper?"

Bill opened the door and stepped out. "Yes, she is, Mom. She promised to call if there were any leads." Lou handed the phone to Bill. He felt a tingle of excitement as he raised the phone to his ear. He had wanted to call Gail a hundred times in the last week and had rehearsed the words he would say, but it just didn't seem to come out right and so he would convince himself that she really wasn't interested in him. Maybe he could use this call to see her again. His heart leaped as he said, "Hi, Gail. How are you doing? Did you get any information for us?"

"Bill, small towns just love to gossip and that article I wrote got everyone in town talking. We've had dozens of calls here at the newspaper from people requesting more information. I'm sorry, but nobody has come forward with information on the mystery person. There's time yet. Some of the papers are mailed out and people don't get them for several days after they go on sale."

"I'm glad you called. I wanted to call and tell you that I enjoyed the time we spent together so much and hoped we could get together again sometime." There, he had blurted it out. Now she could cut him down and tell him she was not interested and he could try to get her out of his mind. How do you get a beautiful goddess with deep blue eyes out of your mind?

"Thank you, Bill. We did have a nice day together last week. You're in luck. My editor wants to do a follow-up story on your grandmother. A human interest/historical perspective type story. I need more information and your help. Are you interested in helping me? If so, when can we get together and start?"

Bill quickly explained Gail's planned follow-up article to his mother and asked her if she had any objections. Lou thought it was a good idea as long as Bill reviewed the information and articles prior to publishing. She felt there were no skeletons in the closet, but if anything did come up Bill could filter it out.

"OK, Gail, Mom and I are in agreement that we will have a celebrity in the family. If you are not busy this evening, come over and we will give you whatever information we can. In fact, Mom just said come at 5:30 and have dinner with us." Bill followed his offer with directions to the house and waited for a reply.

"Thanks, I'll do that. I travel home many weekends to see my mother. Eating here by myself when I stay in town sure gets lonely on the weekend. I'll be there at 5:30 sharp. See you then."

Lou couldn't help notice the smile on Bill's face as he hung up the phone. "Why, Bill," she started, "I believe you have a crush on this girl. I haven't seen that look on your face since you took the Baker girl to the prom. Maybe I should use the good silverware."

"It's true, Mom, Gail's pretty, I enjoyed spending time with her and I wanted to see her again. Are you going to get that published in the paper?" Bill joked.

That evening Lou stuck with the everyday silverware, but she did make lasagna. Her lasagna was the best in the valley and she always made it when she wanted to impress someone. Bill also noted bowls heaped full of fresh home-grown green beans and applesauce made from apples he picked off the tree in the backyard last fall. Now he noticed her in the kitchen putting finishing touches on the chocolate icing of a cake.

Lou had seen the loneliness in Bill's life for some time now. She and her sisters had tried their hands at matchmaking, but Bill seemed to resist all efforts. She was afraid that he would never find anyone. She was determined to make the best of this opportunity tonight. Bill's expression had betrayed his feelings and she was going to try to gently nudge the situation in the right direction. Her mother always told her food was the way to a man's heart. How do you catch the girl? Her thoughts were interrupted by the doorbell. As she moved the knife one last time and swirled the icing across the top of the cake, she glanced at the clock and noticed it was 5:30 exactly.

Bill walked to the front door and glanced nervously around the room to make sure everything was in order. He was nervous and excited as he opened the door. His eyes met the blue oceans in Gail's as he noted her long flowing hair that tumbled gracefully down her back. She wore a light blue summer dress that plunged slightly at the neck to show a hint of firmly tanned breasts. Bill wondered if wearing this dress was a subconscious message that she was interested in him. In any case she was stunning and he hoped she approved of the khaki slacks and dark blue polo shirt that he had finally settled on wearing. His mind was jolted back to reality when he heard his mother's footsteps as she rounded the corner from the dining room.

"Bill, don't just stand there. Let our guest in, please."

Still in awe of Gail's beauty, Bill opened the door and ushered Gail into the house.

"Don't you two make a nice couple," Lou couldn't help noting. "Let's just go to the dining room. Everything is ready."

Once in the dining room, Bill regained his composure and introduced Gail to his mother. During the course of the dinner, Lou explained to Gail that Bill's father had died two years ago from a heart attack. Lou had returned to working part time as a beautician in a local shop. Then Bill explained his job and its duties.

Later the conversation turned to Gail and how she had come to work at the newspaper. Gail explained that she had grown up in Lancaster and had gone to Penn State for a degree in journalism. After graduation, she had worked a few odd jobs around Lancaster. Everywhere she applied she was turned down due to lack of experience. When no local jobs appeared, her mother feared that she would have to move to a bigger metropolitan area like Baltimore or Philadelphia. Then one day Gail went to visit her grandfather and he told her he had heard the Greencastle newspaper was looking for a reporter for local events and news. He thought working for a small newspaper would be a lot more rewarding, less stressful and would give her the experience she needed to break into the Lancaster papers if she decided to return there later. With no experience Gail knew she would not be hired; however, her grandfather persisted and she reluctantly applied for the job and surprisingly was immediately hired. Now she had been on the staff for almost five years. She admitted yearning for the excitement of a big city newspaper, but she liked the freedom and responsibility in the local paper.

As the meal was drawing to a conclusion, Lou suggested that they move to the porch for dessert and coffee. A glass doorway led from the dining room to the porch, which was bright with the light from large windows on both sides and the back. A set of French doors on the back wall opened onto a small deck. A cool evening breeze flowed through the windows. The pastoral view from the windows was dotted here and there with quaint bank barns and sturdy stone farmhouses. The gradual rise in the landscape slowly ascended to the little town of Upton over a mile away.

Gail couldn't help exclaiming, "What a beautiful, peaceful view. I need to bring my camera and capture it. I want to do an article on living in the country sometime."

"Yes, it is a tranquil view," Bill noted. "My father added the porch to the house. We all enjoyed many happy hours reading or playing games out here. Dad also enjoyed sitting on the porch in the midst of a snowstorm just watching the snow swirl and blow around the yard and fields."

"Please, let's stay here during the interview," Gail pleaded as she grabbed Bill's hands and held them. "Let me run out to my car and get my notebook and camera while your mother prepares dessert."

Bill fell into one of the chairs at the small table on the porch as soon as Gail stepped out. What had just happened? *Get real, Bill*, he told himself. *This girl is interested in your grandmother's life. She probably doesn't even know you exist.* Still, she was very excited a few minutes ago and had grabbed and squeezed his hands. He had to talk to her and find out if she knew he existed. His thoughts were interrupted by his mother bringing a tray full of cake into the room.

"Bill, are you OK?" she exclaimed when she saw him slumped in the chair. "You look a little pale. Did something you eat disagree with you?"

"I'm OK, Mom. I just need to work through some issues," Bill stated as he stood up from the chair and walked out of the room. Lou's motherly instinct told her the problem and she smiled. A few seconds later Gail and Bill returned and Lou served dessert.

After the dessert dishes were cleared away, Lou began the story, "My mother, Sarah, was born on a cold winter's night—as she used to like to tell it—at the turn of the century, January 3, 1900, here in Greencastle. When she was five years old her father, William, died from a stroke. By the way, I named Bill in honor of his great-grandfather William. Well, proceeding on, Mom must have had an uneventful childhood. Occasionally she would talk about something she remembered, like the first time she saw an airplane land near Chambersburg or a day at the old school on South Washington Street. I remember the sad look on her face when she told us about marrying a soldier by the name of Brown who was killed in World War I, but she would never tell us anything more about him except that true love only comes once. Right before the Second World War she used to get so upset at people who wanted America to join the war. She told them they would never talk that way if they had experienced the loss of a loved one on the battle field. Getting back on track, Mom got

25

remarried to Richard Myers and Kate was born in October of 1921. Dottie and I followed approximately two years later. Jane is the youngest born in 1929. In 1956 my father died from cancer. Mom never remarried or dated. She became active in charity organizations until she died in September of 1973 from a stroke—an ordinary life with no clues to the appearance of the flowers."

"Well," Gail started, "I think we should research the time period from 1956 to 1973. The answer to our mystery is probably in there somewhere. Did Sarah always live here in town through that time period? Where there any men even remotely in her life? Give me more information on the charities she was involved in."

"Sarah lived her whole married life until the day she died on South Baltimore Street in the same house. No, there were no men in her life. She was active with several local charities through our church here in town. She volunteered at the homeless kitchen in Hagerstown, and she worked with a handicapped children's home in York. Why, she even went out there several times a month to fill in for the staff when they went on vacation or leaves. She said they were always short of substitutes and she couldn't say no because the kids really enjoyed her visits."

"Wait," Bill jumped in, "I just thought of one man we are overlooking in her life. She worked very close with Pastor Jones on many of her projects. He is a widower—lost his wife in a car accident about twenty years ago. We really need to talk to him."

"Good, we have two starting places. We need to see Pastor Jones and we need to visit the homeless kitchen. Bill, I would like you to be with me during the visits. Many times one person will pick up information that the other misses. What is your work schedule?"

"We are in luck. This week we are starting a new line at work and I will be on second shift a few weeks. I need to be home before three to get ready for work. I will check with Pastor Jones tomorrow and see if we can meet with him first thing Monday."

Gail agreed that this would work for her and Bill could call her Sunday evening with a time. Then she glanced at her watch and announced that it was getting late and she better get back to her apartment. Bill announced that he would walk her to her car.

Outside the full moon hung just above the mountains in the distance. Bill marveled at how beautiful Gail appeared in its soft light. He was gathering his courage to tell her about the growing feelings he was having for her when she turned and said, "Bill, I really need your help with this research and I appreciate everything you and your mother have done for me. Working together like this can easily lead to emotional attachment. I need to let you know that I can't become emotionally involved right now. I went through a very traumatic time during and after my breakup with Mike and it drained me. I can't let myself get hurt again. We need to keep our relationship professional and unemotional to be objective. I know you agree with me."

"Sure, Gail, objective and professional—no problem," Bill said as he opened her car door. Later as he walked back to the house he said to himself, *Boy, I almost stuck my foot in my mouth. Now what am I going to do? I want more than a professional relationship with Gail.*

As soon as Bill walked through the door, Lou exclaimed, "Bill, what is wrong? You look like you lost your last friend."

"Well, maybe I have, Mom. Gail's one terrific girl and I can talk to her so easily. I was really getting excited about dating her and I was about ready to ask her when she stopped me dead in my tracks. Before I could say anything she told me she was still recovering emotionally from her breakup with Mike and we need to keep our relationship totally professional with no emotion. What am I going to do? I never met a girl like her before. I don't know how to spend time with her and not get attached."

"Give it time and move slowly, Bill. I commented earlier this evening that you two make a great couple. I have a good feeling that Gail will come around. Trust your old mother's opinion."

"Thanks, Mom, and you are not old. Now I better go to bed."

CHAPTER 3
The Mystery Grows

The room was dark except for the moonlight that slid through the curtains on the side window. He tore off his shirt as he slowly crossed from the door. When he reached her, his lips met hers in a long passionate kiss. With the hot passion in her breath as she returned the kiss, he knew tonight was the night. He delicately unbuttoned her dress and slipped it off her silken shoulders. It fell to the floor and the full beauty of her dark tanned body was fully exposed to him for the first time. His excitement and manliness were growing to the point of bursting as he gently caressed her back and shoulders and fondled her firm, erect nipples. She breathed a low sigh as he gently picked her up in his arms and felt her cool soft skin against his naked chest. A sudden breeze from the open window blew her auburn hair gently over his shoulder and he shivered with anticipation as it slid down his back. The pounding of his heart was so hard in his chest, he feared it may burst. As he moved swiftly toward the bed he was further aroused by the enticing aroma of her perfume. Yes, tonight was the night and he would...

"Bill, get up. You need to leave in an hour. I have breakfast ready." Lou knocked on his door and left.

"Gee, Mom, couldn't you give me five minutes more?" *Yeah, Bill old buddy, that's all the time it would take as excited as you were*, he chuckled to himself as he slid out of bed. "And, why, Miss Gail, do you walk

28

around wearing no underpants and bra?" he mumbled aloud.

"Bill, who are you talking to? Did I hear you say something about a bra?"

"No, Mom, I said I have to borrow a couple dollars to buy gas." Bill knew that would get her thoughts off what he really said. How would you explain a dream like that to your mother?

She mumbled as she fumbled through her purse for her wallet. "Kids, why does he think I am the local bank?"

By seven-thirty in the morning Bill was on his way into town to pick up Gail. They had an appointment with Pastor Jones at the church at eight. Bill had not told him anything except he and Gail needed to talk to him. Bill had also spent a lot of time thinking about what Gail had said to him and his mother's comments. A part of him just wanted to break and run. Get done with helping Gail today and tell her he would not be able to help in the future and trump up an excuse. Another part of him wanted to grab her and make passionate love to her just like he was about to do in his dream. But, right now, she was in control and he decided to heed his mother's advice and let things develop.

As soon as Bill stopped in front of Gail's apartment, she came running down the sidewalk. Today she was dressed very business-like in a pair of dark blue slacks and a simple white blouse. Bill ambled around his truck and started to open Gail's door when a sudden gust of wind stopped him in his tracks. That perfume fragrance, he remembered it clearly from his dream. How can you remember a perfume from a dream?

"I really like the fragrance of your perfume. What kind is it?"

"Thank you for the compliment. It's Summer Passion, a new fragrance I found at the mall yesterday afternoon. It kind of reminded me of the scent of the flowers flowing in on the breeze that I smelled on your back porch."

I never knew flowers could be so erotic, Bill said to himself as he walked around the truck and slid into his seat. Both deep in thought, they drove quietly the short distance to the church parking lot.

Pastor Jones heard them entering the church and met them at his office door. "Good morning, Bill and Gail. I've enjoyed your articles in the paper, Gail. You have a wonderful way of freshening up our local news. I confess, I sometimes skip the world news and read your section first. My, you two make a handsome couple. How can I help you?"

"It's Gail's article about my grandmother that brings us here today," Bill started, hoping Gail had picked up the pastor's comment about them making a handsome couple. "Gail is researching for a follow-up article and we knew Sarah spent a lot of time with you helping the less fortunate. Maybe you know someone who might have grown close to her during her work."

"Well, your grandmother was very active with the shut-ins from our church. Each Sunday she would work up a list of anyone unable to make it to church due to illness or infirmity. By Friday she would make sure she had visited everyone on the list and she would pass me the names of anyone requesting or needing a further visit. She was a very big help in this ministry. I have discussed your article with many of our parishioners. It has created quite a stir in our little community. Everyone loved Sarah and many related stories of receiving cheerful visits from her over the years. Sarah was a very friendly and outgoing woman and we miss the warmth she passed on to us, but nobody had any explanation for the roses. If anyone from our church were putting those flowers in the cemetery, they would have told me."

"Do you know of anyone in the congregation she might have dated or had a special relationship with?" Bill asked, hoping to lead Pastor Jones to reveal his own feelings toward Sarah.

"In our little town, church gossip on this type of thing spreads quickly. I never heard any gossip on your grandmother."

"What about you, Pastor Jones? You're a good-looking eligible bachelor Sarah's age," Gail said in a joking tone, but Bill knew this was a probing question.

"Thanks for the compliment, Gail. I loved my wife very deeply and after her death, I devoted myself totally to the church and my son's family. I am very content and have no time or desire to form a new relationship. I am a one-woman man. As for Sarah's soup kitchen involvement, I don't think you'll find anything there either. Most of the guests were transients and street people. Sarah told me her work with many of them to help improve their lives was very disappointing. Few had the strength to break from their environment and forge better lives."

"What do you know about her work with the children's home in York?" Gail tried a different direction.

"Why, I never knew she worked with the children's home," Pastor Jones responded surprised. "We talked at great length about her other efforts. I wonder why she never mentioned going there."

Bill and Gail closed the interview at this point, and as they prepared to leave Pastor Jones said, "I'm sorry I couldn't shed any light on the mystery. It was nice meeting you, Gail. Please come to church with Bill next Sunday."

As Bill drove away, they agreed with Pastor Jones that he was not able to provide any helpful information. On the drive to Hagerstown, Bill brought up the pastor's invitation to come to church. Gail explained that she had not gone to church since she was a teenager. Her parents separated and had gone through a bitter divorce at that time in her life. She had prayed repeatedly that her parents would get back together. Instead they fought daily even after the divorce was finalized. She told Bill if God really cared he would not have let this happen to her family.

It was apparent to Bill that Gail was still bitter over this episode in her life. He explained to her that it was his faith that had pulled him through his father's sudden death. He and his father had been very close. They hunted, fished and camped together. They worked together around the house. Only prayer and faith that some day he would be together again with his father in heaven eased the pain and gave him strength to go on. Bill urged Gail to give God another chance and let Him back into her life.

"Bill, that was a powerful sermon," she joked. "Pastor Jones better watch out or you'll be taking over his job. Seriously, I have some skeletons hanging in my closet. I usually keep them locked up. It's just so easy talking to you. This one slipped out before I knew it. I'm not ready to get religion, but I feel better now that I shared this with you."

Soon they arrived at the Hagerstown soup kitchen which fed the destitute and homeless a nourishing meal every evening. Bill and Gail talked at length with the manager of the kitchen. She remembered Sarah very well. They worked together in the kitchen preparing the meal. She told them Sarah usually only helped two nights a week and many times they were alone in the kitchen. She said Sarah was always talkative and openly expressed her feelings. There never was any mention of a romantic involvement. When she told everyone that Sarah had died, a few of the guests had shown remorse. However, when Gail's article came out in the paper none of the regulars could remember who Sarah was. Once again Bill and Gail had come up with a blank sheet of paper. It was late in the afternoon when Bill dropped Gail off.

"Thanks for taking me, Bill. I guess we struck out today. I'll look at my notes and see where we go from here. I have some other pressing stories at the paper and we may need to drop this one for a while. I'll call you in a few days." Gail jumped out of the truck and trudged toward her apartment.

At this point Bill was depressed and ready to throw the towel in. Being near this girl drove him crazy because she made it plain that she was not interested in him. Trouble was, he enjoyed her company, and even Pastor Jones felt they looked great as a couple. Women—what man could understand them? He looked at his watch and noted it was 2:30. He needed to go home and get ready for work.

Bill was not used to working second shift and it had been a long evening. Now as he crawled into the cab of his truck he was thankful he turned down the offer his buddies made to go to the local bar and unwind with a few beers. As he drove home he reviewed the day in his mind. It had started with the dream. Hopefully he could experience a rerun to completion tomorrow morning. Then there was the quick breakfast with his mom. Since his dad's death, he and his mother had grown much closer together and she was always there when he needed her or just wanted to talk. Then he had spent the rest of the morning and most of the afternoon with Gail. Mixed emotions flowed again as he reviewed this part of his day. It was great being near her for such a long time, but she really seemed to draw away from him after he told her that religion had given him the strength to continue his own life after his dad's death. He wondered for a moment if he made a bad decision in speaking out, but he was what he was and that was something he couldn't change. *Bill, old buddy, it's time you make a break with this girl and move on before you get in too deep and can't pull back,* he told himself as he turned into the driveway at home. Now he was exhausted and ready for bed.

He slid out of his truck and quietly opened the front door. A light his mother had left on in the kitchen dimly lit the area. He moved sleepily toward the kitchen, turned off the light and headed toward his room. His thoughts were totally focused on sliding between the cool, soft sheets and quickly falling into a deep sleep when the sharp ring of the telephone interrupted his hopes. He quickly retraced his steps, hoping he could reach the before it woke his mother. *Now who could this be? It's probably some drunk who dialed the wrong number,* he moaned as he flipped a light on and reached for the phone. At this hour in the morning he managed a curt, "Hello."

"Bill, thank goodness you are home. I hope I didn't wake your mother up. I've been crying for the last hour and I couldn't stand it any longer. I need you to come over right now." It was Gail. Her voice was strained and she stopped a couple times to regain her composure.

"Are you alright?" Bill was confused and his mind was struggling to comprehend why Gail had called at this hour.

"No, I'm not alright. Would I have called like this if I was alright? I need you. Please come over." She was almost yelling hysterically into the telephone.

"I'm sorry, Gail, I just got home from work. Your call took me by surprise at this time of night. I'll be right over." Bill hung up the phone and turned toward the door. His mother came down the hall as he turned the doorknob.

"Bill, I heard you talking to Gail on the phone. It's terribly late for her to be calling. Is something wrong?"

"I'm not sure, Mom. She was very upset and wanted me to come over right away. I'll run over and see what I can do. Go back to bed. I'll call if I need you."

All thoughts of sleep were erased from Bill's mind as he drove quickly through the night back to Greencastle. His focus was on his last conversation with Gail. Something had happened to upset her and she needed him. He was on his way to help her, but other thoughts were rolling around in his head also. Twice she had said, "I need you." Was this the same girl who had told him a couple of days ago that she didn't want to have a relationship with him? Since he was the one she called when trouble occurred, was this a signal that her feelings for him were growing? Or was it just that she had no one else in the area to call? He would soon find out.

He slid into a parking space in front of her apartment and ran to her door. It seemed like only a second later that Gail opened the door and flung herself at him. It looked like she had been getting ready for bed. She was in her bathrobe and slippers. In the soft light of her living room he noted she wasn't wearing any makeup, and her eyes were red from crying.

"Thanks for coming right away, Bill. I know the last thing you probably wanted to do was come back to town after working all night, but I couldn't stop crying and I knew you could help me." Her voice was low and hesitant. She was crying again and she clung tightly to Bill with her arms around his neck.

Bill's heart went out to her and he just wanted to embrace her, kiss her and tell her he would care for her and everything would be alright. Instead, realizing she had called in need of a friend, he said, "Why don't you begin from where I dropped you off this afternoon and tell me what happened?"

She released her grip around his neck and he took her hand and led her to the sofa where they sat down. He noted as they walked that the room was very small and opened on one side into a tiny kitchenette area with a table and two chairs. Two doors on the other wall probably led to the bathroom and bedroom. The living room itself was sparsely furnished with a sofa, reclining chair and small TV on a stand with a stereo radio beneath it. On another small table next to the sofa a few pictures of Gail, apparently with her mother, were neatly arranged. All gave the appearance of order and neatness.

"Well, when I got into the apartment I rolled up my sleeves and did some chores. As you can see, I cleaned the place up. Then, I got busy writing a couple articles for the paper. I have a desk in the bedroom for my typewriter. I became so engrossed in what I was doing, I didn't realize how late it was. Finally about 10:30 I finished the articles and realized I was hungry. I took a quick shower and made myself a sandwich and then sat down to read the mail. It must have been a little after eleven when I got through the sales flyers and bills, and I noticed this."

Bill noticed her hand shake as she reached over to the table next to the sofa and picked up a letter. She handed it to Bill and wiped her eyes again as she began to cry.

"It's OK, Gail. I'm here. There's nothing to worry about." He put his arms around her and hugged her.

She put the tissue down and turned to him and smiled. "Thanks, Bill, I don't know what I would have done if you didn't come. We haven't known each other very long, but you are a true friend."

Bill released Gail and started to open the letter. *Wow, she really does like me*, he said to himself.

There was a single piece of typing paper in the envelope. Bill pulled out the letter and opened it up. It said:

Gail,
Some things we search for are best left unfound. I did not like the story on Sarah. This story is best left unpublished. Do not share the story with other papers and do not dig into the past for any more research on this article. You and your family could get hurt if you do not heed my warning. I will be watching.

Bill could not believe the words as he read them. Why would anyone threaten Gail and her family over a story about his grandmother? This was beyond his comprehension. Who was putting the roses on the grave and why was this letter written? How could a simple story bring this kind of response? What would he say to Gail?

"Oh, Bill, what am I going to do? I never expected anything like this from any articles I wrote. I write little local news stories. I came here instead of going to the city so I wouldn't have to write about crime, corruption and violence. I just wanted to enjoy writing and make my readers happy with cheerful articles. Now I write a simple article and look what I get. What do I do now?"

Bill put his arm around Gail and held her as she burst into tears again. "I'm sorry, Gail. I knew the person delivering the flowers wanted to remain anonymous. I should never have come to you with that article. It's my fault."

"You didn't know," she sobbed. "How would anyone know my article would produce this response? No, Bill, it isn't you fault."

"We'll take the letter to Jim, your editor, in the morning. As for you, I think it would be best if you came home and stayed with us tonight. We have a nice bed in the spare room and it never gets used. Let me call Mom and let her know we're coming." Bill's take-charge attitude had a calming effect on Gail. She agreed with Bill and went into her room to change and collect her things for the morning.

Bill called his mother and gave her a quick run down of the letter, how it affected Gail and his plan to let her sleep in the spare bedroom. His mother agreed and said she would make sure everything was ready. Bill reread the letter, folded it and put it back in the envelope as Gail came out of the bedroom dressed in jeans and a loose-fitting sweatshirt.

As he helped her into the truck she burst out laughing and said, "I can't believe I just did what I did. In my rush to get dressed I just grabbed this old sweatshirt and put it on like I do lots of times when I'm just lazing around the apartment. I never put my bra on then and I didn't do it now. Do you mind riding to your mother's with a half-naked lady?"

"No problem, miss, it'll just make it easier to ravish your gorgeous body later," he joked as he slid into his seat.

"Why, sir, would you take advantage of a helpless lady and ravish this tired body?" As she joked she grabbed the bottom of her sweatshirt and raised it slightly, exposing her thin waist and navel area. Suddenly Bill felt himself becoming aroused and hoped that Gail didn't notice. The thought of her sitting next to him with no bra on and now seeing her bare midriff was too much.

Gail suddenly turned serious and said, "Say, Bill, that part about my gorgeous body—thanks for the compliment. I was the tall, goofy-looking, clumsy girl growing up. I guess I've always been self-conscious of my height and lack of coordination, and so I became a loner and spent a lot of my time reading. Guys seldom asked me out and usually didn't call for a second date. After I came to Greencastle, I was just content working and partying a little with a couple of girl friends. Then after the episode with Mike, I swore off men. You treat me like a lady and make me feel good about myself. I appreciate that, but it's scary. A part of me wants to let go and enjoy the time we spend together. Another part keeps telling me not to get close to you because I'll only get hurt again."

Bill felt that he needed to convince Gail that he wasn't like Mike. He began, "Mike and I have been friends since high school. Sometimes when I'm feeling a little lonely or life's getting me down we get together and get drunk. I could never live his life of excessive drinking on a regular basis. As for our relationship, I have too much respect for you to ever treat you differently than I do now. You are a beautiful woman and deserve to be treated like a lady. I am just doing what my mother taught me. Again, I am sorry for getting you in this mess."

"Like I told you earlier, it's not your fault. I feel much better since you arrived at the apartment. It was really nice of your mother to let me stay at her house." Gail seemed more relaxed.

As they drove out of town Bill noted that the tension had disappeared from her body. "Mom's a peach. She's a lot like my grandmother Sarah was. She has a warm, giving personality and she genuinely cares about people."

Within minutes they were at the house and Lou greeted them at the door. Gail was exhausted from the long day and the emotional experience. Within a few minutes she was in bed and fell asleep almost immediately. Lou returned to the kitchen and saw Bill sitting pensively at the table. He handed her the letter and she slowly read it.

"What do you think, Mom?"

"Well, someone definitely wants Sarah's mystery to remain unsolved. I'm sorry Gail got pulled into this thing. She took it pretty bad. She is a sweet girl. I never thought I'd let you bring your girlfriend home to bed after only a couple of dates. This kind of thing has to stop, young man!" Bill's mother tried to lighten things up. "Well, it'll soon be three a.m. Let's get to bed. Perhaps Jim will have some ideas in the morning."

Bill awoke in the morning to the clatter of pots and pans in the kitchen. He slid into a pair of jeans and walked down the hall. Lou saw him coming and said, "It's 8:30. Go knock on Gail's door and wake her up and I'll pour coffee for everyone."

When Bill returned the coffee was on the table and Lou was busy at the griddle preparing pancakes.

A few minutes later Gail padded down the hall. "Good morning, Bill and Mrs. Henderson," she said sleepily. Then she leaned over and whispered into Bill's ear, "Are you trying to get me excited first thing in the morning, Bill, by showing me that muscular, hairy chest of yours?"

"Well, who had me all aroused last night by running around half nude?" he whispered back to her.

"Yes, I saw."

Her whispered response in Bill's ear made him blush and he said no more, but he noticed the warm, broad smile on Gail's face and he knew she really liked him. He glanced quickly at his mother. Thankfully, she was busy stacking the pancakes on a plate and had not seen his red face.

"The pancakes are ready. Let's eat." Lou was enjoying Bill and Gail's company. Since Fred's death her life felt so empty when Bill was absent. Getting back into doing beautician work had filled some of the time and her sisters were very supportive, but she had a loving, fulfilling relationship with Fred and she missed him so much. Jim, Gail's boss, had recently asked her out. She wasn't sure she was ready. It seemed like ages since she dated and he was a divorced man. Why did life have to be so complicated?

For the moment all problems were forgotten and a light banter followed throughout the meal. As coffee was being poured, the conversation returned to the letter and all agreed Jim would give them the best advice. Everyone helped clear the table and then Bill and Gail left to get dressed. It was after 9:30 when the two of them finally left for the newspaper. Bill stopped at Gail's apartment and she picked up the articles she had written yesterday. When they arrived at the paper, Jim was waiting for them. Lou had called in to let him know Gail was going to be late and she briefed him on the reason.

"Good morning, Bill and Gail. Lou called earlier and told me you would be late, Gail. She told me about the letter. May I see it?" Jim greeted them and quickly got to the point. He was a no-nonsense man respected by the community for his efforts to keep the struggling weekly local newspaper afloat.

Gail pulled the envelope with the letter out of her purse. Jim removed the letter and slowly read it. Placing it on the desk he said, "My, we stirred up quite a hornet's nest with someone. Except for the vague reference to someone in your family getting hurt, there is no specific threat in this letter. I would like to keep the letter and have the police look at it. This article was not on organized crime or any similar story that understandably might bring retribution from someone wishing to remain anonymous. Therefore, I suspect some local crackpot probably wrote the letter to see if he could get his name in the paper. I still want a follow-up article in the newspaper. Just give me any information you have gathered to date and I'll write the next article and make sure it clearly states that you are off the story. I don't scare easily and this paper will not let threats from anyone sway our opinion on printing articles. Will you be comfortable with me writing a follow-up article?"

"Sure, Jim, Bill and I haven't found much information. I was going to present it more as a human interest story of Sarah's life. I'll get my notes together and bring them in tomorrow."

"You're a good reporter, Gail. People in the community like your stories. I'm sure the police will have some idea who this guy is. We'll flush him out." Turning the envelope over, Jim exclaimed, "Wait a minute, this is weird. This letter is postmarked from York., PA. Who in York would be reading our paper?"

"Ethel," he yelled, "get me a list of all the addresses in the York area that we mail the paper to."

Ethel, the newspaper's secretary, soon came into the room with a slip of paper. Jim picked it up and asked her, "This is the full list—just one address?" Ethel nodded her head and left. "Well," Jim continued, "it seems that we have sent a copy of our weekly newspaper to the children's home in York for the last eight years."

"The children's home," Bill and Gail uttered almost simultaneously.

"What do you two know about this place?"

"Sarah helped out there as a volunteer," Bill responded. "I have a feeling the answers to the letter and the mystery may be at the home. Gail, would you be up to visiting the home with me and clearing this up? I could call and set up an appointment."

"Yes, I will go as long as you are with me. I want to get to the bottom of this and maybe we will have that follow-up story."

"Spoken like a true newspaper reporter. I knew from your first day that you had it in your blood to go after the story. Ethel can make a copy of the letter for you to take along. I think this letter was only meant to scare you. However, if there is a person at the home who feels cornered by your visit, he may try to put actions to words. Just be careful."

Gail and Bill got up to leave Jim's office when Gail suddenly stopped and turned back. "Say, Jim," she began, "I always did wonder, why did you hire me for this job? I was fresh out of college and the ad said you were looking for an experienced reporter."

"You owe this job to the mystery woman, Sarah. On the day I interviewed for the position, I had three applicants. You were the last. As you walked out Sarah came in the front door."

"Gosh, I remember it now!" Gail exclaimed. "I was sure I had blown the interview. Jim had asked me about experience and I had none. I wanted the job so bad. I was ready to cry as I was walking out of the office and then I saw this lady coming toward me. She had a broad smile on her face and her eyes twinkled as she said to me, 'Don't worry, dear, everything will be alright.' That was your grandmother, Bill!"

"As I was saying, Sarah came in and picked up Gail's resume. She glanced at it for a minute and then she handed it back to me and said, 'Hire her, Jim.' I figured she knew you through a family connection. I explained that I really needed an experienced person, and you had none. She looked at me with determination in her eyes and said, 'You owe me one, Jim, and I'm calling it in. Hire her. I promise you'll never be sorry.' She was right. I owed her big time for all she had done to help during the last few months of my mother's life. So, I took a chance and gave you the job, Gail. In the beginning I had a few days when I regretted not picking the most experienced candidate, but I had to give you the time to get the experience. I couldn't face Sarah and tell her it didn't work out. Fortunately, you are a fast learner and within a couple months you had mastered your duties and things smoothed out. I realize now the other applicants would never have been satisfied in a struggling, small town paper and probably would have moved on as soon as other opportunities came up. Sarah was right and I am glad she gave me the incentive to hire and train you."

Bill noticed the color draining from Gail's face as Jim was talking. He put his arm around her to help support her and eased her back into the chair by Jim's desk. "Jim," she exclaimed, "this is getting weirder all the time!"

Bill noticed she raised her voice as she continued to talk and she began to shake. "Are you OK, Gail? You look a little pale. Can I get you a drink?" Bill started to cross the room to get Gail a drink.

"No, come back here, Bill, and tell me what you know about this. Why would your grandmother, who I never met until that day in Jim's office, tell Jim to hire me and promise that he would never regret it? And why did someone write that letter to me when I wrote an article about Sarah? What do you know about this?" Gail continued to shake as she fired her questions at Bill and she burst into tears at the end of the questions.

Bill walked back over to Gail's chair, kneeled down beside her and gently took her head in his hands and raised it until their eyes met. "Dear Gail," he began, "the first time I ever met you was a couple months ago at Mike's apartment. My grandmother never mentioned your name to me at any time. I may have noticed your name in the newspaper when I read one of your articles, but I never knew who you were. This news is as shocking to me as it is to you. I respect you and I will not withhold any information from you now or in the future. Grandma could look at a stranger and tell you what type of person he or she was. My guess is she saw the desperation in your eyes that day and wanted to help. She knew from looking at you that you were a determined individual and would succeed if given a chance. So, she gave you that chance by telling Jim to hire you."

"That letter has really rattled me," Gail sobbed. "I'm sorry I accused you of holding something back, Bill. You and your mother have been so kind to me and here I am blowing up at you. Please, forgive me. See, I told you earlier, I am good at pushing people away. I will understand if you don't want to help me anymore."

"I'm not sure where this whole thing is going yet. I know our lives are intertwined thanks to my grandmother. At this point we are in this together until the finish. I am sure that we will find a logical explanation and it may be in York. As for you driving me away—you had a very upsetting night last night and very little sleep. It will take more than this to drive me away. I like you and want our friendship to grow." Bill felt confused, but he put up a strong front for Gail. He still hoped to build a relationship with her.

"Thanks, Bill. I really needed you to say that." Gail reached for Bill, pulled him to her and gave him a big hug and a kiss on the cheek.

Jim had quietly left the room when Gail started to question Bill. He now came back in and suggested, "Gail, take the rest of the day off and relax. I know the letter was upsetting to you and then I increased your distress. The articles you gave to Ethel this morning will fill page two and I can finish up the rest of this week's edition today. Tomorrow, if you are up to it, we'll start on next week's articles on the upcoming Old Home week."

"Thanks, Jim, you're right. I still am very distraught from last night, and as Bill reminded me, I did not get very much sleep. Can we go to your house please, Bill, and see if Sarah ever talked to your mother about me?"

"Sure, I don't know why she wouldn't have told me, but we can check with her."

"Take good care of my best and only reporter," Jim told Bill as they left the office. "And, Bill, please tell your wonderful mother that invitation to dinner at the inn still stands."

As they drove to Bill's home, Gail calmed down and said, "Gee, Bill, I think Jim's got the hots for your mother."

"My parents were very much in love, but Mom could use some companionship. Jim's a good guy. He's just too involved with the newspaper. I can't see him taking the time to develop a relationship. I've driven by the office at ten-thirty at night and seen the lights on in there. I don't think old Jim ever goes home."

"Err, Bill, as long as we are being honest, that was probably me at the office. As I told you earlier, I don't have much social life, so many evenings I go back into the paper and work until late at night. Jim's told me that I spend too much time in the office. He offered to take some of my work load. I refused because I didn't know what else to do with my time."

"Well, I guess I stuck my foot in my mouth again. It just seemed obvious that Jim worked those late hours. I wonder if Mom will have anything good there to eat for lunch. I'm starting to get hungry."

Since it was noon when they returned to the house, Lou ushered them to the small table in the kitchen area and prepared egg salad sandwiches. As they were eating, Bill told Lou the story Jim had related on how Gail was hired. Lou thought for a minute and then responded, "Now that you told me this story, I remember an incident that occurred shortly before Sarah's death. Bill had been dating a girl from the bank. She was too short for him and she didn't know how to cook."

"Please, Mom, don't tell Gail my sordid past," Bill interjected.

"Well, anyhow, Bill finally broke up with that girl. The next week when I talked to Sarah she told me that there was a girl down at the paper that would be perfect for Bill. I reminded her that I didn't play Cupid. She said not to worry—she would arrange everything. You know how she was, Bill. I'm sure she had a plan, but God had other plans for her. That girl must have been you, Gail."

Bill was afraid that Gail would become upset again and glanced at her apprehensively. However, she was now in control of her emotions and said, "Do you have any idea, Mrs. Henderson, how Sarah came to know me and why she would want your son to date me?"

"Please call me Lou, not that formal Mrs. Henderson. No, dear, I never asked Mom how she came to know you. She had spent a lot of time with Jim's mother during her illness. Many times after a visit she dropped by the newspaper to update Jim. I just assumed she met you on those visits. Now, on further reflection, I realize you were not working at the paper at that time. Funny how things seem to fit at first, but later we realize it was all wrong."

"I think we can clear this up with a trip to the home in York." Bill got up, picked up the phone in the kitchen and dialed information. As he talked on the phone, Gail and Lou carried on their own conversation and soon Bill returned to the table. "I'm beginning to think that Grandmother Sarah was a secret agent. The more we dig into her life, the more mysterious things become."

"Why, dear, what are you talking about?" Lou asked.

"That was Mr. Jenkins at the home I was talking to. He's only been there three years. I told him that we were doing some research on my grandmother, Sarah Myers, and since she had been a volunteer at the home, we wanted to talk to some of her acquaintances there. Mr. Jenkins checked with his secretary who he said was there forever and she said Sarah never worked at the home. I told him about the plaque she received one year with her name on it for her service. He agreed to meet with us if we brought the plaque along. What's going on here, Mom? Are we in another dimension like in the *Twilight Zone* on television?" All the pressure and confusion from last night and this morning had finally pushed Bill to a point where he was venting his frustration.

At this point Gail stepped in, "It's OK, Bill. Somewhere we will find the piece that puts this whole puzzle together. Probably the secretary didn't recognize the name. This morning I was still shook up by the letter when Jim told his story. I am sorry I got upset at that point. Since then, I have become determined that we must see this thing through to the end and solve this riddle. If we don't get to the bottom of this it will always hang over our heads. Now, Mrs. Henderson, or forgive me, Lou, where is this plaque?"

"Kate has the plaque. It's a fairly large wood plaque with the wording in brass. Sarah was very proud of it. She kept it in her bedroom. When she died, Kate insisted that it belonged to her. Nobody objected and she became the keeper of the plaque. Let me call her and see if we can borrow it. Bill, take Gail to the porch while I make this call. The chairs are more comfortable and as you know Gail loves the view."

Bill took Gail's hand and led her to the wicker sofa on the porch. The bright afternoon sun flowed through the open windows and French doors on the back wall. A soft breeze carried the songs of a host of birds into the room. The apple tree lazily responded to the breeze and revealed a splendid young crop of fruit. It was an ideal, romantic moment and Bill turned to Gail and on impulse embraced her in his arms and kissed her gently on the lips. There, his feelings were out in the open. *Please, God,* he prayed, *let her tell me she cares for me as much as I care for her.*

"Bill, I've been on an emotional roller coaster the last twenty-four hours. I never met a person as kind, gentle and caring for me as you have been. You have also been strong and level headed as we work through problems and ever so patient with me even when I yelled at you. You are a true friend and possess the qualities I always wanted in a person to spend my life with. However, like I told you the other night, give me some time. These new developments have my senses reeling and I still have that closet of skeletons to clean out."

"OK, Gail, I'll try to keep my hormones in check, but it isn't easy being around you. You're beautiful and sexy and, as you saw last night, you can easily arouse me. What's a guy to do?"

"Take a cold shower," she teased. "I do care for you, Bill, just give me a little space. Everything's going to work out. Here comes your mother."

"Kate's on her way over and she's hopping mad. I told her what Mr. Jenkins said and she exploded into such a tirade, I couldn't keep the phone at my ear. Kate always appointed herself mother's protector. If

45

anyone even insinuated anything about Sarah Myers, they had the wrath of Kate to contend with. Prepare yourself for another part of our wild family, Gail."

"Don't worry, Lou. I'll be alright. Besides, I'm really quite impressed with what I've seen of this family."

Lou looked at Gail and noted that she turned to Bill as she spoke and a broad smile spread across her face. Lou really liked this girl.

Everyone stayed on the porch and continued to chat for about a half hour. Suddenly they heard screeching tires and then the roar and whine of an engine wound up to high RPMs. "Well, here comes race car driver Kate," Lou commented as they heard the pitch of the engine diminish and then rise again when Kate shifted. It seemed like only an instant before they heard her jam on the brakes in front of the house and slide into the driveway.

Lou rose to open the door, but it was too late. A loud bang outside told them that Kate had exited the car and was bounding toward the house. Before Lou got to the kitchen, the front door flew open and Kate came charging in under a full head of steam. In her one hand she held the plaque and in her other hand she brandished her keys.

"Who the hell is this Mr. Jekyll? My mother was one of the best aides that place ever had and I have the plaque to prove it. He's going to eat his words or I'll kill the son of a...."

"Kate, please calm down. We have company." Lou gave Kate a hug and led her to the porch. Kate had a rough exterior, but inside Lou knew she had a heart of gold. She had been one of Lou's biggest supporters after Fred's death.

"Kate, please meet Gail Mason, a friend of Bill's and a reporter at the *Daily Post*."

"Well it's about time Bill got himself a girlfriend, and what a looker you are, and smart too, working at the newspaper."

"Gail wrote the nice article on Mom." Lou moved the conversation in a different direction. However, she did not attempt to correct Kate's comment on Gail being Bill's girlfriend. As Lou grew to know Gail, she knew Gail was the girl for Bill. Now somehow she had to get Gail to agree.

With the conversation now flowing, Lou explained all the events of the last day to Kate and corrected her on Mr. Jenkins' name. At first she insisted on going along to York. After Lou explained that Gail had the proper training for the interview and Bill would be there to lend support, she agreed to give them the plaque and stay home.

Bill realized it was getting late and he needed to get ready for work. He rose and said, "Sorry to break things up, but I need to go to work. Let me change my clothes and I'll drop you back at your apartment, Gail, on my way to the plant."

"No, don't go, Gail. Please stay with Lou and me for dinner," Kate pleaded and then asked Lou, "It is OK if she stays, isn't it, Lou? I can drop her off in town afterwards."

"I think that would be a wonderful idea," Lou chimed in looking forward to the company. "We could make hamburgers on the grill and I have part of a cake here for dessert."

Gail was happy a plan had developed to keep her away from her lonely apartment where she was sure she'd get upset thinking about the letter. Besides, she really enjoyed the company of these two women. She told Bill she had decided to stay for a while and Kate would take her home. Bill liked the idea, but he reminded Kate that she needed to drive slowly and carefully back to town.

After Bill left, Lou began to make dinner. Later she recommended a game of dominos and everyone agreed. It was finally close to nine o'clock when Kate and Gail crawled into the car and headed for town. Gail was tired but spending the afternoon and evening with these two cheerful women had raised her spirits tremendously.

As she drove to town, Kate said, "Look, Gail, I am a little rough around the edges and I get excited and yell easily, but I'm no fool. All I need to do is look at you and Bill and I can tell you're made for each other. That's a gift I inherited from Mom. I'm so happy to see he finally found someone to enjoy life with. He loved his father very much and took it very hard when Fred died. Bill's a bright boy and very sensitive. Lou's helped him through the worst of it. Now it's time for you two to kick up your heels and have fun. Not too much, mind you, we aren't ready for any little ones yet. I really wanted you to stay this afternoon so

47

I could check you out a little more and I like what I see. You and Bill are a perfect match. Mom was right again."

Gail was about to interrupt Kate and tell her that she was not Bill's girlfriend when the last sentence made her pull up short and change direction. "What do you mean by Mom was right again?"

"Mom was always giving out advice and folks listened because she was a real good judge of character and seldom steered them wrong. Well, a few weeks before she died she came to my house and told me that Bill needed a new girlfriend and she was going to work with Jim to arrange a date between you and Bill. She told me you two were a perfect match, but it all had to be done in secret because Lou objected. Within days she had a stroke and then she died. We were busy with the funeral and in the process I totally forgot about Mom's last scheme. It wasn't until Lou introduced you that it all came back to me."

"But how did Sarah know me?"

"Well, she was always dropping in at the paper to chat with Jim. I assume she met you on her visits. She never really said any more."

"Did you know that Sarah insisted that Jim hire me and she had never met me except for passing me on the way out from my interview?"

"Well, that was just like Mom. She could look at a person from across the room and tell you all about that person. Why in your case even I knew you were a person I liked as soon as I met you. Thank goodness Bill had the common sense to latch onto you right away." Kate had reached Gail's apartment and she pulled into the lot where they said their goodbyes.

Gail walked to her apartment, opened the door and sat down for a second to reflect. A dead woman whom she had only met once was in control of her life. This woman had manipulated her boss into hiring her. Then this woman was scheming to get her and Bill together as a couple, but she died before completing the scheme. Now five years later a story about this woman brought Bill and his family into her life. She thought, *Oh no, could Sarah have developed this whole scheme from the grave just to get Bill and me together? I could do a lot worse. No, I'm not sure I can accept this whole idea. It's all just a bunch of coincidences.*

Gail picked herself up and got ready for bed. As she drifted off to sleep she was thinking of the idea that Sarah might just be pulling the strings to all these weird occurrences. *We can't publish this in the paper,* she thought to herself as she drifted off to sleep.

It had been over two weeks since Bill had last seen Gail. When he called Mr. Jenkins back at the home he told Bill that he was very busy and the earliest he could see them was on the twenty-ninth of June at one p.m. It was a Thursday and Bill took a vacation day since they would be getting back late. During the two weeks Bill had thought up numerous excuses to call Gail and try to see her. But then he would remember how she told him Mike harassed her and how she needed some time and space to sort everything out. Just when he thought he had her out of his mind, he would wake up from a reoccurrence of the dream where he undressed her and carried her toward the bed. He had the dream a couple more times and each time he awoke just as they got to the bed.

This morning he had woken up at seven a.m. thinking of Gail's radiant smile, the dimples that formed in her cheeks when she smiled, and the sparkle in her eyes when she laughed. He had paced the floor and watched the clock minute by minute until it was finally ten a.m. and he could leave to pick Gail up.

Lou watched him leave with the plaque in his hand. She was beginning to worry about Bill being crushed emotionally if this relationship with Gail did not grow.

Meanwhile in town Gail was also looking forward to being with Bill again. She had been busy over the last two weeks, but whenever a quiet moment came she thought of his strong, muscular body and how gentle he treated her. She hoped he would call, yet she realized he would not. He was giving her the space she had requested.

Gail also was ready long before quarter after ten, which was when they agreed he should pick her up. She had gone through everything in her closet several times this morning to pick out the right outfit. Eventually she settled on a short black and white print skirt with a black short-sleeve silk blouse. She knew the skirt would reveal as much of her long, curvy, tanned legs as possible and she purposely unbuttoned the top two buttons on the blouse to reveal a slight hint of the top of her breasts. To compliment the outfit, she applied an extra dash of the Summer Passion perfume that Bill had complimented her on wearing and she dug out a pair of pearl earrings her mother had given her. As she looked in the mirror for a final check, she smiled in approval of what she saw. Yes, this outfit would drive Bill wild.

Bill pulled up in front of the apartment exactly at quarter after ten. He quickly slid out of the seat and almost ran to Gail's door. When he rang the doorbell, she slowly opened the door to catch his expression and she was not disappointed. Bill stood there speechless for a few seconds and then finally stammered, "Good morning, Gail. You are absolutely stunning in that outfit and you are wearing that new perfume. Why are you trying to get me excited so early in the morning?"

"Why, Bill, don't be silly. I am not trying to get you excited. This is just an outfit I threw together today to keep me cool. You know the weatherman says it's supposed to go over 90 degrees this afternoon."

"Nice try, Gail. I suppose that you are also wearing those stunning pearl earrings to keep you cool?"

Now it was Gail's turn to blush as they walked toward the truck. "You're right, Bill, I really wanted to impress you and make you notice me. I thought about you many times over the last few weeks. I decided this morning when I got up that I was going to make this a special day and your compliments have certainly helped. Thank you. As for the pearls, my mother gave them to me. They were my grandmother's. Gramps had given them to her on their first anniversary. They are very special to me and I am wearing them today for you."

Bill put his arm around Gail's waist to help her into the truck. He could almost touch her flesh through the thin silk blouse. He was excited by her body so close to his and he bent over and gently kissed her on the lips as she slid into the seat. He was pleased as she responded and returned his kiss.

Then she giggled a nervous little giggle and said, "Enough of this, Mr. Henderson, we have places to go and things to do. If we do not stop this kissing and get our emotions under control, we may never solve this mystery."

Bill walked slowly around the front of the truck. He didn't want Gail to see how aroused he was, though, he was sure she already knew. Well, maybe when they returned from York he could take care of this problem. He was sure Gail was warming up to the idea, but he was beginning to get very fond of her and if they ever got to the lovemaking stage he wanted it to be special. He would just have to see what today would bring. For now he was very happy. The sun was shining on a warm summer day and he was going to spend it with a very beautiful, sexy woman. Now if he could just keep his body parts under control. That was embarrassing.

It was an hour and a half drive to York. As Bill drove up the interstate to Chambersburg he told Gail about his ancestors coming to the valley shortly after the revolution and their part in helping the town of Greencastle grow. He figured that was why he had developed a passion for the local history.

In high school, Gail had almost flunked her history classes. She always thought they were so boring, and who could remember all those dates and names? She enjoyed listening to Bill, though, and the personal touch he added made it interesting.

In Chambersburg they got off the interstate onto route 30 east and headed toward Gettysburg. Bill explained that this road was called the Lincoln Highway because it was the road Abraham Lincoln supposedly traveled on his way to Gettysburg to deliver the Gettysburg Address. At first the road was heavy with shopping areas on both sides of the road. Gradually the roadside opened up to scattered houses and small businesses and soon these also disappeared and a thickly wooded area encroached on the road on either side. As they approached a slight bend in the road, an intersection appeared. Bill explained that this was one of his favorite areas. To the right the road led a short distance through the woods to the Totem Pole playhouse. This was an open air summer stock theatre that ran from early June through late August. He explained that famous actors and actresses came here in the summer to get away from the big city and the normal pressures of their jobs. He came to see a couple plays a year with his mother and had seen Jean Stapleton one time in *Oklahoma*.

Gail also knew the area and enjoyed spending warm summer evenings watching the comedies, murder mysteries and musicals. Many times she came to write reviews for the paper. She spoke up and told Bill the names of a couple plays she had seen at the Totem Pole. Bill was not surprised to learn that he had also attended some of the same plays. He was beginning to realize that they shared many common interests. Gail may have been one of the pretty girls he used to pick out from the crowd and pretend was his date for the evening. He was confused if this was a date or if he still had to go on pretending.

"Say, Gail, since you dressed up for me today, is this our first date?"

"No, Bill, this is not our first date. When we have a first date, I want it to be very special. I'll get elegantly dressed up for you at that time."

Bill was quiet for several miles as he reflected on the recent conversation. Would he someday have a real relationship with Gail? They were always on newspaper business when they got together. Maybe Mike was right about Gail being too involved in her work to ever have a normal relationship. She did seem to devote all her time to the paper. Still, as she talked about their first date she had said when, not if. She had been very clear about that. Again he heard his mother's advice to be patient and everything would work out.

Now the truck was moving up a large hill and Bill explained that this was the direction most of Robert E. Lee's army had marched in July of 1863 on their way to Gettysburg. They both tried to imagine trudging up this long hill with a gun and knapsack on a hot, dusty morning while the sound of gunfire at Gettysburg just a few miles away reminded you of the grisly job ahead. Talk proceeded along this line and soon they were traversing a series of small ridges on the outskirts of the battlefield. The last of these, McPherson's Ridge, is part of the National Battlefield Park and the site of some of the heaviest fighting during the first day of the battle.

Gail told Bill that she had never been to Gettysburg. He figured he could point out a few of the highlights and pulled the truck off the road near a monument. To the left in the distance on Oak Hill stood the

Eternal Peace Light dedicated by Franklin Roosevelt at the last great encampment of survivors of the war held on the 75th anniversary of the battle, July 3, 1938. Bill told Gail that one of the most beautiful views in Gettysburg was standing on the hill behind the light as the sun went down. He went on to explain that when John F. Kennedy visited the battlefield he saw the light and told his wife that when he died he would like an eternal flame over his grave site. His wish was fulfilled and the flame burns today at the Arlington Cemetery. President Kennedy had also been invited back to Gettysburg on November 19, 1963, for the hundredth anniversary of the Gettysburg Address celebration, but he declined because of a planned trip to Dallas.

Bill also pointed out the railroad cut on the left, parallel to the road. Some of the bloodiest combat of the first day's battle occurred in this cut. To the right front he pointed out the serene buildings of the Lutheran Theological Seminary which was used as a lookout post by both armies and a hospital for some of the 51,000 or more casualties from the three days of battle. The seminary sits on another of the rolling ridges about 500 yards east of McPherson's Ridge. Seminary Ridge was the location used by the confederates to place their cannons the second and third day of the battle and stage their troops before attacks on the Union lines on Little and Big Round Top Hill and Cemetery Hill to the southeast beyond the town. In McPherson's Woods on the extreme left the highest-ranking general killed in the battle, Union General Reynolds, was hit by a confederate sharpshooter and died instantly on the first day of battle.

Numerous statues and monuments dotted the scenery and groups of tourists moved among them stopping occasionally to read the inscriptions. Bill enjoyed coming to Gettysburg and wished he could show Gail Devil's Den, the Pennsylvania Monument, the High Water Mark and other key sites, but they needed to move on to be in time for their appointment.

As he drove on into town he pointed out General Lee's headquarters during the battle, a small white house sitting on the left near the top of Seminary Ridge. Shortly beyond this point, they turned to the left and proceeded through the bustling main street area of

Gettysburg lined with Civil War memorabilia shops. In the center of town they came to a large open square area. In the center of this area the road was blocked by a round park-like area ablaze with blooming summer flowers. Around the square stood historical old hotels, restaurants and shops busy with the hustle and bustle of the tourist season.

As Bill waited for his turn to proceed in the traffic slowly circling the island of flowers, Gail said, "Gettysburg is a very picturesque town and the little tour of the battlefield was very interesting. You will have to bring me back sometime and show me more of the sights. Maybe we could sneak out to the Peace Light after dark and make passionate love on the lawn beneath its flickering flame."

Bill glanced at her and her impish grin told him she was teasing. However, her nearness and her provocative appearance in the outfit she wore excited him every time he looked at her. No, this was not a joking matter. Yet, he felt a light response was needed at this point in time, and he quipped, "Well, why wait, let's turn around and head for the light right now." He hoped the smile on his face hid his true feelings.

"You men are all alike, can't wait to jump behind a monument with every woman you meet," she continued to tease.

"Not true, Gail, I only ever went that far with one other girl who I had a relationship with. The feelings I have for you are special. I've never had them for any other girl." Even as it slipped out of his mouth, Bill realized he had gone serious when she was joking. Immediately he was mad at himself for blurting out his true feelings. Now he had ruined the moment. What would her response be?

Gail noted the disappearance of the joking smile from Bill's face as he spoke and she was silent when he stopped. They traveled on down the road several miles before Gail finally responded, "Wow, Bill, you continue to shock me. All my life I've wanted a romantic relationship with that special someone I pictured in my dreams. Like I said before, I have not been very active on the dating circuit and then when I met Mike I got serious. At that point in my life I was very lonely and depressed and I just needed someone. I could talk to Mike and so we fell into a relationship. From the beginning, I knew it was wrong, but I was weak and I let myself get in too far. When I finally pulled out I was a wreck. Just when I was getting it all sorted out you came along. All girls dream of a strong, tall, handsome guy stepping into their lives and sweeping them off their feet. When you called me from Mike's apartment, I tried to remember what you looked like. I had an argument with Mike that day and everything was a blur. So when you walked into Rosie's it was really the first time I had ever really seen you. As you walked across the room, I realized you were a match for that man in my dreams. I quickly hid my shock and put up my defenses because I still tied you to Mike. Then you said, 'I didn't come here to trick you. Let's start over and pretend this is the first time we ever met.' At that point I took your advice, relaxed and enjoyed the rest of the day.

"When my parents were going through their divorce, I built a wall around myself to protect me. Then the boys in school teased me about my height and clumsiness, and the wall got taller. It opened a little for Mike. But after the breakup I built it even higher. After the first time we met, I knew that I had a problem. The very foundations of that wall shook from one meeting. So when we met at your mother's I had a plan. I told you there would be no emotional involvement between us and I convinced myself that I had things under control. Then the letter came and I needed you so badly. That night I knew in my heart that there was already a crack in the wall. I don't know what to do, Bill. You're the man of my dreams. You battered down my wall and my defenses are weak and then you tell me that the special feelings you have for me have never been there with any other girl. A big part of me is ready to fall for you. But I'm scared. If I let myself go and we don't make it, what do I do then? How do I know if you really are my Prince Charming? Are we moving too fast? After all, we have never really had a date."

As Bill listened he realized how deeply he had affected Gail's feelings. Now he knew that she also cared for him. At this point he realized that he needed to reassure her that everything would be alright. "Relax," he started, "I don't want to hurt you. We make a good team on this research project. I agree, we need to date and build a relationship away from your work. May I take you out on our first official date this Saturday night?"

Gail was relieved that she had revealed her feelings to Bill, and the rest of the time on the trip was spent planning the details of the date. When they arrived in York they stopped for a quick sandwich and then followed the directions to the home. It was a sprawling two-story brown brick building with a large glassed-in entryway.

As they pulled into the parking lot, several of the residents were parked at the corner in their wheelchairs awaiting their turn to be loaded on a bus. They cheerfully greeted Bill and Gail as they walked toward the front door of the building. Right inside the doors, they saw the reception desk and announced their appointment with Mr. Jenkins. While they waited, another wheelchair-bound resident approached and used an electronic communication device to greet them. They were continuing a conversation with this girl when Mr. Jenkins arrived.

"Good afternoon. Well, I see you've met Jessica. She is also from the Greencastle area. Her parents live outside of town on a farm. Come into my office where it's quieter to talk."

Bill and Gail followed him around the corner and into his office. Mr. Jenkins took a moment to explain that the goal of the home was not just to meet the needs of the handicapped residents, but also to integrate them as much as possible into the local community. He explained that the bus they saw on the way in was taking a group to the local mall shopping. Then he switched to the business at hand, "As for your grandmother, Sarah Myers, we have no record of her ever serving in any capacity here at the home and we keep records on all the staff and volunteers. I also talked to several of the long-time staff and they said they never heard the name. I'm sorry. Your grandmother never spent any time here."

Bill handed the plaque to Mr. Jenkins and countered, "We appreciated your efforts, Mr. Jenkins. The problem is we have this plaque from the home recognizing the work she did here."

Mr. Jenkins took the plaque and said, "Yes, I've seen one of these before. They were given out before I arrived here. Hey, Hank, can you come here?"

Hank was walking down the hall. He turned and came into the

office. When Mr. Jenkins questioned him about the plaque, he responded, "These plaques were ordered one Christmas by your predecessor and given to the volunteers as a gift for the services they provided. I did the ordering. They are rather nice and were not cheap. We really should have put the money to a better use. Why has this one been altered?"

Bill questioned, "What do you mean it was altered?"

"See here. The name has been etched on a separate piece of brass that has been fastened to the plaque with these two screws. All the plaques we ordered had the name etched in a piece of brass inlaid in the wood. Someone has added the brass piece with Sarah Myers' name on it. I don't remember her name."

"Do you have a screwdriver, Mr. Jenkins?" Bill continued. "Let's take the piece with my grandmother's name off and see whose name is underneath."

Mr. Jenkins fumbled around in his desk drawer for a few moments and produced a small screwdriver. He carefully backed the screws out and lifted the nameplate clear of the plaque. By this time everyone had gathered around his chair. "Well, whoever did this made absolutely sure we would never find out the original owner's name. See, they've ground off the name on this underneath plate."

Bill asked, "Do you have a list of the names of the people who received the plaques?"

"No, but even if we did have a list, I could not show it to you. All information pertaining to our employees and volunteers is held in the strictest confidence. Just like you, I am curious as to why your grandmother went to all this effort to make it appear she did volunteer work here at the home. However, I don't know of any way we can help you any further."

Gail jumped in at this point, "Perhaps you can still help us, Mr. Jenkins, with one other item. We checked at my paper, the Greencastle *Daily Post,* and a copy of the paper is sent here every week. Do you know why the home buys a copy of the paper?"

Now it was Hank's turn to speak, "Well, I can at least clear up that mystery. You both met the reason on the way in. Remember Jessica is from Greencastle. She came to us about eight years ago and was a very homesick girl. Her mother recommended we get the paper and read it to her. Since Jessica never was able to learn how to read, she had always done that at home. We bought the paper and one of the volunteers read it to her from cover to cover and it's been a tradition ever since. Sometimes some of the other residents even sit in on the reading. I confess, I sometimes borrow it and browse through the pages. It's nice to see a newspaper filled with local news and good events instead of the world problems that are always on the front page of our paper. I remember that interesting article about the flowers on Sarah's grave. I suppose your visit here is tied somehow to that story."

"We have evidence that led us to believe our mystery admirer worked here," Gail explained. "One final question, Hank, does the same person always read the paper to Jessica?"

"No, with our mail system we don't always get the paper on the same day. Every now and then we get the paper the Monday after it hits the streets. Jessica usually gets someone to read it as soon as it arrives. So, whoever is helping out in her area that day gets the chore."

Bill and Gail prepared to leave and thanked Mr. Jenkins and Hank. Gail gave them her telephone number. They promised to call if they obtained any information on the mystery. Back at the truck Gail told Bill that she had the envelope that was mailed from the York post office. She asked if they could drive to the post office and she would talk to the clerks on the slight possibility that they might remember who sent the letter. They stopped at a service station to obtain directions. Shortly the post office came into sight and Bill pulled into a parking space directly across from the entrance. He told her he would wait at the truck while she went inside.

She returned a few minutes later and appeared a bit irritated. "That guy was very rude to me," she began. "He said, 'Lady, we process thousands of pieces of mail every day and you expect me to remember who dropped that piece off. Besides, it was probably placed in the box outside. Now unless you need stamps, step aside and let me help the next person in line.' The people in our post office always try to answer everyone's questions and I've never seen them speak to anyone like he did to me. I have half a notion to report him."

"I know you're on a roll here, Gail. I hate to interrupt, but I think we are being followed. Don't turn around, just look in your side mirror and check out the old green car on our side of the road three blocks back. I first noticed the car at the service station where we pulled in for directions. I saw it parked at the far corner of the lot and when I pulled out it followed. Since then it's made every turn I did and when I pulled into this spot, it quickly pulled in back there. Nobody got out of the car the whole time you were gone."

Gail glanced in her mirror and then said, "Oh, Bill, I see the car. Now what do we do?"

Bill heard the nervous tension in her voice and saw that her hands were shaking as she returned the envelope to her purse. "Don't be afraid, Gail. I'm going to get out of the truck and walk back down the street toward the green car. Hopefully I can get close enough to see what the driver looks like. Maybe I'll be able to walk up and ask why he or she is following us. You stay here and if the car comes past get the license number. Whatever happens, stay in the truck."

Bill opened his door and slid out. Gail appeared to be reassured by his words. Now if only he could calm his own fears. All sorts of thoughts sped through his mind. Worst case, he figured, was if the person in the car was armed with a gun. What then?

"Please be careful," Gail shrieked as he shut the door and walked around the front of the truck.

When he reached the sidewalk he turned to the right and slowly began walking toward the green car. Now he turned his face toward the stores and tried to make it look like he was interested in the window displays as he walked. Occasionally, he would turn his head far enough toward the road to catch a glimpse of the car. By the time he reached the end of the block he could feel the hair on the back of his head standing up.

Two blocks to go, the tension was unbearable and mounting by the minute. It seemed like an eternity since he left the truck. He forced himself to move slowly across the street and step onto the curb on the far side. Slowly he eased his way down the block. Step by step he approached the middle of the block. He barely noticed the people that passed him.

Suddenly he heard an engine grind into action and instantly he swung his head toward the car. The driver was holding what appeared to be a handkerchief over the right side of his face and in an instant the car jolted out of the parking space. Bill began to run toward it. Even as he did, he saw the driver spin the wheel to the left and shoot up an alley between the buildings on the far side of the road. By now Bill was almost directly across from the alley and hoped he would be able to get the license plate number.

As the car started to turn, Bill heard a truck horn and suddenly saw a tractor trailer rapidly approaching in the far lane. The truck driver locked up his brakes and the screech of tires added to the bedlam. The truck brakes slowed the huge vehicle just enough to allow the green car time to slide across the road and safely into the alley. However, Bill's view of the rear of the car was blocked as the truck slid in front of the alley. The driver of the truck had his window open and Bill could hear him swearing at the retreating vehicle. By the time the truck cleared the view of the alley, the car was gone.

Bill turned around and walked back to the truck. He was relieved that the tension of a few moments ago was over, but he was upset that he had not been able to read the car's license number and he had no description of the driver. Still his suspicion that they were being followed was confirmed. When he slid back into the truck he was pleasantly surprised by Gail throwing her arms around him and hugging him tightly to her.

"Oh, Bill, I was so worried for you. I am glad you are safe. That crazy driver almost got himself killed. Why was he following us? Did you get his license number?"

Gail continued to cling to Bill as he explained that the truck blocked his view and prevented his getting the license number. All he knew for sure was that it was a fairly rusty, old, green Nova. Slowly Gail released her grip and then Bill started the truck engine and they pulled out of the parking space. They decided they had enough adventure for one day and Bill turned the truck toward home.

As they drove out of town and back toward Chambersburg and Greencastle, they talked about the events of the day. Every couple miles they glanced in the rearview mirrors, and whenever a green car approached, Bill would slow up until they were sure it was not a Nova. When they reached Gettysburg, the time was approaching five o'clock. Bill recommended they stop at one of the pubs on the square, eat dinner and have a beer. Gail agreed that she needed a drink after the day's experience.

It was almost seven o'clock when they emerged from a leisurely dinner at the cozy little pub. As they left town and rode through the battlefield again, the sun was slowly sinking in the western sky. Bill had to stop at the red light in the intersection that led to Oak Hill. On inspiration he glanced at Gail and smiled. Then when then light turned green he turned the wheel to the right and they headed toward Oak Hill.

With apprehension in her voice Gail said, "Ah, Bill, I was only kidding about the passionate love on the lawn near the Peace Light."

Bill said nothing as he continued to drive. After parking in the lot next to the light, he got out of the truck and pulled a blanket out from behind the seat.

As he opened Gail's door she continued, "Bill, stop fooling around! You are beginning to worry me. Get control of your hormones and get back in this truck right now. I really mean it. I will not have sex with you out here in plain sight." Gail's face had turned red and it was easy to see she was flustered by the situation.

At this point Bill burst into laughter. His whole body shook as he laughed so hard he almost dropped the blanket. "Thank you, dear Gail, I really needed that release after today's tension. Come with me now please. I only want us to sit here on the grass and enjoy this beautiful sunset together."

"Well, why didn't you say so? And, mister, I don't appreciate your laughter at my expense." Gail's smile told Bill that she also was enjoying the moment now that she understood his intentions. As she slid out of the seat her skirt slid up and Bill enjoyed seeing the full length of her long, thin legs. He pulled her to himself and planted a firm kiss on her lips. She wrapped her arms around him and returned his kiss with equal zest. He moved his hands down to her legs and slowly caressed her bare thighs as they continued to kiss.

"Oh, Bill, you make me feel so good," she moaned as his hands moved up and gently massaged her firm backside. The heated moment was interrupted at this point by an approaching car. Slowly control returned and they separated as the banging of doors and chatter of children told them that a family had arrived to also view the sunset.

They moved up the small hill behind the monument and Bill spread the blanket on the grass. As they sat down to watch the last rays of the sun slip below the distant horizon, two small girls from the car came running up the hill toward them, sat down on a corner of the large blanket, and struck up a conversation as children usually do. Bill and Gail laughed and joked with the children and their parents who came up the hill a short time later. Time seemed to fly by and soon it was dark and everyone headed back to the vehicles.

On the way home Bill and Gail agreed that stopping at the monument and meeting the tourist family had been a perfect ending for the day. Neither spoke of the passion that had erupted prior to the arrival of the tourists, but both pondered on the emotional high they had experienced. Each secretly yearned to be in the other's embrace again and vowed to themselves that next time there would be no interruptions.

Arriving at the apartment, they walked hand in hand to the door. Gail yearned for Bill to pick her up at the door, carry her to the bedroom and spend the night. Bill had equal thoughts flowing through his mind, especially after the encounter at the park. But the frustrations and fears from York also flowed through his mind. He wanted that first time with Gail to be special, something they could look back on forever. This time, this place was not it. He gave Gail a hug and they kissed. This time the deep passion from early was not there. They parted looking forward to their planned date on Saturday and each hoped it would be that special time.

CHAPTER 4
The Search Intensifies

Bill awoke Saturday morning and felt like he was sitting on top of the world. Today was the day of his first date with Gail and he knew their special moment would be tonight. He became excited just thinking about it at the breakfast table and he tried to hide it from his mother.

"So, tell me about this big date tonight," Lou prodded him as she poured a second cup of coffee for both of them.

"We're going to the Inn by the airport in Hagerstown for dinner and a movie afterward." Bill hoped the passion from the other day would return and he would spend the night with Gail. This he could not tell his mother. Even though he was twenty-nine years old, he knew she would not approve. He would face the music tomorrow if things worked out.

"Wow, you are going all out for this first date. The Inn's about the most expensive place in town. It will be very romantic, though. I remember my first date with your father. He took me to Howard Johnson's on the strip in Hagerstown for the Wednesday night all-you-can-eat fish fry. It's hard to believe I fell in love with him after a start like that. Your father was solid, dependable and caring, but not romantic. His idea of romance was sharing a six pack of beer with me while we watched football on TV. Funny, I really miss those times we spent together."

They had finished breakfast and retired to the porch to read. Bill glanced at the clock every half hour or so hoping it would soon be afternoon and he could begin to prepare for his evening. At a little after 10:30 the telephone began ringing and Lou jumped up to answer it. Bill continued to browse through a favorite hunting magazine to which he subscribed. He was sure that the telephone call was from one of his mother's friends or sisters. It seemed they spent most of the weekend calling back and forth to each other. He heard her pick up the telephone and then she yelled to him, "Bill, it's Gail and she sounds upset. I hope it's not more problems from Mom's story in the paper. She needs to talk to you."

Bill leaped from his seat and bounded into the kitchen. He picked up the telephone and greeted Gail.

"Bill, I've got to go to Lancaster. They just took my mother to the hospital. She fainted in the store and they rushed her to the hospital. I'm sorry about tonight. Please call me next week."

Bill expressed his concerns for Gail's mother and hung up the telephone. He told his mother what Gail had said. They talked for a long time about Bill's feelings for Gail and his hope that a relationship was finally growing. He also filled his mother in on Gail's hesitancy to become emotionally involved in another relationship. Finally they talked about the evening's canceled date. He knew she had to go to her mother's side and he wanted her to do that. If things were reversed, he would cancel everything to be at his mom's side. Still, tonight was to be their first real date and he told his mom he couldn't help it, he was disappointed and perhaps a little frustrated. Lou knew there was little she could say at this point.

On Monday morning Bill called Gail at work to get an update. Her mother was still in the hospital. It appeared to be a blood sugar problem which the doctor said could be controlled with diet. He was keeping her for a few days more for testing. Gail was leaving that evening to spend tomorrow, the fourth of July, with her mother. His hopes of spending the day with Gail shattered, Bill called Mike after hanging up with Gail. Mike was free and recommended they get together and have a few beers.

It was almost one in the afternoon when Bill climbed the steps to Mike's apartment and banged on the door. Mike, dressed as usual for the summer in an old pair of shorts and a tee shirt, opened the door and thrust a beer in Bill's hand. "Here, man, have a cold one. It's hotter than hell out there. Where've you been lately? The last time I saw you, you were on you way to meet Attila the Hun. Please don't tell me you hooked up with her."

"OK, I won't tell you I hooked up with her, but I guess I did." Bill walked across the room and sat in the sofa. The blast from the window air conditioner bathed him in cool air. It felt great after the hike up the hot stairwell.

"What do you mean when you say, 'I guess I did'?"

"Well, we saw each other several times working on my grandmother's story."

"I read the article. It was a great piece. Old Gail always had a way with words. Maybe that's what attracted me to her." Mike slid into the kitchen and returned with two more beers.

"Let me finish my story. We have a good time together. Trouble is every time we've seen each other we've been working to get information for a follow-up article. We were supposed to have a real date last weekend, only her mother became ill and was hospitalized."

"Didn't I tell you all she thinks about is work? She never wanted to party with me. Don't tear yourself up trying to get into that broad's pants. I can line you up with some real action. Come out with me this weekend."

"I don't think so, Mike. I'm really very attracted to Gail. Once her mother recovers, we're going to get together. You'll have to drink my share for a while. Gail's really not into the bar scene."

"To each his own, just remember when you're sitting in the loony bin I told you that's where you'd wind up if you insisted on pursuing this girl."

Was Mike right? He was already deeply committed to making this relationship with Gail work. What would he do if she dropped him and walked away? How would he fill the void? He wasn't going to let Mike know he harbored some of the same fears and doubts.

"Soon Gail and I will be the hottest thing in this town. When that happens I'll buy you a case of beer. For now, grab a couple more of those cold ones and your trunks and let's head out to Aunt Dottie's to swim a couple laps. She and Eddy are going down to Waynesboro to the fireworks tonight. While she's gone we'll hit the liquor cabinet and get old Jake drunk. You know how much that old dog likes his beer."

Bill rolled over and looked at the clock next to his bed. It was a couple of minutes before seven. Even though he worked last night and went to bed after midnight, he was wide awake. He awoke this morning remembering watching the sunset in Gettysburg with Gail. She was monopolizing his thoughts lately and not seeing her made it even worse. Yesterday when they talked, she told him she was going to her mother's again this weekend.

Even his mother had abandoned him. She and Kate had left last night on a bus trip to the casinos at Atlantic City and would return late tonight. He was feeling a little depressed. While he was taking his shower, he decided to ride into town and get breakfast. He and his mother frequented the Franklin House, a large white two-story structure with ornate windows. The restaurant was an old converted hotel and movie theater that sat on the corner a block east of the square next to the only stoplight in town. His mother enjoyed sitting next to the windows near the corner and watching the traffic. They had spent many a lazy Saturday morning at this spot chatting with friends. Perhaps he'd bump into someone he knew and it would raise his spirits a bit. Later he could track Mike down and drown any remaining depression.

It was another one of those beautiful summer mornings in central Pennsylvania. The sky was light blue with a few wispy white clouds floating about. An abundance of rain through last month had turned lawns a lush green and the corn in the field across the road was already knee high. Out in the distant, the green mountains flowed in an unbroken line from north to south as far as the eye could see. A profusion of yellows, blues, oranges and reds covered the well-tended flower beds along the walk near the front door. The temperature was only in the mid-seventies and a cool breeze played with Bill's hair as he walked to his truck. He paused for a moment to watch two rabbits playfully chasing each other in the side yard. Just stepping out into the fresh clean air and experiencing all this was enough to buoy Bill's spirits.

On the way into town Bill had to drive past his grandmother's grave and he wished she were here to enjoy the morning. She liked taking walks. He used to come to town on mornings like this and together they would hike across town or walk to Dottie and Eddy's house. Then they'd return to her house and she'd make him a heaping plate of pancakes and sausage. That was her favorite breakfast and she always made it for Bill when he visited. She always wanted to take care of him. It seemed like even now she was doing that. He would never have taken a serious look at Gail if the newspaper article hadn't come up.

Bill was greeted at the entrance to the Franklin House by Emma, a friend of the family and long-time employee of the restaurant. She led Bill to the corner window table which, as luck would have it, was unoccupied. Emma served Bill's coffee and took his breakfast order. Bill glanced over at the entrance occasionally as people entered, hoping he could engage them in conversation and invite them to sit with him. Pastor Jones came in and Bill's hopes rose. However, a group of parishioners followed behind him and it was apparent that they were all together. Pastor Jones saw Bill and exchanged greetings as Emma led his group off to a table near the buffet.

Bill was dreamily staring out the window when he heard Emma ask about the size of party.

"I'm alone. Do you have anything by the windows?"

Bill snapped his head around as he realized the voice was Gail's. His spirits soared as he stood and said, "Oh, miss, I have an empty seat here you could use."

"Bill, I never dreamed I'd meet you here. I look a mess this morning," she said as she hurried toward his table. She was wearing a black tube top and a pair of short cutoff jeans. Again she had her hair tied in a bun on top of her head revealing her long graceful neck and bare shoulders. A silver necklace and small silver earrings in the shape of hearts were the only jewelry she wore. Emma poured her coffee, took her order and moved off.

"You'd look great in anything and even better in nothing," Bill joked. "I never dreamed seeing you here. I thought you were going to your mother's house." Bill noted a slight blush on her face from his first comment.

"Thanks for the compliment. Well, I think it was a compliment. Anyhow, I called Mom last night to let her know I was getting ready to leave for Lancaster. She said she was feeling much better and didn't need me. She told me instead to stay home and see that fellow I spent all last weekend talking about. Really, Bill, I didn't think I was that bad. Maybe I did go a little overboard. I don't exactly lead an exciting life with lots of things to talk about. So, I guess you were the number one topic of conversation. Do you mind?"

"No, I'm flattered. Why didn't you let me know you were in town?" They sat directly across from each other at the small corner table and he couldn't help noticing her large, firm breasts outlined by her tight-fitting top. Thankfully he was sitting down.

"I called Lou as soon as I hung up from talking to my mother. She was just about ready to walk out the door and told me that you normally sleep in until about nine on Saturday. I decided to surprise you and call after nine. When I woke up hungry, I decided to get a bite to eat here first. That was odd because I never came here for breakfast before. The other day I had this weird feeling that your grandmother was controlling us from her grave. When you think about it, it's like we're following the plan she put together before her death."

Emma delivered their food and both ate in silence for a few minutes.

"As I passed the cemetery this morning my thoughts were along a similar line. Grandma always liked to walk with me and make breakfast for me. She liked caring for me and it occurred to me that it was like she was still doing that now. Maybe she is looking down at us from heaven and giving a little nudge to push us together. In any case, I'm very thankful that I met you. After we're done eating, come with me to meet my Aunt Dottie and her husband Eddy. They have a beautiful house in town here on Apple Drive. They're leaving this afternoon for a week's vacation in Maine. I'm going to spend the week at their house with Jake. He's nine years old and you hardly know he's around unless I give him some beer."

"I'm a mess, Bill. What kind of impression would I give them looking like this? And what are you doing giving a nine-year-old boy beer to drink?"

Bill laughed. "Aunt Dottie and Uncle Eddy never had any children. That's why they spoil me. Jake's their yellow Lab. He's very calm and affectionate. Whenever Dottie and Eddy go away, I stay at their house and take care of Jake. He gets very upset if they put him in a kennel. As you can see, I've got my shorts and an old shirt on. It's Saturday and they are down-to-earth people. We'll just stop at your apartment and you can pick up a swimsuit. They have a big in-ground pool behind the house. It's a great place to swim or just lie in the lawn chairs and get a tan."

"That sounds great. I'm not sure I have my suit here. I usually pack it when I go home. We have a pool in the backyard and that's where I spend my summer afternoons with Mom."

"Let me pay Emma and we'll head out."

At Gail's apartment Bill sat in the living room while she went to search for her suit. She returned a few minutes later carrying a bag. She had also released the clip in her hair and it cascaded down her back. After a short drive up the main road through town, Bill turned right into the area locals called the Orchard, which received its name from an apple orchard that grew there in the fifties before the development was built. Bill snaked around the roads and soon turned left into a long driveway leading up to a long, light brown brick house.

As he pulled into a parking area on the back side of the garage, a large glassed-in patio appeared in front of them. The pool was on their left side at an elevation about three feet higher than the porch. A set of steps led from the back of the porch up to a brick patio about six feet wide that ran completely around the pool.

"Come in and meet the family and then we'll change and take a dip.

It's starting to warm up out here and the water will feel good by then."

They entered the porch, which was about twenty feet square, and turned right to enter the spacious eat-in kitchen area of the house. Four people were seated at the table playing a card game and Jake stood up and walked toward them with his tail wagging. Bill greeted Jake and then introduced Gail to his Aunt Dottie and Uncle Eddy and his cousin Jessie, Aunt Kate's daughter, and her husband Randy. Dottie asked them to sit down as they finished the card game.

"We're all packed and ready to go. Eddy couldn't wait and loaded up the bags about an hour ago. We pick up the Wilsons at two and then we're on the road. When Randy and Jessie dropped in to say goodbye we talked them into a game of 500 to entertain Eddy for a while."

Jessie, who had been sitting quietly up to this point, cut in and said, "Gail, my mother speaks very highly of you. Take good care of my cousin. He and I grew up together. Aunt Lou kept me when I was little and Mom worked. Ask her to show you the picture of the two of us in the bath tub together—buck naked." At this point Jessie began laughing and Bill blushed.

"Really? I will have to get Lou to show me those pictures. I think Bill has a cute butt and I've never seen it in the buff."

"Seriously, Gail, we are a close-knit family and we spend a lot of time together," Jessie continued. "Say, where do you go to church?"

Bill cringed at Jessie's question. He knew it put Gail on the spot. He glanced at her to see if she was mad at him. She winked and said, "Right now I'm between churches. Perhaps you could fill me in on yours."

Jessie jumped in with her sales pitch about the old church on North Washington Street that the family had attended for generations. Bill breathed a sigh of relief. He had seen Jessie totally destroy people who gave the wrong answer to her question. From this point on Gail and Jessie carried on a conversation that threatened to stop the card game. Eventually, Jessie glanced at the clock and noticed it was after noon. She announced that it was time for her and Randy to leave.

After they departed, Dottie and Eddy excused themselves to get a few last minute items ready for the trip. Gail went to change in the laundry room and Bill took his suit up to a small bathhouse behind the pool to change. He was swimming laps when Gail climbed up the steps from the porch and jumped in. Bill thought she looked great in her modest yellow bikini. They swam a few laps together and then climbed out and sat by the pool in the reclining chairs and talked. After a while Dottie and Eddy came up the steps.

"Well, guys, we are leaving. Be sure to take Jake for a walk and lock the door when you leave. Oh, I almost forgot, we have two tickets for the Totem Pole playhouse tonight. It's a classic musical, *South Pacific*. Can you use them?"

Bill and Gail looked at each other and said in unison, "Yes, thank you."

Dottie pulled the tickets out of her pocket and said as she turned them over, "Bill, this is not the place for your pickup. It's a great vehicle, but you know people treat this evening as a formal thing. Eddy, give the kids the keys to the Lincoln."

Eddy smiled and dropped the keys in Bill's lap. "Have fun, guys, but be careful. It turns into a pumpkin at midnight. Let's get moving, Dottie. I don't want to be late."

When they were alone again Bill said to Gail, "Let's make this our first date. There's a little restaurant on the way that serves great steaks and good wine."

"Bill, that's a wonderful idea. It's almost two o'clock now. If you could pick me up at five-thirty we'd have plenty of time to eat and make the show at eight. Let's get back in the water to cool down and then we can go home and get ready."

Everything happened so fast that Bill was on his way home before he began to reflect on the day's events. How rapidly and completely things had changed from this morning. With Gail around everything always seemed so relaxed. Time always seemed to travel faster when they were together. Here it was a little past three. Where had the day gone? At least they would be together again this evening and afterwards—well, who knew.

By the time Bill got home, performed some chores, showered and dressed it was approaching five o'clock. He knew that people dressed up to attend the plays. He put on a pair of black dress pants and a light blue short-sleeve shirt. He had a grey summer sports jacket and black dress shoes that completed his outfit. A few minutes after five, he began his drive to pick up Gail. He was very anxious to return to spend the evening with her. He knocked on the door and she called from the bedroom, "Come in, I'm almost ready. Have a seat in the living room."

When the bedroom door opened, Bill stood up and turned to get the full effect of Gail's grand entrance and he was not disappointed. She wore a full-length, black evening dress with thin shoulder straps. A single strand of pearls accented her shapely neck and tanned shoulders. Again she wore the pearl earrings he had seen the other day. Her outfit was completed with a small, simple black purse and black high heels. Bill crossed the room, embraced her and kissed her gently on the lips. "You are absolutely stunning tonight. Please bring your camera and we will get someone at the restaurant to take our picture."

Gail went for the camera and Bill draped her shawl across her shoulders when she came back. "I feel like Prince Charming taking Cinderella to the ball," he said as they walked hand in hand to the car.

"Well, Bill, tonight you are my Prince Charming. Remember, we have to be home by midnight unless you know how to drive a pumpkin chariot."

It was easy for the staff of the restaurant to see that this was a very special night for the young couple that drove up in the new, white Lincoln and walked through their doors at six o'clock, and the staff reacted accordingly. Two waiters jumped to assist when Bill asked for someone to take their picture. Bill was not a wine expert, so he fell back on his favorite and ordered two glasses of a Riesling recommended by the waiter. After lighting the candle on their table, the waiter poured the wine and left.

Bill decided to satisfy his curiosity, "I have a question from this morning's meeting. First, I wanted to apologize for Jessie cornering you on the religion question. She can be a real zealot at times. Secondly, I want to ask, how did you handle her so effortlessly? I've seen her make even Pastor Jones cringe when she gets in her evangelistic mode."

"I'm just a great politician, my dear," Gail replied as she took a sip of her wine and smiled. "Truthfully, as you recall I spent an afternoon with your mother and Aunt Kate. We talked about you a lot of the time. In between I was introduced to most of the family members. When Jessie's name came up, Kate made sure I understood her religious zeal. Then we discussed my, shall we say, lack of religion. Kate felt a direct answer on my part would turn the wrath of Jessie on me. She coached me on a couple of approaches to deflect the wrath. I ran them over in my mind and came up with the non-committal answer of this morning. I'm rather proud of how effectively it worked. Once we got over that hump, I really enjoyed Jessie's wit and humor."

"Yes, I noticed how you had her eating out of your hands by the end of the card game. Perhaps you should become a politician."

"No, I don't do well in crowds. Besides, I enjoy what I do now; although, since meeting you, I've had a few tense moments. Here's to our first date and the beginning of a long and rewarding relationship." At this point they both raised their glasses in a toast.

Soon their steaks came and they laughed and chatted as they ate. Over a second round of wine they contemplated dessert and kissed in the low light of the restaurant. At seven-thirty Bill paid the waiter and they walked to the Lincoln.

"Gosh, Bill, I'm having such a good time. Maybe it's because you got me half drunk plying me with wine."

"Only half drunk, we can fix that. Let's go back and have another and then we'll skip the play and go home to bed. Just kidding, but you must admit the thought has some merit."

Cars were streaming into the parking lot when they arrived. The Totem Pole playhouse is advertised as the theater in the woods. It is completely surrounded by tall trees from the mature forests that surround it. A gentle evening breeze rustled the tops of these trees as the couples weaved their way to the entrance doors. Although the theater was not air conditioned, louvers in the doors and sides of the building and ceiling fans kept a cool breeze moving through the spacious structure.

Bill and Gail were ushered to a pair of seats in the center aisle close to the front of the building. Shortly after they arrived the lights were dimmed and the curtain rose on an island in the Pacific during the

Second World War. The play, a classic story of two couples falling in love during wartime, totally engrossed Bill and Gail. During intermission between the acts everyone mulled around the open courtyards on both sides of the theater and enjoyed the starlit night. Bill thought of the many times previously he stood alone in the crowd and wished one of the girls he saw was his date. Tonight was so different. Tonight he led the most beautiful girl at the theater around on his arm. They stopped occasionally to greet friends he and his mother knew, and Bill beamed with pride as he introduced Gail. All too soon the lights blinked indicating time for everyone to return to their seats for the final act of the play.

It was after ten o'clock before the final curtain came down and everyone headed to the exit. On the way home they spent the time discussing the play and the actors' performances. They debated Emile's relationship with the deceased Polynesian girl and the resulting children. Bill supported Emile's new girlfriend, Nellie, when she recoiled from the relationship upon learning of the children. Gail, on the other hand, felt that true love demanded that Nellie accept Emile's children as her own. Both agreed they couldn't pick a favorite song from the many great ones: "Some Enchanted Evening," "Bali Ha'I," and "I'm in Love with a Wonderful Guy." They vowed to check the schedule of future plays and come back again soon. With the spirited conversation on the play monopolizing their time, soon they were exiting the interstate at Greencastle.

"If it's OK I need to stop by and check on Jake before I take you home. He's been penned up in the house since five when I put him out just before I picked you up."

"Sure, I'm in no hurry. I have all weekend and it is a gorgeous evening."

Bill turned the car into the Orchard area and drove to his aunt's house. When they let old Jake out he was ready to do his duty. "Let's sit up by the pool while Jake gets some exercise," Bill said. Many evenings when he stayed at the house he would just sit by the pool and enjoy the night air, the stars, and the reflections of the moon on the water.

"That's a great idea. It's so beautiful out here tonight." Gail moved up the steps ahead of him and sat down in one of the chairs surrounding a small table in the patio corner. "Oh, listen to the traffic on the interstate. Where do you think they're all going?"

"That's a good question. Lots of times I sit here and try to imagine what the people are like and where they are going. I am quite the traveler myself. I've been up to New York a couple times and down to Norfolk about the same number of times to visit relatives. Why, I drove all the way to Ohio once on company business and they flew me down to Florida to a school. Unfortunately, I was in the wrong area of the state to visit Disney World. Where have you been?"

"My parents took me to Disney an age ago. When I was in college, I went to England and France one summer. Like you, I've done the visit-relatives-in-neighboring-states thing."

"Wow, I'm with a celebrity international traveler. But seriously, where do you want to go from here? What do you want to do with your life?"

"I haven't really developed a plan. I want to get married at some point and own a home in the country with a white picket fence. I'm not real career oriented, but it would be nice to write human interest type stories for a major newspaper some day. You know the type where someone saves another person's life or overcomes a handicap and wins a race or is successful in business. Someday I'd like to write a book. Don't ask me what it would be about. That's my life—now tell me yours."

"I've been saving money since I started working and I just about have enough in my account to buy my own home. Sometimes I think I want a house in the mountains surrounded by trees. A place where I could sit on the back porch and watch the deer, turkeys and other wild animals wandering through the yard. Then at other times I think I should buy a house in town where I could go for walks and greet my neighbors or sit on the corner by the bank and watch the cars go buy. And I want to travel. I want to see the Grand Canyon, Las Vegas and all the other places this great country has to offer. Then I want to travel to Europe like you did and visit several of the major countries there."

"Those are great plans, but I didn't hear any plans in there for marriage and kids," Gail interrupted.

"I'm glad you asked. I haven't bought that house yet because I am waiting for my partner in life to help me make the decision. And then I want us to do some of the traveling I talked about before we have our first boy. I think two boys will round out my family nicely. Hey, I didn't hear you mention children in your plans. How many are you planning to have?"

Gail paused for a minute and Bill saw that something was troubling her. Finally she responded in a non-committal manner, "I suppose two children is the ideal family size."

When Bill asked if there was a problem she needed to talk about, she turned the conversation by responding, "Someday I will tell you. Let's not ruin the moment tonight. Now, Mister Henderson, we were talking about children. I didn't hear you mention girls."

"Well, aren't boys also children? I mean, you can do so many things with boys. You can take them camping, hunting and fishing. I can coach their football and baseball teams and we can sit together and watch sports on TV."

Gail laughed at Bill's enthusiasm and spontaneity. She could see that he was relating to his own childhood and the happy times he had with his father. She drew from her own past and countered, "Well, dear, girls are fairly versatile children, too. They also like camping, hunting, fishing, and sports coached by their fathers. But with girls you get so much more. There's tap dance, ballet and piano lessons to get involved in. You can make them doll houses and miniature kitchen sets." Gail giggled as she talked and was totally enjoying herself.

The start of her last remark hung in Bill's mind. This was the second time tonight she had called him "dear." He wanted to tell her more about that partner he was looking for. He wanted her to be bright, witty and able to enjoy life. She must be understanding and caring and someone whom he could share the pleasures of life with, but also count on her being there to help him through the troubled times. Tonight as they sat by the pool talking and laughing he knew he had found the person he wanted to be that partner. But he knew she wasn't ready to hear those words. After all, this was really only their first date.

"Well, Jake appears to be ready to go back. Aunt Dottie tells me he usually is in bed around ten every night. I hope he will forgive us for keeping him up late." Bill stood up and headed toward the patio door and Gail followed.

"It's such a beautiful evening. Look there, Bill, a shooting star. I sure hate to go home."

"We could go for a swim and talk some more. The water is very warm and would feel good. Let me put Jake to bed and get our suits." Bill felt Gail grab his shoulder. He stopped walking and turned toward her.

She looked into his eyes and said, "I think the swim is a wonderful idea. We don't need the suits. Just get us some towels."

Bill stammered, "Ah, sure, OK, right away." He turned around and walked right into the closed sliding patio door. It was quite clear that he was in shock from Gail's remark.

"What's the matter, Bill, haven't you ever skinny-dipped with a girl before?" She wasn't about to tell him that she had never done anything like this before and she didn't know what possessed her now. She only knew that inside she ached to have him hold her, kiss her and make love to her. She wanted him and tonight she was going to have her way.

"No, I never have. Let me get the towels." Bill had regained some of his composure. What was going on here? Was he in a new dream and would wake up in a few moments? Things like this just didn't happen in his life. *Better get the towels quick before I wake up.*

Gail had remained on the porch and he returned with two beach towels in his hand. He walked to the corner of the porch opposite the kitchen entrance and used his key to open a door to the house on that end. "You can use my bedroom to change. Err, I mean to get undressed. I'll go back in the laundry room."

"Relax, Bill dear. It's only a swim." Gail planted a passionate kiss on his lips as she slipped the one towel from his hands and headed for the bedroom.

Bill was confused by the turn of events as he headed for the laundry room. He had dreamed for weeks of making love to this beautiful, sexy girl. He had developed several schemes to get her into bed. But in the end he abandoned them because he wanted the time to be special and a little bit spontaneous. Somehow he never dreamed tonight would be the night and yet somehow it all happened so naturally. His thoughts were interrupted by a splash of water and he hurriedly finished undressing. When he reached the pool he heard Gail splashing about in the far corner and could faintly make out her form in the pale moonlight.

"Come in, Bill, the water's lovely. It's so warm and refreshing. But, wait a minute, we need some rules. You stay on the side near the house and I'll keep on the far side. After all, this is our first date and we don't want to get carried away, now do we? Jump in and swim over to this end. I'll race you across then."

Bill did as he was told and soon they were racing across the pool. He led a very active, physical life with his job and sports. However, Gail had spent many hours swimming in her mother's pool and her sleek body easily slid through the water. They were almost at the opposite wall before Bill finally pulled ahead and reached the wall ahead of his competitor.

"That was great. Do you want to race back to the other side?"

Breathing a little heavily, Gail responded, "You won that fair and square. Let's just swim across slowly and talk."

Bill and Gail swam back and forth for a while. At first they kept to the outside edges of the pool per the rules established by Gail. Gradually as they talked, Bill noted that they both were moving toward the center of the pool until they finished a lap only inches apart. Bill saw the moonbeams glistening in her hair and the soft outline of her breasts beneath the water. "Gail, I don't think the rules are working," he panted, the passion of the moment overcoming him. "Being this close to you and knowing we're both naked just makes me the horniest guy in the world."

"No, I guess my idea isn't going to work. Kiss me then, Bill. Kiss me and hold me. Kiss me like you never kissed me before."

Bill swam the short distance to Gail and gently embraced her. As her naked body touched his, he could feel his heart pounding in his chest from the excitement. They swirled about in the shallow water for many minutes as they continued to embrace and kiss. Finally separating, they leaned back against the edge of the pool and caught their breath.

"I heard bells from that kiss. Did you, Bill? And this guy was in the way all the time," she joked as she reached down and stroked his firm, erect manliness.

"The ringing of those bells is another first for me," he agreed. "Let's go to the bedroom where we will be more comfortable."

They crawled out of the pool and walked hand in hand to the porch. Near the door to the bedroom, Bill stopped Gail and said, "Ever since meeting you I've dreamed of doing this." He picked her up in his muscular arms, opened the door and carried her to the bed. As he carried her he felt her breasts gently brushing his chest. The strong muscles in her bottom and her smooth soft legs rested in his powerful hands. She laid her head on his shoulder and her long hair flowed down his back.

Just like in the dream, only a thousand times better, he thought to himself as he gently laid her head on the pillow and draped her long, lean body down the center of the bed. The pale moonlight flowed through the window and revealed the contented smile on her face. Then his eyes followed the light as it danced off her firm breasts with their excited erect nipples, flowed down her lithe waist, across her long legs and ended its journey at the tips of her toes.

Meanwhile Gail had been watching the light flow around his gentle eyes and warm smile, down across his broad, hairy, muscular chest and down his waist to his, well, still very firm, swollen manliness. "Come to bed with me now, Bill," she pleaded.

He needed no further coaxing to slide his body next to hers. They rolled on their sides and kissed again as their hands explored each other's bodies. As he played with Gail's swollen nipples, she felt her whole body pulsate with passion. She wanted to tell Bill that she was falling in love with him but she was afraid it would ruin the moment if he didn't feel the same way. Now as his strong, large hands roamed over her breasts, waist, hips and legs she quivered with excitement. He lay her on her back and gently massaged the soft warm area between her legs as they continued to kiss. By now Gail was so excited, she felt like she was going to explode.

Bill heard Gail's heavy breathing and felt her body quiver. His excitement grew as she also continued to caress him with her hands. Slowly their passion rose to an uncontrolled state. He knew tonight was a night they would always remember. He was in love with her even if they had known each other only a short time. Legs were entwined and both bodies were glowing with sweat. When Bill positioned himself on top of Gail, she couldn't stand it anymore. She pounded on the bed and panted, "Oh, Bill, I need you now. I need you in me right now!"

As Bill gently entered her she thought she had died and gone to heaven. Now their bodies moved in unison and the sweat rolled off of Bill as Gail continued to emit long low moans. Later, old Jake was jolted from his sleep by Gail's scream and a moan from Bill at the wonderful moment when they experienced the joy of releasing their passions together. A short time later two sweat-soaked naked bodies streaked up to the pool and splashed back into the water.

"That was a good idea you had to come up here and cool off under the stars, Gail. I never dreamed a person could get that turned on or could make love with such intensity. It was great. No, it was fantastic. I'll remember this night until the day I die."

"There truly are no words to describe it," Gail sighed as she floated in the water. "Come on, let's swim a little. Look at the sky. The clouds are gone now and the moon is almost full. We must be in the midst of a meteor shower. There goes another one."

Bill lay on his back and slowly stroked across the pool. A question was forming in his mind. Dare he ask her for her feelings toward him? Even if she answered, considering the passion of the moment, would her feelings be the same tomorrow? He did not want to risk losing the moment. Yet, he knew his own feelings. "How's that wall you built doing these days?" he said in a joking tone. Not threatening, but hoping to get a response.

They finished their lap and Gail stood near the wall to face him. "It's got some mighty big holes in it that you put there. If you keep up with this kind of behavior, the whole thing will be tumbling down." She moved close to him to hug him and give him another long kiss. "So, Prince Charming," she continued, "keep up this behavior and knock my wall down. Oh my gosh, Bill, speaking of keeping it up, you are up again!"

"Well, I'm a viral young man standing naked in a swimming pool next to the most beautiful girl in the world. I can't help but get excited."

"Yes, but we just spent over two hours making—oh, never mind, come to the bedroom and we'll do something about this." Bill was out of the water in a flash.

As the sun rose in the eastern horizon and its warming rays peeked through the bedroom window, they revealed Bill and Gail lying on the bed, holding each other and engaged in conversation. "Look at the window. The sun is coming up. We spent the whole night together. Bill, how many times did we...?"

"I lost count. I am just so happy. I've enjoyed this time holding you and talking almost as much."

"Yes, it's been a wonderful evening. It started with the trip to dinner and the play and then, wow, ended with this. I am always so happy when I am with you. I have a confession. I am falling in love with you." Gail's heart skipped a beat. She had wanted to tell him her true feelings all evening and now it was out. What would he say?

"Gail, you just made me the happiest man in the whole world. I wanted to tell you the same thing earlier, only I thought you might get upset. Listen, I promised Mom I would see her at church this morning. The service is at ten-thirty. Come with me please."

"No, Bill, I couldn't do that. Honestly, I...I'm just not ready for that yet. In the last twenty-four hours I admitted to myself and you that I am falling in love with you. I can't embrace religion at the same time."

"Oh, but you just took the first giant step. You love me and I love you. God brought us together because he loves us. You see, we can make religion as complex or as simple as we like, but in the end it comes down to three words: God is love."

"I just don't think I can do it, Bill."

Lou pulled into the church parking lot and walked to large red doors on the front of the church. She tried not to get upset at Bill. Yes, he had promised to come to church with her this morning, but he was still young and didn't always make it. Still, he should have called her and given her an explanation. True, she had arrived home too late last night for him to call. He could have easily called this morning. There was plenty of time before she left the house.

She moved through the entrance to the sanctuary and was thankful that nobody asked where Bill was. As she moved down the center isle, she greeted several friends and finally sat down in the pew near the front that she sat in every Sunday. Bill was nowhere to be seen and she was convinced now that Gail did not get in contact with him. He probably wandered off to Mike's house and had too much to drink. It had happened a couple of times in the past and he was in no shape to come to church the next morning. Oh, if only she had written a note to let him know Gail was in town. The bells in the large white steeple began ringing and she closed her eyes to say a prayer.

As she bowed her head she heard the old doors at the back of the church creak open and a shuffle up the center aisle. Someone was late. It always bothered her when late arrivals interrupted her prayer and meditation before the service began. This morning it seemed to annoy her double because of the vacant seat beside her. For a moment she was tempted to look around and scowl at whoever was hurrying down the aisle, but she knew that was not a proper way to react.

She restarted her prayer when a hand rested on her shoulder and gentle squeezed it. Now this was going too far. Coming in late and then interrupting her in the middle of her prayers. Irked, she was going to let this person know her feelings. She turned her head and raised her eyes to shoot a disapproving stare. Her countenance immediately changed when she saw Bill standing by her, and no, that couldn't be Gail standing behind him. Only a couple weeks ago she had confided that she hadn't been to church in years.

Lou slid over in the pew and noticed the smiles on their faces, and the way Bill's whole face seemed to glow when he looked at Gail. Lou knew her son and she knew he had taken this relationship to the next level. Yes, he was in love and the looks Gail was giving him told her she was probably experiencing the same feelings. Lou had a pretty good hunch of what had happened last night and she admitted to herself that she didn't approve. Still, seeing the love and joy that radiated from the two of them, how could anyone be angry? All she really wanted was to see her son happy like he was now.

After church several of Lou's friends rushed to her side and chided her for not letting them know that Bill had a girlfriend. All agreed they made a perfect couple. Just outside the sanctuary doors Jim caught up with her. "Lou, how in the world did you and Bill convince that girl to come to church today? She almost ate my head off one time when I tried to get her to come here with me."

"I had nothing to do with it, Jim. God moves in mysterious ways. I asked Bill how he did it. All he told me is that it was the power of love."

"So, those two are dating. I've seen a change in Gail recently. She's been singing to herself and seems to enjoy life so much more. Now if only I could work the same miracle on that boy's mother." There was a joking tone in Jim's voice as he uttered his last comment. He had worked hard on trying to date Lou and he thought this was a good time to put in a lighthearted plug to prepare her for a call later in the week with another serious try.

"Times are changing and I guess we all better be moving on with our lives."

Jim felt a sickening sensation inside himself as he prepared for Lou to continue. Here was where she told him to go get lost. She had always told him she was still mourning Fred and maybe with time they could work things out. But deep down inside he knew a dull, middle-aged, balding, small town editor never had a chance with a sophisticated lady like Lou.

"So, Jim," she continued her conversation as Jim steeled himself for the worst, "why don't you join us for dinner out at the house this evening at five?" Lou saw the look of shock on Jim's face and laughed in spite of herself. "Jim, I've never seen you at a loss for words before. There will only be the four of us. Dress casual and bring a swimsuit. Dottie's away and we may go over to the pool later."

As Bill helped his mother set the table for the evening meal, he noticed she was using the best silverware and china and there were four place settings.

"OK, Mom, what's going on? I'm setting the table for four people and we are using your best silverware. Who's coming to dinner?"

"Well, I met Jim as we were leaving the church. You know he spends Sunday afternoon alone in that apartment of his reading newspapers. I just felt sorry for him. He's bringing a bathing suit. If you have no plans, we can all go over to the pool afterwards. You look tired, dear, didn't you sleep well last night at Dottie's house? It's probably that old mattress on the spare bed."

Bill looked at his mother and knew he could not tell her a lie. "The mattress is fine, Mom. I believe you know I'm tired because I spent the night with Gail. It was the most wonderful evening in my whole life and we were awake all night until the sun came up. Then we dozed off and almost missed church."

"I don't approve of what you did. But when I think of how happy and full of life you and Gail were this morning, I can't be mad at you. I love you, Bill, and I am so glad things are working out for you. Just don't make this a habit." Even though he was 29, Bill cared very much about his mother's opinions and he was glad she had not lectured him on spending the night with Gail.

'Thanks, Mom, for trying to understand last night. I love you, too. I know it gets lonely around here at times. Jim's a good friend and it will be nice to have him come to dinner."

Five o'clock came quickly and soon everyone was seated at the table. Gail had ridden to the house with Jim and was pleased that Lou had invited him. As they ate, the conversation turned to Old Home week which had been a triennial tradition since 1902. Indeed, Sarah's father had been on the committee that assembled the first event, which was a reunion of between 50 and 60 "old boys" of the community. Gradually, every third year it evolved into a reunion celebration for all past and present residents of the town. This year the programs would run from August sixth through twelfth. On Sunday night the traditional welcome back opening program would begin on the square at 8 p.m. and as usual would continue through midnight. Monday night a special Civil War re-enactment was scheduled near the Corporal Rihl monument. Tuesday night would be the usual parade. Wednesday and Thursday nights' showing of the play on the founding of Greencastle would be followed by the grand ball on Friday night and fireworks at 9:30. Closing ceremonies were scheduled at the park for Saturday. There were many other events too numerous to mention.

They all decided to attend the opening ceremonies together. Jim was a Civil War enthusiast and had planned to cover the re-enactment for the paper. He screwed up his courage and asked Lou if she would accompany him. Again she caught him off guard when she accepted without a moment's hesitation. Bill knew he would be busy Monday night helping Eddy get his 1905 Reo ready for the parade. When Gail learned about the car, she asked to come along and write a story on the car which had been in Eddy's family many years.

Dinner ended and everyone retired to the porch for coffee and more discussion. Bill was into his fourth cup of coffee trying to stay awake when Lou announced it was time to go for a swim. Jim suggested that Gail ride with Bill and he would take Lou and bring her home later.

There was little conversation on the way into town, since the occupants of the truck were rather exhausted at this point. However, Bill did speak up as he pulled into Dottie and Eddy's driveway. "Will you be needing your suit tonight, madam, or just a towel?" he joked. She laughed and he continued along a more serious line, "Now that you've met most of my family, I would like to meet yours."

"Oh, dear, that's so sweet. I only see my dad around Christmas time when he comes back to the area for a brief visit. I'll call my mother and grandfather next week to see if the twenty-ninth of this month will work."

The water was refreshing and everyone perked up again. At eleven Jim and Lou took Gail along to drop her off at her apartment. As soon as Bill and Jake returned from their walk, Bill collapsed on his bed and fell asleep immediately.

As usual it was after midnight as Bill drove home from Tuesday's shift. The new line was running smoothly and soon he could return to the day shift. He liked that idea now because he wanted to spend the evenings with Gail.

As he parked in Dottie's driveway, he saw someone lying on the couch on the back porch. He almost ran to the door as he realized it was Gail. She was asleep and did not hear him enter the porch. She was wearing an old pair of cutoffs and a halter top. The soft silken sheen of her legs and navel area started his hormones working again, but tonight he just needed to hold her.

After letting Jake out, he unlocked the door to his room, came back and gently picked her up and carried her into the bedroom. She awoke and sleepily said, "Sorry, Bill, I just missed you real bad. I had to come see you tonight. Please don't be mad."

He lay down beside her and put his arms around her. "I'm not mad. I'm so happy to see you." They kissed and chatted a short time before both drifted off to sleep. Early in the morning Bill awoke and drove her home. The rest of the week the pattern was repeated and soon it was Saturday morning. At breakfast Gail announced that the plans were set for the 29th. Bill also had good news and told her that he was moving to first shift next week and now they could spend more time together.

The weekend and following week passed quickly and Bill woke up on the 29th a little apprehensive about meeting Gail's mother and grandfather. He and Gail had spent a lot of time together this past week and things were going very well. What if her family didn't like him? It was almost a three-hour trip to Gail's mother's house. They decided to leave at eleven and Bill could spend time getting to know Gail's mother, Lauren, and her grandfather, Ted, before dinner.

Lauren lived in a small brick ranch house on a quiet street near the heart of Lancaster. This was the house Gail grew up in and stayed in through college. Several neat little flower beds meticulously maintained were scattered around the front lawn. As Gail opened the door and announced their arrival, a short, average build woman in her early fifties came around the corner. She was followed a few minutes later by a tall, elderly gentleman.

"Mom, Gramps, I want you to meet Bill Henderson." Gail began her introductions. As she started to speak, Lauren put her arms around Bill and gave him a hug. Then standing on her toes she managed to kiss him on the cheek.

"Bill, at last we meet. I feel like I already know you. All my daughter talks about anymore is you. She calls me in the middle of the night to tell me about the dimples in your cheeks or how your smile lights up her day even when things are going bad at work. She even calls you her Prince Charming."

"Mother, please don't tell all this to Bill. It will go to his head."

Bill looked at Gail and she was clearly blushing from Lauren's revelation.

"Well, it's true, Gailee, you've got a crush on this man. I must admit, he's every bit as handsome as you said he was and such a gentleman." Gail was blushing again. "Oh, I am sorry, dear. It just slipped out."

Bill leaned over and teased her, "Nice blush, Gailee. I think I'll use that as my special name for you, Gailee Girl."

"Well enough of this. Please meet my grandfather, Ted Price."

Bill noticed that Gail's grandfather hesitated a moment before extending his hand and when their hands met he felt Ted's tense up.

Lauren broke in again, "As you can see, Gail inherited her stature, her looks and her beautiful blue eyes from my dad. When we show you the pictures you'll also see that dad's silver grey hair was auburn in color when he was younger. Bill, please sit on the sofa and Gail can get the picture albums."

"Oh, Mother, don't bore him to death."

"Alright, Gailee, at least show him some of your pictures when you were little. She was so cute. If you have any trouble recognizing her, just look for the tallest girl in the class."

"Yes, I always looked like a zombie, a tall skinny one."

"Nonsense, you were always very pretty, and look at you now. You are a beautiful, smart woman of twenty-six. Isn't she, Bill?"

"She's the most beautiful woman I've ever met and she has made my life complete. Mrs. Mason, I must tell you that I am in love with your daughter."

"Oh, Bill, that's so wonderful to hear. Gailee went through some rough years during and after my divorce. Then in high school and college she hardly dated. You're the first boyfriend she's ever brought home. And now you love her. I always told her to be patient and she would meet the right person. Isn't it great, Dad? They're in love."

For the first time Bill noticed a smile on Ted's face. Now he seemed to warm to the conversation as they talked about Bill's job and his hobbies. Ted had been a hunter for many years and he and Bill swapped hunting tales for a while when the women left to finish the dinner preparations. Later at the dinner table a lively conversation picked up again. As everyone was seated around the table drinking coffee, Lauren said, "Gailee, Gramps is very upset about the letter you received after publishing the article on Bill's grandmother, Sarah."

"Gail, we want you to stop researching this article right now." Her grandfather suddenly cut Lauren short and jumped into the conversation. He raised his voice and pounded his fist on the table as he spoke. "Your mother and I love you very much and we will not allow you to continue to put yourself in harm's way. Bill's family needs to solve this mystery without your help. Do you understand?" By this time Ted was almost yelling the words and his face was red from the exertion.

"Dad, calm down. Gail is a woman now. We need to let her make her own decisions."

Ted stood up and stormed out of the house into the backyard.

"I'm sorry about this outburst, Bill. Dad was a soldier and he always ran his family like a sergeant leading his troops into battle. Dad was the leader in his house and nobody ever dared to question his orders. I can't make him understand that those days are over. Truth is I'm just as scared as Dad about this whole thing. Gailee and I talked about the whole affair on the phone and I understand why she can't cower in a hole whenever someone doesn't like something she writes. She has also assured me that you will be with her whenever she does any more research on the article. Please, promise me you will keep my daughter safe and protect her."

"Mrs. Mason, like Gail I need to find out who is behind this threat. We will only be completely safe when we have uncovered the person who wrote that letter. I promise to protect Gail with my life if needed."

When Bill and Gail got up to help clear the table, Lauren said, "I really wish Dad wasn't so upset about this whole thing. It's ruined my day. Maybe it's best if you leave and I'll talk with him. After Mom died he got very secretive about things and now this outburst makes me wonder if he needs to see a doctor."

Lauren led Bill and Gail to the door and hugged them both. "I'm so sorry things turned out this way. Bill, please come back soon with Gailee. I really want to get to know you better. Next time if Dad's here I'll put a muzzle on him."

As Bill helped Gail into the truck, he smiled and said, "I like your mother. She is so understanding and caring. Now get those hot little buns of yours into the truck, Gailee."

"Why, Bill, are your hormones bothering you again? And stop calling me Gailee. It's embarrassing enough when my mother does it."

"My hormones are always running on overtime when we're together and you wearing those red hot pants today doesn't help things. Call me a romantic, but when I make love to you again I want it to be just as great as the night at Aunt Dottie's." At that point Bill leaned over in the truck and kissed Gail. Lauren was watching at the door of the house. In spite of her father's outburst she had a really good feeling about Bill.

On the way home Bill voiced his doubts, "Gail, I know we sounded real convincing to your mother, but I'm not sure I believed what I said. I was very scared the other day when I walked down the street toward that car. What would have happened if the person in the car was carrying a gun? Maybe your grandfather is right; we should just drop this whole thing. After all, everywhere we search we just come up against a brick wall."

"Don't give up on me now, Bill. Like you told my mother, we can never feel truly safe again until we discover who is behind the letter and why it was written. We need to go back and look at all the information we've gathered so far. Somewhere there is a clue to tell us where to go.

I'll review my notes this week and see if I can find anything. The next two weeks I'll be very busy reporting on Old Home week. Jim wants me to write the article on the opening ceremonies and the parade for next week's paper. Then I have to write about the pageant and closing ceremonies for the following week. He's going to cover the re-enactment and the play. I'll be able to give Sarah's story all my attention after that. Oh, and while we're on the subject of reporting on Old Home week, will you attend the activities with me? We make a good team and I really enjoy your company."

Monday evening, the last day of July, found Bill working on his truck. He was under the truck changing the oil when he heard the telephone ringing. He suspected it was Jim. He either called every night now or Lou would be out on a date with him. He was beginning to think that they were more inseparable than he and Gail. Come to think of it, he hadn't heard from Gail this whole day and it was five-thirty. He would have to call her when he was done.

"Bill, Gail's on the phone."

He quickly slid out from under the truck and walked to the kitchen phone. "Hi, Gail, what's up?"

"Bill, I found it. I found the clue. Can you meet me in the library in an hour?"

"I'll clean up and be there. What's this all about?"

"Meet me there and I'll explain."

Bill finished his job and quickly showered. It was almost an hour later when he walked through the door of the library. He spied Gail sitting at a table near the librarian's desk and asked her, "Now can you tell me what this is all about?"

"I was awake most of last night pouring through my notes on your grandmother's article. There was nothing there that jumped out at me. Then I picked up the letter one more time and I saw it right away."

"Saw what? We've read that thing a dozen times or more. Jim's checked it out and so did the police. What did we miss?"

"Read the fourth sentence." Gail handed him the letter.

"*Do not share the story with other papers and do not dig into the past for any more research on this article.* I don't see any clues. It just says not to have any other papers publish the article and don't do any more research on the article."

"We all missed it because we only picked up on the key words just like you did now. We keep looking for the answer in the last seventeen years of Sarah's life. It's not there, Bill! Reread the sentence and look for the words we keep jumping over. Those words meant something to the writer."

Bill reread the sentence slowly and then exclaimed, "I see it now— *do not dig into the past.* We jumped over that phrase. But I still don't see how that leads us anywhere."

"Bill, think about it. Go way back in Sarah's past. Who is the mystery man that she only spoke of vaguely?"

"Oh, you're talking about that Brown fellow. He was killed in the First World War."

"We need to know more about him. He's the key to this mystery. I feel it in my bones, Bill. Dead or not, we need to know everything about this guy."

"OK, well how in the world do we track down a guy who may or may not have existed when all we know is his last name may have been Brown?"

"That's why we're here. Sarah grew up in Greencastle, Franklin County. Even today there are Browns in the phone book. I called the library and they have a book here listing all the men killed in World War I who came from Franklin County. Here comes the librarian with the book now."

The librarian explained, "The book is broken down by local towns and townships with the county. Do you know where your relative came from, Mr. Henderson?"

"No, Bill isn't sure where he lived in the area. Is there just an alphabetical listing of names somewhere?"

"Why, yes there is. Here it lists all the names and the page where we can find information on that person. Hmm, are you sure the name is

Brown? There were no Browns from this area killed in the war."

"See, I told you Great-uncle Freddie Brown wasn't from this area. Thanks for the help."

When they got outside Bill asked, "Why did you tell that girl this Brown guy was my great-uncle and where did the name Freddie come from?"

"I was just embarrassed to say we really knew nothing about this guy so I invented a story. Freddie just came out of the top of my head. Now what do we do?"

"Well, you're searching in the wrong town anyhow."

"What do you mean the wrong town? Your mother told me Sarah lived her whole life here in Greencastle."

"Mom told you she lived her whole life here in Greencastle—after marrying my grandfather. He met her in Hagerstown. Somewhere around nineteen-fifteen my great-grandmother moved to Hagerstown. After the marriage Sarah moved back here."

"Look, Bill, it's not even seven o'clock. Let's run over to the Hagerstown library and see what information they have."

Bill agreed and soon they stood in the historical room at the Hagerstown library.

"Oh, we have a really good book on Maryland war veterans," the librarian bragged when they asked about Browns killed in the war. He returned shortly carrying an old book. "Now what was the last name? Brown, let me see under the Bs. Yes, here we are. You are in luck. There were five Browns from Maryland and two were from Washington County. The others were from Baltimore. Here are the local ones with their full names and addresses."

Bill excitedly picked up the piece of paper. He was wondering how to determine which one married his grandmother when Gail asked, "Can you tell me why they both have an asterisk behind there names?'

"Sure can. An asterisk means they were black. As you can see, this is a rather old book and black versus white distinctions were still made."

"Well, there were very strict racial divisions in Sarah's day and we can be pretty sure she didn't marry either of these men. I think we are running after a shadow that we can never catch. We have no proof Mr.

92

Brown existed and certainly no way to determine if he ever married my grandmother."

"Have you checked the census?" the librarian volunteered. "The 1920 census would certainly list her under her married name. We have copies of that census at the desk downstairs."

Bill and Gail thanked the librarian and hurried down the steps. It was now eight and the library would close in an hour. The attendant at the desk gave Bill a microfilm reel with the 1920 census for Hagerstown, Maryland. The reel was very large and difficult to read.

"We'll never get through this reel in an hour," Bill complained. "The names are not alphabetical. They are just listed sequentially on their street. We should give up and come back some other time."

"Sit down, Bill, and watch this thing with me as I wind the film forward."

Almost twenty minutes later Bill suddenly yelled, "There near the bottom of the page. It's my great-grandmother Elizabeth Springer. See, we're looking at the Potomac Street residents. Now I remember Mom showing me a house on that street and telling me that my great-grandmother used to live there. There on the next line is Robert, Sarah's brother. And on the next line is Sarah A. Brown, twenty years old, with a 'Wd.' in the marriage status column. We found the proof."

"Yes, we know Mr. Brown really existed. But who was he, where did he come from, where did they meet, and how does he fit into the puzzle? We need to know more. Where would he have left a trail?"

They made a copy of the census page and left the library. "You know, Bill, this is the first time we haven't come home empty handed when we searched for the answer to this mystery. I have a feeling that the pieces will start to fall together now."

Bill didn't share Gail's confidence. "I don't think it will be that easy. All we proved is that my grandmother was a widow in 1920. How do you expect to fill in the story?"

"It's almost nine o'clock. Let's go back to Rosie's and I'll buy you an ice cream. While we eat it, we can plan our next move."

As they sat and ate their ice cream Gail began, "Here's the plan. You already told me that your great-grandfather was a lawyer and politician.

I know he died when Sarah was very young. But in small town newspapers of that time period local gossip sold papers. I think your family may still have been newsworthy and there may have been little tidbits in the paper on their lives. When I called the library here in Greencastle I asked her if she had newspapers from 1914 through 1918. The librarian thought they had them all. I can take one year and you the next. We'll read through the headlines looking for any articles on your family members until we work through all of them. Are you with me on this?"

"That's five years of papers. We have to read two hundred and sixty weekly papers. How many years will that take?"

"It's not that bad, really. I have to scan through old papers at work sometimes to find articles. Tomorrow night the library is closed. If we start Thursday night, I am confident we can finish Saturday."

"It's a good thing I love you. We'll do Thursday night. If nothing crops up, then I think we need to reassess going further."

"Fair enough, pick me up at five-thirty. That will give us about three hours until the library closes at nine."

Bill and Gail were sitting at a table in the library Thursday evening when the librarian dropped two large thick books on the table in front of them. "You take 1915, Bill, and I'll search through 1914. Just read headlines and stay out of world events. We should get through these two this evening."

About fifteen minutes later Bill exclaimed, "Gosh, Gail, you were right. There's an article in here on February thirteenth about Sarah recovering from scarlet fever in a hospital in Pittsburgh. My grandmother never talked about Pittsburgh. I wonder if she lived there."

Bill found his answer about twenty minutes later and told Gail, "Bingo, the date is July 3, 1915, and the article announces that Sarah Brown from Pittsburgh is visiting with her mother Elizabeth. Wow, this is opening up a whole chapter in Grandma's life nobody ever knew anything about. She was married somewhere between February and the end of July because the earlier article used her maiden name. She was only fifteen. This Brown fellow was robbing the cradle. Why was she living in Pittsburgh?"

Gail was enjoying Bill's change in enthusiasm as he found the articles. "Formal schooling usually ended with eighth grade. Families were usually large and there were not a lot of jobs for women. Economics sort of dictated that women get married shortly after the end of school and started their own families. I'm into August in these papers and there have been a few minor notes on Elizabeth visiting in Hagerstown and converting the second floor of her house into apartments. So far I have found nothing exciting."

They were quiet only a few minutes when Bill spoke up again, "Here in August there is a little snippet on Sarah and her husband, Leo, visiting Elizabeth after vacationing in Washington. Mr. Brown has a first name—Leo."

Now all was quiet at the table until Gail was into the last paper in her book. She exclaimed, "Here's your answer, Bill! There's a small announcement that Sarah left for Pittsburgh on the morning of the twenty-sixth of December to attend nursing school." As she closed her book, she continued, "More pieces of the puzzle fell into place tonight. We know that Sarah went to Pittsburgh to become a nurse, met Leo Brown, fell in love and married him."

"Good, we know Leo's name now so we don't have to read those other papers, correct?"

"Wrong! Trust me on this one, Bill. Leo has something to do with this mystery."

"Well, it was kind of exciting. I guess I can labor through another night. Tomorrow night we'll take on 1916 and 1917. Let's go get an ice cream."

Friday evening, Gail took 1916 and Bill took 1917. It was a very quiet evening except for a small announcement in August of 1917

stating that Sarah was now living with her mother, Elizabeth, and brother, Robert, on Summit Avenue in Hagerstown. Bill and Gail agreed that Sarah had probably returned home to live with her family when Leo joined the service. Since the war ended in November of 1918, they knew there was only eleven months to search through on Saturday morning.

Saturday dawned a bright, sunny day and Gail and Bill both had other things on their minds as they entered the library. Since there was only one year to research they shared the book. It was Bill who found the first article of family interest. In the April paper he found out about Robert's enlistment in the Medical Corps. And then in early May he found a second article on Robert recovering from pneumonia.

A little while later Gail exclaimed, "I found it. The article is titled 'County Girl's Husband Dies.' It's good you're sitting down for this one. The article was written in Ottawa, Canada, on August twenty-seventh. I'll read it to you, 'Today's Canadian casualty list includes the name of L. F. Brown who died as a result of wounds he received at the front. Brown was a Canadian by birth and while working in Pittsburgh he met and married Sarah Springer, daughter of the late William Springer of Greencastle. He had been in the army for several years. After Brown had been transferred to France for foreign service, Mrs. Brown took up residence with her mother. They were married about four years ago.' No wonder we couldn't find anything on Leo. He was a Canadian. The plot thickens. Let's check a few more pages."

There were no further articles on the family. As Bill drove away from the library he said, "Let's get your swimsuit and spend some time at Aunt Dottie's. We can fill her and Eddy in on our finds. They may have some ideas on what our next steps should be. Besides, I'm ready to get another look at that great body of yours and put my hands on it."

"Oh, Bill, if you keep up with these compliments it will surely go to my head. Thank you, I always feel special when I'm with you."

Dottie and Eddy were sitting on the spacious back porch drinking coffee. "Look at the radiant beams of sunshine that just flowed through our door, Dottie. It's been a long time since I've seen two people as happy in love as you two are. It kind of reminds me of another couple I know. I think their names are Dottie and Eddy."

"Eddy, that was a nice compliment, but it isn't going to work. You are not going to buy that sporty little Porsche. You're too old to cruise the streets in one of those. And all the young girls would be chasing you."

"Well, I have noticed a few good-looking young girls who could force me to take them for a ride."

"Oh, Eddy, you are incorrigible. You just love to ruffle my feathers. I'm not going to get upset today. Buy that car if you want. But if I see or hear about anybody other than me in the passenger seat you'll be sleeping in the bathhouse."

"Get a red one, Uncle Eddy. Gail and I will keep the battery charged when you're out of town."

"Nobody but me is going to drive it."

"It's not nice to hoard your toys, dear. Bill has always done the pool maintenance and taken very good care of Jake for us. If you insist on getting this plaything, we are going to share it with him. I see you kids have come for a swim."

"Well, we also wanted to update you on our research on Grandma." Bill proceeded to explain Gail's theory that there was a connection between Leo and the mystery flowers. He continued by revealing their discoveries in the library.

"I'm impressed with the work you two are doing. I am also amazed at your findings. I never knew my mother studied to be a nurse. She also never told us that she lived in Pittsburgh. I am beginning to realize how very little we really knew about her. She only told us what she wanted to. This whole story about her never volunteering in York really unnerves me. She purposefully deceived us. Do you have any theories on that?"

Gail responded, "Yes, we have reason to believe that she was meeting someone in York. From the letter I got, I believe that someone is tied to her dead husband, Leo Brown. My theory is that it is a friend or relative of Leo's from the time they lived in Pittsburgh. I do not understand her desire for secrecy. When we actually track this person down he or she will have the reason."

Dottie left to prepare lunch and Eddy spoke up, "Well, I have a friend in Washington who owes me a favor. Jot down the information you have on Leo Brown and I'll have him get us Leo's war records from Toronto. I'm sure they maintain those records for their troops just like our government does."

"Thanks, Uncle Eddy, I told Gail that you and Aunt Dottie were the right people to talk to because you come up with good ideas. We owe you one for this."

"Go get your suits on and let me see this charming friend of yours in that little yellow bikini of hers. That will be payment enough." Eddy winked at Gail and his warm smile showed that he was joking.

"Eddy, you're a dirty old man, but I like you in spite of it." Gail smiled back and leaned over to plant a kiss on his cheek.

As Bill showered it occurred to him that summer was almost over. Today was August sixth. Tonight would be the big celebration in the square to kick off Old Home week. Everyone was worried about the weather and hoped rain would not interfere with the outside activities. This morning the skies were clear with not even a hint of clouds and the prediction for the evening was more of the same. Bill hoped to spend most of the day with Gail.

They had been seeing each other almost every day for the last couple weeks as their relationship grew and matured. Gail was more open and affectionate now. Bill noticed that the empty feeling inside him was gone. Now his only problem was the desire to grab Gail and drag her to the bedroom every time he saw her. The short shorts, halter tops, tube tops and that skimpy new bikini she bought didn't help matters. They had talked about the whole sexual thing and decided not to get into a casual sex rut. Instead they would save their lovemaking for special occasions. As time went on, his hormones told him this was a big mistake. They wanted him to declare every day he spent with Gail a special day. Gosh, even just thinking about her was getting him turned on.

And what about Jim and his mother? The other day he caught her folding Jim's shirt and underwear that were in a load of laundry she just brought up from the basement. When he asked her what they were doing in the wash, she blushed and made up a lame excuse. He didn't ask about the extra toothbrush he found in the bathroom, or if she knew anything about the extended lunches Jim began taking recently. After all, she was the one who berated him for his wild night with Gail. Perhaps the shoe was on the other foot now. Anyhow, they both had someone with whom to enjoy life. Everything was going so good. Sometimes he worried that he was still in one of those dreams and would wake up soon.

Bill and Gail walked hand in hand to the town square as the old town clock in the cupola on the bank struck eight. With an approving glance Bill inspected Gail's outfit for the evening, a sleeveless brown print dress with a wide belt that accentuated her slender waist. Traffic had been diverted and it seemed like the whole town was milling about on the streets. As they greeted friends in the square, Gail would occasionally write in the small black notebook she carried. From a distance they could see Jim and Lou standing on the opposite corner. Jim was busy taking pictures. The mayor had just finished his welcoming speech as they stepped up on the curb beside Jim.

"Hi, kids. You two are looking very distinguished this evening. Did you see that hussy from the realty standing over near the shoe store? If her dress was any shorter it wouldn't cover her underwear and she isn't wearing a bra. I think she's half drunk," Lou began the conversation.

"I didn't think her dress was that short. And I didn't notice she was parading around without a bra. This sounds like a newsworthy story. I had better go over there and get a picture."

"You stay right here and check out my foundation garments. Oh God, what did I just say? Since I started dating you, Jim, I am beginning to act like the hussy around here."

Jim kissed Lou and said, "Run quickly, kids. Here comes old Susan

Moore, the nosiest woman in Greencastle prior to her moving to Harrisburg. She knew every body's business and delighted in passing it around. Who invited her back for this shindig? Too late, she saw us and is coming over."

"Lou, I see you finally let this handsome gentleman catch you. If I was only a few years younger I would have given you some competition. And, Bill, you've turned into such a handsome young man. Please introduce me to this stunning woman at your side."

Bill introduced Gail and explained that she worked for Jim.

"So, your family has monopolized the staff of the paper. Now I know how you convinced this bright young girl to write that charming little narrative about Sarah. Which reminds me, Lou, if you really want to know who is delivering those flowers, you should check in dear departed Sarah's diary."

Everyone responded in unison, "Diary, how did you know Sarah had a diary?"

The smug look on Susan's face told everyone she was enjoying this moment. Once again she had information even the Greencastle newspaper was not aware of. "A year after Rich died, I stopped in to console Sarah on the anniversary of his death. She was writing in a book at her desk when I stepped into her living room. When she noticed me, she rose quickly and turned to greet me. Later when she went to make us a cup of tea, I noticed the diary was still open. Well, wanting to make sure she wasn't overly distraught on the anniversary of her dear husband's demise, I naturally read a few of the recent entries. I can assure you she was very candid with her remarks in the diary."

"In your readings in Mom's diary, was there anything about a man?"

"Dear me, no there wasn't. Like I said, I only glanced through a few pages. Sarah was not a very complex person and seemed content throwing herself into work for the church. There goes Old Man Hess. I must tell him what I heard about his daughter-in-law. Mr. Hess! Mr. Hess, please hold up a minute." Susan was gone in an instant, weaving through the crowd after Mr. Hess.

"That woman's a bitch," Jim mumbled under his breath.

"Jim, we are Christians," Lou reminded him.

"I'm sorry, Lou. Forgive me, Lord, for calling that bitch a bitch." Everyone laughed at Jim's response.

The band was in full swing at this point and the crowd had turned their attention to the wooden stage when Gail was suddenly knocked off the curb from behind. Bill moved quickly and grabbed Gail as she was falling.

"Leave her fall, B-Bill. She messed up my mind and now she's after you." The words were very slurred and a strong odor of alcohol permeated the air. Mike tripped off the edge of the curb and staggered in front of them. A beer bottle crashed to the ground and shattered in pieces.

"Mike, you're drunk. I don't know what your reason was for coming here, but drop it before we lose our friendship. Let me take you home." Bill reached out to steady Mike and to lead him toward his apartment.

"No, I'm not leaving. That whore ruined my life, and now she stole my friend from me. I haven't seen you in weeks, Bill." At this point Mike shrugged off Bill and staggered in front of Gail. Wagging his finger at her, he proceeded, "You're just a slut that takes people to bed and then ruins their lives. You leave my buddy Bill alone. You don't deserve a nice guy like that."

Gail pushed him aside and ran crying toward the edge of the crowd. At that instant Bill lost his temper and placed a well-aimed punch on Mike's jaw. Mike fell to the black top and blood oozed from his lip.

"Mike, you're a drunken ass. You and I are through as friends. If you ever hurt Gail again I won't stop at one punch. I love that girl and she doesn't know it yet, but I'm going to marry her." At that point Bill pushed through the crowd and ran after Gail.

Sobered up by the punch, Mike dragged himself to his feet, wiped the blood off his lip and sulked away.

As Lou started to follow Bill, Jim held her back. "He needs to do this alone. When Gail comes to work in the morning, I'll talk to her and make sure she understands that the problem tonight was the drunk— not her. Bill did the right thing. If he didn't slug that guy, I was going to."

Lou and Jim stood stunned for a few minutes. Finally Lou continued, "Jim, did I hear my son right? Did he just say he was going to marry Gail? He's told me how much they cared for each other, but he's never said that before. I hope he doesn't bring marriage up to Gail. After Mike and other problems in her past, she's not ready to even think about commitment and marriage."

"Don't worry. Bill's very levelheaded. Gail tells me a lot about him. He'll do the right things. That drunk just pulled the deepest, hidden inner feelings from Bill. He's a very determined young man. If I were you, I'd begin planning for a wedding."

"A wedding," Lou started and paused for a while as she was thinking. "Where shall we have the reception?"

"What do you mean by 'we'?" Jim glanced at Lou and the mischievous grin on her face told him that he, too, was getting deeply involved. "I'm beginning to realize that Bill is not the only determined person in this family that has long-term plans."

"Well, Jim, you've been single a long while. I know you've enjoyed these last few weeks and you've raised feelings in me that haven't been there since Fred died. I was thinking the other day of how great it was to have a man around the house again. Maybe in the not too distant future we can discuss long term plans too."

Meanwhile Bill had forced his way through the edge of the crowd and raced after Gail. However, by the time he reached her apartment she had locked the door. He rang her doorbell and knocked on the door, but she would not open it. From the faint sobs coming through the door, he knew she was inside.

Not knowing what to do, he slowly walked back to the square and told his mother and Jim that she would not talk to him. Lou felt that she just needed to be alone for a while and Jim assured Bill that he would talk to Gail tomorrow.

Still confused, Bill returned to Gail's door and tried again to no avail. All thoughts of revelry gone, he drove home and spent a sleepless night. His only thoughts were how he could make things right with Gail. Right now he couldn't care less about Mike and the loss of his friendship. Who needed friends like him?

Monday, on the way in to help Eddy get the antique Reo ready for the parade, Bill decided that this was one of the worst days of his life. First thing in the morning he had called Gail's apartment. She didn't answer the phone. Later he called the paper and Jim talked to him. Gail had come in very upset and crying. She blamed herself for the episode last night. Also, she told Jim maybe it would be better to end their relationship before she hurt Bill like she did Mike. Jim pointed out to her that Mike wasn't hurt, just extremely drunk. When it was evident that Gail was not able to work in her emotional state, Jim sent her back home to the apartment.

Bill tried the apartment again, but the ringing of the telephone still went unanswered. He needed to talk to Gail and tell her he loved her and nothing else mattered. He didn't care what Mike said, he desperately needed to make Gail understand she was the most important thing in his life and he was not afraid of her hurting him. Right now he wished Mike were here. One punch was not enough punishment for the mess he had created.

As soon as Bill parked his truck, Eddy saw how depressed he was. Dottie and Eddy had witnessed the altercation in the square and Lou had filled them in on the whole story.

"Hi, sport. Boy, I'm glad you showed up. They just delivered the Reo from the storage garage and we have our work cut out. She's pretty dirty and we have a couple oil leaks. Before we get started, come into the kitchen and have a sandwich." Eddy led Bill into the house where they sat down with Dottie to eat. Eddy opened a couple beers while they talked about the events of the night before.

Bill felt relieved telling his story to Eddy and Dottie. They were very sympathetic and understanding. Eddy was able to draw experiences from his own life that related to Bill's situation and he knew when to throw in a remark to get a laugh. Gradually Bill's spirits rose and by the time he finished a second beer he was in the mood to tackle the cleanup. Eddy promised to accompany him to Gail's apartment after finishing work on the car. Hopefully Eddy could help him get Gail back.

Meanwhile, approximately a mile north of town on Route 11, Jim was busy setting up his camera in an open field on the east side of the road across from the Corporal Rihl monument. Lou had come along to help. As she pulled a tripod from its box she asked, "Who is this Corporal Rihl and why does he deserve a monument in Greencastle? The battle was at Gettysburg."

"Didn't you read my article in last week's paper?"

"I confess I passed over it at the time. Reading historical articles never interested me. Then you invited me and I couldn't find the paper."

"Well, to give you a quick history lesson, Corporal William Rihl was in the First New York Cavalry. When the confederate army's advanced cavalry crossed the border on June 22, 1863, they met Corporal Rihl and the union cavalry here. In the small battle, or skirmish as they called it, Corporal Rihl was mortally wounded. The union cavalry was greatly outnumbered and then retreated. The confederates buried Corporal Rihl and proceeded on to Chambersburg. A few days later everyone marched to Gettysburg and the rest is history. So Corporal Rihl goes down in history as the first union casualty on northern soil during the battle of Gettysburg."

"So why are we having this little mock battle today?"

"A publicity stunt, a few of the local Civil War re-enactors got the idea. They got permission to hold the event and rented this field. It's really more show than an accurate re-enactment. In the real engagement the Union soldiers were cavalry and mounted on their horses. These boys don't have horses, so we will be seeing an engagement between foot soldiers. For effect they've also rolled a cannon that one of the boys owns onto the field. Everybody gets excited when they fire one of those. It should be a good little show. The script may not be accurate, but the dress and weapons are. To join one of these re-enactment outfits your uniform, weapons, shoes and everything you carry must be an authentic reproduction. I'm hoping to get some good pictures of the charge. That's why I set up over here on this little rise close to the Union line."

"Shouldn't we be over there in the roped-off spectator area where it's safe to watch?"

"It's OK. I got permission to be here from the leader of the group. Besides, they only load powder into the guns and cannon. Nobody ever gets hurt."

"Well then, why is the ambulance pulling in behind the confederates?"

"In case somebody has a heart attack when that cannon goes off. Here, you take pictures with this small camera and I'll use the one on the tripod. Let's get ready, they're about to begin. See, the Confederate general down there is telling his men to lie down and hide because they just spotted the Union soldiers they plan to ambush."

The Union soldiers, fifteen men, marched into the opposite end of the field from the Confederates. They were halted by their leader, and after a few minutes of discussion, two of the men hunched down and cautiously advanced forward toward the hidden enemy. At the determined moment, the thirty or so men in grey opened fire. Several minutes of rifle fire ensued, and the two Union soldiers, representing Corporal Rihl and a companion wounded in the skirmish, fell to the ground pretending they were hit. The air was filled with smoke and the acrid smell of the powder. Then several men wheeled the cannon in place aimed at the distant Union troops and loaded it.

Lou took several pictures of the cannon being loaded and she even got one just as it was fired. Jim was very busy taking pictures of the Confederate line and then he swung his camera and took a series on the blue soldiers returning the fire.

The cannon fire stopped and Jim, in his excitement, shouted to Lou, "Be ready with the camera, now the charge is about to begin."

At that instant the confederates stood up and charged across the field. The Union troops, greatly outnumbered, fired a last volley at the confederates and began retreating.

"We're getting some great pictures, Lou. The smoke from the cannon is still lazily floating in the air. It's going to give these pictures a look of realism. I'm so glad you came along to help me."

As the Union troops withdrew, the grey line halted for one final volley of fire. Lou was busy snapping pictures as fast as the camera permitted. She heard a thud and a moan from Jim. As she lowered her camera and turned toward him, she saw a look of confusion on his face and then he crumpled to the ground knocking the camera over. Lou screamed and two of the grey-clad re-enactors, now only a couple hundred feet away, ran to her side.

"What's the matter, lady? Did he faint or something? Help me roll him over and loosen his shirt. Oh shit, Joe, he's bleeding. He's been shot. Get the ambulance."

Joe ran toward the ambulance yelling that someone had been shot. Tears rolled down Lou's face as she knelt down beside Jim still clutching the camera. Now the ambulance came bouncing across the field and rolled to a stop next to the small crowd that had gathered around the group on the ground. The ambulance attendants grabbed a stretcher and everyone parted to let them pass.

The driver quickly checked Jim and said, "He's got a weak pulse. There's a small wound on his chest which is bleeding. We need to get him to the hospital in Chambersburg right now!" They placed Jim on the stretcher and carried him to the ambulance. Lou stood dazed by the door as the driver yelled, "Come on, lady, get in there with your husband. Every minute is critical now."

Lou did not correct the attendant. She stepped into the ambulance and, seeing a friend, called out, "Frank, please get the camera and tripod. Bill's at Eddy's house. Tell him what's happened." She saw Frank nod his head as the door was slammed shut and the ambulance took off with a jolt.

As the technician worked on Jim, she sat in the corner of the ambulance. What had just happened? Only moments before she and Jim had been happily taking pictures of the mock battle. For two years she had grieved the loss of Fred. The love of Bill and her family had kept her going. Then that morning had come when Gail and Bill showed up in church. Their love of each other and the joy of being together just seemed to radiate from their bodies. When Jim met her at the door, she just knew she wanted to feel as happy as they were. So she invited him over to dinner. She couldn't believe how much she enjoyed his company and how deeply she had grown to care for him. And now in an instance, just like with Fred, it all seemed to be ending again. Lou began crying again, but the wail of the siren muffled her sobs.

Back in Greencastle, Bill and Eddy were putting the finishing touches on the Reo when Frank suddenly flew up the driveway and slammed on his old truck's brakes. As he jumped out of the cab Eddy admonished him, "Slow down, Frank. You almost hit my antique car. Who taught you to come flying in the driveway like that?"

"Sorry, Eddy, I got to talk to Bill."

Bill, with a big grease stain on his shirt, slid out from under the car and stood up.

"Your mother sent me to tell you that they took Jim to the hospital and she went along in the ambulance."

"Why did they take Jim to the hospital?"

"It appears like he was shot by one of the re-enactors. The sheriff arrived just as I left and he collected all the guns. One of the fellows was late and in his hurry to get in the final charge he didn't check his gun. The sheriff thinks he may have had an unfired ball in it from target practice yesterday. I have Jim's camera. I'll just put it in your garage."

"Thanks, Frank. Uncle Eddy, I need to borrow a shirt. You take Dottie to the hospital and I'll get Gail, even if I have to knock her door down." They went in the house quickly to update Dottie and clean up.

Bill raced out of the driveway a short time later. When he got to Gail's apartment he saw movement through the front window. He rushed to her door and banging hard on it he yelled, "Gail, there's been an accident. One of the re-enactors shot Jim and Mom's on the way to the hospital with him."

The door opened and Bill noticed that Gail's eyes were red from crying. "That's impossible. The guns they use are not loaded."

"One of the re-enactors was late and apparently his gun was loaded. I'm on my way to the hospital. We don't know anything about Jim's condition."

As Bill and Gail sped toward the hospital, she began, "Bill, I'm sorry I ran away from you last night and didn't answer the telephone today. I was so embarrassed and just needed some time to think. Mike really hurt my feelings last night. Then Jim related how you punched Mike. I never dreamed I would make you break up with your best friend. Maybe I'm cursed. Mike said I hurt him and now I'm hurting you. Please let's just end this relationship before I hurt you badly. I could never live with myself if I did that."

"My dear, Mike hurts himself with his drinking. He's a depressed person and when he gets drunk he lashes out at people. I've talked to him about it before. This time he went too far and destroyed our friendship. It was bound to happen. He did that—not you. I'm a big boy and can take care of myself. The only way you can hurt me is to break up with me. I love you very much. You are the light in my life. Now slide over on that seat next to me and let me hold you."

"I don't deserve you. I only hope and pray I can make you as happy as you make me." She saw him smiling at her and she smiled back. "Yes, Bill, I said pray. Ever since that first morning I went to church with you, I've been praying for us. Now you know another one of my secrets."

"Well, let's pray now that Jim is not seriously hurt."

When they arrived at the hospital emergency room they were sent to the waiting area near the operating rooms. Lou, Dottie and Eddy got up as they entered. Lou spoke in a hushed voice between her tears, "The doctor says it's not good. Jim's heart stopped beating on the way to the hospital. They were giving him CPR until he was wheeled into the emergency room. They wouldn't let me go back with him. Later the doctor told us he needed to operate immediately. The bullet hit a rib and shattered it. Then it turned and shattered the next rib down and turned again going through the lung, grazing the heart and finally lodging in the spinal column. There was a lot of blood building up in the chest cavity. They needed to operate to stop the bleeding, repair damage to the heart, and remove bone splinters and the bullet. If he survives the operation, he may be paralyzed from the damage to the spinal column. I'm so glad you kids came. It hit me as I was riding in the ambulance this morning that I am falling in love with Jim. Now I'm going to lose him like I did Fred two years ago."

"Mom, Jim's a strong man and he has you to live for. Don't write him off so quickly."

Almost two hours later the tired doctor appeared from the operating room. He slumped into a chair near Lou and began, "Well, we have good news and bad. On the good news side, by the time the bullet hit the spinal column its energy was spent and it only damaged two discs. We removed the one and fused the other. When the swelling goes down there's a good possibility he should regain feeling and motion in his legs. On the bad side, the bullet tore through the lung and the muscle of the heart. We've repaired the damage as best we could. The next forty-eight hours will be critical. He's in recovery now. Why don't you go home and get some rest? We'll call if there are any changes."

The doctor moved off and Lou began, "The doctor said he will come out of recovery in about an hour and then I can visit him for five minutes every hour. He will be unconscious, but I'm sure he will still be able to hear me when I talk to him. I need to stay here. Go home and get some sleep. It is after nine."

"Well, Mom, Gail and I talked it over and we are going over to the paper. Jim was holding a spot open for his article on the re-enactment. We thought we'd put a story in that section on the accident and request that the readers send Jim a get well card here at the hospital. I'm sure getting the cards would cheer him up when he wakes up."

"That's a great idea. Go ahead. I'll call Eddy if I need anything and he can get you at the paper."

Bill took the camera his mother was still carrying. Then he and Gail rode to the newspaper office. Bill helped Gail develop the pictures and they selected one of the cannon firing to put in the paper. Then Gail wrote the story to go with it and Bill edited it. Next they added the finished article and picture into the paper and rolled the presses. It was after two in the morning when they finally had all the papers folded and ready to deliver that morning. Bill drove Gail home and then went home to collapse on his bed.

In the morning Bill called into work and took an emergency vacation day. After calling the hospital and talking with Lou, he helped Gail get the papers delivered. Later he relieved his mother at the hospital. That evening passed in a blur as he helped Eddy get the Reo in line for the parade. Then he and Gail took pictures and notes for an article in the paper. With Jim in the hospital, Bill and Gail and Ethel decided to work together as a team to put out next week's paper. Ethel, with her years of experience in the office, would be able to handle the daily chores that were Jim's responsibility. That freed up Gail and Bill to gather the news and write the articles.

Soon it was Friday evening and Bill rushed home from work to shower and change into a tuxedo for the ball. This was one part of the festivities he usually skipped. He was very uncomfortable on the dance floor and had never mastered any of the special dances. A few weeks back when Gail had teased him about his lack of enthusiasm to dance and promised that she would teach him, he had reluctantly agreed to cover the ball with her. Now he wished he had refused. Jim was still in a coma and Lou was spending most of her time with him. The doctor was very concerned with the large amount of blood still draining from Jim's chest cavity and feared he would have to operate again. Bill felt he would really rather be at the hospital supporting his mother and would have to stop over there later after leaving the ball.

Bill was running late when he finally pulled up in front of Gail's apartment. She had been watching for him and came out of the apartment immediately. With all that had happened this past week, Bill scarcely had time to think about his relationship with Gail. Now he could see her warm welcoming smile and he was suddenly reminded of how graceful and beautiful she was as she walked toward him in the full-length blue silk dress she had chosen for the evening. Very little of her silken shoulders was covered by the two small straps that ran over them.

As he helped her into his mother's car, he saw that the backless center potion of the dress plunged down to her waist. Her long auburn hair swung to the side and tantalizingly revealed her tanned bare back as she slid across the seat. Once again his excitement peaked as his hand brushed against the soft warm skin of her firm breast while he pinned a pink corsage on her dress.

As Bill slid into the driver's seat Gail snuggled up next to him and all his reluctance to go to the ball vanished. Between the episode with Mike and Jim's accident this had been a very difficult week. But now it was obvious that his relationship with Gail had grown stronger and they were closer together than ever before.

Later at the ball, they had a good time. Gail made a small amount of headway teaching Bill some ballroom dance moves and they both laughed a lot over some of his clumsy mistakes. Their favorite was the slow dances when they embraced and moved leisurely across the floor. Bill noted that Gail's eyes were a deep blue like the ocean and her hair seemed to glow in the dim light. As they danced he felt like they were the only ones on the floor. He was pulled from his mood by a sudden tap on his shoulder.

"Sir, may I exchange partners with you that I may complete this dance with your enchanting date?" Eddy and Dottie had arrived late and had danced over next to them.

"Yes, you may borrow her for a trifle, if I can steal this charming young vixen by your side."

"Oh, Bill, for heaven sakes, you're making me blush. Don't tell stories like that."

Now it was Eddy's turn. "My dear wife, you are the most beautiful women at this ball. The only other woman I have eyes for is this auburn-haired goddess that our nephew has enticed here this evening. Come, my dear, let's trip the light fantastic."

Eddy was an accomplished dancer and Bill was envious at how easily he glided across the floor with Gail. Bill took Dottie's hand and clumsily tried to follow.

Later as they took a break and sat near the dance floor, Eddy asked, "How's the paper coming? Do you think you'll be able to print next week?"

"Well, I've been writing the local articles for several years. Ethel's been great on picking up the advertising end. The front page and the sportsman's corner are new to me. Fortunately Bill's been an avid reader of both of those areas. He's come up with good ideas for the sportsman's corner and we're both reviewing the daily newspapers to figure out what condensed world, national and state news to put on the first page. After I started here, I was surprised to learn that some people in this area still get all their news from our little paper. I'm still struggling with the format and getting all the pieces put together. Yes, we will have a paper next week. It may lack a little professionalism, but all the news will be reported."

Eddy waved to a business associate and continued, "Dottie, Lou and I are very proud of the maturity you two showed when you jumped in and accepted the responsibility of getting the paper out. A lot of people would have panicked and just cancelled the paper until Jim recovered. Oh, I almost forgot, my contact in Washington called today and is sending the information on Leo that he obtained from Canada."

Gail picked up her drink and responded, "That's great. Now if we only had a clue as to what happened to Sarah's diary. Maybe then we could clear up this mystery."

Dottie became excited and said, "I think I know where the diary is. I just remembered something Kate said that day at Lou's after she almost killed us."

Bill looked puzzled and asked, "I was there too, Aunt Dottie. I can't remember Kate saying anything about the diary. Can you refresh my memory?"

"She didn't mention the diary specifically," Dottie answered. "But remember she talked about Jane sneaking into the house the day after our mother's death and taking the valuables. She probably picked up the diary at the same time. I know it wasn't in the desk when I cleared it out after the funeral."

Bill beamed, "Yes, now I remember the conversation. Why would she have taken the diary? It has no monetary value. And, if she did take it, how will we get it from her? She's so nasty, she'd burn the diary before giving it to us. The only way we could ever see anything she took is if she could benefit financially from showing us. Maybe Kate could persuade her. She's the only one Jane ever listens to."

"Here's what we'll do. We need to have a meeting with Lou and Kate included. Right now Lou is too distraught. We'll wait until Jim is improved. Perhaps next week when Eddy gets the information on Leo we can all meet and review it before planning how to get the diary from Jane if she has it. Oh, Bill, I hate to ask a last minute favor. Eddy's taking me down to the bay house for the weekend. We're leaving from the ball and going down tonight to avoid the traffic. Can you watch Jake?"

"Sure, Aunt Dottie, I'll let Mom know. We're going over to the hospital in a few minutes."

"Excuse us, kids, they're playing our song. I need to borrow my wife and take her to the dance floor."

Eddy and Dottie danced away from the table and Gail inquired, "What's the bay house?"

"Eddy, as you know by now, is a successful businessman here in town. He and Dottie own a second home heading toward the shore on Kent Island right on the other side of the Bay Bridge. The back of the house looks out on the Chesapeake Bay and at night you can watch the cars crossing the bridge. The large container ships also move up the channel in front of the house to deliver their cargo to Baltimore. I'll talk to Eddy and see if he'll let us visit some time they go down. Teach me one more dance step and then we had better leave for the hospital."

Bill dropped Gail off at her apartment and then he went to Dottie's to change. A short time later they were on their way to the hospital. Lou was sitting in the waiting room when they arrived.

"Any change in his condition?"

Bill noted the weariness from long hours at the hospital on his mother's face as she responded, "Yes, today when I was talking to him and holding his hand I was sure he tried to move his fingers and squeeze my hand. The doctor thinks it was an involuntary twitch, but I know he did it on purpose. I had been sitting there talking to him like I usually do and I started crying. Then I leaned over and kissed his forehead and told him that I love him. It was at that instant that his fingers moved. I know he heard me and was trying to tell me that he loves me too. Then a little while ago when I was in the room, his eyelids quivered like he was trying to open them. Soon he will be better."

"Mom, you've been here almost continually for four days. Let's go in to see Jim and then we'll take you home. Get a good night's sleep and come back in the morning."

"I do need to get some rest. But I hate to leave Jim. Since we couldn't find any of his relatives, he needs me here. Let's go in and say good night and I'll come back early in the morning."

They stayed the allowed five minutes and then Bill drove his mother home and picked up his truck. As Bill drove back to town, Gail was resting her head on his shoulder. He teasingly ran his one hand up and down her left leg. "It sure is a hot night."

"Are you thinking what I'm thinking? Oh, I didn't bring my suit."

"Who needs a suit?"

"Now, Bill, I thought we were going to save sex for special occasions and build our relationship."

"Well, tonight is special. We went to the ball. Besides, any time I'm with you is special."

"That's very sweet, thank you."

"I don't know if I can keep our commitment. You are the sexiest woman on this planet and whenever you are this close to me my hormones just go berserk. All I want to do is tear your clothes off you, kiss you all over your body and make passionate love."

"My goodness, we'd better do something about this problem of yours." Gail slid across the seat as far away from Bill as she could get. "Are you feeling better now?" she joked.

"That doesn't work. Get that pretty little butt back here next to me."

Gail laughed and slid back across the seat.

When they arrived at the house, Bill unlocked the kitchen door and while Jake took a walk, he collected a couple of towels. Then he led Gail to the back bedroom he used and shut the door. He kicked his shoes off as he pulled his shirt over his head.

"Bill, aren't you undressing in the bathroom?"

"Tonight we do this together." Bill kissed Gail as he unzipped her dress and slid it off her shoulders. As it fell to the floor the vision of her lithe body raised his anticipation. He pulled her close and reached around her back to unsnap her bra. Meanwhile Bill's pants fell to the floor as Gail successfully loosened the belt and zipper. He felt the tug on his underwear as they were pulled down. Now he moved the bra straps off her shoulders and left it tumble to the floor.

As they continued to kiss, his hands moved up and down her bare back and he slowly moved her toward the door in the room that led to the pool. At last his hands reached her silk underwear and, with a quick motion, downward they fell to the floor. For a few minutes they continued to kiss and caress each other, reveling in the tingling excitement they inflicted on their partner. Then he opened the door leading to the porch and picked her up. Her slender bare legs dangled over his right arm and her long hair cascaded down his back as he carried her toward the pool.

"Oh, Bill, I'm the luckiest girl in the world, having you as my friend and lover." At that instant, Bill threw her into the pool.

When she surfaced he laughed and she commented, "I think I just changed my opinion on that lucky thing." She laughed at this point and pulled her wet hair away from her face.

As the light from the stars reflected off the pool and illuminated Gail's face, Bill thought she looked more beautiful than he had ever seen before. He jumped in and swam the short distance to her side. "I know I'm a very lucky man to be able to love and enjoy life with such a beautiful woman."

They swam a few laps quietly together. As their naked bodies touched, the excitement rose to a fevered pitch. Then Bill pulled himself out of the pool, took a couple chair cushions, laid them on the deck by the pool and draped towels over them. As he helped Gail out of the pool, he grabbed an extra towel and unhurriedly dried her face, hair, and upper body. Then he knelt and completed his chore.

As she bent over and playfully ran her fingers through his hair, he looked up and rubbed the towel gently over her nipples. Now a low moan rose in her throat and he lowered the towel, slowly moving it up and down her legs and across the tuft of hair where they met. "Oh, Bill, I love you and I love what you do to me," she whispered as he reached around to her backside and gently lowered her to the bed he had made by the pool.

Rock hard now, he slipped into Gail. She moaned again louder as he caressed her breasts and they moved together. Gasping for breath, Gail stopped him, motioned for him to lie on his back and positioned herself over him, gently running her hands over his hairy chest. Soon their heavy breathing returned as she rhythmically moved. The warm night air seemed to crackle with the electric excitement in their bodies now glistening with sweat from the heat of desire and the excitement of the moment. The stars in the sky shone down and dimly lit the two figures locked in ecstasy. An eternity in time seemed to pass before they could no longer control their passion.

Later as they lay resting by the pool, Gail kissed Bill and commented, "How funny life is. For a long time I convinced myself that I was content in life. I knew I did a good job, and if I kept busy, I could convince myself that I was happy. A couple months ago I would have laughed at anyone who would have told me my life would change so drastically and so fast. Yet, here I am in the buff lying next to the man I love, looking up at a star-filled sky and it all seems so natural, so great. It's scary though. Now I know what true happiness is and I don't think I can ever go back to being content. You have made this drastic change in my life and I'm scared about losing you." Then she raised her body up and leaned on one arm so she could look into his eyes. "Tell me, Bill, that I have nothing to worry about. That wall I built has all crumbled to pieces and is gone and now my feelings, like my body, are naked and vulnerable. Only you can protect them and nurture them. I don't know what to do or where to go if this relationship should end."

"You have nothing to worry about, dear Gail. I love you very much and I'm here for the long haul. Now kiss me and let's swim."

Slowly, as Bill awoke from a deep sleep, he became aware that he was in the bedroom lying on his back and Gail was snuggled up next to him with her head on his chest. After a night like he just had, how could he wake up horny? God, this girl drove him crazy. All he had to do was see her, touch her, or even just smell her perfume and he wanted to make love with her. He was contemplating whether you could wear it out from overuse when the phone began to ring. Gently he moved Gail's head and slid out of bed. On the third ring he picked up the phone in the living room.

"Bill, is Gail with you?"

He sensed the excitement in his mother's voice and asked, "Are you at the hospital and is everything alright?"

"Everything's alright. Well, no, I'm not sure if it's alright. I need you and Gail to come down here to the hospital as soon as possible. You can't fool your mother. I know she's with you."

"Has something happened to Jim? Just tell me, please."

"No, I can't do that. I need you here. OK, I'll tell you this much, when I arrived this morning Jim was awake and sitting up in bed. That's all I can tell you now."

"We'll be there in an hour." When Bill hung up and turned back toward the bedroom, he saw Gail standing in the door with the bedspread wrapped around her.

"Bill, aren't you worried about standing there with no clothes on? If someone comes in the porch, how will you explain this?" She giggled and he blushed as he realized that the curtains for the sliding glass doors beside him were wide open allowing anyone standing on the porch to see him in the living room. He beat a hasty retreat to the bedroom and related his mother's weird conversation to Gail.

"That's great news about Jim being awake. Let's get a shower and we'll go find out why your mother wants us at the hospital. Come on, we can shower together."

"Err, ah, I'm not sure that's a good idea."

"Oh, I see what you mean. I can hardly walk now from last night. Well come on, we can use it for an extra towel rack until we figure out what else to do with it." They both laughed and walked to the shower.

When they arrived at the hospital Lou met them in the waiting room. "We can go in now. I was waiting on you two."

Jim's bed had been elevated and two pillows were propped on his sides to support his weight. It took all his effort to raise a hand and greet them as they leaned over his bed. "Thanks for coming and thanks for running the paper for me. Lou has told me how great a job you two are doing. If I stay in here too long, you may have me completely replaced. I wouldn't be here this morning except for Lou. While I was in the coma, I had this sensation or experience, call it what you like, of walking down this long corridor toward a bright light. I was happy and at peace, yet I could hear Lou talking about the good times we had and how she enjoyed being with me. I continued on toward the light feeling good about our times together. Then I heard Lou with a lot of emotion in her voice tell me she loves me very much and needs me. At that moment I felt a tear fall on my face as Lou bent over to kiss my forehead. I no longer wanted to enter the light and I tried to move to let Lou know I heard her. Next thing I knew, there was another light bothering me. My brain was still very foggy, so it took me a while to realize it was the light of day streaming through my closed eyelids. I opened them and the rest of the story is history as they say."

Jim breathed heavy from the exertion of his speech. It was obvious he had more to say. Lou picked up the story at this point, "Bill, Gail, Jim has asked me to marry him and I have accepted."

Now the room was quiet except for Jim's labored breathing. He saw the shock in the eyes of the couple and gathering his strength he continued, "Now I've made it perfectly clear to your mother, Bill, this marriage will only occur when I am fully recovered and can walk again. I, too, have grown to love your mother. Now I owe my life to her love that would not let me cross over. Whatever time I have left on this earth I want to enjoy with Lou. Bill, can you accept me as your stepfather?"

Bill was finally able to speak again and he said, "I only want to see my mother happy. I know she's missed Dad terribly. But since you two started dating, I've seen joy creep back into Mom's life. I will be honored to have you as my stepfather."

Jim smiled and fell asleep. As they were getting ready to leave, the doctor arrived. "Good morning. Jim's return from the coma is a good sign. We are not out of the woods yet, but he should make steady progress from here. As soon as he is strong enough we will move him to physical therapy. Remember, it will be a long time before the spinal cord swelling subsides and we will be able to determine if he will walk again."

Everything moved in a blur during the next week. During the day Bill worked at the plant and at night he worked with Gail at the newspaper. Once again they spent the wee hours of Wednesday morning printing and bundling papers. Now, Thursday evening, Bill, Gail, Lou and Kate were meeting for dinner at Dottie and Eddy's house. Eddy had received the packet from his contact in Washington and they would open it after the meal.

After the dishes were cleared and Eddy had poured another round of wine for everyone, he produced a manila envelope which he proceeded to open. Inside was a large bundle of papers bound together with a cover letter attached. The cover letter was brief and Eddy read it first.

Dear Ed,

Good to hear from you. When are you coming to Washington again? Please bring that lovely wife of yours and we will take in the theater.

I am forwarding everything I received from our contact in Toronto. Nothing spectacular here. The records all seem in order for a soldier killed in action in the First World War. Were you looking for anything in particular?

Well, they are calling me for a meeting. Do come down soon, I enjoy our lively discussions of the time we spent together at State.

John

"Well, let's get into the good stuff. Here's Leo's attestation papers to sign up for the Canadian Expeditionary Forces." Eddy separated the bundle of papers and began to spread them out.

Everyone gathered around as Bill picked up the first paper and began to read, "Well, now we know Leo's middle name was Fitzmaurice and he was born October 10, 1896. His address is listed as Hamilton, Ontario, and he was a salesman. He's our man. Married to Sarah Brown, with her address listed as Greencastle, Pa. Now we come to the vital statistics. A rather tall fellow like me, he's listed as being six foot one inch tall with dark blue eyes, a dark complexion, and dark brown hair. Last page, here we have his signature and date of joining up—July 12, 1917."

Gail picked up the next piece of paper. "The official death certificate, name, rank, age all match Leo's information. The date of death was August 26, 1918. Now listen to this. Place of death is listed as France, and cause of death states 'Died of Wounds.' That's pretty vague. Do you think they were covering up something?"

Eddy answered, "Sometimes there were thousands of men killed in a single charge across no-man's land. There weren't enough staff people to record in detail the location a person died in and exact nature of wounds. What you have there is the standard information."

Lou was next around the table and filled everyone in on her find, "Well, I've got the name and location of the British cemetery in France where he's buried. Sarah is listed as next of kin and his mother's and father's names are also listed."

Dottie picked up the last piece of paper. "I have the triage center report here. It just looks like the medic recorded that he was dead on arrival."

"Just as John said, nothing earth shattering here. Now I think it's time for Dottie to get us all a piece of that apple pie I smelled baking earlier, and be sure to put a scoop of ice cream on mine. After dessert we can talk about the mystery diary. Hopefully it will be more informative than these documents tonight were. I think it's time to close the case on Mr. Brown. It was a good idea to track this out, Gail. Now we need to move on."

As they ate, Gail picked up the document nearest her, the triage center record, and idly read it. "Bill, can you remember how tall Leo was?"

"I'm not sure. Let's check. Pass me those attestation papers, Kate. Now let's see. Here it is. He was six foot one inch tall."

"I thought that was his height. On this record, the medic jotted down the corpse's hair as brown, eye color blue, and height of five foot ten. How did Leo lose three inches in height?"

Eddy volunteered the answer, "It's just another one of the hurried mistakes made when processing a large number of dead and wounded.

The note that Dottie read earlier states the commanding officer confirmed that the deceased was Leo. Either the doctor measured the height wrong or recorded it wrong."

"Or the deceased was not Leo."

"You're trying to make something from a bad measurement on a scrap of paper. Next thing you'll be telling me is that Leo didn't die in World War I and he's putting the flowers on Sarah's grave. I'm a businessman. I work with facts and figures every day. What you've got there is a piece of circumstantial evidence. If that isn't Leo in a grave in France, who is it and where has Leo been all these years? Why didn't he come home to his wife? We need to stick with the facts and at this point we have no factual information on who our mystery delivery person is. But, I can tell you this, he's no ghost from the First World War."

Now Kate, who had spent most of the night listening, spoke up, "Get off your damned soap box, Ed. You're not running your company here. Cut these kids a break. They've spent many a frustrating evening and weekend hunting for the answer to this mystery. Along the way they've been threatened and spied on, and still they have very little to show for it. I don't know if this Leo thing will ever take us anywhere, but right now it's all we have. We need to appreciate the work they've done. Let's give them a hand." At that point Kate stood and clapped. Dottie and Lou quickly followed and finally Eddy stood up with the others.

When they were done, Eddy announced, "You are right, Kate. Forgive me, Gail. As Kate pointed out, it's the businessman, take-charge part of me that came out. I should not have jumped on you like that."

"I needed that little reality check to keep me in line," Gail said. "I still believe there's merit to what I said. However, we need to move on and keep an open mind. How are we going to find out if Jane has the diary?"

"Oh, that part's easy," Kate spoke up. "With four kids in the house, Mom needed help raising us. Dad never seemed to know what to do. Since I was eight years older than Jane, I took care of her most of the time while you twins went off and did your thing. So, in some ways, I was like her mother figure. You can always tell when your younger siblings are lying. So any time she tried to pull anything on me I turned her in to Mom and if it was serious she got her bottom tanned. She learned quickly never to tell me a story and it stuck. All I have to do is ask her if she has the diary and she will tell me. If she says no, I can guarantee she doesn't have it. Now comes the hard part. She's very stubborn and very possessive of everything she obtains. If she has that diary, getting it from her will be next to impossible."

Bill asked, "Why is she so hard to get along with? That house she lives in is falling down around her head. When I offered to go over and help her fix things up, she nearly jumped down my throat telling me to mind my own business. She's the only person in the family that Gail hasn't met. Trouble is, you never know when she will go into one of her tirades and pick you as a target."

"Jane was a perfectly normal child, a happy child. Then she married that husband of hers. She was deeply in love with him. He turned out to be a skirt chaser and ran around on her from almost the day they got married. She did everything for him and was blind to the affairs he was having on the side. Finally he got tired of Jane and ran off with her best friend in Frederick. When I tried to warn her, she told me that I was just jealous because she was so happy.

"Well, she sat in that house and just stared at his picture for months, insisting it was all her friend's fault and her perfect husband would come back. After the collection agencies almost evicted her, she was forced to get a job. In time, the love in her heart was replaced with bitterness. Losing the jerk also turned her into a fanatically possessive person. In her mind when he left she lost the most important thing in her life and she is determined never to give up anything else.

"Every now and then when I visit her, she will drop her guard and I will see the old Jane, the little girl I helped raise and love. She still needs me and that's why I can never turn my back on her. But, like I said earlier, I doubt she will relinquish the diary if she has it. It's time for me to visit her. She hasn't been feeling the best of late. I'll call her tomorrow and see when she will have time for me to visit her. After the visit I'll let you know what she says."

"Good, we have a plan." Bill picked up the coffee pot and poured everyone another cup as he talked, "Now, Mom, you gave us a brief update on Jim's condition. Is there any news on when he will be discharged from the hospital?"

"As I said earlier, his says he feels great and the doctor tells us his internal wounds are healing perfectly. He still has no feeling in his legs. The doctor says this is normal and we need to give it time. He has started therapy and is learning how to get out of the bed and into a wheelchair. We have decided that he will come home to live with me when he's discharged until he can walk again. We can set up a desk in the spare bedroom and he can do some work for the paper there at first. He really feels bad about dumping his work on Bill and Gail. Oh, by the way, he read last week's paper from cover to cover and thought you guys did a terrific job. He joked that if he stays away too long you may tell him not to come back.

"He talks to me constantly about getting married and insists we should plan a May wedding. I keep telling him that we have to wait and see how things go. He's constantly talking about the places we will go when he's walking again. I don't want to dampen his spirits by reminding him that the doctor told us it will be a long road until he's completely recovered, and there is a possibility he may not walk again. Whatever happens I will stand by him and love him. I just hope he knows that."

CHAPTER 5
The Journal

Kate was in an agitated state as she crept along the street behind the school bus. There was no particular reason to be in a hurry to reach Jane's house. Kate was just an impatient driver and following any slow-moving vehicle bothered her.

Today she knew it was more than just following the bus. She loved her sister and knew something was wrong. Her sister's voice usually came through the phone very strong and clear and she spoke her words with conviction. This time it had been different. She seemed less sure of herself and her breathing was heavy. At first she told Kate she was too busy to see her, but when Kate persisted, she agreed to the visit.

During the trip of almost fifty miles from her house to Jane's in Frederick, Maryland, Kate had been thinking about the telephone call and her sister's sad life. Jane was the shortest of the girls at five foot seven inches and from her youth she had struggled with a weight problem. After her husband left she had grown even heavier and then she was diagnosed with diabetes. She worked long hours in a department store in town ever since she was forced to go to work to support herself. Kate suspected that Jane had few friends and she never left Frederick. Lou, Dottie and Kate had all tried unsuccessfully over the years to build relationships with her. Kate was the only sister Jane tolerated visiting with, and then, only infrequently.

Finally the bus passed Jane's street and Kate turned into the dead end. The homes were all small ranches built in one of the building frenzies after World War II. Jane's house was halfway down the street on the left. Kate noted that the lawn was uncut and the weeds were taller than the flowers in the usually immaculate flowers beds. Yes, she was right. Something was wrong here. There was barely enough room for Kate to park her car in the short driveway behind Jane's aging Ford, which normally was parked in the garage.

Kate rang the doorbell and waited. After a few minutes she knocked loudly on the door. Then she heard shuffling inside and soon the door was thrown open. Between heavy breathing Jane said, "Come in, Kate. It's good to see you. How was your trip?"

There followed a barrage of small talk in the kitchen as Jane made tea and served cookies. As Kate talked, she noted the dirty dishes in the sink, the dirty floor, and a basket of wash sitting in the corner waiting to be folded. Jane usually kept her house spotless and everything in order.

Kate knew she was treading on dangerous ground to deviate from the small talk, but she was worried about her sister. "Jane, is something wrong? You look tired, and I noticed you were breathing heavily when you opened the door and while you were making the tea."

"It's none of your damned business how I feel. I knew I shouldn't have invited you here to snoop into my life. You and my other goody-two-shoes sisters have been out to get rid of me for years. Well, you may finally have your wish."

Kate expected the attack. Something was bothering Jane and in her usual manner, she had gone on the offensive rather than talking about the problem. This was one time Kate couldn't let it drop, which she knew was what Jane wanted. "Now listen here, Jane, I wouldn't have brought this up except that I'm concerned about your health. I took care of you when you were a little kid and helped raise you. In some ways I love you like a mother. If you have a problem I want to help. Please, let me." Kate looked at Jane and saw the anger growing in her. She was bracing for another attack when she saw the color drain from her sister's face. An expression of fear and anguish replaced the anger.

"You're right, Kate. You are the one person in our family that always did care for me. I need to talk to someone. I barely have enough energy to complete my work at the store anymore. When I come home I spend my time resting or sleeping. My family doctor is sending me to a heart specialist next month. I'm only forty-nine. What's to become of me if I can't take care of this house? It's all I have in life."

Kate groped for the proper words, "Don't worry, Jane. I don't work and I can help if you want. I'm sure the doctor will give you some medication to help."

"Yes, pump another medicine in me to keep old Jane alive. Sometimes I think it would be better if I just died."

"Oh, don't say that. You don't want to die."

"You have Jessica and that truck-driving husband that you seldom see which gives you a lot of free time to do what you want with your life. What do I have? Memories of a worm of a man who broke my heart and the years I stupidly sat here waiting and hoping he would come back. What do I have to look forward to except work and death?"

They sat in silence for a few minutes and then the conversation returned to small talk. As Jane huffed and puffed her way to the door at the end of the visit, Kate decided it was time to ask about the diary. She had softened Jane up as much as possible. It was now or never. "Say, Jane, you know Bill is working with the paper to unravel this mystery of someone placing flowers on Mom's grave. We think her diary may shed some light on who is delivering the flowers. Do you know what happened to Mom's diary?"

"You know I have the diary, Kate. I took it when I picked up the jewelry Mom promised me. You can tell Bill he's an idiot wasting his time chasing after some nutcase sticking roses on a dead woman's grave. That diary is private and there's nothing in there that would interest him. Goodbye, Kate." Jane slammed the door shut before Kate could respond. It was obvious that she had no intention of letting Bill review the diary. It was also obvious that she had no intention of discussing the issue any further with Kate.

Worried by her sister's health and discouraged with her inability to get the diary, Kate slid into her car and drove away feeling like she failed everyone. She had failed to find the right words when her sister needed comfort and she had failed to find a way to convince Jane to give her the diary.

As was the custom since he was a little boy, Bill rose early to go into town to help Dottie and Eddy prepare for Thanksgiving dinner. Since Lou needed to help get Jim ready, she was breaking with custom and would come in later. This was Eddy's favorite holiday and he needed to surround himself with family. Eddy depended on Dottie's family to fill the back porch. Today there would be a banner crowd.

As Bill and Eddy set up the tables on the back porch, they set four places for Kate and her family. Then there was one for Eddy's aunt, his only remaining relative in the area. As they went for more chairs Eddy commented, "This year we'll need three chairs and a spot for Jim's wheelchair for your family, Bill. That was nice of Gail's mother to change her plans so Gail could spend the day with us. Maybe next year when Gail's part of the family, we'll invite her mother and grandfather here."

"Where did you get the idea that we'll be married by this time next year? The subject of marriage has never come up."

"Well, my boy, what are you waiting for? She's been by your side almost constantly the last few months. I know you two are in love. And nosey old Mrs. Biddle across the street has informed me that you no longer stay here alone when you watch Jake. I've never seen two people happier together. Since Dottie and I could never have children, we have always loved you like a son. We are so pleased for you."

"Truth is, I've know I wanted to marry Gail since our first date that night you gave us the tickets to the play. She's everything I ever wanted in someone to spend my life with. She's had some trouble in her past which has made me cautious about rushing her into making such a monumental decision. I want it to be a super special moment when I ask for her hand in marriage. I want it to be so special she can't refuse. I don't know what I'd do if she turned me down."

"You've confided in the right man to help you. Old Eddy knows just how to make this happen. Let me lay the groundwork with Dottie and I'll get back to you."

Soon it was time for Eddy, Bill and Dottie to move to the kitchen to stuff the holiday bird. Bill assumed his usual position at the chopping block to dice the ingredients. Eddy cleaned out the turkey and carefully began filling all the nooks and crannies with Dottie's mouth-watering dressing. Bill helped Eddy put the finishing touches on closing the now swollen cavity in the turkey and together they carefully picked up the huge bird and placed it in the mammoth roasting pan. In an instant they popped it into the oven.

Next they all returned to the porch to complete the setting of the tables and worry over the seating arrangements. Later there were pies to retrieve from the basement refrigerator, a mound of potatoes to peel and numerous other chores to attend to. Old Jake, attracted by the tantalizing aromas emitted from the kitchen area, had joined the group and was sitting in a corner by the oven excitedly wagging his tail. All too quickly the busy morning ended and the men settled down to catch some football on the television before being called to the table.

Gail arrived slightly before noon impeccably dressed in a dark blue fall suit with a mid-length skirt. Her smile spread almost from ear to ear as Bill rushed to kiss her. "We've been working so hard at the paper. It's going to be so great to just kick back and spend some quality time with you today. I'm so glad Mom and Gramps volunteered to have our family dinner tomorrow. Mom thinks you are the greatest thing since sliced toast. Every time I go home she says I appear to be happier and bubblier. We spend so much time together, whenever I tell her about anything going on in my life, you are in the conversation. She wants me to bring you back to her house for dinner again soon. Even Gramps tells me how I've changed and seem more confident and assured of myself. He promised me he would not get upset again, and he never breaks a promise."

"I'll go with you any weekend. Look, here comes Mom and Jim. Let's go help Jim get into the wheelchair." Bill noticed that his mother and Jim seemed in high spirits today and she would begin to laugh whenever Jim looked at her. Since moving into the house, the two of them liked to play harmless little jokes on Bill and he suspected they were planning something today. Bill always played along because he realized Jim had been through a lot of pain in the last few months and his chances of walking again were getting slim. As long as they were laughing it kept the harsh realities of the moment at bay. Recently Lou took Jim into the office three days a week and he said he was beginning to feel like his old self.

By two o'clock everyone had arrived and the house was abuzz with conversation. Eddy excused himself to fill the wine glasses at the table and take the turkey from the oven. Then Dottie announced it was time to move from the living room to the tables on the porch. Dottie was jockeying everyone into the proper position when Lou wheeled Jim onto the porch. Eddy had left the chairless position near the door for easy access. Suddenly Lou announced, "May I have everyone's attention. Jim would like to speak."

"Well, I know the tradition here is to go around the table and state one thing you are thankful for before eating. I have so many things to be thankful for this year. I am alive and working again. But most of all I am thankful to have Lou in my life. Every time I was depressed or ready to give up she would be there to crack the whip, get me back on track and buoy my spirits. Last week we began a new therapy routine and she insisted we show it to everyone here. So, here goes nothing. Lou, dear, please lock the chair."

Lou locked the wheels of the chair and positioned herself in front of Jim. The room was completely quiet as Jim placed his hands on the armrests of the chair. As he pushed up Lou grabbed his arms and balanced his weight. The sweat formed on Jim's brow as he slowly eased himself out of the chair and after what seemed like an eternity stood erect in front of it with the Lou's help. Everyone clapped and cheered until Jim interrupted, "No, wait. There's more."

As Lou continued to balance Jim, he slowly slid one foot in front of the other. As he struggled to slide the other foot forward, Lou fought to maintain his balance and Bill prepared to grab him if she failed. Slowly Jim shuffled a couple of feet until he reached the table. "I'm done now. Please hold your applause until Bill gets a chair behind me before I collapse."

Bill moved quickly, slid the chair behind Jim and helped lower him into it. Once again the room erupted in clapping and cheering. "Alright, you two. I'm upset. I live with you and was never informed of this fantastic improvement. When did it occur and why didn't you tell me?"

Lou answered, "Well, remember that day about three weeks ago when you came home from work and we were sitting around the table drinking wine and laughing uncontrollably? It all started earlier that day. I had helped Jim with his bath and getting dressed. Then since we were going to therapy, I put his shoes and socks on. I had other things on my mind and yanked hard on the shoestrings. Jim cried out, 'Ouch, that's too tight.' As what he said sank in we both sat there in shock. Then we looked at each other and burst out laughing and we laughed the rest of the day. Each day from then on more sensation returned to Jim's feet and legs. He decided we shouldn't tell anyone until today while he worked on walking and standing."

Eddy broke in at this point, "Please, everyone take your seats and I will say a blessing. The turkey is cooling and we need to hear what everyone else is thankful for."

After the blessing Eddy started next to Jim and they moved around the table. They were hitting the highlights—peace, health, a good job—as they moved around the table. When they got to Kate she told everyone she was most thankful for her family including her sisters and their families. But, most of all, she said she was thankful for her husband, son-in-law and especially her daughter Jessie.

At this point Jessie spoke up, "Gee, Ma, great minds think together. I was prepared to do the family thing also. Aunts, mother, father, husband—the same list you went through. Oh, I almost forgot to add our baby that I'm carrying to that list."

Kate burst into tears of happiness and hugged her daughter, "My little baby is going to have a baby. You've made this a thankful day indeed. Hey, everybody, I'm going to be a grandmother. Can you believe it?"

Now several conversations burst out at the table and Eddy realized his standard format before dinner was destroyed. He took his spoon and tapped on his wineglass until he had everyone's attention one more time. "The food is getting cold. I will make a toast and we will eat. I toast this wonderful family that has enriched my life. I toast the new life growing in Jessie and the return of life to Jim's legs. I toast the blossoming of romantic love between Bill and Gail and the birth of a second love in Lou's life. Finally, I toast my loving wife and the early Christmas gift she gave me yesterday."

Everyone raised their glasses and drank. Bill put his down and asked, "Uncle Eddy, could this Christmas gift be red and have the numbers 911 on its side?"

"Give the lucky man in the back another drink for correctly guessing that my new red Porsche 911 convertible is sitting in the garage where it was delivered yesterday. Dottie says if I'm good I can take her for a ride in it tomorrow and as we all know I'm very good. Pass the turkey, please."

The hearty conversation during the meal made it an enjoyable experience. When Lou saw everyone was done eating, she stood and announced, "May I have everyone's attention. Jim has one more announcement."

"While in the hospital I made a commitment and today I wish to fulfill that commitment." Jim pulled a small box from his pocket. As he opened the box gasps swept through the crowd when the gorgeous diamond ring inside sparkled in the sunlight. Jim slipped the ring on Lou's finger and asked, "Will you marry me, Lou Henderson?"

"Yes, Jim Martin, I am in love with you. I want to enjoy the rest of my life with you."

"I want everyone in this room to know that I owe my life to this woman. With unceasing energy and total commitment, she spent every waking moment at the hospital while I was in a coma. It was her wonderful voice that called me back from the pearly gates. I don't know how I can pay her back for that or all the months since then of caring for me. But I will spend the rest of my life trying. Now, the date is May twelfth next year. Put that date on your calendar. No excuses, I want everyone there to see me walk my beautiful bride down the aisle."

Eddy, always ready for a speech, arose and said, "A toast to the newly engaged couple. May your lives together always be filled with contentment and happiness." After the toast he continued, "This has been quite a day. We have witnessed a miracle, received a birth announcement, watched a marriage proposal being accepted and my beautiful wife gave me the car of my dreams. Who could ask for anything more? Now before we serve dessert, anyone interested in seeing my new play toy please follow me."

Everyone except Jim marched to the garage and complimented Eddy on his new car. Bill was standing near the garage door and said, "Listen. Someone is pulling into the driveway."

"I wonder who that could be. Let's go find out."

Back on the porch, Kate looked at the car and exclaimed, "That's Jane's car. Did you invite her, Dottie?"

"Of course I invited her. I do every year. And every year she gives me an excuse. When I called this year, she told me she wasn't feeling well and could not come. I know I told her we were eating at two. It's almost five now. Why did she come now?"

As they talked Jane got out of the car and slowly hobbled toward the porch. She stopped a couple times to catch her breath.

Lou spoke up, "She's so pale, and using a cane. And she's lost weight. I've never seen her look so sickly. Come on, let's help her get to the porch." Bill and Lou left the group. Bill took Jane's bag and they escorted her to a sofa on the porch.

After several minutes of heavy breathing, she was able to speak. "It's so good to be here. I know I told Dottie I wasn't coming. When I got up this morning, I suddenly had this need to see everyone again. Now I know what you're thinking, Dottie, Lou, Kate. I'm a grouchy old woman who loses her temper too often. You don't want me here spoiling this day. Well, I promise to control myself. Now, fill me in on what's been going on."

Still in shock that she had shown up and was attempting to be civil, the sisters were quiet. Eddy seized this opportunity to introduce Jim and tell her about his ability to reuse his legs. He finished this account with the news of Jim's engagement to Lou. At that point Lou showed Jane her glittering new ring. Expecting a snide remark, Lou was stunned when Jane complimented her on the luster of the ring and extended her congratulations. At this point, Eddy continued with an announcement of Jessie's pregnancy. Once again, Jane issued her best wishes and surprised everyone by admitting that not having children was her deepest regret.

Now Eddy was on a roll and he proceeded to tell Jane the minute details of his new car. When he stopped to catch his breath, Jane ended the conversation, "Oh, Ed, you're too old a fart to be cruising around in a little sports car. Now my nephew Bill and that vision of beauty next to him are the perfect couple to sport around town in your red roadster. Bill, will you do me the honor of introducing your girlfriend?"

"Aunt Jane, please forgive me for not introducing you to Gail Mason."

"Gail Mason, I know that name from somewhere. Now I remember. You wrote the article on our mother. Hand me my purse please, Bill, I brought something along today to give to you. Instead I'm going to leave it with Gail. We girls need to stick together. By the way, nephew, she's a keeper." At that point Jane reached into her bag, pulled out a small red book, and handed it to Gail. "I've paged through this diary several times. What you're looking for is not in it unless I missed something. You can call me anytime if I can be of further assistance."

Sensing a good point to turn the conversation, Dottie suggested they clear the table and serve dessert. Jane stayed for dessert and then announced that she was tired and needed to go home. It was obvious that she had expended all her energy to come to the celebration. Kate insisted that she would drive Jane home. Bill and Gail would follow in Lou's car to bring Kate back.

As they pulled out of the driveway, Jane noted, "I'm so glad I came. I was really scared that everyone would reject me after I was such a bitch for all those years. I really didn't mean to be that way. At first it was anger and frustration, later it was jealousy, and always I was afraid of being hurt again. I've been such a fool. They all seemed genuinely happy that I came. Eddy even joked with me."

"Jane, you've always been in our hearts and prayers. With Jessie's announcement about the baby and you showing up, this is my best thanksgiving ever. Next year when you come we'll have the baby to play with."

"I won't be back next year."

"Stop talking like that, Jane. That's the old Jane coming back. We love you and want you here."

"I can't come next year, because I will not be here. Kate, I-I-I'm dying. The doctor gave me six weeks at the most. I have a degenerative heart condition."

"You're only forty-nine. The doctor must be mistaken. We need to get a second opinion. I'll call Denny's doctor tomorrow. He's a specialist and can refer us to an expert."

"Kate, please, I've already gone this route. Believe me, there is nothing more the doctors can do. I quit my job about a month ago. Now I want to spend my final days in my house. Through all my problems in life, my house was always there and now it will be there for this one last thing. Look, I got off on the wrong foot early in life and I never could get things turned around. I have a lot of regrets and no time left for change. Through it all you've been a faithful sister. I did a good job of pushing Dottie and Lou out of my life. I couldn't bully you into leaving me alone. You have persistently let me know that you care about me and want us to spend time together. I want you to know that has always been very important to me. When I'm gone, don't ever feel sorry for me. I made this miserable life I lived. There's nobody to blame but me."

Little more was said on the rest of the trip to Jane's house. When they arrived, Bill helped Jane into the house and Kate put her to bed.

Later, on the way back to Greencastle, Gail started the conversation, "I had an entirely different picture of Jane. From the descriptions I heard, I pictured this plump, robust, fire-eating woman that would pounce on my every word with a vicious verbal attack. Instead she was so frail and all her words seemed complimentary. This can't be the women you described to me."

"We were all shocked by how calm and complimentary she was. She did look very sick. Do you know why she was so pale and weak, Aunt Kate?"

Kate had been sitting quietly in the back seat of the car until this point. Now she began crying and said, "Jane will not be with us much longer, kids. On the way to her house, she told me that she has a degenerative heart disease. The doctors say she only has a few more weeks to live. Poor Jane, she's had a rotten life. At least the doctors say she will have very little pain."

When they arrived back at the party, Kate's news on Jane's condition dampened everyone's spirits. One by one the guests began leaving for home.

Bill stood in front of the altar next to Pastor Jones. He was vaguely aware of several of his friends standing next to him. He looked down through the church and everyone had turned around and was staring at the open double doors at the rear of the church. Now the organist began playing the wedding march and all eyes were glued to the doors as Gail's grandfather led her into the church. All were transfixed by the beauty of the bride in her white gown with the long train. Majestically she moved toward the front of the church where Bill waited apprehensively. Now his happiness with Gail would be complete as they vowed in front of God and man to love each other forever. Gail was almost at the altar when he heard the muffled sound of the telephone. The sound grew louder and louder, drowning out the organ music. The vision of Gail smiling at him through the wedding veil faded slowly.

Bill lay still and enjoyed the memories of his dream for a moment. Some day soon he would make it come true. Then he opened his eyes and, glancing quickly at the clock, noted that it was after nine in the morning. As he stumbled toward the telephone in the kitchen, his memory slowly cleared.

It had been almost eleven at night when they finished helping Eddy and Dottie clean up and put away the dishes, silverware, tables and chairs from the Thanksgiving dinner. After dropping Gail off at her apartment, he went home and found Lou and Jim at the kitchen table in lively conversation. They had opened a bottle of wine and were discussing possible honeymoon plans. Lou asked Bill to join them. It was almost three in the morning when they finally broke up and prepared for bed. All things considered, it had been a wonderful Thanksgiving.

Finally, he reached the telephone and picked it up.

"Hello, is this the residence of Mrs. Lou Henderson?"

"Yes, this is her son, Bill. May I ask who is calling?"

"My name's Marty. You don't know me. I'm your Aunt Jane's neighbor. We both moved into this neighborhood about the same time. Since Jane's been so sick lately, I look in on her every morning and help arrange things for the day. This morning when I knocked, she didn't respond. I unlocked the door with the key she gave me. I found her in bed. Oh my, I don't know how to tell you this. She died peacefully in her sleep last night. The doctor warned her about any exertion. I warned her not to drive up to Pennsylvania yesterday. She got quite upset at me and you know how she gets when she's mad, so I backed off. I was so glad to see you folks brought her home. But I guess it was still too much for her heart. She gave me your phone number a while back and made me promise to call you if anything happened. She had a pre-arrangement agreement with the local funeral home where they took her body. Let me give you the name and phone number."

By now Lou and Jim had entered the kitchen. Bill excused himself from the telephone and broke the news to his mother. Seeing that emotionally she was not ready to handle the telephone, he picked it back up and took the information from Marty.

As Bill hung up the telephone, Lou slid into a chair at the kitchen table and dried her eyes with a tissue. Jim wheeled his chair next to her and put his arm around her. "Life's not fair, Jim," she said in a low voice. "For twenty-five years I lost my baby sister. I've always been real close to Dottie and Kate. Jane has resisted every effort I made to build a relationship. I am ashamed to admit it, but I gave up trying. Then yesterday she pops back into our lives and finally I feel like we can get to know each other and be a complete family. Now we've lost that opportunity forever."

Bill responded, "Now I understand why it was so important to her that she come visit us yesterday. She knew it was her last opportunity to seek the forgiveness from the family that she desperately needed. I'm so thankful that all of us welcomed her with open arms and gave her what she needed. We were there for her when she was finally ready to admit she needed us."

Monday night was spent in the traditional viewing at the Frederick funeral home. The family members almost filled the small sitting room. As the night progressed, several associates from work and a couple of close friends paid their last respects. Marty, the neighbor, showed up and filled everyone in on Jane's rather uneventful life.

Tuesday dawned a cold and dreary morning. Jane would be buried in the family plot on the gently rolling slopes of Cedar Hill cemetery about a mile west of town. The graveside service was planned for family only. True to form, as the hearse pulled in, the skies opened. The torrential downpour that ensued drenched the family as the coffin was placed above the open hole. After a brief service by Pastor Jones, everyone met at the Franklin House to dry out. A large table in the back was prepared. As Emma came to take their orders Kate noticed tears in her eyes.

"Emma, I'm so sorry, I almost forgot that you and Jane were the best of friends from grade school through high school. When she moved to Frederick, I remember you stayed in contact until the jerk left. Then she isolated herself from everyone in her past life."

Emma wiped her eyes and said, "Life is never what we expect. When Jane moved to Frederick it broke my heart. She was my best friend and I didn't even have a boyfriend. I saw how happy she was and I just knew I would die a miserable old maid. For a while, I resented her for leaving me and being happily married and in love. Then it was my turn. I met Abe, fell in love and got married. We went to Frederick several times to visit. Then Jane called and told me her husband ran away and she needed some time alone. I never saw her again. At first I tried calling regularly, but she was always short with me on the phone. Now here I am with three wonderful children and a good husband, and it's Jane that winds up living a sad, lonely life and dies alone in an empty house. I feel so bad for the way I resented her." Tears welled up in Emma's eyes again. She quickly turned away. "I've stood here too long. I must get your meals."

Later when Bill and Gail were alone with Lou, Gail pulled the diary out of her purse and handed it to Lou. "You and Bill need to keep this. Since Jane gave it to me to review, I took the liberty of checking for information on our mystery flower delivery person. Far as I can see there's nothing there. I guess this is one mystery we will never resolve."

Lou asked, "When did my mother start the diary?"

"Well, I would prefer to call it a journal, not a diary. The first entry was made early in 1957. Sarah was struggling with the loneliness in her life since Richard's death. She stated that she loved her children and had a good relationship with them, but there were some things she could not discuss with them. She felt writing about these things would help her. She went on with a couple of pages elaborating on her relationship with Richard. Surprisingly she mentioned Leo in this area. I didn't know your mother or anything personal about her until I read those pages. Now I know she was a very intelligent, complex and sensitive person.

"Getting back to her relationships with Richard and Leo, she wrote of her love of these two men in detail. With Leo it was the first love that only comes once in a lifetime. It's apparent that she was still madly in love with him when he was killed. Do you mind if I read a few paragraphs to you?"

Not waiting for a reply, Gail opened the small red book. Turning the first couple pages over, she began to read aloud.

There are those who would say that I do not love Richard and never did. As long as I live and breathe I will harbor the youthful love of another inside my heart. He is the one who kissed me in those innocent days so long ago and romantically swept me off my feet.

For four wonderful years my every breath revolved around loving him. During this brief interlude the world seemed to stop. Just he and I existed in complete marital bliss. What a man! He was so handsome and virile. Wherever we went I always felt safe and protected by this tall, masculine guy. We danced; we sang together; we toured Washington and Hamilton, Ontario; we visited our families. Mother was so pleased that he was so gentle with me and I was so happy with him. Then war came and took him away. Oh, I wish I would never have answered the door that terrible day in August. My whole world caved in and a part of me was forever locked in a time warp of love for this man I will never see again.

Into this backdrop of catastrophe stumbled poor Richard. How was he to know that I could never love him like I do Leo? I have pledged my heart, my soul, my body to my slain lover buried in an inaccessible grave in France. I was an empty shell of grief that he stumbled onto. Still, Richard was lighthearted and could make me laugh. We dated almost a year until one night in a moment of passion we gave into human weakness. Unfortunately, my reproductive system finally worked perfectly and I was soon pregnant with Kate. Richard was elated. He was deeply in love with me as I still was with Leo. How could I tell him the feeling wasn't mutual? What was I to do? For Kate's sake, the only proper thing for me to do was to go away *and quietly marry Richard.*

He was a basic, down-to-earth man and the security of our marriage and our adorable children satisfied him. Since he was a very private person and never showed affection in public, it was easy for people to surmise that we did not have a loving relationship. I was never able to give him the passionate, all-consuming love that Leo and I shared, but over the years I grew to love him as a friend and the father of our children. I never told Richard about my feelings or relationship with Leo and, thankfully, he never asked.

Now I am alone again and mourning the two men who made my life worth living. Dear God, where do I go from here? I do not want to be a burden on my children.

There were tears in Gail's eyes as she closed the book. "Those paragraphs were so beautifully poignant. I just had to read them aloud one more time. Oh, Bill, I wish I could have known your grandmother. She was so perceptive, and she knew you and I were destined to have this wonderful relationship. I know she was a terrific person."

"She was a very unique person. All my life, she always knew when I was troubled and had the words to console me. If I was sad, she would have me laughing in five minutes. If had done wrong, she would be stern but forgiving. When and why did she stop writing in the journal?"

"Well, the journal goes on for over four years. At first there are regular entries. Then weeks and even months pass before Sarah puts a new entry into the book. As I said earlier she uses it as a place to openly express those inner feeling she needs to get out. Here's the last entry dated March 9, 1961. I like the way it begins."

That little Billy is such a cute kid. He and Lou stopped by after school today. He ate four of my chocolate chip cookies and an apple. I hope I didn't spoil his dinner. It makes me wish I would have had a boy.

Anyhow, the doctor is very worried about my blood pressure. Everything we've tried has not lowered it. I guess I am a walking time bomb. I told the doctor I am only 61 and my family needs me. He referred me to a specialist in York who is having great success with other patients like me. I go to see him tomorrow. Dear God, please let him be able to help me.

"That's the last entry. The rest of the pages are empty. There really is no indication why Sarah stopped the writing in the journal. Maybe it had something to do with the doctor visit."

Gail handed the book to Bill and he absently paged through it as she and Lou continued to talk about Sarah. He stopped at the last entry and read it again to himself and smiled as his grandmother referred to him as Billy.

When he finished he absently ran his fingers over the words Sarah had written. It helped him connect to the past. For an instance he was that little boy again sitting in the warmth of his grandmother's kitchen with a heaping plate of homemade cookies next to him and a tall glass of milk in his hands. He could almost see his mother and grandmother sitting across the table chatting about the upcoming school play.

Suddenly he felt a sharp pain pull him back to reality. Looking at his hand that rested on the page of the open book he saw blood start to ooze from a paper cut on his index finger. Mystified by the cut, he spread the pages of the journal near where they were bound.

"Ah, Gail, Mom, there's a page missing from this journal. I just cut my finger on the edge of a piece of paper left from the page. The last page of the journal has been torn out. Why would Grandma or Jane have torn that page out?"

Gail took the journal back. This time she looked closer and saw the edge of the missing page. "Maybe the news from the doctor was so bad she wrote it down and then tore out the page to keep from looking at it again."

Now Lou became very excited. "No, wait, it's starting to come to me. Monday of the following week we met at Kate's house for a planned card party. Mom was very agitated about something. I knew she had the doctor's appointment in York. When I quizzed her on the visit she showed me new pills and a diet the doctor gave her that he told her would lower the blood pressure. She seemed relieved about her medical problem. Something else was bothering her. Now it all fits together. A couple weeks later she announced that she had met one of the residents from the children's home at the doctor's office, and after talking to him, she decided to volunteer her time there. But we all know now that she never worked at the home."

Gail thought for a moment and said, "Sarah met our mystery flower person that day in the doctor's office. Meeting this person upset her very much. She came home and recorded it in her diary. From then on she made regular trips back to York to see this person. For some reason, she didn't want anyone here to know what she was really doing so she fabricated a story with this person's help. Then she panicked because she had recorded the meeting in the diary and she tore the page out of the journal. She couldn't trust herself to write in the journal anymore and that's why there are no more entries. Bill, Lou, it all fits together."

With excitement rising in her voice, Lou continued, "Mom was a meticulous record keeper. She never threw anything away. I can almost guarantee that she kept the missing page hidden somewhere. Now the only people who knew that the journal existed prior to homecoming week were Jane and Susan Moore. When Jim gets up in the morning, I'll talk to him. I believe he has Susan's address and can get in contact with her. Susan may know where Mom kept the diary and where the missing page is."

"It's time I get Gail back to town. I think her theory has a lot of merit to it. Still, we have no proof. Hopefully Susan can shed some light on things. Kate has Jane's house key. We can ride out to Frederick and search the house if we know what we are looking for."

Now the Christmas holiday season broke into full swing. All the stores in town were decorated and a large evergreen tree ablaze with multicolored lights was erected in the center of the square. On the first Saturday of the month the traditional Santa Claus parade was held. The jolly old man and his helpers took up residence in a small building placed on the corner near the bank. That evening everyone came out to celebrate the season as carolers strolled amongst the crowd and sang the old familiar tunes. Hot chocolate and spiced cider kept the chill away.

Bill was waiting in front of the shoe store when Gail arrived and he produced two tickets for the next horse-drawn buggy ride around town.

"Oh, this is so romantic!" she exclaimed as they climbed into the back seat of the buggy. As they slowly moved down the main street of town she continued, "This is my favorite time of year. All the shop windows are decorated for the season. The singing of the carols and the shoppers filling the streets make it special. Look at the manger scene in the drugstore window. It's so realistic. I feel like a kid again. I'm so glad we met and are sharing this time together." She snuggled up tight against Bill as the buggy turned a corner and the cold night air made her shiver.

Bill was also enjoying the evening. "This is my favorite time of year, too. I hope we spend every Christmas like this."

At his comment, Bill felt Gail tense up and she replied, "Now we must not think about the future. Let's just enjoy tonight. Hold me tight, that night air is really chilly. You need to buy me a large cup of hot chocolate when we get back to the square. Look over there, I can see Eddy's big glowing star hanging from the flag pole behind his house. Now there's a man that really gets into Christmas decorating."

Later as they strolled around the square and sipped their hot chocolate, they saw Jim and Lou cutting across the street. "I'll be glad when I'm out of this wheelchair. The therapist thinks I can graduate to a walker around Christmas. Getting out of this chair would be a great Christmas present. I've been a burden on Bill and you long enough."

"Nonsense, I will miss having you around when you return to your apartment," Lou interjected.

"Not as much as I will miss living with you and Bill. I felt like part of a family again. Look, there's Bill and Gail coming across the street. Hi, I have something to ask you guys. I talked to Susan Moore today. She remembered a large, cherry-stained, wooden jewelry box on the desk the day she saw the journal. We think she kept it in the box. Lou and I rode over to Kate's and picked up Jane's key this afternoon. Can you two come with us to Frederick tomorrow to look for the box?"

Gail looked excitedly at Bill and asked, "Can we please, Bill? I know we are finally close to the answers we are looking for."

"Sure, we'll all go right after church."

Everyone in the car was very excited as they drove to Jane's house after church. When they arrived each person took a room in the small house and searched every corner for the jewelry box. The house was very small with two bedrooms, an eat-in kitchen, a living room and bath on the main floor. In a short period of time all the closet and cupboards had been searched.

Bill proceeded to the unfinished attic where he found a multitude of boxes filled with a collection of unused things that Jane had stored. He was about halfway finished when Lou and Gail joined him. They had searched the basement. Other than some old tools, a neat laundry area and the furnace, the basement was bare. With their help the boxes were soon searched. "Well, that's it, no cherry-colored jewelry box anywhere," Bill announced as he trudged down the steps.

"Better check the garage," Jim ventured. "Maybe there's a storage area out there."

They moved to the garage and returned in a few minutes. "There isn't much out there, Jim. Jane's old car and some yard tools. We even checked the trunk of the car. No missing bodies there, just the spare tire. Come on, kids, let's wrap it up. We'll check with Kate. Jane may have had a safe deposit box at the bank large enough to put the jewelry box in."

Gail seemed a little depressed as they drove away and said, "I thought we were finally going to end this search. Somehow we always come up empty handed."

Jim glanced over his shoulder at the retreating house and asked, "You did check the crawl space above the garage, didn't you, Bill?"

"No, there's no access to it. I checked in the garage. There were no pull-down steps in the ceiling."

"I wonder why there's a window in that area if there's no access," Jim mused.

Suddenly Bill jammed the brakes on and wheeled the car around. "Jim, you're a genius," he announced. "Jane did a good job of hiding the entrance to the crawl space. I would never have thought about it if Jim hadn't noticed the window. Let's go back and check out Jane's hideaway."

Bill parked the car and they wheeled Jim into the house. Lou asked, "Now what are we going to do? Knock a hole in the garage ceiling? Even you said there was no access to the crawl space."

Bill began ascending the attic stairs and yelled back, "Follow me and ye shall see." In the attic Bill worked his way through the piles of boxes to a large chest at the far end of the room.

Gail was following him and said, "I checked through that chest earlier. It's just filled with old clothes."

Bill grabbed the chest and easily slid it toward the side of the room. As he did, a small door approximately two feet wide and three feet tall appeared from behind the chest. Bill unlatched the door and as he opened it light from the window on the end of the garage streamed through the opening. Bill stuck his head into the opening and said, "Now let's find out why this door was hidden."

Bill's upper body disappeared into the hole. Then his hand came back through the hole holding a grey metal box by the handle. Gail grabbed the box and the hand disappeared only to reappear holding a bag. The third time the hand reappeared holding a large, cherry-colored wooden jewelry box. Bill pulled his head back out of the hole and dusted himself off. They carried the three items downstairs and sat down with Jim.

"Well, Jane had three things that she valued enough to hide in that hole up there. Let's see what they were." First Bill opened the bag and pulled a stack of money out of it. "These are all fifty and hundred dollar bills. Apparently Aunt Jane was not as financially strapped as we thought."

Bill passed the stack to Jim and he began counting it as they turned their attention to the metal box. Opening it, he revealed several small jewelry boxes.

Lou opened several and exclaimed, "These boxes contain mother's missing necklaces, bracelets and pins. See this necklace with the triple diamond setting? It was given to my mother by my father on their wedding day. After he died, she never wore it again. It's so beautiful. I can't understand why Jane would hide it in a place like this. What if we had not found it?"

"Well, it's a good thing Bill discovered that door in the attic," Jim interjected. "There's five thousand dollars in this stack of money. Jane's mistrust of people must also have included bankers. The proper place to store these valuables is a safe deposit box in a bank. Do you think the wooden box has more jewelry in it?"

"Well, let's find out." Bill dusted off the wooden jewelry box and raised the lid. The inside was empty except for several envelopes yellowing with age that lay on the bottom. He picked up the first envelope turned it over and exclaimed, "I can't believe this. It's a letter Grandma sent from Pittsburgh to her mother in Greencastle. Her name on the envelope is Sarah Springer. Look, these two also come from Grandma in Pittsburgh, but her address is different and she has her married name, Sarah Brown, on the letters."

Gail had been quiet until this point. Now she recommended, "I know we all would like to hear what Sarah wrote in those letters. I think we need to wait. They are from Sarah's private life. I believe Lou, Dottie and Kate all need to decide our next step together. They will certainly want to review the letters in private before opening their contents up to others. As we all know Kate was quite upset that Jane gave me the journal and I read Sarah's confession that she was pregnant with Kate when she married Richard. It's getting late and we're all hungry. Let's head back to Greencastle and call Dottie and Kate."

"That's a good idea," Lou piped in. "Kate was upset because Mom never told us anything about her meeting and marrying Dad. Mom was a very private person and she would not tell us anything she thought would hurt us. However, she did write those things down in the journal. I doubt there would be any private secrets in the letters to her mother. Still, it's best we proceed cautiously."

Everyone agreed with Lou. When Dottie and Kate were contacted, there didn't appear to be any time to get together for a review of the letters until after Christmas. It was already December tenth. There were gifts to buy, packages to wrap, decorations to hang and parties to attend. It was decided that the jewelry box would be placed in Eddy's safe until after the holiday.

Soon everyone was gathered around the tables on Dottie and Eddy's porch for another holiday feast. A large tree covered with multicolored ornaments and twinkling lights stood in the one corner. High mounds of packages cascaded from under the tree and flowed out into the room. The glass doors to the living room were open and a fire crackled on the hearth in the fireplace. Elves, Santa Clauses, mistletoe and all the other seasonal decorations added to the festive feeling. Throughout, the air was permeated with the odor of roast turkey and pies baking in the oven.

Bill and Eddy had finished their chores and gone for a ride in the Porsche when Gail arrived. She met Lou and Dottie in the kitchen gathering dishes and utensils. As they greeted her, Lou noted that something was wrong. Gail didn't smile and seemed down. She wandered out to the porch and stood staring at the small snowflakes falling on the pool cover.

Lou crossed the porch and stood by her side. She asked, "Is there a problem, dear? You know I've become very fond of you. In addition to making Bill so very happy, you and I have forged a special relationship. Whatever is bothering you? Please tell me. You are important to us and we want to help."

"Bill came into my life in an unexpected way and everything happened so fast. While working together on Sarah's story and the paper, I dropped my guard and fell in love with him. He is just so caring and gentle I couldn't prevent it. I didn't mean for things to happen this way. For a while I thought I could just pretend everything was fine and live for today. I just couldn't let him make plans for the future. That was working alright until today."

"Gail, what are you talking about? Today is Christmas, a happy day. Dottie has even invited your mother and grandfather and they are coming to dinner."

"There's the problem. Today the happiness that I know will be shattered by my past. I can't keep this deceit within me anymore, especially with my family here. They know. Please don't hate me, Lou. I saw how excited you got when Jessie announced that she was pregnant. Bill has also talked about the sons he will have one day to take hunting and fishing. I...I was in an auto accident when I was a teenager. The doctor said my reproductive system was damaged and I can never have children. I should have told you and Bill a long time ago. It's just that for the first time in my life I was happy, really happy and I didn't want it to end. I'm so sorry."

Lou hugged Gail affectionately. "Gail, I love you like a mother loves a daughter. I can never hate you. Now dry up those tears. I understand why it became difficult for you to tell us this information. I am sure it hurts you just to talk about it. I want very much to have grandchildren and Bill wants his own family. But adoption is a very good alternative. You need to share this conversation with Bill. I know my son. There is no way he will leave you or hurt you. Together, you and he are going to continue to build this relationship and I will babysit your children some day. Come into the kitchen now and help me make the mashed potatoes."

"Thanks, Lou, I do love you like a second mother. I feel so much better now that I told you. I will talk to Bill. Just give me some time."

"Take whatever time you need to tell him. Here they come now. I have to finish those potatoes."

Bill and Eddy burst through the door talking excitedly. When Bill saw Gail, he crossed the room to hold her in his arms and kiss her. "Gail dear, Uncle Eddy just gave us a wonderful Christmas surprise. He wants us to meet them Friday night at the bay house and stay for New Year's Eve and he wants us to bring the Porsche down. There's a restaurant at the bridge that has a party we can go to. Doesn't it sound like fun?"

Gail's mind was still on her conversation with Lou as she smiled and responded, "Yes, that sounds wonderful."

Soon after everyone began arriving. Once again the whole family gathered around the tables on the warm glassed-in porch. This time they were joined by Ted and Lauren, Gail's grandfather and mother. Jim kept his commitment and walked to the table by himself with the help of a walker. After dinner, the table was put away and Eddy placed holiday music on the stereo. Everyone gathered around the Christmas tree to sing carols and watch the opening of the packages.

Lauren was sitting next to Lou. As she opened a package from Bill and Gail, she said, "I'm so glad to meet Bill's family. Gail has told me a lot about the area and the family. It's just as I pictured. Everyone here's been so nice to us. Thanks for inviting us down."

Lou leaned over close to Lauren and whispered, "Gail confided in me this morning that she cannot have children. She was very upset that she had not told us earlier. I told her that I loved her like a daughter and everything would work out, but she needed to tell Bill. Bill would be upset if I said anything to Gail, but I know he intends to ask her to marry him."

"Oh, thank goodness, she is finally getting this off her mind. I told her you would understand. It's so hard for her. She feels like she can never be a whole woman because she can't have children. Since she's returned to church with you and Bill it's helped. For a long time she was so bitter about her life. Now faith and hope have been reborn in her again. Gailee calls Bill her Prince Charming. Sometimes I think he's a miracle from God."

"I, too, am glad you and Ted came today. He seems to be enjoying himself. He's spent a lot of time talking to Bill. They seem to have a common hunting interest."

"Dad's a good man. A friend of his told him about the job here at the paper. Gail was reluctant to apply for the job. Dad insisted she try and the rest is history. He's just overprotective. We've had a couple of long talks on that issue. I think he understands now that we have to let Gailee live her own life."

Later that evening after everyone left, Bill and Gail sat alone by the fire. "It was a wonderful day, Bill. Growing up we always had a small, cozy Christmas. Here the whole family gets together in a big celebration. It was so different, yet so satisfying. And your family just accepted me and my family like we've been here all the time. They're a great group of people and they really know how to celebrate. I think I gained five pounds today."

"Eddy always says, 'when it comes to the holidays the more people enjoying themselves the better.' Everyone in my family enjoys having you here. It just seemed like a natural extension to invite your family. Your grandfather and I talked a long time about hunting and about you. He's so proud of you. By the way, I heard Mom, Kate and Dottie planning today to read the letters right after New Year's."

"Sarah was a very interesting person. I hope they decide to share the letters with us. I'm looking forward to spending this coming weekend with your aunt and uncle. I can't wait to see the bay house. I've heard so much about it. Why are we going down in separate cars?"

"Uncle Eddy needs to work late Friday. Since you and I are taking the day off from work, we can get an early start. Besides, Eddy insists that I drive the Porsche down. It's his special Christmas present to me. You know he has strict orders from Aunt Dottie to share it with me."

Bill walked into the garage and slowly walked around the shiny red automobile. "Today you're mine, wow. I am going to be the envy of every driver on the road."

"Did you say something, Bill?" Eddy had walked into the garage behind him.

"I was just commenting on how great this car looks. I am a little nervous about driving it down to the bay. Do you want me to take the Lincoln and you can drive the Porsche?"

"Nonsense, we settled this earlier on Christmas day. Just remember, only you and I know Dottie and I will not be down until tomorrow afternoon. I'll tell Dottie that a meeting came up for Saturday morning and I'll call you at the bay house so Gail doesn't suspect anything. Good luck." Eddy winked as the door opened. Dottie and Gail stepped into the room.

Dottie still anticipated arriving that evening and she stated, "Now we'll see you tonight around five. After dinner we can play cards at the house. You can see the big boats anchored out in the bay. Their lights dot the horizon on the lower bay side of the house. Almost directly in front of the house, we can watch the traffic crossing the Bay Bridge from the mainland out to Kent Island. You'll get there early enough today to see it before dark. Take a ride around the area and have fun."

Bill and Gail loaded their suitcases into the car's small trunk. As Bill carefully maneuvered out of the garage and down the drive, he commented, "This is like a dream. I have the girl I'm in love with sitting next to me in one of the most expensive sports cars in America and we are on our way to a romantic weekend by the bay. What more could I ask for?"

Gail agreed that it was a great feeling. Still, the conversation with Lou was running through her mind. She needed to talk to Bill. Maybe the opportunity would present itself this weekend. She decided to enjoy the trip. Perhaps one night or on the way back she would unburden her soul. Now they talked and joked together. It was fun to watch the expressions on the people's faces as the sleek red sports car passed them. Gail waved and put on a pair of sunglasses. "I feel like a celebrity riding in this car. It was so considerate of Eddy to let us use it."

"Uncle Eddy and Aunt Dottie treat me like I am their son. We have a great relationship. When I'm depressed, I can always depend on

Uncle Eddy to cheer me up and find a way to solve my problems."

At the Bay Bridge there was a short line to the toll booth. Bill's ego was flying high when the attendant doted over the car. As they crossed the bridge Bill pointed to a row of houses on the distant shore of Kent Island off to the right. "Uncle Eddy and Aunt Dottie's house is the middle one in that row along the shore over there. We'll make the right turn here at the end of the bridge near the restaurant. That's where we'll be eating tonight. Now we go down this road about a half mile and turn into the development."

Once in the development, Bill expertly maneuvered through the streets and soon was driving down the road parallel to the edge of the bay. Near the end of the street he pulled into the driveway of a grey house. A large garage ran across the front of most of the house and opened perpendicular to the driveway. Bill pulled the car up to the garage doors.

After picking up the luggage, they walked up a couple steps to the door aside of the garage. Bill opened the door and they stepped into a large entrance foyer with a marble floor.

As Gail's eyes took in the dining room and living room beyond, she commented, "Your aunt and uncle have great taste in homes. This house is so warm and cozy looking." She walked to a set of French doors at the back of the living room. "Wow, an enclosed porch looking out on the bay. I could live in this place year round. Come look at the sailboats, Bill. It must be cold on the water today. See, over there in the distance is Annapolis. It's beautiful."

Gail was interrupted by the telephone ringing. After answering the call, Bill joined her. "I knew you would like this view. That was Uncle Eddy on the phone. They won't be here until tomorrow. Let me take you on a tour of the rest of the house."

Bill led her down the hall to the back of the house. "On the left here is my bedroom. It's a nice room, but the garage blocks any view toward the front of the house. Now let's step into your room on the left. Here, let me open the drapes." Bill pulled the rope and the drapes slid open to reveal a row of large windows on the bay side. "Both this bedroom and the master bedroom next door have an excellent view of the bay."

Next Bill led Gail into the master bedroom. It was a slightly larger version of the room next to it. It also had a side door that opened onto the porch that ran behind the living room and dining area. Bill finished the tour with a stop in the kitchen where he dug two beers out of the refrigerator.

He pulled a chair out for Gail and they sat at the dining area table. "My aunt and uncle bought this house about six years ago. It was a small rundown ranch. They enlarged and remodeled it to what you see today. Come on out back. We'll walk down to the seawall."

Bill led Gail through the porch and down the yard to the edge of the bay. "I like to walk along the wall and check out what floats up on that little beach area. This is where we found that gnarled old piece of drift wood in Mom's flower bed." As they walked, seagulls flew overhead and a large container ship moved up the channel in front of them and slipped under the bridge.

"Bill, this is all so wonderful it almost overwhelms me. I didn't think I could ever be any happier than I've been recently with you. Now you've brought me here and I know I was wrong. My whole life used to center around my job and visits to my mother. Now my life revolves around the time I spend with you. I'm so happy and yet I'm scared. We need to talk, Bill. There are some things I need to tell you. Could we do that tonight after dinner?"

"Well, as a matter of fact, I had something to talk to you about after dinner also. Let's not spoil the moment with any more of this. I'll race you to the car and we'll take a tour of the rest of the island before dinner." Bill was off in a flash up the hill. Gail sprang after him and caught him at the corner of the house. Her long legs served her well as she pulled ahead of him along the side of the house and reached the car an instant before he did.

"Got you that time, Mr. Henderson," she panted delightfully.

Bill locked up the house and then they spent about an hour riding through the small town of Stevensville and around the bays and slips on the northern end of the Kent Island. At five o'clock they returned to the house to prepare for dinner.

Bill slipped into his dark blue suit and was waiting patiently on the porch when Gail appeared in a full-length black dress with long sleeves. After putting on their warm winter coats, they drove the short distance to the restaurant. The waitress seated them in a quiet corner near a window looking out on the bridge. Bill ordered wine and they ate an excellent meal of Maryland crab cakes while they talked of the day's adventures.

Finally over coffee, Bill steered the conversation in a new direction. "I believe you had something you wanted to talk about."

Gail's curiosity had been raised by Bill's earlier comment and she loathed bringing up her subject so she responded, "No, you go first please. It's my preference tonight and I want you to be first."

"Well, first I have a confession to make and don't tell Aunt Dottie. Uncle Eddy never intended to come down tonight. He wanted you and me to have this special romantic evening alone. I don't know where to start. I'm not very good at speeches. Since that first day I met you at Rosie's my life has never been the same. Something told me you were going to be a special part of my life from that very first meeting. By the time you came out and had dinner with us, I knew I was falling in love with you. Your smile lights up my life and I can't bear to see you cry. Over the past six months I have grown to love you as no man has ever loved before. I have experienced more joy in this brief period than in all the rest of my twenty-nine years. I don't ever want to be separated from you again. I feel so relaxed and content with you. It doesn't matter whether we are feverishly working side by side to get the next edition of the paper out or just snuggling in front of the fireplace, there is a warm glow inside my body telling me I want to spend the rest of my life with you. Keeping that thought in mind, will you marry me, Gail Mason?"

At that point Bill pulled a small box from his pocket. As Gail looked on in shock, he took a large, sparkling diamond ring out of the box and slipped it on her finger. Gail picked up her glass of wine and drained it. As she gazed at the ring, she stammered, "I...I...I never dreamed, well I know we love each other, but it just didn't seem. Err, give me a moment to catch my breath."

Bill watched as Gail closed her eyes and breathed heavily for a few moments.

"OK, I think I can handle this now. I can see now that I should have gone first. We need to talk before I can answer your question." Bill looked on puzzled as Gail continued. "I've tried since meeting you not to let this happen. You don't want to marry me, Bill. I am damaged merchandise. I was in an automobile accident when I was sixteen. I can never have children. I should never have let this get so serious without telling you. It's just that I was so happy, too. I just knew if I said anything you'd leave me. Now I've really messed things up. Oh, Bill, please don't hate me. I love you very much. I'm sorry. Here, you can have your ring back."

As Gail pulled the ring off her finger she looked at Bill and he began to chuckle. Then he broke out into a fit of uncontrolled laughing. Angered, she countered, "Bill, there's nothing funny about my situation. Did you hear me correctly? I am half a woman. I can never feel a child moving in my womb, hold my baby to my breast and feed it or enjoy any of the other blessings of motherhood. I never thought you were so insensitive." Gail was ready to burst into tears and started to leave the table.

Bill gently pulled her back. Wiping tears of joy from his face, he began, "I am so sorry my laughing has upset you. Let me explain. Asking you to marry me is the single most important thing I have ever done in my life. The pressure on me has been tremendous the last few days. I knew that every time I remotely mentioned a long-term commitment, you would tense up and change the subject. I was sure it was because you really didn't love me. I've driven myself crazy over the last several months trying to figure out what I have been doing wrong. Somehow I needed to convince you to marry me. Then Eddy suggested this romantic evening. In desperation, I made my plans for the evening. I couldn't imagine how I was going to cope if you turned me down. See, the joke's on me and I'm laughing at myself. I was such a fool. I never realized you were holding back because of a problem in your life. I was so sure I was the problem. Forgive me for being so insensitive to your needs.

"Gail, I love you with my whole heart, soul, and body. I love you just the way you are. Together we can overcome any challenges in life. I realize one of the greatest joys in our lives would be conceiving and raising our own children. I also want to experience the joys of fatherhood. God has closed this door for a reason. He knows we both desperately want children. There is an urgent need for couples to adopt special needs children. God may be leading us in that direction.

"I also want to challenge your comment that you are half a woman. You are a very hard-working, successful career woman. In addition you are an intelligent, sensitive, caring person. You make me very happy when I am with you. You are also a very sexy female. The way you dress, walk, talk, even wink at me, drives me crazy. And, in bed, you are the greatest. Half a woman—I think not. Half the women out there wish they had your talents, abilities and body.

"Yes, I wish you would have talked to me earlier, mainly because I would not have made such a fool of myself. Now we need to try this again."

At this point Bill picked up the ring and carefully slipped it back on Gail's finger. Now he pushed his chair away from the table and on bended knee repeated the question, "Gail Mason, will you forgive me and marry me? I promise that I will always try to make your life as happy as you have made mine."

"Bill, for almost half my life I shamefully carried the scars of that auto accident. Tonight you have made me see that they could be a blessing in disguise. You have made me a whole woman again. How can I say no to a man with your wisdom and gentle caring? Yes! Yes! Bill Henderson, I will marry and support you in all of life's adventures."

As Gail spoke her voice steadily rose until she almost shouted the last sentence. This attracted a small crowd in the restaurant and one of the patrons exclaimed, "Well don't just kneel there, take her in your arms and kiss her." Now the spell of the moment was broken and Bill followed the onlooker's directions, planting a passionate kiss on Gail's lips. Suddenly the room broke out in applause. Bill blushed and sat down in his seat as the waiter approached.

"Congratulations and excuse me for interrupting. The older gentleman with the cane and his wife sitting over there wish to say congratulations. They also have told me to put your expenses for the evening on their bill. Is there anything else I can get for you?"

"No, thank you. Do you know the older couple?"

"Yes, they are regulars."

On the way out Bill and Gail stopped at the couple's table. "Good evening, how are both of you tonight? My name is Bill and my girlfriend, excuse me, my fiancée, is Gail. Thank you for being so kind to us."

"Oh, it's the least I could do. Watching you tonight took me back fifty years to a similar night when I proposed to the fantastic woman across from me. We've had fifty wonderful years together and I wish the same for you two young lovers. Please accept our congratulations again."

Bill and Gail thanked the couple again and walked hand in hand to the car.

Later Bill and Gail changed and snuggled under a blanket on the couch on the porch and watched the lights of the boats dancing on the bay and the car lights darting across the bridge. Bill stroked Gail's bare legs and felt his excitement rising.

"Somehow I feel Sarah is responsible for all this. If she hadn't pressured Jim into hiring me, I'd probably be in some low-level position in Pittsburgh or Philadelphia hating every minute of my life. It's amazing how our lives seem to pivot on one decision like that. Instead of hating my job I have a great one that gives me a lot of freedom and I'm engaged to marry the most wonderful man in the world. Thank you, Sarah, wherever you are."

Bill moved his hand beneath the skimpy negligee Gail had changed into and idly rubbed her back. "Well, don't forget that wonderful man is her grandson. Also, she decided years ago that we would make the perfect couple. I wonder if I inherited any of her talent for matchmaking."

Gail rested her head on Bill's bare chest as he rubbed her back. "Sometimes I think I am in a dream. Everything here is so perfect and I am so content. Please tell me it won't end."

Bill moved his other hand around to Gail's firm waist. "From here on our future will be what we make it. There will be many times when it will not be as perfect as tonight. But if we work hard at it, we can have fifty wonderful years like the couple at dinner." By now, Bill was moving his hand up and down Gail's chest and gently massaging her breasts.

"Bill, how do you expect me to continue to carry on a conversation when you are getting me so hot?"

Bill pulled Gail on top of him and kissed her while he continued rubbing her back. "Maybe it's time we stopped talking." At this point Bill slipped off Gail's negligee and drank in the beauty of her lithe body in the pale light of the room. Rolling her onto her back, he continued to kiss her and fondle her breasts as he slipped her panties off.

"It's time you show me what you bring to this marriage," she joked as she flipped off his pajama bottoms and left her hands wander across his naked body.

Their passions aroused, they continued to gyrate as the cover slipped to the floor. Gone was the concern to keep warm as the two bodies heated up the room with their zeal. Soon Bill was on top moving with a steady rhythm as he caressed Gail's long, flowing hair and shoulders and gently kissed her.

"Oh, Bill, you are so good to me," she moaned.

Now positions were switched and Gail's hair fell lightly across Bill's chest as he moved his hands over her back and firm breasts. She writhed from the excitement and yelled, "I can't take much more of this." Suddenly Gail's fervor peaked. She screamed and fell across Bill's chest as his passion exploded.

The early morning rays of the sun the next morning found Bill and Gail asleep in a tight embrace on the bed in the room facing the bay. Bill opened his eyes and smiled as he realized Gail was cuddled up next to him. "Hey, are you always going to steal all the blankets?"

Gail opened her eyes and stretched. Then she pulled her hand out from under the blanket and looked at the ring. "Well, once we're married we can save a lot of money on pajamas. This ring is gorgeous. The stone is so large and sparkly. I don't ever want to take it off. I can't wait to tell Mom all about it. Do you think Eddy would mind if I called from here?"

"Uncle Eddy will be overjoyed that you are now a Henderson-in-training. He assured me that a trip in the flashy car and a dinner at his favorite restaurant would make you say yes. I guess he was right. The way to a woman's heart is through her stomach. And I always thought it was the great sex that they liked most."

"Oh, Bill, you are such a tease. Diamonds are a girl's best friend, and I have the most dazzling rock in Greencastle. I love you, Bill Henderson, and I'm going to show you just how much."

"Here we go again."

Bill and Gail were sitting on the porch when Dottie and Eddy arrived around one o'clock. Dottie rushed through the front door and sped to Gail's side. "Your Uncle Eddy is a lousy storyteller, Bill. Well, don't just sit there calmly, Gail. Show me the ring."

Gail proudly raised her hand and Dottie exclaimed, "Wow, what a rock! Honey, this guy really knows how to treat a lady. Like Jane said, he's a keeper."

Eddy came through the door at this point carrying the bags. "Sorry, Bill, she tortured me until I broke and told her the plan for last night. Say, can I see the ring? It sure does sparkle. Who is this rich man you're marrying, honey? I'm starved. Dottie was in such a rush to see the ring, she wouldn't stop to feed me. Let's all take a ride up the road about two miles. There's an old-fashioned hamburger joint there and you can fill us in on the details of the proposal last night. This is so great. Our Bill is getting married. Look at me, Gail, I bet I'm almost as excited as Bill was last night. Well, considering that the two of you were alone, I know I lost that bet."

Later when they returned, Eddy lit a fire in the fireplace and the two couples played cards past midnight. Sunday passed rapidly and soon everyone was dressed and on their way to the New Year's Eve party. Once again Eddy and Dottie proved themselves exceptional dancers. All too quickly it was midnight and a television was turned on to watch the ball in Times Square fall.

The next morning Bill and Gail planned to return to Greencastle after breakfast. However, Dottie and Eddy convinced them to stay until late in the afternoon. Bill packed his bag first and carried it to the car. Then he returned to help Gail. "Are you about ready for me to take your bag?"

"I just need to put my cosmetics in the overnight bag on the shelf in the closet. Can you get the bag down for me?"

"This was a great weekend. I was thinking about Grandma again this morning. She would be so happy if she knew that we are getting married. She tried to get us together before she died, but time ran out. You and I were meant to be together so it happened without her help."

"What makes you so sure she had nothing to do with our meeting and falling in love?" Gail's hands were filled with bottles and containers as she waited for Bill to pull the cosmetic bag down and open it.

"Don't be silly. Grandma's been dead for five years. Here's your bag." As Bill pulled the bag off the shelf, he saw something fall from the shelf to the closet floor. "Did you put anything else on the shelf?"

"No, why do you ask?"

Bill swung back to the closet and bent over to examine the article. "This piece of cloth fell when I grabbed your bag. Oh my God, Gail, you aren't going to believe this. Grandma did get us together."

Bill handed the slip of material to Gail. She examined it and asked, "SAM, what does that mean?"

"That's one of Grandma's hankies. She embroidered her initials on many of them—Sarah Ann Myers. Everywhere she went, she always carried one of her hankies."

"Wow, Bill, that is spooky. Do you really think she's able to manipulate our lives from the grave?"

Just then Dottie came into the room. She saw the hanky in Gail's hand and commented, "I see you found Mom's old hanky. It became mixed up with some of my linens I brought from home. In the unpacking I misplaced it. Now that you found it, I can get it back with some other keepsakes I have at home. Thanks, guys. Bill, why are you looking at me like that?"

"We were just talking about the possibility of Grandma manipulating our lives to bring us together even after she's dead. I said that was impossible and suddenly this handkerchief appeared."

"Well, I don't believe in ghosts. However, you two are a perfect match, and if Sarah had anything to do with it, all I have to say is, 'Thank you, Mom.' There's Eddy calling for me. That man can't do anything without my help. Come out when you're ready."

"Aunt Dottie's right. It really doesn't matter who or what brought us together. What really matters is that we are now engaged and officially together. I am the happiest man in the whole world and I thank anyone living or otherwise that help bring us together."

"I agree, let's roll. Take me for one more ride in that fancy red car. We'll see how many faces we can turn on the way home. When they stare at the car, I'll flash them my diamond. Riding in that car with this rock on my finger will make them doubly jealous."

Saturday, January 20 was a cold, clear winter's evening. Dottie, Lou, and Kate had decided that all members of the family would be invited to tonight's discussion on Sarah's letters. Kate arrived alone. Denny had an emergency delivery and Jessie was sick. Lou arrived with Jim gaining speed and confidence with the walker. Bill and Gail were the last to arrive after a busy day at the paper.

Jim saw the couple come in and said, "Here come the stragglers. I have good news. In about a month, the therapist wants me to try a cane. When I graduate to the cane, I will be able to take over a lot of my duties at the paper that you two have assumed. Then I can start carrying my own weight in this family again."

Bill hung up Gail's coat and commented, "It's no problem, Jim. We enjoy working together setting up the press and running the papers. Come sit in the living room, dear. They are waiting on us to start."

Lou began, "Mom's writing was very articulate. As we studied these letters the story of her life with Leo almost jumped out of the pages at us. We thought it would be fun if each one of us just took one of the letters and read it to the group tonight. I'm taking the first one. Now as we all know from Bill and Gail's research, Sarah left home late in December 1914 to attend a nursing school in Pittsburgh."

"But she was only fourteen years old," Kate interjected. "She was just a child."

"Yes, but her birthday was on January third. So she would have been fifteen when the school began. In those days, fifteen was the age a girl left home. Many got married or went to work as servants. In Sarah's case she was going to school for a profession in nursing. In this letter Sarah gives us a glimpse of life in Pittsburgh shortly after the turn of the century as she tells her mother about meeting Leo and falling in love with him. It's dated March 29, 1915. Now let me begin to read."

CHAPTER 6
The First Letter

Dearest Mother,

Finally I am returning to work. I have written you numerous times over the last several weeks. Now it is necessary that I write this letter and tell everything about Leo. I know I had mentioned our meeting and dating, but there is more you need to know. It all started about a month after I began working at the hospital.

As Lou read the letter, Sarah's story jumped off the pages. It was as if they were there living the adventure with her…

Sarah hurried along Sandusky Avenue thankful that it was Wednesday. Like the other new nurses at Allegheny General Hospital, she worked from six in the morning until six-thirty at night with a half hour for lunch. On Wednesday the head nurse was tied up in meetings most of the morning and gave the trainees an hour lunch while she caught up on her work. If Sarah hurried, it usually took her ten minutes to cross Stockton Avenue and reach the drugstore on the corner of Church and Sandusky Avenue. Here she could slip inside to the fountain service area in the back of the store. Instead of ice cream in the winter they offered soup and a sandwich at a very reasonable price. A welcome change from the hospital-provided food she ate the rest of the week. If she were lucky, one of the three small tables would be empty and she could spend a half hour reading as she ate lunch.

The bitter cold February air kept pedestrian travelers to a minimum and Sarah reached the door of the drugstore in record time. Inside, the glow from a pot-bellied stove in the center of the room warmed her cheeks. The wooden floor echoed with her footsteps as she slid past the medicine counter. "Good afternoon, what is on the menu today?" She smiled at the dour-faced matron behind the counter as she made the request.

"Same thing as every Wednesday, miss—vegetable soup and a ham sandwich. You have a choice of rye bread or white."

"That sounds delicious. I'll have the rye, please."

Sarah paid for her lunch and, spying an empty table, she grabbed her bowl and sped to the closest chair. She arranged her bowl and sandwich near her book and began reading. Turning a page she became aware that a man had seated himself at the opposite side of the table and was staring at her. She looked up at him and said, "Don't you know it's impolite to stare?"

"Oh, I'm sorry. It's just that you have the most beautiful hazel eyes."

"Thank you for the compliment. Now if you don't mind, I only have a half hour and I would like to read." Sarah had noticed the man's accent, but she decided not to comment on it. She did not want to engage him in conversation. All she wanted was to enjoy these brief moments with her book before she went back to scrubbing floors, making beds, and emptying bedpans. Last week one of the patients died while she was washing him and this morning one had thrown up on her. This was not the exciting career she envisioned when she left Greencastle.

"So how is Bartley Alexander's bridge building doing today?"

"You've read *Alexander's Bridge* by the new author Willa Cather?"

"Yes, after I saw you in here last Wednesday reading it I bought a copy. Would you like to know the ending?"

"Don't you dare tell me the ending! Now wait just a minute, are you spying on me? And why did you buy and read a book just because I was reading it?"

"Good questions, but first, I need to introduce myself. My name is Leo Brown. I am originally from Hamilton, Ontario. Now I live in Pittsburgh and sell grease and lubricants to the railroads and factories here in Allegheny City and across the river in Pittsburgh. You, my hazel-eyed beauty, caught my fancy when I stopped in here for lunch last Wednesday after landing the Graff Carriage Works up the street as a new customer. I noticed that your total attention was focused on that book. You were completely oblivious to everyone and everything in this store. I bought the book and read it in the hope of understanding you better. Now it's your turn to tell me who you are and what brings you to this corner drugstore."

"I came to this corner store to read my book and escape from that hell hole called a hospital just up the street. Now why don't you move to that vacant table over there and let me read."

"Ah, you are one of those poor unfortunate creatures called nursing students that the hospital staff uses to complete all the undesirable tasks. Still, this is no way to treat the man who's lived in this store during lunch time for the last week hoping for your return."

Sarah slammed her book shut and, glaring at Leo, she exclaimed, "Well, I can see you are not going to let me read. My name is Sarah Springer from Greencastle, Pennsylvania. Yes, I am a nursing student at the hospital since the fourth of January. I had these great notions of being a nurse and saving people's lives. Instead I clean up people's messes, empty the garbage and deliver bodies to the morgue. In return the hospital gives me room and board and a whopping salary of $50 per year. You still didn't answer my question. What is your interest in me? I have no use for your grease, Mr. Salesman."

"I make a decent living selling lubricants, thank you, but it is not my life. I like your feisty disposition and you're not afraid to stand up for your rights. You are a very beautiful young woman, Miss Sarah, and I wish to show you the sights and sounds of our fair city."

"Look at the time. It's quarter to one. I must go. I am flattered by your offer, Mr. Brown. Miss Hill is our dormitory resident. She is responsible for making sure that we obey the rules. I will check with her on getting some time off for your tour. You can meet me here next Wednesday if that suits you."

"That suits me just fine, Sarah Springer. I will be here."

On the way back to the hospital Sarah thought about Leo. He was a very handsome, dashing sort of man, and he had an interesting accent. She knew she had taken out her frustration with the hospital on him. He seemed so intent on dating her, he hadn't even noticed her hostility. There was a new motion picture at the theater that she wanted to see. Hopefully Miss Hill would let Leo take her. After all, it was only a short walk down to the Allegheny River and across the Seventh Street Bridge to the theater.

Sarah cursed the hospital, her supervisor, and the old lady who decided to die at two minutes to twelve. Her supervisor insisted that the body must be moved immediately to the morgue. She had rushed the gurney downstairs only to find the attendant gone to lunch, which is where she should have been. It had taken almost ten minutes to find someone who would accept the body. She considered leaving it in the hall covered with a sheet, but she knew that would get her in trouble and approval to date Leo would be revoked. Now it probably didn't matter.

The clock on the bank chimed the half hour as she swung open the door to the drugstore. Her eyes quickly darted to the tables in the rear of the store. A large old man with a handlebar mustache was the only customer. She walked to the nearest table and sat facing the street. Taking out her handkerchief, she wiped the tears from her eyes.

"Hello, it is my hazel-eyed nymph. Hopefully those tears you shed are for me."

"Oh, Leo, I thought I had missed you. I was detained at work, and I was sure you had given up on me. Miss Hill was so kind and got me the whole afternoon off on Saturday so we could go to see a moving picture show. Can we do that, Leo? There's a western one of my roommates saw."

"I can't think of a better way to spend the day. I read in the newspaper the other day that Mr. Edison is working on an invention that will bring sound to the picture show, kind of like a phonograph. We live in an exciting time, Sarah. Automobiles, phonograph, moving pictures and airplanes—never in the history of the earth have there been so many revolutionary new inventions and I doubt there ever will be in the future. I just purchased this paper while I was waiting on you. Ah, there's the timetable for the picture shows. The one you are interested in is at two. I will meet you at your dormitory promptly at one."

Leo grabbed his fob chain and pulled an ornate gold watch from his vest pocket. Sarah stared in awe at this expensive piece of jewelry as he opened the cover. "I see you like my watch. A successful salesman impresses his clients with his clothing and jewelry. You arrived just in time. I must leave you now for a meeting with some Western Pennsylvania railroad officials at the freight station across the street." Leo grabbed his bag and hurried through the door.

Sarah couldn't help admiring how professional he looked in his suit and hat.

Saturday was usually a busy day at the hospital. Today Sarah worked feverishly to complete her chores by noon. Then she rushed to her dormitory and changed into a warm dark blue winter dress with a matching hat. Sitting in the reception area at one o'clock, she saw Leo coming up the walk. Smiling as he came through the door, he exclaimed, "Look at you out of that uniform. You're very pretty. I'll be the envy of all the chaps in the theater today. Here, let me help you with your coat. The air is warm today and the sun is shining. It should be a pleasant day for our jaunt to the theater. Did you know that the first theater in the whole world to show moving pictures opened here in Pittsburgh in 1905? It was called the Nickelodeon because it cost a nickel to get in. I learn a lot of history about this town as I make my rounds."

As they walked in the warm afternoon sun, Sarah questioned Leo, "I've been thinking about your line of work—sales. Every day you must meet dozens of eligible young professional secretaries. They probably all throw themselves at a tall, handsome, smooth-talking bachelor. Why are you interested in me—a plain country girl?"

Leo put his arm around Sarah as they started across the steel suspension bridge that spanned the Allegheny River. "When I first came to Pittsburgh about two years ago, it was my first experience with the big city. I took out a lot of those secretaries that threw themselves at me at first. They all wanted to latch onto a successful man, get married, quit their jobs and have a dozen kids."

"Well, I must admit that I hope some day to get married and have children also."

"Ah, but there's the subtle difference; you came here with the goal of getting a profession in nursing, not a man. You weren't even interested in me at the drugstore. I've had to work very hard at getting this date. I liked the challenge, and it makes me appreciate you far more than I ever did any of those secretaries. Look how busy the river is. The Carnegie Steel Company is increasing its employment rolls by eight thousand people to meet the increased demand for steel as a result of the war and I've got a contract with them."

"What is your opinion on the war? Can we remain neutral and when will it end?"

"Sarah, I am a Canadian. The day Great Britain entered the war, we entered also. The United States on the other hand is attempting to stay neutral while supplying Great Britain and France. If this war drags on any length of time, your country will be forced to take a stand and join us."

"And you, Leo, where do you stand? Will you march off to war?"

"Our government currently is only asking for volunteers. I hope and pray that the war will be over quickly. But if we reach a point where my country needs me I will go. Oh, look, we are at the theater. There is a line at the door. I hope we can get good seats."

Leo and Sarah enjoyed the show. In the next few weeks Leo faithfully met Sarah at the drugstore every Wednesday and they went for walks in East Park next to the hospital when Sarah was able to slip away for brief periods. Now it was the third of March and there was a hint of spring in the air as Sarah rushed to meet Leo at the corner near the hospital. She saw him leaning against a light pole watching a group of workmen cleaning the fountain in the middle of the street. She snuck up behind him and, putting her hands over his eyes, teased, "Guess who?"

"It's my pretty date coming to have lunch with me."

"Look at me in this dirty uniform with this silly hat. How could you even dream of calling me pretty?"

"I wasn't looking at the uniform, I was looking at the beautiful woman inside."

"Boy, you sure know how to boost a girl's ego. Now I have good news. We have quite a few empty beds in the hospital right now. The head nurse has agreed to give me the whole day off on Saturday. Can you take me into Pittsburgh and show me what it looks like? The first day we met you told me you wanted to give me a tour of the city. At night I look out my window at the lights in the tall buildings across the river and wonder what it's like over there. The only time I've ever set foot in the city was when we went to the picture show."

"Hmm, did I offer to take you on a tour?" Sarah saw by the twinkle in Leo's eyes that he was joking. She laughed and he continued, "Miss Springer, on Saturday I will dazzle you with the sights and sounds of yonder town. I will even take you to see my room at Mrs. Finnigan's boarding house. She doesn't usually let strangers in the house, but I'm her favorite boarder."

"It's all so exciting. I can hardly wait. Look, our table is vacant. Let's hurry and get it."

That night, as the girls in the dormitory were preparing for bed, Sarah proudly told them all about Leo's plans to show her around Pittsburgh. Several of the girls were impressed that Sarah, the youngest of the group at only fifteen years old, was the first to find romance. However, all were excited for her. Sarah pulled out a couple of dresses she had brought with her and asked, "Do you think either of these would be appropriate for the day?"

Hallie, the oldest girl in the group and a close friend of Sarah's, spoke up, "Honey, they would do just fine if you were back in Greencastle dressing for the Saturday night sing along at the church. This beau of yours wants to stroll up the main avenue with a mature, sophisticated woman. Now I have a tight-fitting burgundy dress with a revealing neckline in my wardrobe. Men go crazy when I wear it. I think you and I are almost the same size. Your bosoms aren't quite as developed yet. Come on, let's see if we can add a little padding and make it work."

Sarah felt ready to conquer the world as she walked down the stairs to the dormitory lobby. Hallie had spent the last two hours helping her primp for this date. At the bottom of the steps Sarah slipped into the bathroom. There, in a full-length mirror in the corner, she had an opportunity to view their handiwork. Who was this mature woman staring back at her? Even her smile of approval with the dark lipstick made her look older. And the tight fit accented her trim waist and slender legs. Look out Pittsburgh, Sarah Springer the woman has arrived.

As she rounded the corner to the lobby, Leo stood up. Never at a loss for words, he stared at her and was speechless for several moments. Finally he stammered, "Sarah, you're stunning in that outfit. I always knew you were beautiful with those hazel eyes and long brown hair. Today you are dazzling. God, I am so lucky to have found you."

"Thank you for helping me with my jacket. Now I need to set the record straight. I am the lucky one. I hated my life before you showed up. Endless hours of toiling at menial tasks with no end in sight. The only escape I had was my book, which has lain unopened the last several weeks. I can't even remember what chapter I was on."

Leo opened the door and joked, "Remember I did offer to tell you the ending. If you beg me, I may be able to still remember what I read. Well, the sun is out and it promises to be a beautiful day. Once we get across the river, we'll take the trolley. Let's go down this street to get started."

There followed a wonderful day for Sarah as she experienced all the sights and sounds of the big city. Leo took her first to the Point where the rivers met to see the Pittsburgh Exposition building. Then as they worked through town he showed her the Soldiers and Sailor's Memorial, city hall and the grand splendor of the Pennsylvania Railroad's Union Station. They lunched near Forbes Field and then walked across the expansive grounds of Carnegie Institute. As they walked, Leo told Sarah they were heading for the best part of the tour. Soon they were riding the incline on Mount Washington.

Leo filled her in on the history, "This area used to be called coal hill due to the rich deposits of coal on the mount. From 1867 to 1877, these inclines were built to solve the transportation problem. Now tourists like us use them to get to the terrific view of the city at the top. See, the whole panorama of the city spreads out before us. Directly below us in front of center city is the Monongahela River running parallel to the mountain. Flowing in from the north is the Allegheny River. See how they form a triangle at the Exposition Building and form the Ohio River. Across the river out there in the distance you can see the hospital where we started this morning."

"Oh, Leo, it's all so fascinating. The exposition building is so big. You could almost fit the whole main street of Greencastle in it. Just look at all the tall buildings on the skyline. And the buildings are so ornate like the Grand Opera House and Union Station. I could spend days just walking through them. There must be a dozen bridges crossing the rivers. I can't begin to count all the boats tied up at the docks and scurrying about on the water down there. Everywhere we went today people were so busy and there were automobiles everywhere on the streets. It's all so different from the sleepy little town I grew up in. I just feel so alive and excited by the pulse of life that ebbs and flows around us here. It makes my job at the hospital seem so insignificant."

"Oh, Sarah, nothing you do can ever be insignificant. Spending the day with you has been wonderful. I'm afraid I have grown immune to the beauties of this city. In my drive to succeed, my life focused on the industrial sectors of town. I only saw the dirty factories and the sweaty workers toiling away their lives in them. Now through your innocent eyes, I see it all in a new light. This is home to over a half million amazing people. Together they have built massive architectural wonders, a colossal ballpark, universities of higher learning, and all the other wonders spread out before us. Amongst these they have placed many all-important green areas of solitude like Shenley Park, Grandview Park and East Park near the hospital. Yes, I have missed the beauty and might of this city as I focused on my own little insignificant job. But now with your help, I stand here on the slopes of Mount Washington and realize how great this city is and how truly wonderful you are. Look at me rambling on like a school boy. This is what you do to me. We need to leave now. There is just enough time left to stop at Mrs. Finnigan's on the way back. When I mentioned our plans for the day, she insisted I bring you by to meet her."

It was a short ride across town to Mrs. Finnigan's boarding house. She met them at the door and ushered them into the parlor. "Please sit down, Sarah. I have some tea and cookies ready. It's so nice having a woman in the house. Since my husband died I have three young men living upstairs that take up much of my time. Leo has told us so much about you when we gather for dinner in the evening. It's a welcome relief from the business stories he usually brings home. You know, my dear, he's rather taken with you. And I can see why. She's even more beautiful than you described, Leo."

Both Leo and Sarah were blushing at this point. "Please, Mrs. Finnigan, don't tell Sarah all my secrets. How will I ever get her to marry me if she knows that I am just a boring businessman?"

Sarah dropped the cookie she had been eating at Leo's announcement.

Mrs. Finnigan looked startled and said, "Oh dear, Leo, you never discussed marriage with us. I can see that Sarah is a wonderful person. Still, you have known her for less than two months. Don't you think it would be wise to get to know each other longer?"

"Sometimes I get these feelings in my life and I know exactly what I must do next. That's how I came to Pittsburgh. I was frustrated because

172

I couldn't find a job back home in Hamilton. I saw an advertisement in the paper one night about an opportunity in the States. Immediately I knew what I had to do. I left home the next day and the rest is history. I had that same feeling this afternoon when I stood on Mount Washington. I looked at this wonderful girl and realized I am in love with her. At that instant I knew we were made for each other and I would ask her to marry me. Pass the cookies, please."

Sarah regained her composure and picked up her cookie. A thousand thoughts raced through her mind. She really liked Leo, but did she love him? Where would they live? Did he intend to move to Canada? How would she tell her mother?

"Well, love, are you coming to see my room?" Leo's voice interrupted her thoughts. "Is something wrong? You don't look so good."

"Leo, you just sort of proposed to me. How do you expect me to act? I'm in shock. I hardly even know you, and I don't love you."

"Look, I know there is a lot we don't know about each other. I also know that you have changed my life and I never want that change to stop. I will give you some time, Miss Sarah Springer, to get to know me and then we will talk in earnest."

The rest of the day Sarah seemed to walk around in a fog as Leo's words rang in her ears, "I am in love with Sarah....And I will ask her to marry me."

When she returned to the dormitory, Hallie and the other girls demanded to know the details of the day. Sarah told them about all the wonderful things she had seen and done. However, she did not reveal the conversation at Mrs. Finnigan's. Right now, she needed to ponder Leo's words without any outside pressure.

Sunday dawned a rainy, dreary day as the vestiges of a cold winter returned for one final grand display. The rain seemed to beat incessantly against the windows in the wards as Sarah rushed to catch up with her weekend chores. By the time the day ended she felt totally exhausted and drug herself back to the dormitory.

Hallie woke Sarah up shortly after two the next morning. "Sarah, get up, please. There's been an accident at the steel plant. Some of the new employees were trying to start a furnace and it exploded. They're sending twenty of the workers to us. Some are badly burned."

Sarah fought off the fatigue in her body and sat up. She noticed a slight sore throat as she swallowed. She realized she had probably picked up a cold from the day in the city. Miss Hill poked her head in and yelled, "Hurry, girls, the first ambulance will be arriving any minute. Dress quickly and report directly to the emergency room."

In the hospital everyone was busy preparing for the patients. Sarah was busily stacking bandage material when the first ambulance arrived. Nobody had prepared the new nurses for the grisly scene that met their eyes as the first two victims were wheeled in. The first man was writhing with pain from burns all over his body. His hair was singed and the charred remains of the fingers on his one hand stuck out from beneath the sheet. The second gurney presented an even more grisly scene. The mangled body was not covered. A tourniquet was applied to the remains of the right arm above the missing hand and the bone from the left thigh protruded out the side of the man's lower leg. Worse still a large piece of steel was thrust into his abdomen. A doctor rushed to the man's side.

Sarah and Hallie stood transfixed in horror as the victim's body convulsed several times and then lay motionless.

The doctor checked the pulse and then looked at the two nurses, "Take this one to the morgue, his suffering is over." At that point a second ambulance arrived and the doctor wheeled to grimly face his next patient.

Sarah moved hesitantly to the gurney containing the now lifeless body. She looked back and saw Hallie's ashen face and glazed eyes. "Help me get this body to the morgue." Hallie stood motionless as if she were rooted to the floor. Sarah tried again, "Hallie, this gurney's in the way. I can't get it out of here alone. Help me, please to get it down the hall."

Now Hallie moved stiffly to the base of the wheeled cart. They were maneuvering the cart past the new arrivals as the doctor carefully cut the shirt off the patient on the next gurney. It appeared the man had been hit with many small flying pieces of steel. As the doctor pulled the shirt off, a sharp piece of steel that had penetrated a major artery in the neck stuck to the shirt. A stream of blood gushed from the punctured artery and covered Hallie. Running screaming from the room, she frantically tried to wipe the splattered blood from her face.

Desperately trying to stop the bleeding, the doctor gruffly yelled at Sarah, "Didn't I tell you to get that gurney out of here? We need that area to work on this patient before it's too late. Move that thing out of here now."

Sarah mustered all her strength and maneuvered the cart around the other patients, doctors and nurses. Then with a final supreme effort she pushed the loaded gurney up the ramp to the hallway leading to the morgue. She left it sit at that point and went to check on Hallie. She found her in the bathroom bent over the toilet. Sarah found a towel. After getting it wet in the sink, she tried to wipe the blood from Hallie's face and hair as she continued to throw up.

Eventually Hallie sat whimpering near the toilet as Sarah completed her task. "Oh, Sarah, what am I going to do? This was my first opportunity to perform as a nurse and I go to pieces and throw up. I can't do this job. The doctors and patients needed me out there and I ran away. Go back, Sarah, they need you. I'm a failure."

Sarah searched for the right words, but none came out. The door to the bathroom opened and the gruff old head nurse stepped into the room. Feared by doctors, staff and administration, her tirades were legendary in the hospital. Even a minor infraction of the rules could bring her wrath upon you. Sarah cringed and waited for the explosion as the head nurse marched toward her objective. Hallie looked up to see her approaching and burst into tears.

Sarah gathered her determination to spring at the old witch to protect her friend from the verbal abuse. Hallie did not deserve her wrath this morning. Then a strange thing happened. The head nurse knelt down beside Hallie and tenderly stroked her hair. "I know how you are feeling, dear. I had a similar experience many years ago as a young woman growing up in the little town of Gettysburg." Now she raised Hallie's head and stared directly into her eyes. "My dear, even today over fifty years later, I still feel the urge to run away when I see

175

these mangled bodies and hear their agony. You will always have these feelings. But they need us desperately. They are crushed in body and spirit. Only trained professionals like us can ease the pain and give them the courage to go on. We must go back and do our job."

The head nurse rose and gently pulled Hallie to her feet. "Three of the men have less severe injuries. I have sent them to a ward for cleaning and dressing their wounds. I need you to take care of these patients. Together we'll get through this. Come along and I will show you what needs to be done."

Hallie obediently followed the head nurse. Sarah watched and remembered an old saying about not judging a book by its cover. She had learned a valuable lesson this day. For the rest of her life she would never judge anyone by their outward appearance. She would always look for the subtle little clues that revealed the inner feelings and personality of the person.

Sarah heard another ambulance arriving. She finished her chore of delivering the body and returned to the emergency room. The hours sped by as she was pulled into the thick of administering to the new patients. Finally near noon the emergency room was cleared and the nurses were sent to lunch.

For the first time, Sarah noticed her throat hurt worse and she had trouble swallowing her lunch. Now she felt weak and achy as she performed her afternoon duties. It was after ten in the evening when she finally collapsed in her bed. Feverish and feeling worse all over, she spent a restless night in bed.

As the sun peeked through the windows, she decided she was too sick to return to work. Miss Hill was moving through the dormitory making sure everyone got up after yesterday's long hours. When she came to Sarah, she took one look and exclaimed, "Sarah, what is wrong with you? You have a rash all over your face. And your head is hot. You have a fever. Do you have a sore throat?"

Sarah timidly answered, "Yes, Miss Hill."

Hallie had heard the questioning and moved to Miss Hill's side. She turned to Hallie and told her, "Report to the head nurse and tell her that I suspect Sarah has scarlet fever. I will take her to the quarantine area. When you get back we will need to strip her bed and disinfect the area."

Sarah wished she could die. Her temperature was 102 degrees and her whole body was covered with the itchy rash. Worse still, she was in quarantine. Nobody was allowed in to see her except the doctor and attending nurse. Hallie had snuck in for a few minutes yesterday evening and brought her book.

On top of all this, it was Wednesday and she was supposed to meet Leo at the drugstore. She racked her brain, but there was no way to let him know that she was now a patient in the hospital. In a little while he would enter the store and she would not be there. She couldn't bear to think of him getting mad at her because she didn't show. Tears came to her eyes at the thought of missing him. She reached for a hanky to dry her eyes and realized with a start that the head nurse was staring at her. Several thoughts ran through her mind and she began, "I'm sorry I left the body in the hall yesterday. I know I should have taken it all the way to the morgue. I was just so worried about Hallie. And I'm also sorry I got sick and risked infecting everyone in the dormitory. Please forgive me."

"My dear child, I did not come here to reprimand you. Yes, you should have taken the gurney all the way to the morgue. On the other hand, you left it to comfort and protect a fellow human being in need. Isn't that really our prime job? No, I came here to thank you for working so tirelessly yesterday. The doctors told me that you were everywhere trying to help them and then you worked late into the night last night helping others catch up. You had to be feeling sick, yet you put everyone else's needs before your own. I am very proud of you, Sarah Springer. Yes, we are concerned that you may have spread the infection and we have taken steps to contain any further outbreaks. However, I cannot be angry at you for this. As you told Miss Hill, you thought you had a cold and you were too busy to realize how sick you really were. Now tell me why you were shedding tears when I came in."

Sarah needed to talk to someone about Leo and she filled the head nurse in on her dilemma.

"If this man cares for you as you say he does, he will never be angry at you. Now, I know how uncomfortable you are. I have convinced the doctor to give you something that will help you sleep. Here take these. Good, now sleep, Sarah, and all will be well."

Sarah closed her eyes and dreamed of Leo. She dreamed they were together and he told her he loved her. She felt happy and relieved and she told him she also loved him. Time passed and she drifted in and out of deep sleep. She dreamed about opening her eyes and seeing Leo dozing in a chair next to her. What a silly dream. He should be embracing her in a passionate kiss instead of sleeping. "Wake up and kiss me," she commanded to the air in her room.

Suddenly she felt a pair of hands embrace her and an affectionate kiss was planted on her forehead. Now she forced her eyes open and saw Leo standing over her bed. "Is this a dream or is that really you, Leo?"

"You've been delirious with a high fever since Wednesday. I came as soon as Hallie told me about your illness. I cancelled most of my appointments and have been here by your side the last two days. You do look better."

"I didn't ask Hallie to meet you. How did you get in here? I'm in quarantine. You can't stay here with me. You'll get sick and lose your job."

Leo held up his hands. "Hold on, let me explain and it may answer a lot of questions. Your guardian angel has been at work. The head nurse here at the hospital was very impressed with your performance the day of the steel mill accident. Wednesday morning you told her about our meeting in the drugstore at lunchtime. She had Hallie bring me here and approved my being in the room with you since none of your family lives in the area. I've been told to wash my hands thoroughly if I touch your drinking glass or eating utensils. Unfortunately, I also promised not to kiss you on the lips. As for my job, it will be there when I get back. I doubled sales in the last two years. They won't get rid of me. Can I get you anything?"

"Yes, a new body. Look at me, Leo. I have spots all over my body like a leopard. How can you love me looking like this?"

"My dear Sarah, I will always love you however you look. It is your selfless desire to help others, your small town innocence and the way you see the beauty in life's little things, and a multitude of other good qualities that I love. I am told that these red splotches will fade in a few more days and then you will start to feel like your old self again. Now I do have a few things at the office I need to take care of. Since you are on the road to recovery, I am going to go attend to business. I will return tomorrow morning with a surprise to cheer you up. Try to sleep now, my darling."

Sarah wished Leo would have stayed longer. He had left before she could tell him that she loved him. No, wait, how could she tell him that? She remembered her confusion after Leo's revelation at Mrs. Finnigan's. At fifteen was she old enough to know true love? Yet, how could she not love this tall, strong man? He was gentle and considerate and worshiped the ground she stood on. He showed her wonderful things and together they laughed and enjoyed life. She dreamed about him all the time and missed him terribly whenever she was alone. All she talked to the girls about anymore was Leo. With a start, she remembered her last letter home. *Leo took me to the moving picture show. He's so handsome in his suit....Leo says picture shows will one day have sound.....Leo says the steel mills are unsafe with all the new, inexperienced employees.* Her whole letter was filled with references to Leo. She smiled as she reached her conclusion. Yes, she was in love with this man from Canada. Now she must tell him. She closed her eyes to picture his face and soon fell into a restful sleep.

Saturday morning found Sarah feeling more like her old self. Her temperature was normal. There even seemed to be some fading of the rash on her face and body. Hallie came by early in the morning and updated her on the news from the hospital. "We lost another of the steel mill accident victims. I feel so sad when I think of their families. Oh, that ancient old lady with the stomach problem finally went home.

All the girls wanted me to tell you that they were thinking of you. If I were you, Sarah, I'd get a permanent hold on that man of yours. If you weren't my best friend and so sick, I would have tried to steal him away from you the other day. Seriously though, you should have seen the concern on his face when I told him that you were ill. I had to run to keep up with him on the way to the hospital. Do you realize that he's in love with you?"

"Oh, he's told me he loves me and more. He told Mrs. Finnigan that he intends to marry me. I'm scared, Hallie. I don't know how to be a good wife and Leo deserves the best. I just don't know if I can make him happy. There's so much about life I just don't know."

"Wow, he is serious! Don't worry, Sarah. Your heart will tell you the right things to do. Leo will make a great husband and I know you will make him happy. Sometimes you worry too much. I have to get back to my work now. I'll stop back tomorrow."

Hallie had scarcely disappeared when Leo popped around the corner. "Ah, my little hazel-eyed beauty is up and smiling this morning. I was so worried the last couple days. I love you so very much. I don't want us separated like this with you unable to let me know if you need me. Now you know I earn a good living with my company. I send money home to my folks and still have enough left to put some in savings. I can easily support a wife and family. Here, I stopped at the jeweler's and picked up this token of my love. I noticed it in the store window shortly after we met, and I knew immediately that there was only one person in the world beautiful enough to deserve it. I just had to get this ring for you before someone else bought it."

Leo reached into his pocket and pulled out a small bag. He opened the bag and pulled out a delicate gold ring. A pair of hands clasped together was etched on a wider section of the ring. "This isn't how I pictured doing this. Will you marry me, Sarah Springer, and wear this wedding ring as a symbol of our love?"

Sarah looked deep into Leo's eyes and answered, "I have given this moment a lot of thought since that day at your boarding house. I know you will make a terrific husband. I have worried that I would not be a deserving wife able to make you happy. However, Hallie tells me that my heart will lead me in the right direction. Yes, I will marry you, darling."

I know, Mother, that you will be upset at me for not consulting you on this important step in my life. Please forgive me and rest assured that I have made a sound decision. Remember you and Daddy had only known each other for a short time when you were married in Atlantic City. We love each other very much. Leo is a gentle, caring man who will take excellent care of me. I have never been happier in all of my life. Since I am a Protestant and Leo is Catholic, we have decided on a small civil service on the twentieth of May. Hallie and Miss Hill have agreed to be our witnesses. Leo plans to take a week off in August. He has decided that we will tour Washington. On the way back to Pittsburgh he wants to stop in Greencastle to meet you and the rest of the family. I look forward to this time when he can meet all the people who have guided me through the early years of my life.

Your loving daughter,
Sarah

Lou put the letter down.

Kate spoke first, "I've seen the ring with the pair of hands. After Dad died Mom started wearing it from time to time. I thought she found it at that antique shop she visited. It is part of the jewelry she was wearing the day she died. Remember, the funeral director gave me her earrings and rings after the viewing. All this time I've had her wedding band that Leo gave her, and I thought it was just a trinket she bought because she liked it."

Dottie broke in, "After reading these letters and parts of the journal, I see my mother in a new light. Some of her deep inner feelings and fears which she never spoke of, I now understand. I feel closer to Mom than I ever felt before. Let's get coffee and a snack. Then, I'll read the next letter."

In a little while Dottie began, "This letter is dated April 23, 1916."

CHAPTER 7
The Second Letter

Dearest Mother,

I have lain awake tossing and turning for hours. I keep thinking of your last letter to me. I knew how disappointed you were when I wrote about not returning to nursing school. I was so depressed and short with you in that letter. Today has helped me to turn the corner on this terrible time in my life. Let me start at the beginning and I will end with today's decisions.

Sarah smiled when she saw Leo waiting for her at the intersection of Sandusky and Stockton Avenue. The cold walk to their small third floor apartment a few blocks away always went fast when he met her. She hurried tonight to tell him the wonderful news, "Leo, my darling, our suspicions have been confirmed. Soon our little apartment will be very crowded."

Leo picked her up and swirled her in the air. "That's wonderful. I can't wait for the pitter patter of little feet. When will Leo Junior be born?"

"Now, darling, there is a fifty percent chance that our first born will be wearing a dress instead of britches. Today is the fourteenth of February. I am in my third month. Now, let me see. Six months from now will be the middle of August."

"Did you tell the head nurse and give her your resignation?"

"It's strange how we all feared her so in the beginning. We were told that she has a terrible temper and is very strict about obeying the rules. After the explosion at the mill, I saw her in a different light. She became more like a second mother to me. For an instant she became teary-eyed today when I told her. I feel like I am abandoning everyone at the hospital. I will miss Hallie very much. The twenty-fifth will be my last day. What will I do with my time after I leave the hospital?"

"You will devote it all to making your husband happy. Now we've been through all this before, Sarah. These long days are very hard on you. We must think of the baby first from now on. I earn enough money to support this family. Next month we will hunt for a larger apartment near one of the parks across the river in Pittsburgh. I will be closer to most of my clients over there."

"Taking walks on warm spring evenings pushing the baby stroller through the park sounds wonderful. I am so happy."

They stopped at the butcher shop next to their apartment building. As usual, the selection this late in the day was limited. "I know it will be nice to get here early in the day and buy a decent piece of meat. I will make you great meals every evening. Let's check the bakery next door to see if they still have a loaf of fresh rye bread."

As they ascended the stairs to the apartment a pain shot through Sarah's abdomen and she momentarily winced.

Leo felt her stiffen. "Is something wrong? You should just tell them tomorrow that you cannot continue working."

"Don't be silly. It was just a little gas pain. I feel fine now. I will be careful at work. Besides, they need my help until a new girl can be added. Now help me work a miracle on this fatty little piece of meat. With any luck we may be able to make it edible."

It had been two weeks since the small party at the hospital on Sarah's last day. Hallie disappeared around noon and when she returned Sarah was summoned to the dining room where everyone gathered for a piece of the cake Hallie picked up. It was a sad day of saying goodbyes to all the staff she had grown so close to. As Leo helped her carry out her belongings that evening, she and Hallie promised to meet on Wednesdays for lunch at the drugstore.

Now, on the fifteenth of March, Sarah was on her way to her third visit at the drugstore. It was difficult getting into some of her clothes these days and she had been late leaving the apartment. As she hurried toward the drugstore, the pain in her abdomen returned. It came more frequently and was more intense nowadays. The doctor cautioned against strenuous exercise and heavy lifting. Sarah slowed down until the pain disappeared.

The hour at the drugstore flew by as Hallie updated Sarah on the happenings at the hospital and Sarah described several new apartments Leo had taken her to see. With reluctance, the two girls parted at the end of the hour and promised to meet in a week.

Sarah walked slowly through the streets. The pain did not return and she knew everything was going to be fine. She stopped at the shops along the way and purchased a few items for a surprise dinner for Leo that evening. A gust of wind almost blew the door from her hand at the bottom of the apartment steps. Halfway up the steps a strong pain hit suddenly. Its sharpness made her double over and she sat on the steps to recover. In a minute the pain disappeared and she continued on into the apartment.

Putting things in order and busying herself in the kitchen, she felt like something wasn't right. Suddenly another severe pain enveloped her and she felt the warm rush of blood run down her leg.

Sarah burst into tears and panicked. She walked quickly to the door of the next apartment. The neighbor woman opened her door and Sarah sobbed out her problem. The woman quickly made Sarah lie down and sent her son for a doctor.

Leo came home from work around three. As usual he spent Wednesday afternoon in Allegheny City. His customers had no problems and so he was able to finish early. There was a note tacked to the door telling him to go to the apartment next door. The neighbor woman met him at the door.

"Mrs. Grove, I saw the note. Is Sarah here? Is there a problem?"

"Please come in and sit at the table. We need to talk. Frankie, take the children for a walk. There now, let me get you a cup of coffee. Sarah's in our bedroom with the doctor. He told me to talk to you before you went in. Leo, she lost the baby this afternoon."

"I stopped today and picked up this little rattle for our baby. He'll never get to play with it. We talked every night about all the wonderful things we would do as a family after the baby was born." Tears came to Leo's eyes and he started to get up from his chair. "I must go to Sarah and comfort her."

"Stay here, the doctor is not ready for us. Sarah's had a traumatic experience. When she came to me her eyes were wide with fear, blood was running down her legs. I sent for Doc Wilson right away and put her to bed. He came immediately, but there was nothing he could do. She was hysterical. The doc gave her something to calm her down. I know you two are deeply in love and together you will get through this. She just needs your complete support and understanding. Sarah blames herself right now and that's normal. I went through this same nightmare eleven years ago. My Tom got me through it, and now here I am with five healthy children. Give her some time and then try again."

The doctor opened the bedroom door and motioned to Mrs. Grove. She led Leo into the bedroom. Sarah saw him and burst into tears, "Oh, darling, I've messed everything up. Our baby is gone and it's my fault."

Leo wiped the tears from his eyes and cheeks. "Please don't blame yourself, Sarah. We have our whole lives ahead of us to try again. Right now we need to get you strong and healthy again. What matters most is that we have each other. Together we will solve any problem that comes up. Here, hold my hand and feel the strength. I will give you my strength until you are ready to stand by yourself. Someday we will have a dozen little ones and this will only be a bad dream in our past. Let me carry you home to our bed now."

During the next few weeks, Sarah went through all the stages of grieving. At times she was very sad and moody, and then she would vent her frustration to the point of even yelling at Leo. He tried everything to console her, but she pushed him away and shut him out. At times it seemed like Hallie was the only person in the world that she could talk to about her true feelings.

Finally spring broke and they met for lunch in the park next to the hospital. Munching on a sandwich Hallie began, "It's such a beautiful day today. I don't want to go back to work and spend another five hours inside with sick people while the world is alive with spring. Look, over there's a bed of tulips just opened. You are so lucky to have Leo. It's always better to have someone to share this with."

"If I'm so lucky, how come I messed things up and lost my baby?"

"Sarah, only God knows why he took your baby. It had nothing to do with anything you or anyone else did or did not do. Now it's not the same with Leo. He loves you very much and would do anything for you. Your actions will determine whether he continues to love and support you. Don't drive him away. You don't need this guilt you're harboring, but you do need Leo. Stop blaming yourself for the loss of the baby and start showing your husband the love he deserves. It is rare to be as happy as you and Leo were. Don't throw that away. I must go back to work now. See the hands joined together on your ring. They are strongly bound together. You can find that same strength by binding yourself to Leo."

Sarah sat for a long time and pondered Hallie's words. Now for the first time since that terrible day she cried for the loss of her unborn child. As the tears flowed down her cheeks she realized that her grief had come full circle. There would always be a special spot in her heart for the life that ended in her womb. Now it was time to go on. It was time to return to the man who loved her. She must show him her love.

Leo slowly dragged himself up the steps. This had been one of those days when everything seemed to go wrong. Several customers complained the new lubricant he sold them was not working and the man at the biscuit factory wanted to know how the grease got into the biscuits. How was he to know how grease from the conveyor bearings got into the biscuits on top of the conveyor?

He dreaded returning to the apartment. Most nights he prepared dinner and ate alone. Sarah never greeted him at the door anymore. She rarely combed her hair or changed out of her nightgown and would either sulk in the bedroom all night or yell at him until he left the apartment. It seemed like there was no joy left in his world.

As he fumbled for his key, the aroma of a fresh-baked apple pie perked up his senses. It smelled just like the ones Sarah made, but that wasn't possible. As the door swung open, he thought for an instant that he was in the wrong apartment. A fresh tablecloth was spread across the small table. The candle burning in the middle of the table was surrounded by their best china. He hoped for the best as he announced, "I'm home, dear."

Totally confused, he watched Sarah enter from the kitchen carrying two platters heaping full of food. She was dressed in her best blue dress and her hazel eyes sparkled as she set the food down and embraced him. "Darling, I've been such a fool venting my frustration on you. Hallie made me realize today that I was throwing away the happiest days of my life and replacing them with misery and anger. This Sunday is Easter. All around, I see the rebirth of the flowers and trees. It is time to move forward and have a rebirth of our wonderful relationship. I need you and want our old relationship back. Please forgive me and help me. I will try from now on to be a better wife worthy of your precious love."

"My prayers have been answered. Dearest Sarah, I will do anything I can to make our marriage work. Both of us were grieving these past weeks and I forgive you for any harsh words you spoke. I, too, think Easter is a wonderful time to celebrate the beauty of our lives together. Let's eat and plan the day. No, let's start with Saturday. With your busy schedule at the hospital, you never took time to go shopping. We will take all day Saturday and shop for a new dress and hat for you. It will be the grandest Easter outfit in Pittsburgh. Then Sunday we'll go to church and I have a surprise for you afterward."

"Oh, Leo, I'm so glad to be back to my old self. Tell me what the surprise is. You know you can't keep a secret from me."

"It is wonderful to have you back, and I can keep a secret. You shall have to wait until Sunday before I tell you."

Saturday morning dawned bright and clear as the two shoppers boarded the trolley to take them downtown on their shopping adventure. Sarah was amazed by the variety of products available in Kaufman's and the other large department stores in the shopping districts they visited. She remembered ordering many items from a catalogue in Greencastle because they weren't in the local stores. Here various sizes, shapes and colors of anything imaginable could be found on the shelf or hanging on the rack. It was late in the day when they finally agreed on a rose-colored dress with half sleeves. A dark green hat with a fluffy wisp of white feathers on the front complemented her dress. Leo insisted on completing the outfit with one of the bright new fringed matching parasols.

"There now, let me look at you. I have never seen a more beautiful creature in all my travels through this city. I will be the envy of every man in town as I walk my wife down the promenade tomorrow."

Sarah blushed and giggled. "Leo, I'm afraid this will go to my head if you keep it up. Really you are spoiling me. This outfit is too expensive. Let's go back and get that green one we saw this morning. It was almost as nice and only half the price. How will you pay for this?"

"It's been wonderful seeing the sparkle in your eyes today. I'm always amazed at how much you enjoy these jaunts into the city. I must admit I enjoy coming with you. It really is contagious to see your excitement. No, I don't want the green dress. You are so feminine and beautiful in this outfit. It was made for your complexion. Now let me worry about the money and you worry about keeping your husband happy. After our evening in the bedroom Wednesday night, I felt like I could conquer the world. So I convinced my boss on Thursday to give me a nice pay increase. You are looking at the highest paid salesman in Pittsburgh. Seriously, Sarah, I know my business and the company soon will have half of the business here in town. Go change out of that dress now so we can pay for it and find a restaurant to eat at. I'm famished."

Sunday morning they arose early and walked to a church down the block. When the service was over, Sarah noticed Leo's excitement as he steered her toward the city. "Darling, you are like a school boy on his first trip out of town. You almost rushed past the minister without shaking his hand. I've never seen you this excited. It's time you tell me where you are taking me."

"Hop on the trolley and I'll explain. We are going to view the latest architectural masterpiece in town at the corner of Grant Street and Sixth. Have you heard anything about the William Penn Hotel?"

"I think I read something about it opening in March. After buying this dress we cannot afford to stay at a hotel. What is going through your mind?"

"I earn my living as a salesman, but I enjoy great architecture. This is one of the premier hotels in the world. It cost six million dollars to build. The lobby area is open to the public and I would enjoy seeing it with you."

Sarah laughed. "Well, that is what we shall do then. When I am with you, I enjoy anywhere in this town you take me."

Later Sarah stood in the black marbled entryway to the lobby of the hotel and stared at her image in the mirror. "This is the second time in my life that I have looked in a mirror and wondered who that lady was staring back at me. The first time was on that day you gave me my first tour of the city. That time I stood before the mirror in a borrowed outfit. Today this ensemble is all mine. Pinch me, Leo. I want to make sure that this is not a dream. I will never forget my first baby, but I am so glad I didn't let my grief destroy our marriage. I want to spend the rest of my days with you. I'm ready now. Give me a tour of this architectural wonder." Sarah cocked her hat to the side slightly and Leo kissed her as he took her arm to lead her into the lobby. "Please, darling, we must act dignified now. A refined gentleman does not kiss a lady in public."

"Shucks, ma'am, I guess you caught yourself an unrefined gentleman." Leo positioned himself in front of Sarah and kissed her again. They both laughed when they noticed that they had become the center of attention. Leo explained, "It's OK, ladies and gentleman. She's my wife and I love her very much." The tension in the crowd eased as they proceeded into the main lobby.

Leo began his tour, "This type of design is referred to as the French

Classic period. Notice the thick piers and arches on the side walls supporting that ornate ceiling." .

"The three crystal chandeliers are so beautiful and huge. And everything is trimmed in gold. Wow, this area is so huge. You could put the whole Hotel McLaughlin from my little town in this lobby and have room left over. I must admit, I was skeptical about spending our afternoon in a hotel lobby. It's so grand and elaborate. I'm glad we came. See, I told you I would enjoy being here with you."

Later, as they strolled lazily through the city streets toward their apartment, Sarah said, "This has been a wonderful day. I feel so elegant all dressed up. You must find us other places to go so we can do this again soon."

The last few weeks, consumed by my grief, I was living my worst nightmare. Now I am back from that abyss and going on with my life. This weekend I have felt so alive and happy again as I shared my love with my husband.

Leo and I talked at length tonight before he fell asleep. We want to try to have another baby as soon as possible. I understand now that the stress, long hours, and heavy lifting at work could have caused my loss. Therefore we have decided that I will not return to nursing. I am going to check with the hospital to see if I can volunteer a few hours a week without doing any heavy lifting.

I know you wanted me to become a nurse to be able to support myself. Nevertheless, Leo wants me to stay home and raise our children. He has a very good job and earns enough money for us to live well here in the city. So please do not trouble yourself further with my financial needs. I'm dying to show you that expensive dress, hat and parasol he insisted on buying me Saturday.

Also Leo is concerned about me traveling a flight of steps when I get pregnant again. We are going to continue to search for a first floor apartment near one of the parks in town. We have seen a couple nice neighborhoods. I will send you a new address before we move.

I know you tell me that I am a country girl and want us to settle in Greencastle. I must tell you, Leo and I have decided that we want to live the rest of our lives in this wonderful city. Through Leo's eyes I have experienced the beauty of the architecture of these huge buildings. Every day we discover new things to explore. Day and night the city is alive with the hustle and bustle of industry and expansion. I feel so alive here and have made many dear friends including Hallie that I cannot leave. Please forgive me, Mother, I cannot see myself ever wanting to return to the humdrum, routine life I left two years ago.

Send my love to everyone. We hope to come spend time with you at Christmas for a few days. Since Leo went to church with me last Sunday, I hope he will attend our Christmas Eve service. Write soon, please

Your loving daughter,
Sarah

Dottie laid the letter on the table and everyone stretched.

Bill spoke up, "That letter just doesn't sound like Grandma. She loved Greencastle. She lived here the rest of her life after returning from Pittsburgh. She used to always take me for walks through town and tell me the local history. She was proud of our town. No, that letter was not written by Grandma."

Lou moved to his side and put her arm around him, "I know it hurts you to think Grandma could talk like that about this area which means so much to you. Your dad raised you to appreciate the small villages, farms and woodlands of this rural mountainous area. To better understand we must put ourselves in her shoes. She's a young small town girl only sixteen years old and goes to live in the big city. There she meets and falls in love with a handsome Canadian. He shows her all the wonderful sights and sounds of the big city. Most young men and women placed in that fast-paced, exciting life and experiencing their first true love would chose it over little old Greencastle. In the end she remarried, settled here and grew to understand and appreciate the beauties of this area. Grandma was just overwhelmed by events when she wrote that letter."

Gail took Bill's hand and continued, "Well, it's a good thing that Sarah decided to stay. If she hadn't we would probably not be sitting here today. I really don't even want to think about that, because it means I would never have met my wonderful Bill."

Bill hugged Gail and continued, "Yes, I agree, Grandma's final decision to stay here is what's most important. I wish Grandma had shared this information with us before she died. I always enjoyed listening to her tell me stories about her adventures with Grandpa. I know she had many more stories of those years so long ago in Pittsburgh. I don't understand why Leo left to fight in the war. I know how I feel about Gail. I love her so much I can't imagine ever leaving her for any reason. I know I would never have left her to fight in World War I. He died like millions of other young men and nothing was resolved. Thirty years later we were back in another world war and millions more were killed."

"The boys who signed up to fight in the First World War really believed it was the war that would end wars and bring freedom and prosperity to the world," Eddy broke in. "The Second World War came about because of bad leadership decisions made at the end of the first war. Their decisions set up the chain of events that led to another even more destructive war."

Now Kate broke in, "It's time we read the last letter. I think it will answer some of your questions, Bill. The letter is dated July 20, 1917. To set the stage, it is written approximately a week after Leo enlists in Canada."

CHAPTER 8
The Third Letter

Dearest Mother,

It is with a heavy heart I write to you now. I am so depressed I can hardly function. I haven't eaten in days. Please, Mother, tell me how to accept the fact that the man who is the center of my world has left me to go to war. Dear God in heaven, protect him and bring him back to me. I cannot live without him. We were so happy here. If only I could have borne him a child. I lost my father when I was five years old and my first child when I was sixteen. Now at seventeen my husband has left me and I fear he may never return. Let me put my last glimpse of joy unto this paper. Recording it may boost my spirits for the work ahead.

Racing across the park to his apartment, Leo almost collided with the woman pushing a large baby buggy. "Watch where you are going, Leo. You almost ran me down. Why are you in such a rush?"

"I'm so sorry, Mrs. Fitz. I have a surprise for Sarah and I can't wait to tell her."

"Well slow down or you may not get the chance to tell her. Young love—I can never remember my Harry being that enthusiastic and bringing me surprises home."

Leo sprinted the last few yards to the apartment door and almost knocked it down in his haste to see Sarah. As the door flew open he saw her seated at the kitchen table. He paused a moment to reflect upon her beauty in the soft light coming through the window behind her. Remembering his mission, he bolted the rest of the way to the table. On the way he saw that Sarah's eyes were red and tear-filled. "You've been crying, my dear. Why?"

"I just came back from the hospital. I was so sure I was pregnant this time. The doctor says I am too tense and need to relax. How can I relax when I want a baby so bad?"

"We've tried everything the doctor told us. I'm sure he is right. We are very young and have plenty of time to make this work. The doctor wants us to relax and I have just the thing. Guess what I have in my pocket."

Sarah could see the excitement sparkling in Leo's eyes. She loved him even more when he got this excited. She decided to play along for a while and made up silly responses

Finally getting serious, she asked, "Did you get us two tickets to a show at the theater? I really want to go back."

"Err, no, I'm afraid that's not it. But it's even better. I have two tickets in the center field bleachers under the scoreboard at Forbes Field for tomorrow's game with the Reds."

"And what is so exciting about that? They're in a slump this year. They lost today's game with Cincinnati. That gives them forty losses and twenty wins. What makes you think tomorrow will be any different?"

"Now, Sarah, I happen to know that you are a staunch Pirates fan. Just the other day I heard you dress down the neighbor man when he said the Pirates were a bunch of bums. Do you realize how hard it is to get a pair of these tickets? Your wonderful husband, that's me, dear, used his excellent persuasive powers to convince a business associate that he should sell me the tickets below cost. I did not tell him the late breaking news I had just heard." Leo smiled as he saw that Sarah's interests were aroused.

"And what, pray tell, is this hot news tip that you have, wonderful husband of mine?"

"Dear lady, I have discovered that the manager of our fair city's baseball team has been sacked and the great Honus Wagner will be the field manager of the team tomorrow. I have already placed a ten dollar bet on the mighty Pirates."

"Gee, Leo, that's a lot of money to be betting. Do you think it's wise?"

Leo laughed. "The Flying Dutchman will not let us down. After I collect my bet, I will treat you to an excellent meal at that little restaurant we like on the other side of Schenley Park. Sarah, the weather is supposed to be perfect. Wear your rose-colored dress. It's still my favorite. I want all the men to say, 'There goes that lucky Leo Brown with the most beautiful woman in Pittsburgh.'"

Sarah's face was radiant with a smile as she responded, "I can never be sad with you around. It's settled then, we shall go tomorrow dressed like the nobility we are."

Leo and Sarah enjoyed a wonderful day at the ballpark. Leo was proud of the enthusiasm Sarah showed for his favorite sport. Maybe it did concern him a little when she voiced her feelings a little too freely. One time after what she thought was a bad call by the umpire, he pulled her down gently and said, "Dearest, that name you just called the umpire was not very ladylike."

"Who cares about being ladylike? I'm here to win this game. Come on, Cooper, strike him out! Oh, Leo, this is so much fun." She grabbed Leo to give him a big hug and then she was on her feet yelling further encouragement to the pitcher. Leo feared he had created a monster.

Sarah almost bounced along the path through the park after the game. "I'm sorry I hit you in the eye with my parasol in the last inning. Oh my, it's turning black and blue. I just got so excited I didn't realize what I was doing. How will you explain that eye at work on Monday? We knocked the tar out of those Reds. Can we go again real soon?"

"Please, Sarah, you are rattling on so, I can't get a word in. We didn't knock the tar out of them. The score, if you would have taken time to notice, was five to four in our favor. When I show my friend this eye and tell him you beat me up at the game, he may take pity on me and sell me tickets to another game."

"Tell me you do still love me even after I beat you up."

"Watching you made that the most enjoyable ballgame I ever went to. Next time I bring you, I plan to see if I can borrow the catcher's face mask for protection. I love you, dearest, more than ever and each day my love grows. Now close that parasol and keep it out of harm's way here at the restaurant. And I don't want to hear you uttering any of those unladylike comments like you did at the park."

Sarah was totally enjoying herself as she looked very seriously at Leo and said, "Yes, sir. I will try to make you proud of me." Then she turned and sauntered into the restaurant.

Sarah was still in high spirits all day Monday after the weekend. She prepared Leo's favorite meal, roast beef, and put on a new dress she had bought that day. She rushed to meet him when the door opened. "Leo, what is wrong? There's such a troubled look on your face. Come sit at the table. I made us roast beef for dinner."

"Ever since your country entered the war in April, I was afraid this would happen."

"What happened? What's wrong, Leo?"

"A man from immigration services came by today. The Canadian legislature is about to pass a conscription bill. All draft-age Canadian men like me are being told to report home. Sarah, I've thought about this all day. Last week a letter came from a school friend of mine. He's enlisting in the Canadian Expeditionary Forces the second week of July. Enlisting gives him some flexibility to pick how he will serve. He's going to try to drive an ambulance. He asked me to come with him. I know this is sudden, but I've decided to take up his offer. It will be better to go now and drive an ambulance than to wait to be drafted and become machine gun fodder or freeze to death in the trenches."

"Don't leave me, Leo. Stay here with me. My mother has a friend in Congress. We can work something out."

"We've been all through this before. I've prayed for this war to end quickly, but it keeps dragging on, consuming human life. If I stay here I'll be declared a traitor by my country. I will never be able to return and see my parents. I must go do my duty. At least this way I will return safely to you. Besides, there are signs the war will soon be over. Probably I will get to France just in time to be shipped back to your waiting arms. On the positive side, our company president is very patriotic and he guarantees that anyone joining up will get their job back after it's over. When I come back we will change this apartment in for a big house with a view of the rivers."

"What if you don't come back? I can't survive without you."

"Don't talk like that. I'll be back in your arms before you know it. I'll talk to the landlord. Under the circumstances, I'm sure we will be able to break our contract. I want you to go home to your mother while I am gone. The army doesn't pay me enough to keep this apartment. Besides, I will feel better knowing you are safe at your mother's house. It will really only be for a short time, my dear."

For Sarah the rest of the week passed like a hazy nightmare as she prepared for Leo's departure. She begged him to stay longer, but he told her that the longer he waited the harder it would be to leave. Then, too, he wanted to spend a few days with his parents before he met up with his friend.

Saturday, the seventh of July, dawned a dreary, rainy day. This only added to the mood Sarah was in as she accompanied Leo to Union Station. Several times she burst out into tears as they passed areas that reminded her of the happy times they had together. Finally they reached the station and sat waiting for the train.

"Now remember, Sarah, if you need any more money we still have some savings in the bank. The neighbors have all offered to help in any way they can. Don't forget, you must be out of the apartment by the end of the month."

"Oh. Leo, I can't bear to watch you go. Still, I need to be with you as long as I can. Promise me you will write me every day."

"I will write as often as possible. Here comes the train." They rose and walked slowly out the platform to the boarding area. Sarah clung desperately to Leo. Finally he kissed her gently, and she released her grip. As he walked into the train, he looked back and yelled, "I love you, Sarah Brown. I will always love you."

Sarah turned away slowly and sadly walked back to the station on the platform. Things would never be the same.

> *The postman has just delivered a couple letters from Leo. It has boosted my spirits to see his handwriting on the envelope. Two of the neighbors have helped me with the packing of the items I am bringing home. Next week I will sell off the other items and clean the apartment. I have purchased a ticket to Greencastle on the 28th and should arrive at the station shortly after six. Funny, it was only a short time ago when I boldly boasted that I would never leave Pittsburgh. Life is so unfair. Please do not tell anyone I am coming. I need to be alone with you for a while before the family asks me a lot of questions.*
>
> *Your loving daughter,*
> *Sarah*

Kate folded up the last letter and placed it back in the jewelry box. There was silence in the room as everyone reflected on the contents of the letters.

Lou finally broke the silence, "Right now I feel so sad for my mother. As we were reading the letters I could almost see her as a young girl in her teens watching that train pull away. I just wanted to reach out to her and console her like a parent consoles her child. She loved that man so very much and he was ripped from her by the misfortunes of war. As she walked back on the platform that day, I think she knew he was never going to return."

Bill's appetite kicked in, interrupting his thoughts. "Say, wasn't there some of that cake of Aunt Kate's left? It would be a shame to see it go to waste."

"We're all overcome with the beautiful love between Sarah and Leo and her catastrophic loss at the end. What does Bill think about all this? His only concern is laying claim to a remaining piece of cake. Men, I will never understand them." Gail smiled at Bill and patted him on the stomach to show she was joking. "Come on, my hungry little boy, I will cut you a generous slice of cake to fill your tummy."

"Gee, Gail, while you're up, please cut me a piece too," Eddy added and winked.

"I guess the old saying, 'the way to a man's heart is through his stomach,' is proved true once again. Two pieces of cake coming up."

"I did find the letters very interesting," Eddy continued. "From a historical perspective they were fascinating. However, there is still no connection between our mystery flower person and Leo. Please do not take this wrong, I believe you are chasing the wrong ghost. We should have a brainstorming session and come up with alternate possibilities to pursue. Mmm, this cake is delicious. Can you give the recipe to Dottie?"

"Eddy, Kate uses my chocolate cake recipe! It's that secret peanut butter icing of hers that makes it different. You tell your sister-in-law to show me how she makes it. Now what are we going to do with this box of letters?"

"Just keep them here for now," Kate piped in.

Bill glanced at his watch and stood up. "Well, it's almost ten o'clock. I better get Gail home."

CHAPTER 9
Wedding Bells

As they drove to Gail's apartment, Bill said, "I was thinking about Leo's and Grandma's and Eddy's comments earlier. On further reflection, I don't know what I would have done if I were in Leo's place. At his age I remember I had that I-can-conquer-the-world attitude. I probably would have made the same decision he did, thinking nothing could happen to me and wanting to serve my country."

Gail snuggled next to him and responded, "Don't even think about it, buster. There's no way I will ever let you go away on any dangerous missions without taking me along. As long as I'm there nothing will happen to you. Besides, we can't go anywhere right now. We are going to be busy helping your mother get ready for her wedding during the next few months. We have guest lists to prepare and invitations to send out shortly. Did your mother tell you Jim's latest twist to this wedding?"

"With everything else happening, she hasn't mentioned anything to me. Can you fill me in?"

"Hold on to your steering wheel. You mother and Jim used to slip away to the Hagerstown City Park and take walks around the lake last year before the accident. There's a wooded area next to the art museum. In a rocky area of the woods there's a drop-off down to a spring near the lake. A bridge runs around the top of the drop off with a view down to a quiet pool near the spring below. That's where Jim has decided they will exchange their wedding vows."

"Suppose it rains?"

"Then we take the traditional approach and head for the church."

"An outside wedding in a scenic area could be fun. Mom had the traditional wedding with Dad. If she agrees with Jim, I think they should go for it."

"It gets even better as we move into the attendants. Jim wants you to be his best man and your mother thinks Eddy should walk her down the aisle, or I mean stone walkway."

"What about the bridal party?"

"Well, Dottie is the logical choice for maid of honor. However, since that was Dottie's position when your mom and dad got married, everyone feels we need someone different. Kate was the next logical choice until she assured us with some very descriptive language that she was too old to be in the wedding. Yours truly is now the maid of honor."

"I like it. We hold the number two positions on both sides. It'll get us ready for our big day."

"I can assure you that my mother plans for us to be one hundred and ten percent traditional."

"Gail, while we are on the subject, we haven't discussed a wedding date. Since our engagement, whenever I mention anything about our wedding you seem evasive. Is there something we need to talk about?"

"Yes, I know we need to talk. You have changed my whole world in so many wonderful ways. Yet, I am so scared and confused inside. Becoming engaged to you was a big step for me. I never dreamed I would be so fortunate. I'm very scared that I will fail as your wife and you will wind up hating me. Besides, not being able to have children, I'm a career woman. I really look forward to going to work five days a week. I'm not ready to give that up and become a stay-at-home mom. You know I have trouble boiling water without burning it. We'll starve to death."

"Before I met you I never gave marriage much thought. You've been with my family long enough to see how close knit we are. I've always had someone to talk to, support me and help me. Recently, however, I felt something was missing. Then we met and I knew almost instantly that I wanted to marry you. It all seemed so natural to me. Look, I understand marriage is a big step. When I think of all the things we've been through in the last few months and how we worked together as a team to keep the paper operating and resolve problems, I know we can solve any problems that come up in our marriage because we communicate well with each other. I don't see any reason why you can't stay working at the paper, unless you don't want to work for your future father-in-law. There's no reason to quit even when we adopt children. Mom and Aunt Dottie have already volunteered for all of the babysitting we can give them. My mother and aunts are great cooks. We'll learn from them and buy a few books. We won't starve."

Gail saw that they had arrived at her apartment. She pleaded with Bill, "You are so good to me and always dispel my fears. Don't leave me right now, Bill. We need to get plans for our future started."

Bill looked at his watch and remarked, "But it's almost eleven o'clock."

"Why, Bill, we're almost married. Are you afraid to be alone with me tonight? Whops, you caught me, I planned to get you in my apartment and seduce you." Gail opened her door and waited for Bill to help her out of the truck.

Bill sang a new song he had heard on the radio as they walked to the apartment. He couldn't imagine life being any better than this, but he was saying that an awful lot of late.

As Lou sat in the church pew she reflected on Easter and the theme of rebirth that came with the season. She wished Jane could be here to see the beautiful spring flowers. Jane always found joy in her flowers. Now as she sat there on the fifteenth of April, Lou also reflected on last year's service—Denny was on the road so Kate made an excuse not to come, Eddy and Dottie went to the bay house and Bill was off on a fishing trip. Lou had felt so alone and old watching everyone else file in with family.

She reflected on how much difference a year could make, as Kate, Denny, Randy and Jessie came in and were forced to sit in front of her. With Eddy, Dottie, Bill, Gail and Jim in this pew it was quite full. Still they had managed to find room for Lauren and Ted when they arrived. Yes, God had truly blessed her this year. She looked across the pew and saw that Lauren was embracing Gail's hand as she was Bill's. It reminded her of the phone conversation a few weeks ago. Bill had just come home from seeing Gail and was walking in the house when the phone rang.

She picked up the receiver and Lauren said, "Lou, I just heard. Bill has made such a positive change in Gail's outlook on life. And now she calls me with this news."

At this point Lou wasn't sure if the news was good or bad, so she responded, "Hold on, Lauren, Bill just came through the door and we haven't talked yet."

"Oh, I guess I spoiled his surprise. The kids spent most of the evening talking over their future plans and Gail's fear that she cannot be a good wife. One of the things they talked about was religion. You know we talked and I told you that it was good to see Gail going to church with you and Bill. Lou, Gail called first thing this morning to tell me that she decided to join your church on Easter. Bill called the minister. He said it's not the usual time to accept new adult members. However, after Gail insisted he agreed. I want to be at the service and I think Dad may come. Perhaps we could all go out to lunch afterwards."

As the news spread the whole family decided to come and share in the celebration. Yes, Lou knew God had been good to her this year. Too bad her mother could not be here, she always appreciated having the whole family together in church.

Now the minister was calling for Lou, Jim, Bill and Gail to come forth. He announced to the congregation that Gail was becoming a new member with Bill and his family sponsoring her. As the minister ran through the brief service for new members, Lou glanced back at Lauren and saw the tears of joy in her eyes. Yes, this truly was a blessed day for the whole family.

Later at lunch Ted approached Bill, "I just wanted to apologize for the way I reacted the first day I met you. Sometimes I'm overprotective of Gail. I must confess I was also jealous of you. Before meeting you, Gail would visit me several times a month. I cherished that time with her. As your relationship grew she came to see me less often. I resented you stealing her away from me. When I see how happy she is now and how much her life has changed for the better, I realize that I was just being a selfish, lonely old man. Forgive me, Bill."

"No, Ted, it is I who should ask your forgiveness for not realizing that I was monopolizing Gail's time. Perhaps we could both visit you and set up a day when we could go hunting together."

"That would be a great idea. Lauren is motioning to me. I think she needs to get home."

After seeing Gail's family depart, Bill joined the main conversation as Dottie spoke, "Let's all stop back at our house when we leave here. I want to show you girls the silver pin in the shape of a rose that I bought today. I want your opinion on how it looks with my sequined dress."

Everyone agreed it was a good idea to meet at Dottie and Eddy's house. When they arrived Lou saw Sarah's jewelry box on the table. She exclaimed, "Dottie, I thought you had put the jewelry box away in your bedroom."

"Eddy recommended we make extra copies of the letters for everyone. They're over there on the counter when you leave. Here, I'll take the box back into my bedroom with us. Follow me, girls. You guys have a seat here in the kitchen and I'll be back to model my ensemble."

Eddy and Bill found drinks for the men, and Lou, Kate and Gail followed Dottie as she chatted on, "It is oval shaped with a gorgeous rose in the center. My initials are carved around the rose. I can't wait to wear it." Dottie's mind was on her new find as she proceeded toward the bedroom. She didn't notice the pair of eyes staring at her through the glass doors on the porch. However, the eyes did not go unnoticed. Jake was lying in the corner of the living room near the bedroom. He immediately recognized his enemy, the beagle from the house across the street. In an instant he was on his feet and bounding toward the door to evict this unwanted guest from his property. Too late, Dottie heard his gruff bark and saw the fox-red blur charging toward her. Caught off balance from the collision, Dottie tumbled to the floor. The jewelry box flew out of her hands and crashed into the wall breaking into several pieces.

Eddy jumped up and quickly moved to Dottie. "Are you alright, dear? I can't understand what got into Jake. He's never done anything like that before. Where did he go?"

"I think I'm alright. Nothing is broken here. Oh, I spoke too fast. Look at Mom's jewelry box. There are pieces everywhere. Help me up please, Eddy."

Bill piped in, "I think I just saw a beagle run by the window. They don't watch that dog next door. Old Jake must have spotted him and was trying to chase him off."

Gail was picking up the pieces of the jewelry box. Bill moved to help her. They took the pieces to the kitchen table and Jim examined them. "It doesn't look too bad, Dottie. The hinges broke off the lid. I can glue it back together. What's this other piece, Bill? Turn the box over. There, it's a cover for a little secret compartment on the bottom. We never saw it because there was no need to examine the bottom before. Now wait, there's something in the compartment. It looks like a piece of paper. That's weird. Why hide a piece of paper in that little compartment?"

"I think I know what it is. May I have it?" Bill reached excitedly for the paper as everyone gathered around the table.

Bill unfolded the torn piece of paper. Gail's eyes widened. "Bill, you guessed it right away. It's the missing page from the journal."

Bill glanced at the page for a few seconds and then handed it to Gail. "I believe the honor of reading this page falls to the person who has persistently insisted the answer lay in Sarah's past."

Gail took the crumpled sheet and smoothed it out. "This isn't Sarah's usual neat handwriting. It's jumbled at spots, like she might have been upset and shaking while writing. Dear Sarah, she still took time to date her entry. March 10, 1961. If I remember correctly, that's the day she visited the doctor in York. Oh my, listen to this."

It cannot be. I must be wrong; for, if I am right, I have lived a wretched lie these last forty years. There I was waiting for my turn in the doctor's office. Sure I was nervous. My life hung on the decisions this doctor would make for me. Still I do not believe my fears would cloud my judgment. I sat there awaiting my turn and didn't notice the other patients. I heard a commotion at the receptionist's desk. The man's back was turned to me as he assured the receptionist that he had a three o'clock appointment. Where had I heard that voice before? Suddenly it didn't matter. I had the three o'clock appointment. After spending an hour and a half driving, I was not giving up my spot to anyone. Prepared for a fight, I was relieved to hear the receptionist in a condescending voice tell the man that he needed to get his eyes checked. With finality, she told him that the apparent zero in the date of March tenth was a six. She said his appointment was on the sixteenth—take it or leave it. The man agreed to the sixteenth. When he turned to leave, I glanced at him. Our eyes made contact and he smiled. Dear God in heaven, I saw my Leo at that instant. The voice, the deep blue eyes, and the way he smiled. I knew as he closed the office door that it was him.

I don't know what possessed me. I jumped up like a school girl and ran through the door after him. Flinging myself on him I babbled, "Leo, I love you. I never stopped loving you."

He pushed me away and gruffly said, "Lady, are you crazy? I don't know you."

"You smiled in there just now when you recognized me. Leo, where were you all these years?"

"For an instant there you looked like someone I knew. Like the receptionist said, my eyes are playing tricks on me. Now leave me alone. My name's not Leo."

I stood there in shock as he stormed off. The receptionist stuck her head out and told me I was next. I turned and let him get away again. Later I asked the receptionist for his name. She told me all information on the patients is confidential. I was so mad at myself until I realized he was coming back on the sixteenth at three.

I must go back and find some way to get him to talk to me. There has to be an explanation. There just has to be a logical explanation.

I cannot tell the children. It would break their hearts to know I harbored such feelings all these years. They must never know.

"Oh shit," the words just slipped out of Kate's mouth, "Gail's been on the right trail all along and we didn't believe it. I thought it was nice learning more about Mom's early years before she married Dad. I never believed Leo was connected to the roses. He's dead. We have his death certificate. Can this be possible, Ed?"

"Anything is possible, Kate. However, we have to remember that Sarah was a lonely, scared widow as she even admitted on this page. Secondly, she had not seen or heard Leo speak for over forty years. Under these circumstances, most probably she was mistaken. Also, Sarah came from an age where it was wrong to be married to Richard and still harbor the feelings she had for Leo. Sarah carried a lot of shame and guilt due to those feelings. She was a proud woman and could never let out this secret. That's why she hid this page and the relationship that I suspect grew between her and the man she thought was Leo in the doctor's office."

"It's Leo, Eddy. The doctor's records in the hospital had the wrong height. Do you remember?"

"Gail, you are such a romanticist. In the heat of battle, the doctor made a mistake. Anyhow, we'll never know. This guy changes his flower delivery date every year. What are you going to do—camp out in the cemetery every night in April, May and June?"

"Gee, Eddy, how did you guess my intentions?"

Bill hoped Gail was not serious, but her tone of voice made him wonder. He decided to end the debate, "Wow, we have to get going if we are going to make that movie at the mall. Has anyone seen any more of old Jake?"

Dottie spoke up, "We got so involved in that page from the journal, I forgot to show everyone my pin and dress. Let me go slip into the dress and check on Jake. He hides under our bed when he knows he is in trouble. I'll let him off easy this time."

Later, on the way to the movie, Bill questioned, "Were you serious when you told Eddy you were going to sleep in the cemetery until you caught the mystery person?"

"No, he was just so obstinate after I insisted Leo is still alive. I lost my cool for an instant. Eddy's correct. This man resembled Leo and he's our mystery person. I would still like to meet him. I feel like he should be part of your family. Maybe we could leave a note at the gravesite. He probably doesn't like publicity, but he may come forward in a quiet meeting."

"That's a good idea. We'll compose something to put in a waterproof pouch and attach it to the stone. Let's park here at the back of the mall."

The days leading up to the wedding were filled with the final preparations for Lou and Jim's big day. The small intimate wedding in the park had grown in size to about fifty guests as various friends and some associates from the paper were added to the list. Everyone pitched in to make the unconventional event as memorable as possible. Everybody anxiously watched the weather report as the days rolled toward the twelfth. At dinner after the rehearsal on the eleventh, Eddy broke the bad news, "I just checked the weather report again. Thunderstorms are definitely moving in for tomorrow."

"The service starts at eleven," Dottie thought aloud, "it should be over by eleven-thirty. Was there any indication on when the storms would reach our area?"

"Dear, you know how unreliable the weatherman is. The report said the storms would begin in the morning and be heavy in local areas."

Lou spoke up, "There's been so much planning and effort by everyone at this table. Jim and I are so lucky to have you all help us realize his dream."

"Lou, it's the least we could do for you and Jim," Kate said. "Jim's struggled so hard to come back from the accident; we wanted to do something special for him. Now you all know I like to live on the edge at times. For what it's worth I say we go for it. Let's meet at the park in the morning and bring umbrellas. There are two pavilions in the area that can give us shelter if the rain comes before we are done."

Jim broke in, "As I sat here thinking over the last year I remembered Sarah's words to her mother in one of the letters. She told her mother that she could never return to her old life after experiencing life in Pittsburgh with Leo. Today I feel like Sarah. After falling in love with Lou and being warmly welcomed into this supportive family, I never want to go back to the life I had. From the bottom of my heart, I thank everyone around this table for the support you gave me during the difficult early days of my recovery. Like Kate, I say let's go for it. The worst that can happen is we all get soaked. Is everyone with us?"

Kate's family and Bill and Gail met at the park at ten on Saturday morning to decorate the area and set up a few chairs for those not able to stand during the service. With an uneasy feeling they all watched the cloud cover build.

At quarter to eleven the groom arrived and so did a sprinkle of rain. Everyone was in position at eleven when Dottie approached Pastor Jones and told him the bride was ready. Now the pastor proceeded down to a small ledge near the pond. Bill helped Jim, now walking with a cane, to maneuver down the stone steps. With a nod by the minister, a portable cassette player was turned on and Gail emerged from behind a clump of trees and proceeded to the stone steps as the music began. At this point the music switched to the wedding march and Lou appeared in a simple peach chiffon dress. Together she and Gail maneuvered down the stone steps as a crack of thunder pealed.

Ignoring the rumble overhead, the pastor plunged into the service as Denny moved silently around finding the best angle to capture the moment on his camera. As Pastor Jones announced, "You may kiss the bride," a sprinkle of raindrops bouncing off the surface of the ponds signaled the onslaught of the downpour. Now a flurry of umbrellas unfurled and a mad rush to the cars ensued as the skies opened with a vengeance.

That evening Gail lay on the couch in her apartment unable to sleep. She had convinced her mother to stay over. They had talked for hours before Lauren went to bed. However, the excitement of the day still flowed through Gail's mind. The wedding and reception afterward seemed finally to erase some of the old fears that had been haunting her from the past. Finally she could tell Bill that she was ready for them to pick a date to pledge their undying love forever and ever.

Gail got up and made herself a cup of coffee. As she sat her mug down, it occurred to her that Lou's wedding date was about one week before Leo and Sarah's. As she mulled this thought over in her mind it suddenly hit her that the dates the flowers appeared in the cemetery were scattered around the twentieth of May. With a start she sat upright. Perhaps there was a pattern. She rushed to her desk and turned the light on. Fumbling through a stack of copies, she found a few pages with calendars on them. While in the library doing research on an article one day, she had stumbled on a book of calendars from the past. At that time the years from 1914 through 1920 appeared to hold significance in Sarah's life. On impulse she made copies of these years.

Gail pulled the 1915 sheet out of the stack and began digging through her notes from her first meeting with Bill. There were the dates: April 30, May 11, May 15, May 28, and June 3. She marked them on her calendar and tried to draw a circle through them that would have the twentieth as its center. After realizing that the points did not form a circular pattern around Sarah and Leo's wedding date, she became discouraged. Pushing the calendar aside, her mind returned to thoughts of how handsome Bill looked today. Doodling on a scrap of paper, her mind was busy creating images of her wedding day.

Suddenly the lights flickered and then everything went black. Gail returned to reality and fumbled for a flashlight at the back of the desk. When she flipped the flashlight switch on its beam illuminated her page of doodling that now lay on top of the calendar. Grabbing the pen she drew the outline of a new pattern on the calendar and then rushed to the telephone.

Bill heard the telephone ringing and flipped on his light. Nothing happened. He rolled over to look at his clock, but the illuminated numbers weren't there. He rolled out of the bed and stumbled to the kitchen. He hoped everything was alright with his mother and Jim. They had left after the reception to stay in a motel near the airport. In the darkness he searched for the telephone and finally picked up the receiver.

"Bill, I figured it out. I know when our mystery person will deliver the next flowers."

By now Bill had found matches and a candle his mother left in the kitchen for this type of emergency. Lighting the candle, he saw his watch on the corner of the counter. He glanced at its dial and exclaimed, "Gail, it's two a.m. and our electricity is off. I thought Mom was calling with a problem."

"Gee, I am sorry, Bill. I was so excited, I didn't stop to think what time it is. Go back to sleep and we'll talk in the morning."

"It's a good thing I love you. I'm awake now. Tell me what made you so excited."

"I couldn't sleep."

"So I notice."

"Bill, let me finish! A lot of things were flowing through my mind tonight. Sit down for this one. Today helped me finally throw out some of those skeletons in my closet. Now I am ready to pick our wedding date."

"Terrific, you can wake me up anytime with that kind of news."

"Well, ah, that's not why I called. Still not able to sleep, I plotted the dates the flowers appeared on a 1915 calendar expecting to draw a circle through them that surrounded Sarah's wedding date. It didn't work and I started daydreaming about us. Without thinking about it I was doodling as I daydreamed. You know how I do that sometimes. The lights went out and when I turned my flashlight on I saw a series of hearts I had drawn with our names in the middle. That's when it hit me. The dates the roses appeared are in a heart pattern around the twentieth of May on a 1915 calendar. Our mystery romantic is plotting a heart-shaped pattern of rose deliveries around Sarah and Leo's wedding date. There are a few missing dates on the outline, but there's only one unused day left this year. Bill, our mystery man will show up at the cemetery on the twenty-sixth of May to fill in another point on the heart."

"You're sure of this?"

"It's the only date left this year. If he's coming this year it will be on the twenty-sixth."

CHAPTER 10
A Night to Remember

"I still wish you kids wouldn't do this tonight. I know we are fairly certain that the person putting the flowers on the grave is an old man in his seventies. But how do you explain the threatening letter and car that followed you in York? This guy could get violent," Lou talked as she pulled the biscuits from the oven and carried them to the dining room table. "Jim and I had such a wonderful time on the cruise. Why do you have to take this chance right now?"

Lou sat down and Jim reached for her hand. "It will be OK, honey. Gail has spent a lot of time and energy on this story. She has to pursue every lead. When I was her age, I did the same. Just don't take any chances. Stay low until you're sure this guy's alone. If it looks like he's going to give you any trouble, high tail it out of there and we'll get the police to pursue him. Remember how we practiced. Bill, you flash that bright flashlight on his face and Gail will take a couple pictures. We got him then. If my legs didn't hurt so bad I'd come along for the fun."

Bill was thankful Jim had told him that he didn't want to be referred to as dad. He asked Bill to continue calling him Jim. Bill responded now, "Jim, you overdid it on that honeymoon cruise and need to rest now. Gail and I will do fine tonight."

Gail piped in, "I think it's kind of exhilarating like a safari. I can't help it. Whenever I do something different with Bill I get all excited like a school girl. Say, maybe we should wear some of Bill's camouflage hunting clothes so we can't be seen as we slither through the grass."

Gail still bubbled with enthusiasm as they hiked up through the cemetery, "See, I told you we wouldn't be able to see the truck up here near the road. Now let's see, did we bring everything? I have the camera, a small flashlight and a thermos of hot chocolate. You have the sleeping bag to keep us warm, plastic to put under it, a pillow, the large flashlight and the cookies. Are there any bats around here?"

"Help me spread out this sleeping bag where we won't be seen. Relax, there's no bats in sight. But I did hear they like chocolate chip cookies. Better watch out when you break open those cookies."

"Oh, Bill, you are so silly when you joke around. You were joking about the cookies, weren't you? Let's crawl in the sleeping bag and snuggle. What time is it?"

"It's a little past eleven. Wow, it is nice snuggling inside this old sleeping bag. Let's take our clothes off and get more comfortable."

"Bill, all you ever think of is sex. And what would we do if the mystery man showed up while we were doing the wild thing?"

"Well, he'd have to get his own sleeping bag; we're not sharing this one. Listen, I think I hear a bat. Open the cookies and see if it will come in."

"Don't try to fool me, Bill Henderson. Food and sex, that's all you think about. There are the cookies. Try to leave a few for later."

"First, it's not my fault that you turn me on all the time. Secondly, these cookies you made are really good. Why did you tell me you couldn't cook?"

After a couple hours Gail fell asleep and Bill held her in his arms. He wasn't convinced that anyone would show up this night. At first he was reluctant to spend the night in the cemetery. There were other places he would rather be with Gail. She was right; he couldn't keep his mind off sex when she was this close to him. Anyhow, it really hadn't been that bad. He had enjoyed lying next to her talking as they watched the stars above.

After Gail woke up they took a short walk around the roads in the cemetery. When they returned Bill could not keep his eyes open and he finally dozed off while Gail kept the vigil. He awoke as she shook him vigorously and whispered, "Wake up, Bill, a car just pulled aside the road and turned the lights off."

They hurriedly climbed out of the sleeping bag and started to creep toward Sarah's stone. At that point they heard the creak of a car door and then it slammed shut. Bill felt his heart pounding and glanced at Gail. In the pale moonlight he saw that she was shivering. However, there was a look of determination on her face that told him she would stick to the plan. There was a shuffling of the grass near the road and footsteps approached. The beam of a small penlight barely lit the ground, but Bill was concerned the man might see him next to Sarah's stone. Quietly he slid behind the next stone just before the man stopped and faced Sarah's stone. The man knelt in quiet contemplation for several minutes and propped the flowers in position.

As he started to rise, Bill glanced at Gail and saw she was ready. He jumped up and whistled. The man turned toward Bill and he turned the flashlight on. In an instant, Gail jumped up and the camera flashed two times.

"Oh my God, Bill, it's my grandfather. Gramps, what are you doing here? It's not true. Tell me you aren't the person Sarah saw in the doctor's office that day."

Bill stepped around the tombstone in front of him and said, "Gail, we have a problem here. Your grandfather needs help. Here, hold the light for me. Let me help you back to the car, Mr. Price."

Ted was breathing heavily and was obviously in pain. "Need...my pills...in car," he stammered between deep breaths.

Gail ran to get the pills as Bill helped Ted toward the car. It seemed like an eternity as they slowly crept toward the passenger's side of the car. Gail had the door open and focused the light on her grandfather as he took two pills.

When Bill recommended they go to the emergency room, Ted explained that everything would be fine in a few minutes. Bill changed his approach and said to Gail, "Let's go to your apartment. We'll see how he's doing at that time. We can call an ambulance from there if we need to. You drive his car. I'll pick up our things and meet you there." Gail agreed and Bill rushed back to roll up the sleeping bag and take it with him to the truck. He glanced at his watch and noted that it was almost four o'clock.

Bill jumped out of his truck at the apartment parking area and ran to Gail's side at the car. Ted's breathing was not as heavy and color had returned to his face. "I still think you should go to the hospital, Gramps. It would make me feel better."

"Child, there's nothing they can do to make this old body work right again. Bill, please help me to the apartment. I am very weak right now."

Bill supported Ted into the apartment and helped him lie down on the sofa. Ted closed his eyes and Bill went into the kitchen to help Gail make coffee.

When Bill stepped into the kitchen he saw Gail standing in the corner crying. As he comforted her, she sobbed, "Bill, I'm such an idiot. All the clues were there in front of me. Gramps was wounded in the war. He's tall and has blue eyes. I'm such a great newspaper reporter. Why didn't I make the connection? Now I pulled this stupid stunt tonight and almost killed him. Do you think he will ever forgive me?"

"Gail, we all know your grandfather and none of us ever pictured him as Leo. Don't blame yourself. I just don't understand why he didn't tell us that he was the one putting the roses on Grandma's grave."

"No, Bill, no. Gramps is not Leo. He's Ted Price. Don't try to tell me he's Leo." Gail pulled herself away and went back to making coffee. Bill knew she was still very upset. He needed help at this point.

"Gail, let me call Mom and have her come over. She can help us work through this thing."

Gail wiped the tears from her eyes and nodded her head in agreement. Bill dialed the telephone and heard his mother's voice. "Mom, we caught the mystery person. Trouble is he turned out to be Gail's grandfather. The shock of us surprising him at the cemetery almost gave him a heart attack. We're at the apartment now and things are not going well. I know it's awful early, but can you come in?"

"Gail's grandfather—I would have never guessed he knew my mother. I'll be right there, dear." Lou's reassuring voice calmed Bill.

After hanging up, he checked on Ted and found him sleeping. Back in the kitchen Gail sat at the table staring into space. "Your grandfather's asleep and Mom's coming in. How are you feeling?"

"I was just sitting here thinking about going to visit Gramps and Gram when I was a little girl. They were always so excited to see me. I would go into the kitchen, drag all the pots and pans out and make a mess scattering them on the floor. The whole time Gramps would encourage me and Gram would scold him. It was all a big game and I laughed the whole time. Then one day I came to visit and Gram wasn't there anymore. The laughter went out of Gramps' life. He and Gram were made for each other. He was not married to Sarah. I know my grandfather. He would never have lied to Gram. Sarah was wrong."

"Gail, there is some logical explanation for all of this. Let's wait until my mom gets here. She will help us sort it out. When your grandfather wakes up, I am sure he will explain everything. Let me get you a cup of coffee. It's been a long night."

Bill heard car doors slamming outside. He went to the door and opened it. Lou and Jim entered. "I hope you don't mind, dear, Jim came along. He's going to walk over later and open the paper."

Lou checked on Ted and then proceeded to the kitchen. Gail smiled and they hugged. "Thanks for coming, Lou. I'm just so confused right now and ashamed of myself. What would I have done if Gramps would have died out there? I would have killed him."

"Don't blame yourself for any of this, Gail," Jim came in. "Throughout history great detectives and reporters have missed important clues when they were emotionally involved. As for tonight, well, I'm to blame. Remember, I was the one who coached you on the picture taking. Let's have a cup of coffee and then we'll wake Ted up and see if he's up to talking with us."

A short while later they heard movement in the living room and Bill went to check on Ted. "How are you feeling, Mr. Price? Gail made coffee and has some delicious homemade cookies in the kitchen. Are you up to joining us?"

Ted walked into the now crowded kitchen and sat at the table. "Young man, I have told you before, my name is Ted. Mr. Price is too formal."

Gail poured a cup of coffee and handed it to her grandfather. "Please forgive me, Gramps. I never wanted to hurt you."

"My dear, it is I who must beg forgiveness of you and everyone here. I have been an old fool for leading you on so long. Sarah made me promise not to tell you wonderful people anything and I respected her wish. I realize now that she was wrong. It's time this story be told. But first I must address my granddaughter's concerns. Your gram meant the world to me and I never lied to her. According to the record I was born in 1898 in Chicago. I will return to this later. However, my life as I know it began on a cold September morning in 1918. As long as I live, I will vividly remember that morning."

Everyone felt themselves being transported back in time as Ted told his story.

Ted had a terrible headache and pain shot up his left leg. He realized his whole body felt sore when he opened his eyes and looked around. It was very cold in the small room. Through a pair of open double doors, he saw a large room full of beds with several nurses moving about. Trying to get out of bed, he realized he was tied to the bed. When he yelled for help, a nurse going by the door heard and transferred the message, "Pat, your nutcase needs you."

A nurse slightly older than the others soon walked toward the door. "Now calm down, Mr. Price. I hope we can get some liquid in you." When she saw him staring at her, she stopped short. "You're awake. Thank goodness. I told that doctor you would come around. I saw a man horse kicked in the head a few years back. He was in a coma longer than you were. Then one day he woke up, went out, and shot the horse. Can you speak?"

Ted mumbled, "Why...I tied down?"

"Good question, Mr. Price. You about half woke up several times thrashing about and making terrible sounds. We moved you back here so you wouldn't scare the other patients and tied you down so you wouldn't fall out of bed. I got some liquid into you to keep you from dehydrating before you drifted out again. This is the first time you were able to speak. The swelling in your brain must be going down."

Ted tried to speak again and his words were jumbled. He concentrated and continued slow and deliberate, "Untie me, please. Where am I?"

Pat busied herself with the ropes. "You're in a hospital near Paris. I was in a treatment center near the front when they brought you in. The doctor said you wouldn't last the night with your injuries. I insisted he stop the bleeding and send you here. He didn't like me interfering with his decisions so he had me transferred also. There now, Mr. Price, you are free. Let me get you some food."

Ted tried to sit up and would have fallen out of bed if Pat had not caught him. "You have to be more careful. Your body is weak from not eating and we don't know the extent of the muscular damage from your injury. Just lay there until I get back."

Ted drifted in and out of consciousness. He awoke to the noises of Pat busily setting up a tray of food on his bed. "Col-ld." The word fell in a slur from his mouth.

Pat went into the hall and returned in a minute with an extra blanket. "I checked with the head nurse. She's going to move you to the ward as soon as a bed is open, Mr. Price."

"Why...you...call me Mr. Price?"

"Because that's your name. Now let's see if we can get some of this nourishment into you."

Slowly Ted's strength improved and he was awake for longer periods. After a few days he was able to sit up in bed. Pat smiled as she entered the room. "You look so much better today. There's an orderly coming in a few minutes and we are going to get you out of bed and try out those legs. Remember, Mr. Price, you may need some practice making things work again."

Ted was still having trouble putting sentences together as he said, "I don't remember things."

"People with head injuries lose their memory sometimes. Do you remember anything of the night you were injured?"

Ted made a negative gesture with his head and said, "I can't remember who I am."

Pat wanted to make sure she understood and asked, "Do you remember where you lived, worked, family, friends or anything from your past?"

After Ted indicated negatively, Pat assured him, "Don't worry. Temporary memory loss is normal in these cases. It will come back. Here's our orderly. See if you can swing your legs over the side of the bed."

Ted stopped telling his story and drank from his coffee cup. Gail used this opportunity to ask, "So you met Gram in the hospital in Paris when she was your nurse?"

"Yes, I owe my life to your grandmother. I would have died that first night and also later in the hospital. Gram and the orderly found out I couldn't walk that day. Several more days they came back with the same results before the trouble began. In his haste, the field doctor had not cleaned my leg wound properly before he sewed it up. An infection set in and they had to operate and cut out the infected area. Then while I was recovering, pneumonia set in. Once again the doctor said I would die. Gram was determined not to lose me at this point and she was at my bedside every opportunity she got. Weeks slipped into months and the Armistice was signed in November. Gram and the orderly had just moved me to a chair beside my bed when the head nurse rushed down the center aisle waving a small American flag and yelling, 'The war is over; Germany has surrendered.' We all saluted and a chorus of The Star Spangled Banner broke out. I was ashamed. I didn't know the words.

"Almost immediately they started shipping the hospital cases home. I was scheduled with the first group when I suddenly developed a high fever. Gram sat by my bed as we watched the other beds empty out. She rolled me out in a wheelchair on the last day and turned the lights out. Many years later she told me that she refused to leave until I was ready to be shipped stateside."

Jim stood up stiffly at this point. "I must be getting to work. Someone has to open the paper and get the press running. Gail, stay here with your grandfather today. Ethel and I can take care of business."

Everyone took a break at this point and Gail asked, "Gramps, are you up to this? We can always talk more when you feel better."

"I need to tell the rest of the story. There were no crowds cheering and bands playing when we docked. An ambulance picked Gram and I up and transported us to the new Walter Reed Hospital in Washington. I guess the doctors wanted to study me. I was still having bouts of fever and no memory of the past had returned. As physical therapy continued, they pulled my file to contact my family. That's when they found out I was an orphan from Chicago and my next of kin was listed as one of the other fellows from the orphanage. As the weeks went by, some new drug they gave me finally cleared up the infection. I regained my strength and was able to walk again. Gram was discharged from the service and found a job in the area so she could visit me regularly. By then she was deeply in love with me. I loved her too, but I was a man without a past. What if I was a wanted criminal or had a wife somewhere? My doctor assured me that was impossible. If I had a criminal record, the army would not have taken me. If I had a wife, she would have been listed as next of kin.

"Finally, in the spring of 1919, the doctors decided there was nothing more they could do to revive my memory and I received a full medical discharge from the service. Gram wanted to get married right away, but I wouldn't hear of it. I would not talk of marriage unless I had a good job to support her. We were on a train north to the coalfields in Pennsylvania to meet her parents, when we met a couple former servicemen on their way to new jobs in Harrisburg. We got off the train with them and I was hired almost instantly. The rest is history. We were married six months later and had a wonderful life together. Gram had a rough time when Lauren was born and the doctor told us she was done having children. Later we moved to York when I got a promotion."

Bill took advantage of the break to ask, "Did any of the memory return? Did you ever try to find out more about your past?"

"I asked the doctor why the memory never returned. He said memory loss is usually not long term or permanent. High fever from the infection in conjunction with the severe head trauma may have totally wiped out my previous memory. I even tried a hypnotist with no success. At first we were too busy getting our lives back in order to do any serious research. When Lauren was about six years old, we left her with Gram's parents and we took a mini-vacation to Chicago to see if it brought back any memories. We stopped at the orphanage. I became very irritated when we were told they would not give us any information, citing confidentiality of their records. We rode around town one whole day hoping to spark a memory. I became frustrated because nothing looked familiar. Gram saw how it bothered me and we decided never to discuss my past again unless I had a need to. That's why we never told you and Lauren any of this. Until Sarah stepped into my life, it would have served no purpose to drag this all up again."

Lou spoke, "Then you had no recollection of ever being married to my mother during all the years you and Gail's gram were married?"

"Lou, I had no inkling your mother even existed until the spring of 1961. I still get mad at that receptionist when I think about the way she treated me. I told that impudent hussy that I was there for my appointment. She acted like I was a stupid idiot and insisted my appointment was the following week. As I stormed out of there I thought this one woman looked familiar from somewhere. I smiled at her and the next thing I knew she was hot on my tail calling me Leo. I thought she had lost her mind or something. I was still fuming from my conversation with the receptionist so I just stormed off. You can imagine my surprise when I went back the next week and she was there again waiting for me.

"This time Sarah had a different approach. She quickly told me she meant no harm. I just resembled a man she had married prior to the First World War. Then she asked if she could take me out to lunch to make up for the way she acted. I still didn't trust her. All the stories about scam artists and swindling old people had my defenses up. Still, I was a lonely widower and she was a good-looking woman. I took her to my favorite diner on Route 30. She told me about Leo and their happy years of marriage in Pittsburgh. Then she reached into her purse and brought out a picture of her standing next to a man who she said was Leo. It was her wedding picture. The man staring at me in the picture could have been my twin brother. He was heavier and more muscular than I was when I married Gram, but we had the same facial features. We talked some more and she told me he died on August 26, 1918. I nearly choked on my coffee as I realized this was only a couple weeks before I woke up in the hospital in Paris. Could there be something to this woman's story? Still wary, I did not tell her about my loss of memory. Instead we parted with a promise to meet again in a week."

Gail spoke up now, "When I saw you in the cemetery this morning, I thought the worst and became very upset. I just kept picturing you running out on Sarah to marry Gram. I knew you wouldn't do that. Bill calmed me down and assured me that you would explain everything when you woke up. I feel so much better now."

"Well, it's not over yet," Bill commented. "Are you Leo Brown or are you Ted Price?"

"Bill, the only name I've ever known is Ted Price. I'm Ted. Let me go on. Over the next several months Sarah and I met often and continued to talk. At first I maintained my evasiveness about my past. When I finally told her about my memory loss, she was convinced that I was Leo. She told me stories about her Pittsburgh days, read some old letters she had and showed me her wedding ring to no avail. Nothing sparked any long dormant memory in my brain.

"As we continued to date, one day I insisted on meeting her family. She got mad at me. We didn't see each other for over a month. Finally she called and told me that her family must never know about us. She said she would not bring the shame of what she had done down on her family. I didn't understand then, but now I realize that she never stopped loving Leo. That was a secret she guarded until her death. She even went so far as to use the children's home as an excuse for her frequent trips to York. She had me alter a plaque they gave me for my volunteer work to make it appear like it was hers.

"I need to return to Bill's question. Am I Leo Brown? Many nights I lay in bed with that question racing through my head. The United States government recognizes me as Ted Price, I have my pension check to prove it and people have called me Ted all my life. On the other hand, Sarah had some mighty convincing pictures and a story about a man named Leo Brown from long ago that she said was me. I don't know the answer and probably never will. Sarah and I grew very close and there were times I really wanted to be Leo for her sake. It would have closed the loop for her. She really needed that."

Gail spoke up again, "Gramps, I know you cared for Sarah. That's why you put the flowers on the grave. I also figured out the heart pattern of deliveries around the twentieth of May 1915. Why did you pick Sarah and Leo's marriage date for delivering the flowers, and is there any significance to the four roses with the white ribbon?"

"I never could hide anything from you. Every twentieth of May, Sarah would bring us up a bottle of champagne. We would celebrate that wedding day long ago, which she insisted was ours, by going out somewhere special to dinner and a show and then come home, crawl in bed and drink the champagne. Don't look at me that way, young lady! We were old, but everything worked just fine. Some things improve with age and experience. That's all I'm going to say on that subject.

"Getting back on track, the twentieth of May became our special night—sort of like an anniversary night. We never missed one. I had grown to love Sarah during our years together and needed to continue the tradition after she was gone. Then I remembered Sarah's story she told about her third wedding anniversary in 1918. Sarah told me how depressed she was that day not being with Leo on their anniversary. Then she heard a knock at her mother's door. After all those years her eyes still sparkled and a smile beamed across her face as she told me about the sight that greeted her as she opened the door. There stood the deliveryman with a bouquet of four red roses tied with a white ribbon. Sarah pondered why there were four roses until she opened Leo's note. He told her that three of the roses symbolized their three wonderful years of marriage. The fourth rose was to remind her that he would be home soon to share many more years together. The white ribbon was in remembrance of their child in heaven. Leo had written to a local business in Greencastle explaining that he was a soldier in France and he needed a bouquet delivered on the twentieth of May. It was probably the first FTD delivery.

"I knew Sarah would appreciate my special gift of the flowers. I added the baby's breath to symbolize our time together. Since I promised to keep our relationship a secret, I came up with the pattern of deliveries around the twentieth. It prevented you from guessing when I was coming for quite a few years."

"And Sarah was the friend that told you about the job at the paper."

"We had a lot of fun together scheming to get you hired. I called Sarah with your interview time. It was no accident that she came in right after you left and told Jim to hire you. She called me later that day and told me how forlorn you looked leaving the office. I wanted to call and cheer you up, but it would have made you suspicious.

"Later when we were talking about both of our grandchildren one night, we realized that you and Bill were a great match. We almost pulled that one off before she left me. I'm glad you two got together. I know Bill will always take good care of you.

"I am ashamed of that threatening letter I sent you. I panicked when I saw the newspaper article. I know you are a smart girl and sooner or later you would figure everything out. I thought my only hope was to scare you away. I should have known it wouldn't work. By the way, the car trailing you in York was not my idea. I wasn't working that day you were at the home. A friend of mine was there. He's a very nice person, but a little weird. I think he watches too many spy movies. We had talked about our families during break and he knew your name. He recognized you in the office. After calling my home and getting no answer, he made the decision to follow you until he saw that he had been spotted. I shouldn't have let these things happen. I was just so confused. I gave my word to Sarah and I saw everything was falling apart. I made some bad decisions. I am sorry."

"Gramps, I love you and I understand what you were feeling. Just look at the good that has come out of this episode in our lives. I am engaged to the most wonderful man in the world and his amazing family wants you, Mom and me to be a part of their lives. Finally, I have put my parents' divorce in proper perspective and I have a man who loves me even though I cannot have his children. I have also learned a lot about myself and the reporting business."

Lou had been listening quietly when an idea suddenly occurred to her. "Ted, you indicated that it bothers you a great deal at times not knowing anything about those missing years. Jim has friends in the newspaper business and Eddy has connections in Washington. Would you like to let them do some research? Maybe we could fill those years in for you."

"Lou, like I said earlier, I can't remember anything. That time period is just wiped clean. When I try to remember and nothing comes back, it gets very frustrating."

"Oh no, they wouldn't be trying to make you remember anything. We can do some digging around. Sometimes we leave trails in our lives that we never suspected were there."

"Well, I suppose there's no harm in taking a look as long as you realize there's nothing I can do to remember those missing years. It's all a big blank to me."

A few weeks later Bill and Gail met with Jim, Eddy, Lou and Dottie in Greencastle.

Eddy opened the conversation, "A friend of mine in Washington generously used some tax dollars to research Ted's records. We didn't find any information about his early years. However, we did find the names of three of his friends from the orphanage that joined up the same day as he did. One person was killed around the time Ted was wounded. He's the person that was listed on Ted's military papers as next of kin. We are still trying to track down an address or phone number on the second fellow. The third person appears to be living in Florida. A disability pension check is sent to this address every month. As far as we can determine, there's no telephone at the address. Now here's the interesting part. From his military records, we found out he was wounded August 26, 1918—the same day Leo was killed."

Jim spoke up, "Well, I have some interesting news also. I had an ad placed in the Hamilton, Ontario, newspaper stating that I was looking for relatives of a Leo Brown killed in World War I. I got a short letter from a man claiming to be his brother. Basically it gives his phone number and says call me."

"This is so exciting," Lou said. "Let me call this Mr. Brown right now. Surely he would remember Leo's wife from the U.S." Lou dialed the number and spoke, "Good evening, Mr. Brown. My name is Lou Martin. My mother Sarah married your brother Leo in Pittsburgh in 1915. After his death, my mother got remarried to my father. We are doing some ancestry research on my mother and wanted to talk to you about the years she spent with Leo."

"Listen, I'm 85 and I don't hear so well anymore. Can you repeat what you said?"

Lou repeated her comments, this time much louder.

Mr. Brown responded, "Oh, it was your ad that I answered. Let me see now, Leo did go off and marry an American girl. You say her name was Sally. That doesn't ring a bell. She sure was a looker. I almost followed him back across the border to get me one just like her. How did you say you knew Leo? Why don't you come over to my house and we can talk without this phone problem? I'm here most of the time anymore."

Lou yelled her agreement to Mr. Brown and told him she would call back with a date when they would be in town. She hung up the telephone. "He must be almost deaf. I couldn't get him to understand me on the phone. From our little conversation, I think he can help us."

Bill spoke up, "Well, group, I think it's time for a road trip. Gail and I will fly into Miami and check out this address and then head to the beach for a day of fun in the sun. I have a couple vacation days I need to take."

"Jim can come to Buffalo with me to interview Mr. Albert Brown. He seems like a nice old gentleman. Ethel can cover the paper for a day."

CHAPTER 11
Road Trip

Sweat rolled down Bill's back on the short walk to the rental car at the Miami terminal. "Just our luck, a heat wave rolls in the day we come to town. Ninety-five degrees with a hundred percent humidity; this air feels like a steam bath. Was it my idea to volunteer for this trip?"

"Relax, Bill, there's our car. Everybody has air conditioning. As soon as we are done interviewing this guy, we'll check in at the hotel, get our suits on and take a nice cool dip in the ocean. You drive and I'll be the co-pilot. Let me get that map that the girl at the travel agency laid out for us. She said it was only about fifteen minutes from the airport."

As the air conditioner in the car began to work, Bill relaxed and felt the perspiration on his body begin to dry out. Soon he was weaving through the inner city streets. "Wow, it's hard to believe people live in slums like this. I wonder why that travel agent brought us this way. It must be a shortcut."

"Bill, don't get upset. This is the street our man lives on. Slow down, that building with the boarded-up windows is the address. Is it safe to get out of the car in this neighborhood?"

"There are a couple kids playing over there. We should be fine as long as we're out of here before dark. Stay here and lock the doors while I talk to the kids."

Gail saw perspiration beading on Bill's forehead as he returned a few minutes later and opened the car door. "The kids say there are a couple apartments around back. It's the first one. They said we can't miss it. Just look for the wooden wheelchair ramp."

At the back of the building they walked up a rickety wooden ramp and rapped on the rotted door. A voice inside yelled, "You're early! Give me a minute." The door opened and an old man in filthy clothes glared at them. He barked, "Who the hell are you? If you came to rob me, there's nothing in here."

The man was trying to maneuver his chair away and close the door when Gail said, "Please, sir, we aren't here to rob you. We just wanted to ask you a few questions about Ted Price."

"What is your game, lady? You can kiss my ass if you think I'm going to answer any questions. Ted Price is a dead nightmare from my past. Now get out of my life. I got important things to do."

The old man went to slam the door shut. Gail overcame the nausea caused by the stench oozing from the apartment and stuck her foot in the door. "Mister, my grandfather is Ted Price and service records show he joined up with you in Chicago."

A mean scowl spread across the man's face. "I'm too damned old to believe in fairy tales. OK, you want the story? Here it is. There had been one hell of a fight raging at the Scarpe River near us all day. We heard it was mostly the Canadians involved. Things were quiet in front of us except for one of those whiz-bang artillery shells hitting us every now and then. Night came on and I was trying to get some shut eye when Ted crawled up to me and the boys. Damn idiot was picked for a night reconnaissance mission and he wanted us to go with him. Us boys from the orphanage looked up to him and agreed we'd go. The four of us— Ted, Lefty, Duke and I—went over the top around midnight. You were supposed to crawl over to the enemy's position and have a look see at what he was doing. Hell, we all knew these were suicide missions. Barbed wire, land mines, machine gun nests, enemy patrols were all waiting for us out there.

"We were trying to cut through some barbed wire when a flare went off. The Bosche spotted us and opened fire. Lefty was hit right away and fell on the barbed wire. I wanted to go back to the lines and get help.

Ted said we didn't have time. Duke and I drew their fire while Ted freed up Lefty. Then he carried Lefty toward our lines. We almost made it when an enemy patrol ran into us. They opened fire and Ted was hit right away. They didn't see me and the Duke at first. That gave us time to move in and cut them down. We crawled over to Ted. He was hit in two places and bleeding. Lefty lay in the mud beside him. He had taken another hit and was a goner. We drug both of them back to our trenches. Ted was losing a lot of blood. The sarge knew there was a Canadian medic unit off to our left. He got our report and told us to take Ted to the Canadians since they were close.

"Duke and I carried Ted down the muddy road to the medic unit as a new barrage of artillery shells began to fall around us. The medic did a quick once over on Ted and said he needed to get to the hospital in the rear. An ambulance pulled in and we loaded him up right away."

"Was the name of the ambulance driver Leo Brown?"

"There was a war going on. We didn't stop for formal introductions. Holy shit, I remember. Ted laughed and said, 'Don't worry, boys, I'm with Leo the Lionhearted now. He will take care of me.' Funny, I can see him saying that as clear as day. One minute he lay there joking and the next he's dead. Say, how did you know the driver's name was Leo? What kind of scam are you two running?"

"So why are you so sure Ted is dead?"

"Dumb bitch, can't you see I still have my two eyes. I turned to watch the ambulance drive down the hill. We heard the whiz-bang and then saw the ambulance disintegrate. We ran down and pulled Ted and his new-found friend Leo out of the wreckage. They were both deader than a doornail." The man coughed and laughed sardonically. "Yes, old Leo the Lionhearted sure helped Ted, didn't he? Helped him right into a pine box."

"No wait," Bill broke in, "they couldn't both have died. You must be wrong."

"Were you there, wise ass? Well, I was there that night when the medic declared them both dead." The man's voice softened for an instant as he continued, "I stood there helpless as the medic declared them dead. How did I let this happen to my best friend?" The man regained his composure and spat, "Now get the hell out of here before I call the cops."

Gail pulled her foot back and said, "Go ahead, shut your door. I don't know why you are so bitter over something that happened almost sixty years ago."

The man pushed his chair toward Gail almost running her down. He said, "This is why, little missy," as he pulled a filthy blanket off his lap to reveal two short stumps where his legs should be. "On the way back to my post I was upset and not thinking straight. I stepped on a land mine and this is what's left of me. Ted's, Lefty's and my life all ended that day and what for? Damn it, what for?" At that point he swung his wheelchair around and slammed the apartment door behind him.

Back in the car they drove for several miles in complete silence as the air conditioner dried them out. Finally Gail spoke, "I have never met a man so bitter and consumed with hatred. After meeting him I have a better understanding of that old saying, 'War is hell.' Bill, how can that man be right? He just told us that both Ted and Leo died in that shell explosion. If Gramps is not Ted Price or Leo Brown, who is he?"

Bill glanced at Gail and saw the concern in her face. He responded, "That's a question we are not going to answer today. That fellow is a very bitter man. Still, I am convinced he was not lying to us. Right now I am dying from this heat. Let's get to the motel, check in and go for a swim. I'm ready for you to model that new bikini you told me about."

"Calm down, Bill. You don't want to get yourself all hot and bothered in this heat," Gail teased. "See, whenever I get frustrated or upset you always know how to turn the conversation and make me happy again. That's why I love you."

After checking in at the motel, Bill and Gail changed into their swimsuits and strolled down the sandy beach to the ocean. After a playful dip in the cool water, they lay next to each other on a beach towel. Bill rolled over and kissed Gail. "After this morning's tension, this is so relaxing."

"I was just lying here thinking how intertwined our lives have been and when we first met we knew nothing about this web that seems to almost bind us together. I was so sure we would have all the answers when we discovered who was putting the flowers on the grave. Now we have a whole new mystery trying to find out if Gramps is Ted Price, Leo Brown or someone else. I want to do the right thing for Gramps. I want to help him find the answers to the questions about his past. He's always been there for me when I needed him. This is the least I can do for him."

"We have other leads to follow. Mom and Jim may have had better success than we did. Let's go back to the motel, clean up and go to eat. Later we'll call them and see if they got any information. Come on, I'll race you to the motel."

Later in the evening when they returned from the restaurant, there was a message from Bill's mother. He called the number and Lou answered immediately, "Hi, Bill, it was a long day on the road for Jim. We're in bed resting now. How did your day go?"

Bill thought he detected a hint of excitement in his mother's voice. He decided to make his story short so he could hear about her adventure. "We struck out today, Mom. This fellow told us that Ted and Leo were in an ambulance that was hit by an artillery shell. He assured us that both men were killed. He stepped on a land mine and lost both legs the same night he said Ted and Leo died. He's a very bitter person, but he didn't appear to be lying. Did you have any better luck?"

"Yes, we did. It was a very productive day. Let me start with our arrival in Hamilton, Ontario."

Because Jim's legs had bothered him in the cramped confinement of the airplane seat, Lou drove from the Buffalo airport. The border crossing to Canada went smoothly and about an hour later they approached Hamilton. Lou quickly found Albert Brown's home in one of the older neighborhoods in town. When they knocked at the door, Lou was surprised at the appearance of the man that greeted them. Albert, dressed in an old-fashioned suit, was a short, stocky man with a full head of greying hair. She had to admit to herself there was no resemblance to the pictures of Leo.

Albert opened the conversation, "Hi, you must be Lou and Jim. Come in and sit down. I got new batteries last night for my hearing aids and can hear much better today." When Albert saw Jim limping into the room with his cane, he quickly pulled a chair up. "Here, take the load off that leg, Jim. My hearing and eyesight are going, but I'm still as spry as a spring chicken. Now how can I help you folks?"

Lou sat next to Jim and began the conversation, "As I explained on the telephone, my mother Sarah is the woman Leo married in 1915. We are doing some family research and hoped you could give us a bit of information on Leo. Maybe you even have some old pictures I could get copied."

"Leo was born in 1896, so he was two years younger than me. He was a very outgoing and likeable person. We had a wonderful childhood growing up here next to the lake. Our father worked down at the dock. On his days off, he would take us fishing. My mother didn't work. She always said raising us was all the work she could handle. Leo was an inventive sort of fellow. He made sure we never had a boring day, which got us into trouble sometimes."

At this point Albert told several stories of his youthful adventures with his brother. The meticulous details he wove into the stories made it clear that Albert's memory was perfect. Lou finally asked, "What do you remember of Leo's marriage to Sarah?"

"Leo enjoyed his job in Pittsburgh. He wrote often telling us about the exciting life in the big city. Then one day he wrote and told me about a girl he met and how different she was. Leo and I were exact opposites. He was tall, slim and ruggedly handsome. The women were just naturally attracted to him. Sarah was the first girl he met that didn't throw herself at him. That's what intrigued him about her. She was a challenge and my brother thrived on challenges. His letters soon changed their tone and I knew he had fallen in love with this girl. It was no surprise to me when he wrote our parents and told them he was getting married. Naturally they were upset that he wasn't marrying a good Catholic girl. Still they were happy for him.

"We didn't meet his bride until Christmas the first year they were married. He wrote and told us they were coming for a whole week. My mother went crazy cooking, cleaning, and baking. By that time I was married. The whole family went down to the train station to meet Leo and his wife.

"Sarah was an instant success with our family. She was so childlike and innocent. We were amazed at how excited she became over the normal little things we took for granted because we lived our whole lives here by the lake. The four of us spent almost every moment together. It was one of the most enjoyable Christmases I ever had. One night a friend of mine borrowed a sleigh and we rode through town singing carols. We picked up more couples as we went until the sleigh could hold no more. Everywhere we went people offered us cookies and hot chocolate. It was very cold and the girls would snuggle up close to us trying to stay warm. Those were the days.

"All too quick, Christmas was over and Leo had to return to work. I shouldn't have promised Leo that we would visit him in Pittsburgh. I really meant to go. Then we found out my wife was pregnant and I couldn't afford to take off work. Now I wish I had gone."

"Did they ever come back to Hamilton?"

"No, but we did meet the following year in Niagara Falls. My wife was four months pregnant when we went to the falls. They stayed for several days. We went down one day and came back the next. It was a warm summer day and we had a picnic on the lawn near the edge of the Horseshoe Falls. Sarah and Leo were the type of people you could be away from for months and yet when you met pick right up with the conversation like you had never been apart. I never saw two people as deeply in love as those two were. They were so happy together. Sarah did become troubled for a while when she first saw my wife. Leo quickly filled us in on her miscarriage and told Sarah that she would be pregnant again soon. We changed the subject then and enjoyed the rest of our time together.

"The following Christmas they went to Sarah's mother's house. Then the war closed in and Leo's letters changed. He wrote and told me he was considering joining up. My parents and I wrote back urging him to stay where he was unless he was drafted. But Leo was the type of man with an extreme sense of duty. He came home to sign up with a friend before he was drafted. He was alone this time. He sent Sarah to live with her mother. He spent a couple days at our parents' house. I stopped in, but it just didn't seem right. I had a grim feeling every time I saw him." Albert bowed his head and grew quiet.

Jim spoke up, "I know it's hard on you reliving all this. I see you and your brother had a very close relationship. Is there anything you can tell us about his death?"

"It was one of the darkest days of my life. My boss at work came and told me I was needed at my parents' house right away. He didn't need to tell me any more. I had seen the same message given to other men. With a heavy heart, I walked home wondering what to say to my parents. When I walked in the door I heard my mother crying in the parlor and dad was sitting staring at the wall in the kitchen. They buried him in France. We couldn't even have a proper funeral for our grieving. My parents never got over the loss. It broke my mother's heart.

"Sarah sent us a warm touching letter expressing her sorrow. I knew how terrible she must have felt. It showed her character when in the midst of her grief she found the strength to try to console us. I wrote back and thanked her for the nice letter. She wrote me a couple more letters. In the last one she was almost apologetic when she wrote about getting remarried. That was the last I ever heard from her. I often wondered how she was doing, and now her daughter is sitting in front of me. Isn't life strange? I would never have guessed a day like this would come."

"Albert, I appreciate all you have shared with us. I need to show you a couple pictures and get your comments." Lou pulled two pictures from her purse and handed the first one to him.

"Well, that sure looks like Leo all decked out for a wedding. I remember him being more muscular and heavier. He's standing by the bride like she was his wife. I don't know her. I know it's not Sarah. She's too tall and Sarah was so young, she almost looked like a child aside of Leo. Now this second picture is Sarah, a little older than I remember her. Who's the woman in the other picture?"

Lou looked at Jim and decided it was not the time to tell Albert the full story. They needed to be sure before dropping this bombshell on him. She thought a minute and answered, "We don't have any pictures of my mother and Leo together. We are not sure what happened to those pictures. However, I did have this other picture we thought was Leo at another wedding and I wanted to see if you recognized him."

They chatted for a while longer and then it was time to leave. Lou said, "Albert, I am so glad we got this opportunity to meet with you. If we have some more questions, can we contact you?"

"Well, it's been great chatting with you two young folks and reminiscing. I'll tell you anything I can."

Jim, who had been silent for a long time, spoke up, "One other thing bothers me, Albert. Leo was always close to the rest of the family and there were employment opportunities in this area. Why did he leave?"

"Oh dear, I was hoping you wouldn't ask that. Well, I did promise to tell you everything. Leo was about sixteen when he met a gang of older boys from a bad section of town. In spite of my advice, he started hanging around with them in the evenings. Late one night after Leo had come home the boys broke into a store in town and robbed it. Initially Leo was arrested with the rest of the boys. The police didn't believe my mother and father when they swore he had come home and went to bed. They said it was easy for him to crawl out of his window and go back to the gang. Leo was in big trouble. My father hired a good lawyer and he got Leo off. Still, Leo lost his job and with the publicity nobody wanted to hire him. Leo thought it was best to go somewhere else and get a clean start. He saw an ad in the paper one day about a job opening in the States. When he went downtown to see a man about the job, he was hired on the spot."

"Do you remember how the lawyer was able to get Leo released?"

"I sure do. Fingerprinting of criminals was just becoming popular in those days. The lawyer insisted that all the boys charged be fingerprinted. When their fingerprints were compared with those in the store all matched but Leo's. The authorities knew at that point that they didn't have a case against my brother and released him."

Jim looked at his watch and jumped up. "Come on, Lou, we have to go. Albert, thanks for everything. Can you give us directions to the main police office here in town?"

Albert obliged and Jim hustled Lou to the car. As she drove off she commented, "Jim, you were a bit rude in there at the end. Albert's a nice old gentleman. Why are we going to the police office? You heard Albert, Leo was innocent."

"Lou, didn't you hear how the lawyer proved Leo's innocence? He used fingerprints. That police file has Leo Brown's fingerprints in it. With those prints we can determine if Ted is really Leo."

In a short while they pulled in front of the police office. Jim introduced himself to the sergeant at the desk and explained that his paper was working on a story and needed a copy of a set of fingerprints in the police files. The sergeant responded, "Mister, all fingerprints are confidential. We don't give them out to newspaper men." Jim insisted that he talk to the head of the detectives. By now the sergeant was getting irritated and stormed out of the room. The head of the detectives came in and Jim went through the story again.

After Jim assured the detective that all he needed was a set of Leo Brown's prints, the man responded, "I know the case you are talking about. It's a classic we use here to drive home to new recruits the need to use the latest technology available when investigating a crime. An innocent man almost went to jail for twenty years in that case because cutting edge technology was ignored. Why do you want Mr. Brown's fingerprint records?"

Jim answered, "Leo Brown's military record shows he was killed in World War I. My wife's mother was Leo's widow. Problem is, she met a man who she says is Leo. The man was wounded and can't remember anything about his life before the war. Those prints would prove if he is Leo."

"That's a great story and I wish I could help. However, prints are confidential. We only release them to other police agencies for identification purposes. Now I am busy and have to ask you to leave."

Jim thanked the officer and walked out the door with Lou. She tried to help him toward the car when he said, "Look there, Lou, an Irish pub. I always wanted to visit an authentic Irish pub. Let's go have a drink and a sandwich before we leave."

Lou responded, "I think we should get back to the airport and drop off the car. I'm sure there's a place at the airport to get a sandwich and a drink."

"We have lots of time. What will it hurt to stop there a few minutes?"

"Oh, alright, Jim, you know I can't say no to you. Let's go have a drink and then hit the road." At the door to the pub, Jim said, "I have to go to the bathroom. Get us that table over there in the corner and order me a Guinness."

Lou ordered a domestic beer for herself and a Guinness for Jim. When he didn't return after several minutes, she began to look around and saw him standing at a pay telephone near the bar. She watched puzzled as Jim finished his conversation and approached the table with a large smile on his face. As soon as he sat down, she asked, "Jim, what's going on? You didn't come in here for a beer. You came here to use that telephone. Who did you call?"

"My dear, a good newspaperman does not reveal his sources. Now we need to kill an hour. What sounds good on the menu?"

"Jim, we will miss our flight if we wait that long," Lou fumed. "I am not spending tonight in Buffalo."

"Relax. We have two and a half hours until our flight leaves. That's plenty of time to eat and get back to the airport. Here comes our waiter now. I'm going to try the Irish stew."

Lou kept glancing at her watch as Jim nonchalantly ate his lunch. She was thankful when he agreed it was time to leave the restaurant. As she fumbled for the key to open the car, Jim said, "I need to return to the police office one more time and talk to that nice sergeant."

Jim opened the door to the police station as Lou stormed after him. "Jim, are you crazy? That man almost threw us out of here last time. We need to get to the airport and catch a plane."

By now Jim was across the lobby standing at the sergeant's desk. Lou watched in disbelief as Jim announced, "Sergeant, I've returned for those prints."

In shock she watched as the sergeant reached into his desk, drew out a package, and handed it to Jim. Then the sergeant said, "Here's your information, sir. I still don't agree with handing these over to you, but when our chief gets a call from the Prime Minister, who am I to object?"

Jim thanked the sergeant and headed toward the door. Lou stumbled after him and once outside the office, she commented, "I don't believe what I just saw. You called the Prime Minister of Canada to get these prints?"

"Let's not dally around here on the street. As you keep reminding me, we have a plane to catch." The smug look on Jim's face revealed that he was enjoying the moment. "I never said I called the Prime Minister. Let's just say that the head of the Prime Minister's press corps owed me a favor. I met the fellow on a fishing trip in western Canada a few years back. I was surprised he still remembered my name."

"So you see, I gained a lot more respect for this man I call my husband on our trip. In addition, we can now prove positively if Ted is Leo Brown."

"But, Mom," Bill persisted, "the man we talked to today seemed pretty convincing when he told us that Ted and Leo are both dead."

"Enjoy the rest of your vacation, dear. We'll work this out when you get home."

Bill hung the telephone up and smiled at Gail. "Jim and Mom had a good visit with Albert. Mom showed him the wedding picture of your grandparents. He was sure that the man in the picture was Leo, and he said he did not recognize your grandmother. The best news of the day is that they have fingerprint records for Leo. Hey, look, the moon's come up. Let's change and go for a walk on the beach."

Outside a cool breeze blew in from the ocean. Bill and Gail kicked off their sandals and felt their feet sink into the wet sand. As they strolled along the beach they occasionally passed other couples. Out in the distance offshore they could see the blinking lights from several large boats. Bill stopped a minute to stare off into the distant and said, "The ocean seems so serene at night. This was a frustrating day, but now I feel calm and relaxed. Let's be beach bums and live by the sea when we get married."

Gail rubbed his shoulders and said, "Listen to the waves crashing onto the beach. It's so powerful and yet, like you said, calming. This was a great idea of yours to spend an extra day here. As for living a life of leisure by the sea, I couldn't do it. There's a part of me that thrives on putting that paper out every week. I've always enjoyed my job and now that we are together I enjoy my whole life just as it is. No, I didn't mean that. Bill, it's time we move our relationship to the next level. For a while it was great working together with you, going places and doing things with you. Then we made love and my world was never the same again. I really didn't think it could get any better until you swept me off my feet with this gorgeous diamond and your marriage proposal. When I told you all my deep, dark secrets and you convinced me it didn't matter, I knew I was on top of the world. Still, I needed to pause at that point to enjoy what you had given me and to thank God for bringing you into my life. I can't image ever being happier than I am now. Now I truly am ready to get married to you. I want to come home to our house every night. I want to cook you delicious meals and take care of you. I want to hear the pitter patter of little feet on our kitchen floor. Bill Henderson, my heart, my body and my soul are ready now to marry you. We must pick a date for the wedding and get our plans put together. I hope you don't mind, but I spent a good bit of time talking with Mom on this whole subject last weekend. I think she's just as excited as I am.

"Here's my decision. As I said earlier, meeting and falling in love with you has been the start of a whole wonderful new life for me. You also brought me back to God and fostered a rebirth of spiritualism in my life. I believe a candlelight service on Saturday, December twenty-second would be appropriate. Mom is also in agreement that we should hold the service in Greencastle since you and I are both members of the church there along with most of your family. What do you think?"

"That sounds wonderful. We'll check with Pastor Jones as soon as we get back to town. Then we can let the family know and start making the arrangements."

Gail grabbed Bill's hand and they continued to walk along the beach. "I like your idea, Bill, but I want to put a little different twist on it if you don't mind. Listen to this idea. After we see Pastor Jones...."

Bill got up early and slipped out of the house while Jim and Lou were still asleep. As he climbed into his truck in the driveway, he glanced at the house and a host of old memories flooded his mind. He had spent his whole lifetime living, playing, growing, and maturing in this house. He knew nothing ever stayed constant. Yet, a part of him always felt the house would be there to come home to. It was a real shock last night when his mom and Jim announced that they were selling the house. He had to admit that he was angry at them for a moment. How could they cast aside this solid anchor in his life? His mother's voice called him back to reality as she tried to explain that she and Jim needed a home of their own to begin their new life together. As she talked Bill understood; his father had loved the house and even built part of it. To him and his mother, his father would always be a very real entity in the house.

He wanted his mother to be happy in life as he was with Gail. He also knew that Jim was the man to make her happy. He and his mother would always have a special place in their hearts for his father, but now it was time to move on. Today would be a day of many changes and this was just one more to add to the list. Yes, he understood the decision to sell the house, but it still hurt. Now he just needed some time alone.

Bill turned the key and slid the transmission into reverse. As he prepared to back out of the driveway, he was startled to see Gail's car coming up the road. It wasn't even seven o'clock. Why would she be here? She parked the car and climbed into the truck seat beside Bill. She was dressed in a very short pair of shorts and a halter top. As she smiled and leaned toward him to plant a kiss on his lips, he felt that old excitement rising.

She asked, "Do you mind if we go for a drive? I couldn't sleep last night. I'm still wrestling with all that has happened in the last year."

Bill pulled his truck out of the driveway and headed west toward the mountains. "I have a surprise to show you up on the mountain."

They drove in silence until Bill reached the top of the mountain. He pulled into a seldom used dirt road and parked before he spoke. "I couldn't sleep last night either. When I got home, Mom and Jim told me that they are selling the house and moving into town. That really bothered me. I have so many wonderful memories of times in that house. It seems like all the holidays and important events in my life happened right there. You and I even shared our first dinner together there. I knew I had to get away and come up here. My dad showed me this place. He said he found it when he was a teenager. This is where he came when he needed to be alone or think things out."

"I'm sorry, Bill, I didn't know you wanted to be alone. You should have told me."

"It's OK. I'm glad you came. Talking to you always helps me sort things out. Let me get this blanket for us to sit on later."

As they walked down the road, Gail enjoyed the adventure and soon was asking Bill questions about the times he and his dad had walked the trail. At a turn in the road Bill quickly put his hand over her mouth and pointed to a distant clump of trees. They stood motionless as a doe and two fawns cautiously moved onto the road. The mother, trying to keep her playful children in tow, did not notice the intruders on the path in front of her and headed in their direction.

Bill's frustration disappeared while he watched Gail's excitement grow as the frisky little ones approached. He was amazed at how all his problems seemed to melt away when they were together. Just when it appeared like the romping fawns would run them over, the mother caught the scent of the humans. She stopped to stare curiously at the two people a moment and then turned and led her playful troupe back into the woods.

"Wow, Bill, if they had come any closer, I could have reached out and petted them. Did you see how she looked at us with that inquisitive stare?"

"Yes, I think she was trying to figure out what we were doing in her forest. The area I want to show you is right beyond that clump of trees she came out of."

When they reached the area Bill pointed to, a small trail led to the left. They walked a short distance back to an open meadow. At the far edge of the meadow they climbed on a large rock ledge. The ledge sat on the very edge of the mountain top. The meadow was surrounded by the forest on three sides. The rural valley far below lay in front of them. Small farm buildings dotted the landscape as far as the eye could see. Bill spread the blanket on the rock and took his shirt off.

Gail kicked her shoes off and said, "I understand how your father felt. The view is breathtaking. Let's buy this piece of property and build our house right here."

Bill sat down next to Gail and rubbed her back. "Sounds great to me. We'll talk to Mom when we go home."

Gail felt the desire rising in her body as she ran her hands through Bill's hairy chest. "Why do we need to talk to your mother?"

Bill pulled the string on her halter top and it fell to the blanket as her excitement rose. He sat behind her gently caressing her bare breasts. "This type of mountain land has never been good for anything except hunting and logging. Dad bought this meadow with thirty acres around it years ago. It's where we hunted every year until his death. Have you ever given any thought to the type of house you would like to live in?"

"A rustic A-frame would be perfect in this meadow. Bill, we need to finish this conversation later. You've got me too hot again to think straight."

Now Gail felt Bill's manliness growing as he held her tight against his chest and ran his hands up and down her firm waist. They sat quietly for a while enjoying the moment. Then Bill popped the snap on her shorts. As he stood up she saw him drop his pants. He helped her out of her remaining clothes and they lay together on the blanket letting the morning sun warm their naked bodies. She felt the desire burning inside her as Bill lay on his side and playfully stroked the velvet mound between her legs. "Oh, Bill," she panted. "Tell me again that this will never end. Tell me that you will love me forever and ever. Tell me we will always be this happy."

Bill spread her long, silky legs and she felt like she would explode as she felt him enter her. "I love you, Gail, and want to be with you the rest of my life," were the words she heard him utter as their excitement crested.

For a long time after they lay on the blanket embracing and letting the sun's rays bathe their bodies. Finally Bill rose and said, "I wish this moment would never end, but we need to get ready for this afternoon. We need to come back soon and start plans for the house."

Gail slipped her shorts on and said, "You always find the most romantic ways to make love. Next time we come here, let's bring a picnic lunch and a bottle of wine. Look over there, the squirrels are watching us. Now I'm embarrassed."

They both laughed at Gail's comment as Bill folded the blanket and helped her step down from the rock ledge.

As they walked out the lane to the truck, Bill commented, "Thanks for spending this time with me. I've watched everyone else go through a lot of changes in their lives this last year. I guess it was time for my turn to come. I clung to all the pieces of Dad's existence wanting him to come back. It just hurt so much when he died, Gail. It just hurt so terribly bad."

Gail put her arm around Bill and held him tight as they approached the truck.

Inside Bill regained his composure and spoke again, "Would you really consider building a house in the meadow? It would mean so much to me and it would be a way of honoring my dad."

"I think a house next to that big old rock would be neat. We could have windows all along the back to look down on the valley and a big old porch on the side to sit on in the summer and watch the fawns playing with our children in the yard. I wish we could have stayed longer, but I need to go home and get ready for the party this afternoon."

Bill looked at his watch as he entered Eddy and Dottie's porch. It was almost three. He should have been there an hour ago. When he and Gail got home they went in and talked with his mother about their idea to build a house in the meadow. She thought the idea was great and Jim sketched up some ideas they came up with as they talked. Bill wanted to tell his mother their decision on a wedding date, but he had promised Gail that they would make a surprise announcement this afternoon after everyone had arrived for the big July fourth celebration.

Eddy came through the kitchen door and said, "Hi, sport, we're running a little late. Let's get the grill set up and then organize the chairs. Everything is set up for our surprise later. Let's get cracking."

The two men worked quickly and were finishing up their work as Jim and Lou arrived. Lou commented, "Everything looks great, Eddy. The family is so very lucky to have you invite us all here for these special holiday events."

"No, Lou, I am truly lucky to have your family bless my home for these events. Now if I can borrow Jim we need to sample the whiskey sours that Dottie whipped up. Hey, Jim, how's it going? Dottie tells me the doc has you working on some new back exercises that eliminated the pain when you walk. That's great. Wait till you taste this batch of mix. Dottie has outdone herself. Look, Ted and Lauren are here. I bet Ted wants to try a whiskey sour."

Bill sat by Gail and Lauren sipping a whiskey sour and enjoying the conversation when Jessie and Randy arrived with Daniel. As everyone marveled at the growth of the five-week-old addition to the family, Lauren turned to Bill and said, "He has Jessie's features. He looks so cute in that outfit. I just love babies. I wanted to thank you for inviting us again. I really am starting to feel like part of the family. Dad really enjoys it. Look at him over there fussing over Daniel. He's so lonely sitting in that house in York. I want him to live with me, but he won't hear of it.

"So, have you and Gail settled on a wedding date? Last time she visited we selected a couple for you two to discuss. She's going to make you a wonderful wife. It took your help and some time for her to find herself. Now she's so happy. Look at me, I'm crying just thinking about it."

Bill squeezed Gail's hand and said, "As a matter of fact we have settled on a date." At that point he stood up and announced, "May I have everyone's attention, please? Now that we are all here, Gail and I have an announcement. As you know, we became engaged way back before New Year's Eve. At that time we were undecided on when we would get married. Today I am happy to announce that we have picked December twenty-second of this year to exchange our vows in a candlelight service. Gail has talked it over with her mother and they agree that we should have the service in our church here in town. Pastor Jones has reserved the church. Put that date on your calendar because we want you all at our wedding."

Lou rushed up to Bill and Gail and gave them each a huge hug. "I should be mad at both of you for not telling me this morning. We spent all that time designing your house and not a word of this from either of you. Jim and I were beginning to wonder if you were ever going to make that big step. Congratulations. Oh, Lauren, you and I must get together to plan the reception. Can I come along when Gail picks her dress? It's all so exciting. I can hardly wait to get started."

Gail laughed. "Gee, Bill, I think Lou is more excited than we are. Watching her makes me want to rush out and check out some dresses. What are you doing this weekend, Mom?"

After the congratulations had died down, Bill decided it was time to move on. "Can I have everyone's attention again, please? Over the last year, Gail and I worked diligently to solve the mystery of the four roses that appeared on Grandma Sarah's grave every year. Much to our surprise we learned that the flowers are a symbol of Grandma's love and marriage to a truly remarkable man, Leo Brown, who was tragically killed in World War I. To add a further twist to this love story we discovered that Gail's grandfather, Ted Price, was the mystery man placing the flowers on the grave. Ted and Grandma had met in a doctor's office in York. Grandma believed that Ted, who has amnesia from a wound in the First World War, was really Leo Brown. In the process of Grandma trying to convince Ted that he was really Leo, Grandma and Ted fell in love. Please bear with me on this, Ted. I know Grandma tried her best to keep this story from our family. That was a mistake and it's time we correct it. This family wants you, Lauren, and Gail to be a part of our lives.

"Now our story appears like it should end at this point. We set out to find the mystery flower person and we caught him. Trouble is, we stumbled on a whole new mystery. What happened in those blank years of Ted's life? Why did my grandmother insist he was Leo Brown? To answer these questions Eddy and Jim did some research."

Bill glanced at Ted and noticed the pain and apprehension in his eyes. Bill walked over to him and put his hand on Ted's shoulder. "Relax and enjoy my little story, Ted. I have some answers for you. To continue with our story, we knew from Ted's army paperwork that he was an orphan from Chicago. Eddy contacted a man who kept the now defunct orphanage's records. This man sent Gail and I on a trip to Florida to talk with an old friend of Ted's from the orphanage. Now bear with me here, Ted, and I'll clear this up shortly. In Florida the friend assured us that both Ted and Leo died on August 26, 1918. At this point we were rather confused to say the least. Then Eddy received another call with the name of yet another friend from the orphanage who signed up with Ted. We were fortunate to obtain this person's telephone number. When Gail called this man he filled in the blanks. Now I need to set the stage."

Bill paused for a second as everyone shifted in their chairs. Then he asked, "Is it OK if I go on, Ted?"

Ted nodded and said, "Please do, young man. I've waited fifty years to hear this story and now it looks like I'm not Ted or Leo. Maybe we should just pass a hat around full of names and I'll pick one out. At this point I'm very confused and thinking I should not have given you permission to do this research."

"Really, it gets better from here on, Ted. It's the night of August 26, 1918, and a major battle is in progress in the Canadian sector of the front. Two doughboys help their wounded friend to a triage center. They find out that they have stumbled into a Canadian center. The doctors look at the doughboy and decide he needs to be transported to a hospital immediately. They load him into an ambulance and it takes off only to be hit by a stray artillery round. The driver and patient are dragged out of the ambulance and declared dead by a medic. The two young American soldiers take it hard. This fellow they brought back from the front was their best friend. They start back to their outfit, get lost and wander into a mine field. One of them steps on a mine and it shatters both of his legs. Faced with the prospect of losing another of his boyhood friends, the remaining soldier carries his friend back to the triage center and puts him on an ambulance that leaves immediately. Sick with grief, the man stumbles over to the covered bodies still lying by the road to see his dead friend one more time.

"Now, Ted, here comes the part you've been waiting years to hear. The man bends over his lifeless friend, talks to him, and prays for him. As he gets up to leave he sees the blanket covering the other man move. Thinking a rat was after the corpse he pulls the blanket off to examine the body. That's when he notices a twitching movement of the man's hand and realizes he isn't dead. The soldier gets a medic to confirm that the man lying on the ground is alive."

Eddy broke in, "Since we talked about this the other day, I discovered a flaw in this story. We have a Canadian ambulance driver and an American soldier. Their uniforms were different. How could anyone get them mixed up and think Leo was Ted?"

"That's a good question that Gail and I considered. I must admit, we have no definite answer. However, we did a little research. There were over five million Allied soldiers killed in World War I. In the four years of battle that's one soldier killed about every twenty-five seconds on average. This is only the deaths. There were at least twice as many wounded men requiring attention. With this kind of mass slaughter accurate identification took low priority. Dog tags were used to minimize error. Also, it was important to get the dead buried fairly quickly to limit the potential for spread of disease.

"We hoped we could find out more information from our eyewitness and called him back. He remembered the area of the triage center being very muddy and swampy so the uniforms probably were obscured with mud. Also there was a good possibility that some of the clothing was blown off in the explosion of the ambulance. The rear of the ambulance was on fire from the explosion and he thinks his friend's clothing was on fire when they pulled him out. You have to remember this area had been receiving heavy casualties all day long. The doctors, nurses, and attendants were exhausted and overwhelmed. Their priority was to save and treat the living.

"The most chilling part of the story came out as we continued to talk. Both bodies had been tagged for a burial detail the next morning. If our eyewitness had not noticed the twitch, the driver may have been buried alive. Here's my theory. Whatever minimal record keeping was needed had already been done on the two soldiers lying by the road. The dog tags on both soldiers had probably been pulled to fill out the paperwork or blown off in the explosion. Now an American soldier comes back and says the one man is still alive. Someone assumes it's the American lying by the road that the soldier is talking about and gives his paperwork and dog tags to the ambulance driver. He sees the paperwork says he's transporting an American and takes him to a US hospital unit. At the hospital they cut off the remaining clothing to treat the wounds. The error would have been discovered when the patient woke up. Trouble is the patient, Ted, woke up with amnesia."

"Excuse me for being a little bit stubborn, but I don't accept your story as proof. First we have no real proof that the ambulance driver was Leo Brown. Second, if the driver came back alive, why couldn't I, Ted Price, come back to life, somebody find me, and take me to a hospital? Sorry, Bill and Gail, I'm not buying this story. There's too much circumstantial evidence. But I would like the names and addresses of my old friends from the orphanage so I can get in touch with them and they can fill me in on my life before the war."

"Well, there is one more piece of evidence that supports our story. The injuries on your medical records do not include any type of battle wound. The head and leg injuries could easily have occurred from the explosion of the shell. Finally we suspect Ted should have had burns on his body and you were not treated for any burns. Now I know that what we are telling you affects the very foundation of your life. When a person lives his whole life believing his name is Ted Price, he needs incontestable evidence before he can accept that there has been a mistake. Now I need to let my mom tell you her findings."

Lou stood up and pulled a glass out of a paper bag near her feet. Smiling she asked, "Ted, do you recognize this glass?"

"It looks like one from a set my wife and I bought years ago. I thought Gail broke the last remaining one at my house the other weekend when she visited. After she left I couldn't find it anymore."

"We took this glass hoping to give you that proof you are looking for. The week before Jim and I came to your house we took a trip to Hamilton, Ontario. While there we discovered that the local police force had fingerprinted Leo Brown years ago while investigating a crime. Leo was not involved in the crime, but his fingerprint records were retained. With a little persuasion on Jim's part, we obtained a copy of those prints from the police and Eddy had them compared to the prints on this glass. Ted, your prints are a perfect match to those from Hamilton, Ontario."

"Damn, you kids really got the proof. All the years I knew Sarah, she never gave up hope that I would remember something that would prove I was Leo. I grew to love her so much, sometimes I considered pretending I remembered because I knew how happy she would be if I could remember anything from our past in Pittsburgh. It was impossible to do that because I couldn't betray her trust in me. If only she would have agreed to tell you about our relationship. You could have uncovered this information while she was still alive. It would have made her extremely happy. It makes me very sad knowing that the love of my youth and old age died without my recognition or validation of her love for me.

"As for me, I have always been overwhelmed by the unwavering strength of Sarah's love for Leo. At times I was confused by it. Did she really love me for who I am or was I the recipient of pent-up love for a dead man? Now it doesn't really matter. I am that man. I abandoned her and destroyed our relationship to serve my country. Why? How can I face the knowledge that I willingly made a decision that made her a widow and broke her heart? She carried scars from that decision the rest of her life and now I know it was my fault."

Lou knelt down in front of him and said, "Oh, Ted, it's not a fault thing. You were a responsible individual and you felt it was your duty to join up like millions of other boys did in those days and still do today. You may think it was a tragedy that you lost your memory and didn't return to Sarah. Look at all the loving caring people in this room that came from Sarah's and your second marriages. And in a few months your granddaughter is going to marry Sarah's grandson. The wonderful love these two people share today would never have happened if you and Sarah had stayed together. Indeed, many of us in this room would not have existed. God works in mysterious ways and he did bring you two back together, so you had a chance to know and love my mother again."

"Yes, Lou, you are right. Sarah and I went on and raised wonderful families. We have much to be thankful for. I need to stop feeling sorry for myself and enjoy all you people that care for me. I wouldn't want to give any of this up. Still, I wish I could remember those wonderful happy days with Sarah as my wife and my childhood before I met her."

"Speaking of that, we have one more surprise for you. Dottie, can you get our surprise while I explain? You see, Ted, we found the fingerprints after Jim placed an ad in the Hamilton newspaper. The ad requested friends and relatives of Leo Brown to contact us with information on his life. The person who answered the ad knows an awful lot about your early years and he sent us to the police barracks. We knew you would like to talk to this person and so we brought him here today. Ted, meet your brother from Hamilton, Ontario, Albert Brown."

At this point Dottie led Albert into the room and Ted stared at him incredulously for a minute before he said, "You guys are kidding. He doesn't look at all like me. If this is supposed to be a joke, it's not funny."

Now Jim spoke up, "I assure you this is not a joke. Albert is your brother. He knows all about the memory loss and understands you do not remember him, but he is excited to get to know you again."

"It's OK, Leo. Sorry, I meant, Ted. I couldn't believe you were alive either when they first told me. They showed me pictures from your second wedding and I knew it was you right away. Your wife looked like a nice woman. Too bad I didn't get to know her. Come in the living room with me. I brought some pictures with me and we can be alone for a while. We have a lot of years to catch up on."

Gail saw the tears of joy in her grandfather's eyes as he followed

Albert back into the house. Yes, life was truly wonderful and this was the happiest day of her life. How could anything ever top this?

CHAPTER 12
Future Plans

Gail took a final look in the mirror and marveled at the beautiful woman dressed in an elaborate wedding gown staring back at her. Her thought took her back to last summer's fourth of July party at Dottie and Eddy's. She and Bill had finally announced their wedding date and Gramps had been reunited with his brother. At that moment she was sure she could never be happier. Now in a few minutes she was about to enter the hallowed old sanctuary of this great church and walk down the center aisle. Gail Mason would never return and her new life as Gail Henderson would begin. Now she knew this would always be the happiest day of her life.

The music started and the bridesmaids and other attendants began filing down the aisle. Her father nervously shuffled by her side. This was the first time she had seen him in almost two years. She glanced up at the tall, handsomely dressed man waiting for her at the altar, and she knew it no longer hurt that her father had chosen to live a life without her. Finally, she realized that his decisions had made him the big loser in life, not her. The closet full of skeletons was finally empty.

The wedding march began and everyone turned to see them enter the church. Gail tried to remain calm as they slowly proceeded up the candle-lit aisle with cameras snapping everywhere. It wasn't easy being the center of attention like this. Glancing around the packed church, she picked out the faces of family and friends from her new home and her childhood days in Lancaster. How could she be so lucky to meet and fall in love with that wonderful man waiting for her at the front of the church?

Almost to Bill's side, she glanced at her mother's beaming face. She had always pictured two lonely souls on this pew for her close family. Gramps had changed all that. He insisted they invite Albert and his family. Now the first two pews overflowed with Albert's five married children and several grandchildren. Suddenly she had a large loving family just like Bill. She wanted to shout out her joy and tell everyone how much she loved this man that wanted her in spite of her flaws. They touched and a tingling sensation of excitement flowed through her body. Her past life passed before her eyes and she realized it had all been lived to prepare her for this glorious moment.

The wedding vows were well along when Pastor Jones turned to her and started, "Do you, Gail Mason, take...."

Moments before walking into the sanctuary, she had remembered the old tradition about wearing something borrowed. Everyone was searching frantically through their purses when Dottie had thrust something in her pocket and said, "This is just what you need. Hurry, they're ready for you." Listening to the minister, Gail reached in her pocket and instantly recognized the hanky with the SAM embroidered on it.

Pastor Jones finished and Gail responded, "I do and thank you, Grandma Sarah, for everything."

Gail passed the turnoff to Lou's old house and felt a moment of sadness as she glanced back and saw it. She and Bill had some fond memories there. Why, she remembered the time on the sun porch when she and Bill had....Oh God, she was starting to think like that sex-crazed husband of hers. He meant the world to her, but this was going too far! It really was cute though the way he was so romantic.

In the little town at the foot of the mountain a truck pulled out in front of her and seemed to creep toward the steep slope. Didn't these people know she was in a hurry to see the most wonderful man in the world? Fortunately the truck made a left turn onto a side road and Gail pushed her old car up the rest of the steep incline. At the top she made the right-hand turn onto the rutted dirt lane. Her car jolted along the short distance to the clump of trees where they had seen the deer last summer. The path beyond the trees was gone, replaced by a freshly stoned lane. Gail turned onto the short lane and came out onto the busy meadow. She parked her car next to Bill's truck and several other vehicles.

Gramps noticed her first as she slid out from behind the wheel. He came toward her and said, "Now I know the house belongs to you and Bill. Don't get mad at me if I just made a few suggestions to improve things."

Bill came up and hugged Gail. "Hi, honey, I thought you weren't coming up today. Let's go over to the house. Ted has some great ideas I want to go over with you. I'm glad he agreed to come down and stay for a while to help us out."

Gail caught Bill's wink as they walked toward the rough framed exterior walls that were taking shape. Gramps was like a different person these days. He called Albert every week and they were planning another visit soon. Why, he had jumped at the chance to come down for a few weeks and help Bill after Jim and Lou told him he could stay with them in that big old house they bought on East Baltimore Street in Greencastle.

As they walked to the house, Bill continued, "Come on up to our room in the loft. This is the biggest change. Be careful on the steps, we haven't got the banister up yet." They had hired Bill's high school friend who was now a contractor to build the house. Bill came over on his days off to help. Inside the master bedroom Gail walked over to the glass panels in the rear wall and marveled again at the spectacular view of the valley below.

Ted joined her and said, "Well, kids, this has been some year. A past that was lost has been reclaimed. Love lost has become love reclaimed. Many of us are experiencing new beginnings in our lives. As I stand here in a room that will be filled with love and memories, I'm filled with confidence that God has greater things yet in store for both of you and the family that is to come."

Gail hugged her grandfather and commented, "Oh, Gramps, I like the way you put that. I agree. God has some great things in store for us. Now, Bill, tell me about these changes to the room."

Bill explained, "At first, I wasn't wild about Ted's idea, but it's really grown on me. Ted told me we were wrong to wedge the bathroom in that corner over there. He recommends we integrate the bathroom with the bedroom and put a whirlpool tub in the corner right next to these windows. Like he said, we are on the second floor and we do own thirty acres surrounding this meadow. Just think how romantic it will be. The two of us sipping wine in the candlelight with the bubbles massaging our bodies as we look down at the lights blinking in the valley below. Wow, I can't wait. Maybe we should get the boys to work overtime so we can move in quicker."

Gail laughed and said, "Bill, you are an incorrigible romantic and I love you. Don't ever change. Now how will this affect the rest of our room?"

A long discussion followed while they redesigned the full interior of the room. At the end Gail turned to Ted. "Gramps, I'm so glad you had that idea. It's going to help bring this beautiful view into everything we do in this room. I need your help now in the bedroom next door."

Gail walked out of the room and looked down into the area that would eventually be their spacious living room. A rock-faced fireplace was taking shape on the far wall as she turned and headed through an arch to a smaller bedroom with a double window in the back overlooking the valley.

Bill followed behind her and pleaded, "But, honey, don't you remember we decided not to finish this bedroom right now? We'll use a sofa bed downstairs for guests until I get the time to work on it."

"Now, Gramps, if you were designing this as a little boy's or girl's room what are your ideas?"

Bill persisted, "Now, Gail, you know we decided to wait at least two years before we adopt. That will give us some time alone and Ted can come back later to help us with ideas. We need to get the living area ready for us to move in."

Ted saw Bill was getting frustrated and pulled up a large covered bucket. He eased Bill down on the bucket and said, "Relax and listen to my granddaughter. She has something to say, and if I understand correctly you may need to be sitting down."

"Bill, you are so dense at times. It's like you have a one-track mind. You can concentrate only on the project or job at hand. Let me remind you that I went to see the doctor this morning. When I told him about the problems I have been experiencing he laughed and ran a quick test. You, my dear, will be a father in about seven months."

Bill stammered and finally said, "How can this be? You always told me it was impossible for you to become pregnant."

"Yes, well, they never considered the possibilities of spending a winter in a tiny one bedroom apartment with horny ole Bill. Seriously, the doctor ran a few tests today and apparently everything is just fine. You know, Bill, that God does work in mysterious ways. I know this is a surprise but you're going to be a wonderful dad."

Bill sat on the bucket for a moment grasping this wonderful change of events in his life. Then with one quick movement he picked Gail up and swung her around laughing and crying at the same time.

"I swear, Gail, you have made me the happiest man alive today. Are you sure that you are OK? When is the due date? Is it a boy or girl? What will we name him?"

"Whoa, Bill, hold on a minute. Let me answer one question at a time. First I'm in perfect health. The baby's due date is around October fifteenth, and we will just have to wait until then to find out what the sex will be. I thought that we would name her Sarah after your grandmother, but if it's a boy then you can pick his name."

Bill just stood there hugging Gail and smothering her with kisses. He couldn't believe how lucky he was. Yes, God was very good to him.

All at once Ted cleared his throat and Bill and Gail just starting laughing. Gail asked, "You're going to be a great-grandfather. How does that feel, Gramps?"

"Fine...real fine. Now let's get down to business. We need to make plans for the nursery. I think a window seat along that back wall that doubles as a toy box would be a good start."

Ted joined in the laughter and Gail caught herself thinking that this was the happiest day of her life. Now she knew that being married to Bill meant a wonderful progression of these days for the rest of her life. It was a wonderful feeling she prayed would never end.